THE FALLEN

Kate Martin

THE FALLEN: THE MYST & LABRYNTHS SAGA, BOOK TWO

Published by Outland Entertainment LLC
3119 Gillham Road
Kansas City, MO 64109

Founder/Creative Director: Jeremy D. Mohler
Editor-in-Chief: Alana Joli Abbott
Senior Editor: Scott Colby

ISBN (Print): 978-1-954255-64-7
ISBN (eBook): 978-1-954255-65-4
Worldwide Rights
Created in the United States of America

Editor: Scott Colby
Copy editor: Bessie Mazur
Proofreader: Em Palladino
Cover Illustration: Shannon Potratz
Cover Design: Jeremy Mohler
Interior Layout: Mikael Brodu

Printed and bound in the United States of America.

Visit **outlandentertainment.com** to see more, or follow us on our Facebook Page **facebook.com/outlandentertainment/**

PREVIOUSLY,
— IN *THE SOULLESS* —

Demons once roamed the mortal realm free to deal and bargain as they chose, but in recent years, new philosophies and religious sects have cropped up that have made soul collecting a far more difficult feat.

Unsatisfied with this new development, the mother of all demons, Lillianna, comes up with a plan to raise herself to godhood and change the tides. Using the power of a young witch and the backing of another powerful demon, Olin, she completes ritual after ritual, until finally she is stopped by our group of "heroes."

Bri—A young man of fifteen who has grown up plagued by the ability to see into the Myst (and thus see the future). Unable to touch another mortal being without being thrown into visions that lead to illness, he agrees to sell his soul to the demon Carma one night in order to avoid death. When he meets her soulless, Alec, Bri is shocked to discover that he can touch and be near the other man without his usual ailments. In fact, touching Alec makes everything go silent and calm. He wants desperately to use his power to help people, but it only ever seems to cause more problems.

Alec—Carma's first soulless. Two thousand years into his deal. He sold his soul in an attempt to save his love, Ariadne, and his younger brother, Marc. He was, unfortunately, too late. Alec is tired of life when Carma reappears after going missing for two hundred years, and finds his heart unable to say no when she bids him take care of Bri.

Carma—One of the oldest demons. Just returned after being trapped in another in-between realm for two hundred years, she has secrets that she keeps even from herself. She's been strategically collecting her soulless, occasionally ranting about "pieces" and a game.

Kai—Bri's twin brother, separated since birth. Kai was taken in and essentially raised by Lillianna to serve her as her personal witch. He is extremely powerful, and his perception of reality is twisted because of it. He seeks to reunite with his brother, certain that they will be more powerful together than apart.

Gabriel—A seraph from the holy realm of Haven, tasked with tracking and retrieving Bri because of his ability to see into the future. She has, for these long fifteen years, been unsuccessful in locating him, but as Lillianna's plans come into play, she discovers that Carma possesses the boy she seeks.

Dorothea—A witch working for Carma. She is nine hundred years old, and her mind shows it. All she really seems to care about are her *labrynths* (spells) and besting this new young witch, Kai.

Picadilly—Another of Carma's soulless. Once a demon herself, she was tricked into becoming human and bargained with Carma to get back some of her former power.

Olin—An old demon, former (and sometimes current) lover of Carma. He worked for Lillianna as long as it served him and fed his curiosity to know if a demon could truly become a god.

Ella—Young woman who has befriended Bri and come to his defense and protection when society threatened. An encounter with Ella at his sixteenth birthday party is about to turn Bri's life upside down...

*For anyone who's ever let out a breath
they didn't know they were holding.
Me too.*

PART ONE

— CHAPTER ONE —

A kiss.

So simple a thing, the pressing of two mouths together. The light touch of soft flesh against soft flesh. Breath stills, and under the gentle light of the stars all seems to still for one glorious moment.

Then a flash. Images. Visions. The cold tendrils of the future, always lying in wait, and pouncing at the first hint of weakness.

Pain follows the initial warmth; an all-encompassing embrace that lasts only long enough to drive the body to shock, to twist the heart and seize the lungs.

The visions wash in and out. Stronger than the others.

Then there is only darkness.

"Ariadne."

Her name felt strange on Alec's tongue, something that had been a whisper, a hope, a prayer for nearly two millennia. Seeing her was like a dream all too vivid and too solid. Yet there she was. Ebony hair, golden skin, eyes that seemed to look straight to his soul—that is, had Alec a soul to be seen. His soul had been traded. For her.

She was more beautiful than he remembered.

Her light laughter danced on the air, accompanying the music of the party. "Oh, Alexander, you look as though you've seen a ghost."

"I have. You're dead."

"I'm not dead."

"You should be dead. You must be. How are you here?" His fingers twitched, aching to touch her, but he resisted. What if she wasn't really there? What if she was? The guests danced and mingled about them, twisting and turning under the night sky. Dreamlike. Alec heard their voices, felt the beat of the band's music against his skin, but it all seemed far away. If she was here then he had to be in the heat of home, with the breeze coming off the northern sea, and the gulls screeching above. She didn't belong at this manor, where a demon dictated his life, and times had changed the very world. His hand lifted slightly, but did not make contact. Was that a gull's cry in the distance?

With a good-natured sigh of exasperation and an all too familiar pursing of her lips, she grabbed his hand in hers and set it against her chest where her heart beat strongly beneath warm, smooth flesh. "I live, Alec. Same as you."

Something in her words drew all the slow and muddled thoughts in Alec's mind to a complete halt. The shock was gone, replaced by an intense, burning need to know the truth. The sights and smells of his past turned to dust. He took a step closer, lowering his voice so as to not be overheard by the guests milling about. "You are supposed to be dead. You grew old, you passed, and now your bones are a part of the earth."

Ariadne frowned. "Now, Alec, is that really how you want to greet me after all this time?"

"You can't be my Ariadne. What are you? And why torment me by taking her form?"

"It's me, Alec. You can check my birthmark if you like."

"I just may take you up on that."

"I certainly hope so." Taking his hand from her chest, she lifted it to her lips and kissed it.

Giving Alec a full view of her right arm.

He grabbed her by the wrist, his own breath choking him as his fingers passed over the faded lines that wove their way around her skin at her elbow and disappeared up over her shoulder. "What is this?"

"As they say, we have much to talk about, you and I."

The lines twisted about her shoulder, snaking toward her elbow with sharp-looking thorns where his own had soft leaves. His grip on her tightened, her flesh straining against the force, wrinkling and turning red—he forced himself to release his hold. The very fact that he touched her twisted his heart in his chest, buckling his knees and nearly causing him to collapse at her feet. "You have a demon's mark." With her free hand she caressed his face, and the sheer gentleness of that touch, the familiarity of it, further undid him. "Alec." She whispered his name as though it were a prayer. "I so need to—"

The rest of her words were cut off by the sudden uproar of gasps and hurried shouts from those around them. At first Alec could not tear his gaze from Ariadne, no matter what the guests carried on about, but then he heard one single word among the cacophony, and he turned without further thought.

"Bri?" He echoed the name, rising on his toes to see over the heads of the party guests, to where the boy had been sitting quietly only moments before. He was nowhere to be seen, but the girl—Ella, if he remembered correctly—had knelt on the ground, leaning over something he could not make out. Alec took one step, but was pulled sharply to a halt.

"Ariadne, what—?"

She held his arm with both hands, mouth set in a tight line before she spoke quickly. "Meet me later."

"Ari, I have to go."

"I know. But promise me first. Meet me at the bridge on the west side of town. I'll wait for you all night."

Alec looked back over his shoulder where a crowd was quickly forming around the bench where Bri had sat. "Fine, I will, but I have to—" He stopped. She had left. Not a sign of her remained, nor could he glimpse her moving through the throngs of people.

For the second time in his very long life, Alec walked away from her, refusing to look back, refusing to search.

Shoving the nosey watchers out of his way, Alec jumped the stone bench, knelt beside the young blonde, and found Bri. He lay flat on his back, breathing harsh, uneven breaths, his eyes wide open to the sky above him. Ella was on the verge of tears, her gloved hands touching Bri's face, his shoulders, in attempts to coax some response from him. "I don't know what happened," she said. "He just went still, then collapsed."

"It's all right," Alec assured her, keeping his voice level and calm. He took her hands and gently guided them away from Bri, all the while praying he would not shake and betray his own worry. "I know what to do," he lied, uncertain of Bri's condition. If the boy was trapped in the myst, this was a new reaction they had yet to see. "I'll carry him. Clear a path for me."

Ella stared but nodded, wiping the tears from her eyes, and standing on unsteady legs.

Someone in the growing crowd called out for a doctor. "No need." Carma's voice broke through the din of murmurs and whispers, stilling the night as though by magic. Alec had never been so glad to hear her voice. "I have already taken care of such things. Please, make room."

While she ordered the humans about, Alec gave his full attention to Bri. He didn't dare remove a glove and touch Bri in front of all these people. If the reaction was violent, there would be too much they couldn't explain. Instead, he lifted the boy from the ground, held him close, and charged through the parting sea of people, using his own body as a shield. The less they saw, the better. Brannick opened the house door for him, and Mary met him at the foot of the stairs. She followed him straight to Bri's room, shutting the door and lighting the lamps even as Alec set Bri on the bed and finally placed a bare hand on his cheek.

Bri's wide eyes opened wider and he gasped, sucking in air as though he had been drowning. He flailed, grasping for anything near. Alec took one hand in his own, holding it tight. "You're all right." He repeated the words until Bri stilled some. "Look at me." That silver-brown gaze turned on him, and Alec breathed a sigh of relief when he saw recognition there. "What happened?"

"She kissed me."

Not exactly the answer he had been expecting. "I know, I saw. I meant, what happened when she kissed you?"

Bri groaned and threw his hands over his face, rolling onto his side and curling into a ball of misery.

Alec panicked. "Bri? Bri, what's wrong?"

Just as suddenly, Bri sat up, his hands pulling at his face, before dropping to his lap with an audible thud. "She *kissed* me. She kissed me and I fell into the myst and collapsed in a fit like some kind of invalid *freak.*" He pulled his gloves from his hands and started unbut-toning his shirt and loosening his tie as he scrambled up from the bed. Both articles of clothing were thrown violently across the room. Alec shared a surprised and confused look with Mary—though she then nodded, smiling knowingly before speaking. "I'll get the young master something to drink." With that she left, leaving Alec alone with Bri as he continued to tear at his clothes.

"Bri, why don't you sit?"

There wasn't so much as an acknowledgement that Alec had spoken. "What kind of—of—freak can't kiss a girl? I'm sixteen years old!"

The myst is apparently the least of our problems here. "Stop using the word 'freak.' You're not a freak."

"I am a freak. What other word is there? A girl kissed me and I just—*fall over!* And she *saw.* She saw it all, and now I'll never be able to face her again, and she probably thinks I'm beyond ill, and there's nothing charming about someone who can't even kiss without having a fit!"

Alec could only stare as Bri's rant continued. He'd never seen Bri like this in the three years he'd known him—and raised him. Normally Bri took everything in stride, so much so that it unsettled Alec. There had been so many days when he had wished Bri would rail against his lot in life. Who would have guessed all it took to set him off was a kiss from a pretty girl? Alec was torn between being concerned and amused.

Carma appeared in the doorway, her cerulean dress shadowed, not a silver hair out of place despite her having to navigate the curious guests. She took one look at Bri, who had thrown himself onto his back on the floor, arms locked tightly around his face. "What's going on here?"

"Tantrum of some kind. Nothing for you to worry about."

"Tantrum?" She made the word sound as ridiculous as the reality was.

Alec just shrugged.

"And what should I tell all our guests? Who are now gossiping to their little hearts' content."

"The only thing he's going to die from at the moment is embarrassment, so if we can get past that, he'll be able to go back out. Tell them he drank too much wine."

Exasperated, Carma turned on her heel and left.

"Ella will know it wasn't the wine," Bri said once they were alone again.

"Probably. But everyone else won't."

"What do I tell her?" He still hid beneath his arms.

"That her beauty is so overpowering it knocked you off your feet. Literally."

"Not funny, Alec."

"Honestly, Bri, you should have known better than to kiss her."

"She kissed me. I didn't know it was going to happen until it already had."

Not foreseeing a quick end to Bri's self-loathing unless he took some action, Alec stood and walked over to where he lay on the floor. "Tell her the truth then."

"I can't."

"She already knows you sold your soul; the rest of the story isn't very long."

At that, Bri dropped his arms and glared at Alec as though that was the stupidest thing he had ever heard. Alec offered him a hand. Bri shook his head. "I'd rather stay here. Where no one can see me. Ever again."

Alec reached down and hauled him to his feet. "As dramatic and entertaining as that sounds, I think you'll find things a bit more comfortable elsewhere."

A knock on the door signaled the return of Mary, who came in with a smile and a glass of wine which she pressed into Bri's hands. "It will help."

Bri held the glass as though it had caused him offense. "Carma is telling everyone I had too much to drink, so you're giving me wine?"

"Yes. We'll get you drunk for real so the story holds up," Alec said. "Drink. It will eliminate some of your embarrassment."

"Somehow I doubt that."

"Do it anyway."

Bri drank.

No amount of coaxing could convince Bri to emerge from his room. The guests were assured the man of the hour had simply enjoyed himself a bit too much and had retired for the night. Though they gossiped, they were all more than happy to continue celebrating Bri's birthday without him. The only one truly concerned was the young Lady Ella, who found Alec the first moment he was alone.

"Lord Dusombré?" She approached him, hands wringing together, pulling at her white gloves. A curl had fallen free of her pins, and she had hastily tucked it behind one ear.

Alec, perched on a stone wall trying to lose himself in the relative quiet of the farthest garden, steeled himself for this conversation, seeing the concern in Ella's gaze. "Call me Alec, please," he said, hating when anyone called him 'Lord Dusombré.' He hadn't had a family name in a millennia, but using Carma's assumed name never failed to irritate him. Too much of a reminder of what he had given up.

"I couldn't possibly," she said, standing two arm-lengths away. "It wouldn't be proper."

"Then I would request you refrain from calling me anything at all."

That green gazed narrowed at him, passing judgment over that potentially rude statement. Alec was too tired to care. "All right then," she said, drawing herself to her full height, as though leaving her insecurities behind. She moved to the stone wall, standing beside him, looking beyond to the woods that surrounded the manor on two sides. "Lord Alec," she said it with a clip to her voice that scolded him for creating the need for such a compromise, "I was simply hoping you could tell me how Bri is doing." Everything about her softened the moment she said Bri's name.

"Too much to drink."

"That story won't work on me."

"I know," Alec said.

"I'm not a child. Not really. I know what you are, and what Bri will be. I know he gets sick, but I don't know why."

"It's not my place to tell you."

"I know." She closed her eyes, breathing deep and turning her face to the moonlight. When she opened her eyes again, she looked at

Alec, composed and perhaps a bit resigned. "Will you tell him I said goodnight? And that I hope we can talk soon?"

"That I can do."

Slipping a hand into the small purse that hung at her wrist, she pulled out a folded bit of paper and offered it to Alec. "Will you give him this?"

"Should I ask what it is?"

"Just an address. If he wanted to contact me, send me a letter."

Alec took the paper and put it into his breast pocket. "He'll get it."

"Thank you." She curtseyed. "Lord Alec," she said by way of excusing herself.

"Lady Ella."

She left, and Alec had the sudden nagging feeling that Bri had gotten in over his head with that one. He didn't know her family, but there was training there, manners, and a certain air about her that hinted at something more than merely a sweet girl from a well-off home.

A curiosity for another day. While Carma was conveniently distracted by her guests, Alec swung himself over the stone wall, and headed west.

— CHAPTER TWO —

The bridge was deserted this time of night. The Calla River drifted lazily beneath its mortar and stone, reflecting the moon and stars in its shimmering surface. A soft breeze reminded Alec of home, churning the air as well as his memories. The city lay behind him, quiet and still. Ahead of him, stood the past.

She leaned against the rail, looking over at the river below, her long raven hair loose as it had been in his mortal years. Already he ached to touch it, to run his fingers through those long locks, watching as they fell away, dripping like dark molasses...

Alec shook free of the thought. He had to keep his wits about him. Had to. Having her back was a dream—and dreams were not meant to be real. He remembered all too well the last time he had seen her, fires blazing all around, the scent of blood and death on the air. The skin on his forearm had burned from both the *labrynth* and the mark he had willingly taken on. Too late. Marc lay at his side, unmoving and growing cold. Carma stood over him, all bronze and silver, and ready to take him away from all he loved, in exchange for their lives—her life. Only Ariadne mattered. Marc was lost to him. Too young, too still, too cold. Alec's hands had shaken as he had gathered his brother's body to him, desperate to feel some sign of life. Only moments later was he forced to relinquish the corpse, to lay it gently upon the blood-soaked ground and turn his back on his former life. Ariadne had stirred then, shifting on the ground where her would-be killers lay dead within her reach. Alive. Alec had repeated the word to himself with every step he took away from her. Alive. *Safe.* It made following the demon easier.

He heard his own boots click against the stone of the bridge, lost in memory, not realizing he had completed his walk to her side until he stopped. There was no sign of the past on her now. No ash streaked her face, no blood caked her hair. Her clothes were neat, tidy, untorn by desperate and cruel hands. She looked as she had the first day he had seen her—perfect. The most beautiful woman in the world. Still half-lost in thoughts, he reached out and ran his fingers over the black silk that fluttered in the breeze at her hip.

"Hello, Alec."

"We already said hello."

"So we did." She took his hand in hers, turning to face him. Her deep blue eyes matched the night sky, and Alec couldn't tear his gaze away from hers even as she stroked each of his fingers in turn.

"I don't understand," he said.

"Don't understand what?"

"Why you're here."

She regarded him with an admonishing downward tilt of her chin. "You saw my mark. You know what it means."

"But *why?*"

"You tell me your reasons first."

"My reasons?" Alec stepped back, removing his hand from hers. "I sold my soul so you could live! So you and Marc would be safe from those scribing lunatics!"

She frowned. "You disappeared without a word. Without so much as a goodbye."

"I had no choice. I had made the deal, and she said 'come.' I went."

Her expression spoke of bitterness, her eyes hard and cold. "I didn't know what had become of you. I woke there, on the ground, astonished I was even still alive. And Marc..." She couldn't finish the thought. "How did selling your soul save him, hm?"

Alec felt as if she had twisted a knife in his heart. "I was too late. I didn't know it when I made the deal. Marc was already gone. But you were not. You were alive, and you were supposed to live."

"Without you? Without Marc? What was I supposed to live for, Alec? Who was I to live with? I had nothing."

"You had your whole life ahead of you!"

The meager space between them felt like a gaping gulf. "I had given up everything to be with you. I couldn't go back."

"Did you even try?"

"I searched for you. For nearly a year, I traveled the continent, searching for some sign that you lived. With no body to be found, I was certain you lived, but I couldn't imagine why you would have left me. I thought maybe someone had taken you, or you had lost your mind." She stepped toward him, through that invisible chasm of time, tilting her head upward to make up for the few scant inches he had on her in height. "Then I spotted you. In Vaah. With that woman."

"She's no woman."

"I know that now. But at the time?" He saw her throat tighten. "Imagine what I felt, Alec. Imagine what it was like for me to see you, after not knowing what had happened to you, walking through town on the arm of another woman. Then I found out the truth of it. What you had done, what you were. And so I resolved to take matters into my own hands."

"Who told you? How did you find out?"

"It doesn't matter."

"Of course it matters!"

His face was suddenly in her hands, hands that felt too warm for the night. Hands warmed by a power he knew all too well. "I sold my soul so we could be together again."

A deal like that, resulting in nothing for so long? "Two thousand years, Ari."

"I know."

He could practically see the secrets written all over her face, in some language he didn't know, a part of her he couldn't decipher when once he had been fluent in Ariadne. "Who did you sell your soul to?"

"I can't tell you that."

"Why not?"

"I can't tell you that either."

Alec took both her wrists in his hands, pulling her hands from his face. "This is ridiculous."

"Not all demons are like your Carma."

Afraid of his temper and the power trying to eke past his tenuous hold, Alec threw her hands from his grip and backed away, putting space between them once again. "You should never have done that. You should never have sold your soul. Everything I did, everything I've endured for two millennia, means nothing now."

"Yes, Alec, make everything about you. You do not get to decide my life. It was my choice to do what I did."

To unmake his own grave deal. "You made the wrong choice."

"That is not for you to decide!" She grabbed him by the sleeves, forcing him to look at her. "I sold my soul. I made the deal. Me. Not you. Am I not within my rights to do what I think is best? Would you really have me dead now, and not standing here in front of you? Would you give everything back, give up this moment? I wouldn't. It was worth it. For just this one more time with you, it was all worth it."

"Is that all this is?" They were so close now, close enough he could smell her scent and feel her breath on his face. "One moment in time? For thousands of years of nothing?"

"My hope is that this is the first of many."

"But you can't be sure."

"Nor can you. Our lives are not our own. We both have masters."

"Who?"

"Don't ask me again, Alec. I cannot tell you."

He sighed, setting his forehead against hers and closing his eyes. He felt her fingers along his neck, gentle, uncertain, until they finally settled, half-buried in his hair. Sinking into her, he let his own hands wander to her waist, her hips, pulling her closer. "I feel like my whole world is collapsing around me."

"I feel the opposite."

"Everything within me screams that you should not be here."

"Yet I am."

"Yet you are."

"Don't you want to kiss me?"

"More than life itself."

"Then why don't you?"

Why indeed? He flexed his fingers against her hip, feeling how her skin shifted beneath the soft silk. She seemed real enough. But he had seen too much in his immortal life. Not everything was real, and there were creatures that could tempt weak hearts. "What if this isn't real? It can't be real. Something must have happened. I am trapped in some *labrynth* or monster's lair, and the secrets of my heart are being laid before me as torment."

"No," she whispered, her hands lifting his chin so he imagined her looking at his face. "No. Alec, I'm here." He felt her breath first, then her lips against his as she kissed him, softly, carefully, giving him time to accept. "I'm here," she said again, the words a shiver against his mouth. He parted his lips to say her name, and she took that for the assent it was, her hands tightening around his neck, winding them closer together.

His thoughts nothing more than a shattered mess, Alec gave into his body and the sensations it insisted were real.

The liquor had worn off. Not that it had been enough to change his mind; Bri had made sure it was clear there would be no budging on his part. He would not return to the party. The people there would either fuss—which would result in unwanted touches—or whisper behind his back. He was used to the latter. The former scared him the most.

That, and the thought of seeing pity in Ella's eyes.

So Alec had left, and Bri had remained inside, further loosening his collar and kicking at his already discarded jacket. Being rid of the stifling clothing almost made the embarrassment worth it. Almost.

He could see the guests still milling about below in the garden, as his room overlooked the backyard. So as not to be seen, Bri kept to the edge of the window, with nothing but a single candle lighting his room. When he couldn't find Ella in the crowd he gave up on people-watching, and slid to the floor, propping himself against the wall.

Well, aren't I a prize? A social pariah incapable of human touch, who would rather hide inside than face his reality. The fact that Ella talks to me at all is a charity I don't deserve. He knocked his head against the wall. *Idiot.*

The candle on his bedside table burned steadily, the wax dripping away with the night. The full moon made its way across his window, nearing the end of its journey. Eventually, Bri felt the pull of sleep, and his eyes began to droop.

"*Brother.*" The word whispered against the silence, jarring Bri awake.

Heart slamming in his chest, Bri scrambled to his feet, searching every corner of his room, and finding nothing. A dream, he told himself, a nightmare. He took a deep, calming breath, and headed for the washbasin to splash some water on his face.

Then the voice came again, dancing across his ears like a cold tendril of breath. "*Brother.*"

"Kai." Bri said the name before he could stop himself, water dripping off his face and down the front of his shirt.

"*Let me in, Brother.*"

"No." Suddenly aware of the mirror reflecting his image back at him over the washbasin, Bri stumbled back, away. He turned, facing the larger cheval mirror that stood in the far corner of his room. It was covered, as always, but Bri's pulse did not slow. He held perfectly still, holding his breath, and listened.

Nothing.

He waited until his lungs burned, demanding air. When he breathed again, he felt as if the atmosphere in the entire room shifted, becoming lighter. Still nothing happened. No whispers, no faces.

I must have fallen asleep. Imagined it. Dreamed it. He told himself that over and over again, making his way to his bed where he could sit and regain his composure. His hand shook as he touched the coverlet.

The candle flickered, sputtered, then went out.

A hand touched his shoulder. Bri froze.

"*I'm stronger now, Brother. How about you?*"

Turning, Bri made to shove his brother away—but hit nothing but empty air. Laughter echoed from the farthest corner of the room. "*You can't escape me. I am you; you are me.*"

Bracing himself against the bed, willing his knees to stop shaking, Bri steeled his nerves. "All the power you possess, and you use it to torment me? Haven't you got anything better to do?"

"*Not really.*" Smug amusement dripped from each word. "*Come on, Bri. You have power, too. Get rid of me, if that's what you want.*"

"It's what you want." Bri knew better than to play Kai's games. His twin was mad, but he wasn't stupid. He wanted something from Bri, and this was his way of getting it.

"*Then I shall remain a gnat in your ear. How long will you keep your sanity then? No one can hear me but you. They will all think you mad, talking to yourself.*" He tsked.

"You're the mad one, and we both know it." While he spoke—Kai would be distracted somewhat if he kept up the conversation—Bri thought hard about his own power and what Kai could possibly want from him. If he was going to dispel his brother, he had to do something unexpected. Something neither of them knew Bri was capable of.

Right.

"*How cruel. You shouldn't call your brother names, Brishen. It isn't nice.*"

"There are worse things I could call you, and none of them would be untrue." He struggled to find something to grab hold of, anything he could draw power from. As usual, there was nothing about but the myst, clinging to the walls like snakes, waiting, turning toward him at his attention as if the tendrils had eyes with which to see.

Kai could find him in the myst; it was where they had first met. But Kai's existence there was finite, weak, fragile. He could only exist there so long as Bri welcomed him. Or so long as Kai had access to Bri's blood. Kai had neither of those things now. One tendril of myst crept closer, bluish in hue, and thicker than some of the others.

"*Is it worse to be handsome? Charming? Good in bed? Do you know what that's like, little brother? To lay with a woman? To watch her face as she writhes beneath you?*"

No, he did not. But he would not give Kai the satisfaction of hearing him say it. He hoped the jibe was just a coincidence and not evidence that his brother could spy on him anywhere, anytime. If Kai knew what had happened with Ella…

That blue tendril dropped down from the ceiling, twisting as though cocking its head, making an inquiry. Bri wanted to reach out and touch it, to see what it wanted him to see, but he did not know if Kai had eyes in his room or not. Was it just his voice, or could his brother see everything he did?

To test the theory, Bri sat down abruptly on his bed, grabbing the book he had been reading in the afternoon and flipping it open, though there was no light to read by. "Go to Hell, Kai."

"*Already there!*" The response was far too cheerfully said. Bri flipped a page, and Kai said nothing more. Nothing about books in the dark.

The myst tendril came closer still, almost a nudge, an affirmation that they were alone in one sense if not another, and that Bri should proceed.

"Care to join me?"

Bri reached up and touched the myst, bracing himself for visions and the familiar sensation of falling.

Instead, he felt a gentle pull. An invitation.

He'd never felt that before. And somehow, he wasn't afraid.

"Not at all," he answered his brother, then wrapped his hand around the myst, accepting its offer.

It felt like sinking, rather than falling. Sinking into something thick and viscous, something that lifted you even as it dragged you under. Bri saw his room dissolve, then disappear. He stood, feet firmly on the manifested ground of the myst. All about him blue and silver wisps moved in and out of each other, twisting and turning in a choreographed dance. The tendril that had brought him there shivered in delight, then wriggled its way across his body before returning to the waves of its siblings.

Bri stood stark still, listening for any sign of Kai.

There came no buzzing from the self-proclaimed gnat in his ear. Kai was gone. Bri didn't dare call for him, lest saying his name invited him back. He turned over his hands, studying them in the ethereal light of the myst. He wasn't sure how to explain it, even to himself, but he felt more solid. More present. He had always had a "body" when in the myst, but this was different. He was more completely within the myst than he ever had been. If anyone walked into his room at home, they would not find him unconscious on the floor— they would find him gone.

He felt himself smile. So this was what the myst was supposed to be like. What it had to be like for the seraph who guarded it and walked among it every day of their lives. The myst wandered by him, noticing him, but leaving him be. It waited for him to initiate contact. He was in control.

In control!

One step, then two, brought him further into the myst. A spark of bravery caused him to reach out and touch a passing wisp. White. It would show him something benign, something simple. A moment in one person's life. As it glided over his fingers, he saw a young woman, her hands caressing her belly, which had grown considerably. Even through the vision, Bri could feel the steady drum of the life inside her, and the strong kick as it thumped against her hands.

Releasing the vision, Bri took a third step, feeling both tears and laughter welling up in his chest.

The fourth step sent him to his knees.

Bri gasped for breath, struggling against the weight that suddenly pressed down upon his back. When he tried to stand, it slammed him back down again with crushing power. Bri's arms gave out, and his face hit the ground. The air in his lungs twisted, and through blurry vision he could see the tendrils and wisps focusing their attention on him. Ready to converge. His muscles had no power. Try as he might, Bri could not so much as turn onto his side to relieve the devastating pressure on his chest. Sparks glittered before his eyes, and though Bri recognized them as a sign that he desperately needed air, he could not draw breath. His vision swam, and the pain in his lungs grew.

Gentle hands fell upon him, turning him onto his back, stroking his face. Bri tried to blink, to see better, but could only make out blurred lines and muted colors. Silver, pale, the being above him nothing but soft lines. Pink lips moved, forming words he could not hear, but their shape was familiar. Silver, willowy hair cascaded over a lean shoulder, tickling his face and neck.

A memory. Long silver and brown hair. Smiling pink lips. Kind grey eyes that sparkled when she sang. Hands that combed his hair with slender fingers and held him close when the nights were darkest.

Bri felt his chest twist with pain that had nothing to do with the force driving him into the ground. He forced his voice to work. "Mother?"

The hands wrapped about his face, warm and tingling with power. Bri's vision settled, cleared, and it became obvious that the face above him was not his mother, though the resemblance was there. "I am not your mother, child," she said. "You cannot be here. Not like this. They will find you."

"I—I don't know how to leave."

"You will die if you do not. You haven't the knowledge to stand here in full form." Her gaze darted about the myst, then returned to him.

"Help me." Now he could see the large white wings that spread out above them both, membranous and unfeathered. The myst battered against those wings, whipping in and out of their flesh, gliding along their lengths as they shielded him. He had feared the seraph his whole life, but this one...

She stiffened, her fingers flexing against Bri's cheeks. Leaning further down, her face nearly pressed to his, she spoke. "Take strength from me, and open yourself to the mortal realm. Picture where you last were, where you want to be. Do not give yourself to the myst, it will not help you."

Power melted into his body, a warmth that spread quickly, alleviating the pain of the myst. A few tendrils crept close, but Bri turned them away. For the first time in what felt like ages, he breathed deep.

"Do you see it? Your home?"

The posters of his bed, the rich color of the mahogany. The sheets, and the books usually caught up in them. Bri nodded best he could with his face still in her soothing hands.

"Good. Go. And do not visit the myst again if you can help it. Learn to control this. Gabriel knows where you are."

"Who are you?"

The seraph shook her head. "Go."

She flooded him with power. It burned through Bri's veins and chased away the force of the myst while bringing a sense of dread that made his stomach drop. For a moment the image of his room slipped, but Bri held fast to it in his mind.

The shock of being dropped onto the hard, unforgiving floor knocked the hard-won breath from Bri's lungs. He rolled over on the rug, coughing and gasping until he could breathe.

Once certain breathing would continue, Bri traced the pattern of the rug with his fingers. Familiar. His. Shaking and exhausted, Bri realized he could hear nothing coming from outside. No music from the band, no voices from the guests. It would be morning soon.

He closed his eyes.

Alec stared up at the stone bridge where it arched above them, blotting out a piece of the night sky. If he let his head fall to the left, he could see the bright moon, full and unobscured, casting its light onto the river. With each rise and fall of his chest he could feel the shift of Ariadne's hair, tangled now, and acting as a meager cover for them both. She had her head pillowed on his bare chest, her fingers tracing nonsense patterns on his side. They had been careful to cling to the shadows, regardless of the fact that no one had happened by, but Alec could feel the night waning. Not much longer and the sun's first rays would expose them.

Yet, he had no desire to be anywhere else.

Ariadne stretched, making contented noises before placing a kiss on his chest. "That was worth two thousand years."

Alec couldn't help but laugh, his earlier trepidation fading. How many times had he wished for one more day with her? Did it really matter how it had come to be? The past could not be changed anyway.

"That's good to know. Had I disappointed I think I would have to live as a hermit the rest of my existence."

"No need for that." She glanced at the sky. "But I should go soon."

"Why? What will happen if we both just stay here?"

Propping herself on one elbow, she gave him an incredulous look. "Aside from scandalizing the city populace?"

"Aside from that."

"We both have places to be. You know that." Another glance at the sky, and she rolled off him, reaching for her clothes.

Someplace to be. Alec entertained the thought of not going back to Carma, but it wouldn't hold. It wasn't Carma he couldn't turn his back on.

"Come with me, then."

She pulled her hair free from the bodice of her dress, giving it a shake that did little to improve its haphazard appearance. "I can be summoned with a word. There is no point in earning my master's wrath. Lace me up."

Alec sat up and did as she asked. "I prefer to do the opposite," he said, placing a kiss on her bare shoulder before pulling the sleeve up into place.

"How convenient that your preferences should align with mine." Twisting about, she placed a quick kiss on his mouth. "But I really must go."

Alec twirled a lock of her hair about his fingers. "We wait so long for one night?"

"There will be more. But for now, yes. It's enough to have you know I am here. We will find each other again."

"Stay another hour." He kissed her, his hand trailing down her throat.

She shook her head and pushed him back gently. "I cannot. The sun will rise, and I will be summoned. It was lucky I could get away as long as I did." She threw his shirt at him. "Now, dress. You're distracting me."

Though he grinned at that, Alec pulled the shirt over his head, then sought out his pants. "How will I find you?"

Already standing, Ariadne drew her long hair into a plait and tied it off with a bit of ribbon. "Have faith."

Faith. A word he had long given up on. He thought again of returning home. Explaining himself to Carma would be easy—he would simply tell her to mind her own business—but explaining to Bri would be harder. "Bri is probably worried by now. I doubt he slept."

"Bri? The boy?"

"Yes." He fastened one shoe, then the other.

"He is about Marc's age, is he not?"

"A year or so older now."

"Does this replacement bring you peace?"

The sudden change in her tone had Alec snapping his head to look at her. "What does that mean? Bri is not a replacement for Marc."

Something in her eyes had gone cold again. "No? Do you really expect me to believe the thought never crossed your mind? A second chance? I suppose I should be thankful you never found a replacement for me."

"Where the hell is this coming from?" Alec pushed away from the stone, approaching her. "We spend one night together, after being apart for thousands of years, and you start accusing me of *replacing* you and Marc? There could never be a replacement. Marc was everything to me. He was my brother, my flesh and blood. If I could give my life for him, I would. I *tried*. Don't ever presume to think you can begin to know what he meant to me."

There were angry tears in her eyes. "Marc was as precious to me as he was to you, and you know it. Don't pretend otherwise."

"Then don't accuse me of the unthinkable!"

She blinked, closed her eyes a moment longer than was normal, then breathed, looking over his shoulder at the sky. "I'm sorry," she said, the warmth returning to her eyes. "I'm sorry. I don't know what came over me. Too many thoughts and feelings all at once, I suppose. These years were hard for me, too, you know. There were days when I hated you."

The abrupt change back to her normal self, while disorienting, was welcome. Alec sighed and reached for her, glad when she stepped into his touch, resting his hand upon her cheek. "Understandable," he said. "It killed me to leave, telling you nothing."

"As it killed me to live all this time without being able to tell you. So I suppose we are even."

"Everything is different now."

"Yes." She rose up on her toes, kissing him. Alec could still taste the passion of their earlier activities on her lips, like magic that lingered on the air. It would have been so easy to just forget everything else, pull her closer, and pray the sun would not rise. He wrapped his arm about her waist, fully intending to act on that wishful thought.

Ariadne stiffened in his arms. She broke away from him, hands on his shoulders betraying the strength she had now only because of the mark on her arm.

Alec refused to relinquish his own hold. "What is it?"

"Seraph."

— CHAPTER THREE —

I must go." Scrambling and all but shoving Alec aside, Ariadne batted away his reaching hands and grabbed her shoes from the ground.

Somewhat wounded by her physical rejection of his touch and help, Alec tried to think past that pain to the danger her words presented. "How do you know?"

"I can smell them. You need to go as well." Feet shoved in her delicate-looking shoes, she kissed him one last time. "Go. Please. Now."

"Ariadne—"

She winked out of sight. Gone in a blaze of white-hot fire.

Demon power. Hell power. Alec had never met a soulless with access to that kind of power, not other than Picadilly, and she had never been the norm.

Who had Ariadne sold her soul to?

Clearly, it had not occurred to her that Alec could not make himself disappear as she could. Dressed, but barefoot, Alec ran a hand through his tussled hair, and turned to face the oncoming power of Haven as it descended upon him. He debated drawing power into himself, but in the end, decided against it. Best to look as harmless as possible. He didn't have to be the first one to draw a weapon.

He could just as easily be second.

A flash of light lit the night sky, then faded to the twinkle of a star. That twinkle grew larger and larger, until the shape of a body and wings became distinguishable from that of the sparse clouds. Alec kept to the underside of the bridge, protecting his back. The seraph dropped from flight atop the river, splashing at the edge before righting herself and hopping to the shore with a soft curse. She shook the water from her plain leather boots, lamenting their wetness. In the next moment her expression changed as though she had remembered far more important things, and she searched the area with her gaze, chewing nervously on her bottom lip. Her clothes were nothing more than a long brown skirt and a white blouse, untucked and wrinkled. Brown hair cut past her shoulders hung half in her face and mussed. No armor. The most unkempt seraph Alec had ever seen.

Her frustration grew when she could not find whatever it was she searched for. Her eyes flicked toward the sky, as though checking for something worrisome. As if she was afraid of being caught.

Curiosity getting the better of him, Alec stepped out of the shadow of the bridge. "What do you want?"

The seraph jumped at his voice, clutching her heart, and staggering to regain equilibrium. "Goodness. Haven. You scared me."

Obviously. "What do you want?"

Tucking her hair behind an ear, she checked her surroundings one more time before speaking. "Are you the one called Alec? Soulless of the demon Carma?"

A seraph here, looking specifically for him? "Who wants to know?"

She crept closer, keeping her hands visible in front of herself—though she couldn't stop wringing them together. "I'm a friend. I swear it. If you are Alec, please tell me. No, I know you are him. How could you possibly be anyone else?"

"You're making no sense." He took a single step back when she reached the edge of the bridge, keeping his distance.

"I have watched the mortal realm for years, waiting for this chance. I have seen you with him. You love him."

"Love who?"

"Bri."

At that, Alec felt every muscle in his body change. His expression shifted from that of guarded to confusion to shock—then caution. His legs, which had been ready to run, were now ready to charge, to fight. A warm trickle of power began to grow at the center of his palm. "What do you want with Bri?"

The seraph smiled brightly, with no reserve. "Yes, yes. I knew I could trust you. I see it in your face. Bri is my sister's child. I am

Kadiel. You must help him; you must guard him. He is in more danger than he has ever been before."

"Why?"

"Because Gabriel has seen him. She knows where he is...and what he is capable of. She will stop at nothing to get him."

"I already knew all that."

With a pleading hands, and an equally toned voice, the seraph took one step closer. "You must take him away from here. Somewhere she will not find him so easily. Somewhere he can learn."

Alec countered her with another step back. He wasn't about to let her close in. "Learn what?"

"How to control his power. Please, you must trust me," she said, seeming to sense his lingering caution.

"I do not. Seraph hunt him. You are seraph. Why should I trust you?"

"Because this is all my fault to begin with. Bri is hunted because of me. Because I would not do as I was told."

"And what was that?"

"Kill my sister's child. Give him to the reapers the very day of his birth. They wanted Talia to die that day too. But I could not bear it." She sounded sad, but Alec saw the flex of her fingers, the hatred that lingered behind this old memory.

"So you went against Haven's decree."

Kadiel nodded solemnly. "I only want to help."

Though far from convinced, Alec felt himself beginning to believe her. He knew what it was like to stare death in the face as she came for a loved one. He knew the desperation that could bring—and the decisions it made you willing to make. "What is it you want me to do?"

Her wings stretched in sudden hope. "There are mystics in the far west country of Xia-Lo. There is someone there who can teach him, and the mystics will be able to hide him. He must learn to control the ability my sister passed to him. If he does not, he will end up giving himself to Gabriel, and I fear what will happen then."

"None of this proves anything. How can I trust you? You could have me walk Bri right into a trap."

"No, no." Kadiel shook her head furiously, reaching into her pocket. "Here." Holding out her hand, she revealed a silver ring, a solid band with a single emerald set into the center. "Give this to Bri. He will remember it, and it will prove my sincerity. It was his mother's. I pulled it from the ashes of her pyre, unable to part with her completely."

With just a touch of Hell's power still in his hand, Alec grabbed Kadiel by the wrist and pulled her closer. She winced at the burn of his flesh against hers—he, too, felt it, but had been prepared—but she did not resist, did not fight back. "Why not give this to Bri yourself?"

"And risk leading Gabriel straight to him? No. She has me watched too closely as it is, and I am quickly running out of time here."

Alec released her, swiping the ring from her hand as he did so, and stormed further beneath the bridge. He ran his hands through his hair, then dragged them over his face. "There were two children. Did you know that?"

"Yes," her voice was barely more than a whisper. "But Haven did not. Does not. I let them both live. I see now that was a mistake. Kai is a danger to us all, but that is why Bri must remain safe. Why you must take him to these mystics."

Dropping his hands heavily to his sides, Alec realized he no longer debated this seraph's trustworthiness. There was too much pain in her voice. Too much regret. Too much love. "Who are these mystics?"

"They have learned to live with the myst. Humans who peer within and live without if they so choose. Haven is blind to them. Their leader is powerful and has kept hidden for quite some time. If the council and elders knew about these people, they would certainly eliminate them."

"You certainly know a lot of things Haven is ignorant of."

"I spend my days in study. And I have chosen to study anything the others of my kind relegate to the pile of trivial matters. When I caught wind of the temple, I gathered all the information I could, and kept it secret. Haven has larger concerns and has not yet taken notice of my studies."

"Why can this mystic teach Bri when no one else has been able to? Who is he?"

"One of the Fallen."

The guests had all left, and the manor of the so-called Dusombré family was shockingly quiet with the loss. Alec let himself in through the front door, not waiting for a footman to arrive. He hadn't bothered putting his shoes back on, and had them slung by the laces over his shoulder. The ring Kadiel had given him was tucked safely into his pants pocket. The sun had risen, and its first subtle rays splashed through the entryway behind him. The acting butler, Thomas Brannick, stood in the doorway of the parlor, his normally impassive expression exchanged for one of shock.

"Alec?"

"No time now, Thomas. I will talk to you later." Alec headed for the stairs.

"Alec, stop."

The sheer oddity of being a given such a simple command from the reticent butler who always adhered to the rules of his position stunned Alec into obeying. He stared at Brannick, one foot poised to take the first of the stairs.

Brannick cleared his throat and stood straight, hands clasped behind his back. "Your feet. Mrs. McCallahan will have your head."

"Huh?" A glance at his lifted foot answered his confusion. A look over his shoulder at the path he had taken from the front door to this point in the manor clarified things further.

He had not worn his shoes, and his feet had turned black with the dirt and grime of the streets. Dark footprints marred the usually spotless, shining wood floor. Sufficiently warned of his impending doom if he went any farther, Alec retreated from the stairs a step. Brannick nodded his satisfaction. "I will have someone bring you a damp towel," he said.

"Thanks." With Brannick gone, and being unable to proceed until he returned, Alec shoved his hands into his pockets to wait. The feel of the ring urged him forward, but he resisted. Time was limited, but not so much so that he needed to incur the wrath of Mary McCallahan.

Unfortunately, waiting there put him at the mercy of a demon he had hoped to avoid a few moments more.

"Alec." Carma came around the corner, still dressed from the party in her lavish cerulean gown, though she had let her silver hair down around her shoulders. Her sapphire and gold eyes flared with annoyance.

So, of course, Alec needled her further. "Why does everyone insist on reminding me of my own name today?"

She stormed toward him, the air actually stirring around her. "Where have you been?"

"Out."

"Out? Out where?"

"Just out."

"I do not have time for your games, Alec."

"And yet I always have to make time for yours."

She grabbed him by the chin, pulled him close, and let loose her hold on his soul deep within her, letting him feel its draw. Alec had no choice but to close his eyes at the heart-twisting sensation. It was like the sight of water to a man dying of thirst. "My patience is wearing thin. Where were you?"

His resolve slipped. "At a meeting."

"With whom?"

Just an inch more and he would be able to brush his lips against hers, attempt to let his soul pass back from her body into his. But then he remembered the feel of another's lips against his, and he pulled away, guarding at least one secret. "I have information. Knowledge that may help us with Bri."

Carma let her hand slide from his chin, down his neck, and away. "Help with what?"

"Keeping him safe. Someone who could teach him."

"Where did you get this information?"

Alec thought of Kadiel as she left, pleading with him to do as she asked, to tell no one of their meeting. No one but Bri. "I can't tell you."

The tips of Carma's hair turned red. "I could make you tell me."

"I know."

"Then why say such a ludicrous thing?"

"Because I made a promise." Carma scoffed. Alec forged ahead. "Don't you trust me at all?" It was a feeble argument, but simply pointing out the chink in their millennia-old relationship made him feel better.

Carma studied him, glaring, her duel-colored eyes flaring with anger. Then she did the impossible. She sighed and took a step back, giving him his space. "Fine. I trust you. On matters concerning Bri. Who is this teacher? Don't stare at me like that, Alec. Answer before I change my mind."

It took a moment to find his voice. "A fallen seraph, somewhere in Xia-Lo."

"Fallen?"

Alec only nodded. Brannick arrived then, handing him the promised towel for his feet. Alec sat on the bottom step and began the task of cleaning himself up enough to continue through the house.

"A fallen Singer, I take it," Carma mused. "Do you know the name of this being?"

"I do not. Only that he has a following of mystics, mortals, who will also be able to help. They can hide Bri. Which apparently, we need to do. Gabriel will come after him here."

At that, a smirk came over Carma's lips. "Indeed she will, won't she?"

"That's just what you want, isn't it?"

"Very much so. Though I admit having Bri away when it happens would make things far simpler. But I still do not like it." She paused. "Take him, then. If you think it truly safer."

"If it's not, I'll get him out of there as fast as I can."

"Of that I have no doubt." Stepping over him, she headed upstairs without another word.

Alec knew better than to say anything else. Feet clean, he handed the towel back to Brannick with thanks, and went upstairs himself.

Bri's door was closed, but Alec went straight in with only a single warning knock regardless. The first thing he saw was the single burning candle, little more than a blob of quickly depleting wax on its holder, the flame sputtering in its last moments. The second thing was Bri's empty bed.

Then he saw Bri.

While not completely abnormal to find Bri sprawled out on the floor of his room, rather than safely tucked away in his bed, it nevertheless sent Alec's pulse racing, worry charging through his veins. He crouched beside him, glad to see that he breathed normally, then gave him a gentle shake. "Bri."

Bri stirred, grumbling as sleep left him in a way that further assured Alec of his wellness. Alec shifted to sit, drawing up one knee and resting an arm across it while he waited for the boy to rouse. "Wake up. I have something to tell you."

Scrubbing at his face with the back of one hand, Bri rolled to face him. "Why am I on the floor?"

"You tell me."

A moment passed, in which Bri clearly searched his memories of the night before for the answer. The discovery of that answer came with a groan and a few out of character curses. Bri flopped onto his back, both hands clapped over his face. "I have some things to tell you, too," he muttered.

"Breakfast first? Or would you rather dive into it on an empty stomach?"

"Which is better—wanting to throw up everything you've eaten, or losing your appetite?"

"Is your news really that bad? Mine is actually fairly good."

Bri sat up in one swift motion. The action put him unintentionally almost nose to nose with Alec, who blinked at the sudden invasion of his space. "Good news?"

"Odd, isn't it?"

"What could be good news?"

"Information. Hope. A present."

Bri looked skeptical, a little like he was wondering if Alec had had too much to drink the night before. "A present? From whom?"

Alec didn't see any point in waiting. He reached into his pocket and took out the ring, holding it up for Bri to see. "Your mother."

Bri stared at the ring, tracing its silver lines against the pale flesh of his palm. He had said nothing since Alec showed it to him, having lifted it carefully from Alec's hold as if it might shatter at his touch. He remembered his mother twisting the ring about the first finger on her left hand when she was thinking. So many nights had been spent in her arms, holding her hand and stroking the brilliant green stone that glimmered in the light. A tremble set into his body, threatening to overtake him. He had feared forgetting her, losing the knowledge of the way her mouth would turn up in a smile at him, and the small crinkles by her grey eyes. But with the sight of the seraph so like her the night before, and the ring now—Bri could have cried with each memory that reemerged.

Alec had gotten to his feet and gone to the door. Words were said, but Bri didn't hear them, and Alec shut the door once again before returning. He extended a hand toward Bri, standing over him. "Let's at least get up off the floor."

Bri couldn't tear his gaze from the ring. "Where did you get this?"

"Your mother's sister. Turns out you have allies in Haven." Bri didn't fight Alec when he took him by the elbow and pulled him to his feet. Bri closed his fist tightly around the ring, afraid of dropping it, but uncurled his fingers once more as soon as he had been deposited in one of the armchairs by the table where he had taken to playing Kayos. Alec sat across from him. "Do you want to tell me your story first? That way we can end the conversation with the good news."

Bri started to shake his head, then changed his mind. Telling what happened the night before would help him focus, and he wanted to focus. He *needed* to focus, if he wanted to truly hear what Alec had to say about his mother—and her sister.

He started with Kai's voice, fumbling his words as he tried to explain the myst and the ethereal and ghostly seraph he had met there who looked so much like a silver version of his mother. In the midst of his scattered explanation, a maid knocked and entered at Alec's invitation, setting a tray of food on the table between them before leaving them alone once again.

Alec had let him ramble, clenching fists that turned his knuckles white at the mention of Kai, but saying nothing until Bri had finished. "Kai was here?"

"It was just his voice. I don't think he could see me, and though I thought I felt him touch me, it was only once, and it must have been a trick." He had drawn his knees up on the chair, and now twirled his mother's ring between his fingers.

"So you went into the myst to escape him. Fully into the myst."

Bri flipped the ring around his first finger, where it fit only just past the first knuckle. "Yes."

"You've never been able to do that before."

"I know."

"And the seraph, you said she warned you about Gabriel. That makes two in one night."

"Two?" For the first time since receiving the ring Bri looked at Alec. "How two?"

Alec tapped his fork on his plate, though he had eaten little. "The seraph who spoke to me. She said her name was Kadiel, your mother's sister, but she wasn't a silver Singer like you described. And she said Gabriel knows where you are and is making plans to come for you. She was very insistent I get you away from here."

Bri had so many other questions. What was she like? What did she look like? But he forced himself to settle on the most important first. He could ask Alec personal questions later. "Where am I supposed to go? Gabriel is seraph. A general. She can find me anywhere."

"Kadiel said there's a group of mystics in Xia-Lo. They can hide you, and their leader can teach you."

"That sounds a lot like three years ago." When they'd traveled across country by horseback only to be attacked, ending with a *labrynth* burned into Bri's back.

"Their leader is one of the Fallen. That's got to be a better bet than a crazy old witch."

"If Dorothea hears you say that she'll turn you into a fish again."

"She never turned me into a fish." Alec's voice had raised slightly.

"She says she did."

"She's crazy."

The laughter that bubbled up surprised Bri, but it felt good. "Do you trust her? This seraph?"

Alec didn't hesitate. "Yes. I do."

"Does that mean we're leaving?"

"It's clearly not safe here anymore. Not now, at least. We'll be going alone. Carma is staying here. So I'm sure we'll be back at some point."

Bri slipped the ring onto the middle finger of his left hand, testing the fit. It slid down, no problem. Of course. Slight as he was, Bri wasn't all that surprised that he could wear his slender mother's ring. For once, he was glad for his slim build. "I guess I should pack then."

"A good idea." Alec stood, making as though he would leave, then stopped. "Oh. I almost forgot." He reached into his breast pocket and pulled out a folded piece of paper, which he then set down on the table. "Lady Ella asked me to give this to you." He tapped the note once, then headed for the door. "Make sure you eat something."

The note seemed to stare at him as Alec left. Bri's appetite disappeared completely. *Ella.* He hadn't thought about what leaving meant when Alec had proposed it, but he did now. Leaving meant not seeing Ella again, for however long it took for him to learn to control the myst. Leaving now meant not having the chance to apologize for the night before.

The kiss.

That steeled Bri's resolve. If he ever wanted to kiss Ella again—kiss her successfully—then he had to learn. He grabbed the note and opened it, trying to dispel the nervousness that threatened to be his stomach's undoing.

> Bri,
>
> I do hope this note finds you in better health. Propriety will not allow me to see for myself. Please write me once you are well enough, so that I may know you fair well.
> With all my best,
>
> Ella.

Her handwriting was as beautiful as she was. The address she had placed at the bottom of the note was for a place in the east end of town—not where he suspected she lived. The east end was a place of merchants and artisans, not well-bred young ladies.

Saving that curiosity for later—the morning had been confusing enough as it was—Bri set the note on the table where he could see it, twirled his mother's ring about his finger as he had seen her do hundreds of times, and ate.

— CHAPTER FOUR —

Carma watched as the last of Alec and Bri's meager packings were secured to the back of the carriage. Brannick would take them as far as the border of Chanae. From there, Alec and Bri would make their own way. As a result, they had packed light—one small trunk each, with a bag stowed away in case they needed to travel by foot.

She turned her gaze to the sky, where the blue of midday was completely unblemished, not even with the occasional cloud. Yet she felt more than just the heat of the sun blazing down on her. She knew the view from Haven—two thousand years was not enough to diminish the memory. The stiller the mortal realm, the more clearly the seraph could peer down. A cloud or two would have been nice.

Alec and Brannick had their heads together at the edge of the carriage, talking in hushed tones. Carma couldn't hear them, but she didn't care to. Whatever they were plotting, it most likely had to do with the approaching journey. She trusted them both implicitly, though she would never admit it.

Bri was more interesting, pressing a brown paper-wrapped package into Mary's hands, both eager to hand it over and unwilling to let it go. "You'll make sure it gets there?" he said, not for the first time, his fingers still dancing across the package.

Mary smiled, making no move to take it before he was ready. "Yes, Bri," she said, her lack of the honorific she usually insisted upon a telltale sign of both her amusement and her promise to do as he asked. "It will be there by the end of the day."

Finally, Bri seemed placated, and he stepped back, relinquishing his hold.

Though curious, Carma couldn't dredge up enough compulsion to make herself care what the package was. Bri didn't always have the best judgment, but Mary McCallahan did.

In a sudden pop of cold air, Picadilly appeared at Carma's side. The former demon turned soulless settled back into the mortal realm with a sigh and a crack of her neck.

"You did as I asked?"

Dusting her hands off on the black trousers she'd made for herself, Pica rolled her eyes. "No. I danced around the moon instead. Of course I did."

"And?" Such impertinence in any of her other soulless would have earned them Carma's ire, but not Pica. Pica was an old friend, an ally, and their deal was more an arrangement than anything else.

"I found the place. Very out of the way, nestled in a valley deep within the mountains. There are magical runes and wards everywhere. It's no wonder the seraph have no idea."

"And you believe Bri will be safe there?"

"Safe is a relative term. Sending him to one of the Fallen is risky. Their allegiances are always more skewed than ours."

"No sign of who it is?"

"They don't let outsiders get very close. And they avoid answering questions. Alec will have his work cut out for him getting in."

"I have a feeling a myst-seeing human will be enough to draw our unknown kin."

"Most likely. In any case, I know where they will be, and will be able to travel there easily now."

"Good." It had been agreed upon that Pica would act as liaison between Carma and Alec during their time apart. Carma could easily deliver herself to the location of any of her soulless, but Alec had argued that her movements would be too easily detected by other demons. Nor could she call Alec to her whenever she wanted him. It would leave Bri alone, and she could not send Alec back with a snap of her fingers. If they wanted to remain hidden, they needed a more covert method of communication.

Picadilly had been volunteered. She could bounce around the continent, obscuring her intended destination. That would lead any possible spies astray—if any could detect her in the first place. She was an anomaly, their Pica.

Dorothea appeared from around the side of the house, emerging from her workshop for the first time in days. The old witch was hunched and dirty, her clothes covered in dust and grime, her face smeared with ink and blood. Her hands had been wrapped and bound tightly, but spots of red had soaked through. Carma didn't know what magic she had been working lately, scribing *labrynths* with her own blood day in and day out, but she was surprised it had taken the woman this long to inquire as to the world above.

The witch headed straight for Bri. She caught him by the arm, pushing Mary out of her way despite the housekeeper's protests. "Where you be going, child?"

Bri composed himself quickly, though she had startled him at first. In the last three years, he had learned how to deal with Dorothea. "Alec and I are leaving. There's someone out west who can help me learn. I'm not safe here anymore."

"Bah." She wrested Bri backward, shoving him up against the door of the carriage and lifting his shirt to see his back.

Alec broke from Brannick mid-sentence. "Dorothea." He went toward them, his tone a warning.

Carma decided to join him. Not because she feared for Bri, but because when Dorothea got like this, she spoke words worth hearing.

Bri, for his part, didn't fight. Dorothea gathered his shirt above his shoulders with one hand, using that same hand to hold him still. With her other, she traced the lines of the large *labrynth* she had burned into his back when he was thirteen. She dug one jagged nail into the lowest of the runes and Bri winced. Alec grabbed her by the wrist.

"What are you doing?"

"Testing. Shaping." She pulled free of his grip and returned to her work.

Alec didn't stop her, but he kept close, watching Dorothea, but always aware of Bri. Carma had chosen well with him. Acquiring Alec had never been, and would never be, a mistake. "Testing what?" he asked.

"Yes, Dorothea, testing what?" Carma stood at Alec's side, giving herself a perfect view of both her witch and her soulless, as well as

Bri's back. She watched as Dorothea picked small wounds into Bri's flesh, drawing blood and causing the lines of the scars to light up with power in turn before darkening again.

"His strength. The strength of the *labrynth*. He has never been far from me, and he is growing more rapidly than ever. The spell will continue to stretch; it may break."

"What happens if it breaks?" Bri asked, flinching as she drew more blood.

"Don't know," Dorothea said. "Depends on you."

"What do you mean?"

"The control you have is from this *labrynth*. It activates whenever you use the myst. I feel it. If it breaks, it is uncertain how much control you have on your own."

"It was only ever meant to help him," Alec said. "To teach him until he could manage on his own. Breaking it one day was inevitable, wasn't it?"

Dorothea retracted her hand, ceasing her ministrations, though her gaze remained trained upon her spell on Bri's back. "No. I was going to alter it as he grew, as he learned, until he could manage without it. I will not be able to do so if he is away from me."

At that, Alec shared a cryptic look with Bri. It wasn't a mistake to place Alec in charge of him, but over the years the two had grown close enough that often only a look between them was needed to communicate—a look Carma often couldn't decipher. It was annoying. "So what do you propose to do about it?" Carma said, tapping her clawed fingertips against her thigh.

Dorothea turned her head, looking at Carma over her shoulder like some sort of dangerous bird. "Will your soulless stop me if I open him up?"

"He will if you don't have a good reason," Alec answered for himself, his posture shifting, making ready to do as he had said.

The witch laughed. A deep, throaty sound that resulted in her tossing her head back. By the expressions of all those around, no one knew what was funny.

Snapping her head back, Dorothea reached her free hand toward Alec's face. "Dear Alec, do I ever do anything without good reason?"

He let her trace the line of his jaw the way she had traced the lines of Bri's back. "Sometimes, yes."

Dorothea smiled, then smacked Alec's chin lightly with the back of her fingers. In the next instant, she was all business again. "I can alter the *labrynth* now, make it malleable. It will allow for growth while he is away, but keep the spell from breaking completely. However, he will still need to come to me when it is time to attempt control on his own. It would be unwise to do otherwise."

"How long will it hold?" Carma asked.

A shrug. "A year, maybe more. It depends on how much he grows." Dorothea looked at Alec again. "Don't feed him so much."

Alec was not amused.

Bri, who had quietly turned his face into the carriage door, attempted to look over his shoulder at them all. "Do I get any say in this?"

"No." With a single hand, Dorothea turned his head back around, knocking it against the door.

Alec removed her hand from Bri's head, then leaned in close to the boy. "You don't want to do this?"

"No, I do. There doesn't seem to be any other choice. I was just tired of being left out of the conversation."

That made Alec smile—an expression Carma treasured, but tended to be unable to create herself—and step back again. He glanced at Carma, as though gauging her reaction, then continued on to Dorothea when she said nothing. "How hurt will he be? Will we still be able to travel today?"

"A little bleeding. A little pain. He can sit in a carriage."

"You good with all that, Bri?"

Bri nodded. "It can't be worse than the first time, right?"

"Right." Though he said the word, Alec's reluctance to agree to that was clear in his voice. He knew Dorothea too well to trust when she said something would be simple.

As insurance, Carma stepped up and spoke directly into the old witch's ear. "Do not forget. He is precious to me. I need him. And I need him to make this journey without injury or illness."

"I forget nothing. I will not make him ill. He will be more ill later if I do not do this."

"Then proceed."

Alec slipped a hand into one of Bri's, giving it a squeeze. She couldn't always interpret their wordless language, but Carma knew enough to know what the hand meant. Alec was there if Bri needed him. For anything. Alec would let him clutch his hand through the pain, or pull him away from Dorothea completely if it became too much. Bri squeezed back, taking a deep breath.

Dorothea unwrapped her hands. They were covered in cuts and scars, some of the newest still bleeding. How witches never seemed to do irreparable damage to themselves, Carma would never fully understand. They could cut their flesh almost constantly, and suffer no infections, no permanent damage. Some could bleed more than others without rest—and Dorothea was the strongest witch alive, aside from maybe Bri's brother, Kai—but the wounds always healed. Drawing a small blade from her hip, Dorothea stuck each of her fingertips, raising beads of red blood to the surface. With the blade then stuck between her teeth, she set to scribing along Bri's back.

Her blood must have been warm, but Bri shivered at her touch. Dorothea drew red lines with long practiced ease, making twists and turns that spoke in languages unknown by any tongue. The lines followed those of the scars she had long ago burned into his young flesh, mirroring and echoing their pattern. Then, every so often, she would divert from the established path, pull a loop, or turn in the opposite direction. Each move was deft and precise, without hesitation.

Her fingers met back at their starting point, and Dorothea lifted them from Bri's back. As quickly as she had scribed the new *labrynth* along the old one, she rewrapped her hands once more, staunching the flow of blood and saving it for another time, another spell. She took the blade from her teeth. "Hold still."

Bri turned his face into the side of the carriage, his grip on Alec's hand tightening. The witch's blade cut into his back, carving runes by the *labrynth* and flaring with pale light in the bright of the noonday sun. Remarkably, Bri made no sound louder than a hiss.

A shadow passed over them, as though a cloud had rolled by the sun. But there were no clouds. Carma turned her face to the sky, and felt the unforgettable shiver of the veil parting between the realms. More white shadows joined the first, streaking the sky.

"No time," Dorothea muttered, her blade biting deeper. Bri cried out.

"Seraph," Carma said, cursing her Havenly kin for their impeccably awful timing. She had no doubt who it was. The First File descended upon them. Reverting her hand to its true, clawed form was more a release of her usual restraint than a calling of power. She felt Picadilly draw strength from Hell through her link to her, as did Brannick and Mary. Alec could call nothing, not while he touched Bri. "Pica!" she yelled her name with all the strength of a command. When she saw the nod of understanding, Carma turned her attention fully to the force of Haven that was Gabriel.

She had brought a dozen of her finest, and they gave no indication that they would stop to talk.

Carma let her true form come. Bronze wings tore from her back, stretching and immediately propelling her from the ground. She collided with Gabriel in the air, surprising her and giving her no time to draw her weapon. They crashed to the earth below, a tangle of limbs. Carma clawed at Gabriel's throat—a warning. The blessed armor of her once friend burned her skin when they touched, but Carma had been ready for it. Such pain was nothing compared to the feel of your own hand tearing through your chest. She could stand a little holiness against her flesh. Grabriel snarled, and they both got to their feet. Carma clamped her hand down on Gabriel's when she reached for her sword, holding it still in its scabbard.

"Now, now," she said, her face perilously close to the seraph's. "Let's not sully this reunion with steel."

"You have already drawn my blood." Gabriel tugged at her sword, attempting to loosen Carma's grip. Her neck was bloody where Carma had clawed it.

"So, I have. Is it blood you want?"

"I want the boy."

"Too late."

Through the sounds of scuffling between soulless and seraph, Carma laughed lightly as Gabriel's expression turned darker. She let the general peer over her shoulder, toward the carriage where her quarry had last been seen.

Bri was gone. As was Alec, and Picadilly.

Just as planned.

Brannick stood over a fallen seraph, the white creature streaked with silver blood. But he had been taken captive himself, a strong and capable seraph soldier at each arm, holding him tight. By where the horses scuffled and stomped, alarmed by the fight, Mary had been brought to her knees, and was now held there by a sword to her throat. Dorothea stood, surrounded by a circle of four of Gabriel's First File, their weapons drawn and ready. She looked bored.

Carma could hear Gabriel's teeth grinding together before the seraph even looked back at her. She laughed as two of the unoccupied seraph came and took her by the arms, wrenching her away from their general. With great force they pressed on her shoulders until she went to her knees.

Taut as a wire, Gabriel's face had turned as red as Carma's hair. "What is so funny?"

"The fact that you are surprised."

"You should have had no warning I was coming. You were not ready for me."

"I am always ready for you, Gabe." She did not struggle against her guards. There was no point. Not yet.

"How could you have gotten him away so quickly? He is human. Mortal. He cannot pass through Hell. What have you done? It is impossible."

"Gabriel, I have bested you since we were children. And now, I am restrained by nothing."

"Nothing but the truth."

There was that. "A small and inconsequential caveat."

Sword finally drawn, Gabriel stepped forward and placed the tip of her blade at Carma's throat. "You will tell me where he is."

"I cannot tell you what I do not know."

"An evasion. A way to make it sound as if you do not know, without lying about it."

"I do not know where he is, Gabriel." She spoke each word carefully, enunciating so there would be no misunderstandings. "I can speak nothing but the truth, as you pointed out. There is no evasion here."

Gabriel's feathered armor creaked as her fist tightened around the hilt of her sword. "You may not know exactly where he is, but you know what's been done with him."

"Very true. I have hidden him from you. Tell me, Gabe," Carma enjoyed watching her old friend bristle as she continued, "what do you think of this situation? Two beings come together over a child. One to kill, one to preserve. Who is the villain?"

The tip of Gabriel's blade bit into Carma's throat, burning with its blessedness as it cut. "You do not know the whole of it. You do not know what damage he could wreak on the mortal realm. Or... perhaps you do. Perhaps that is exactly what you want. It sounds demonic enough for me."

"Oh, Gabriel, you have no idea what I truly want." No one did. It was her secret. Her burden. She wouldn't even allow the truth to the front of her mind. A demon couldn't lie, even to herself. So Carma had trained herself against even thinking about her true intentions. The First File, no matter their reputation, was not enough to change that.

"Stand up."

"Is that really what you want?"

"I said stand up."

"Think carefully before you command me."

With a tilt of her wrist, Gabriel forced Carma to lift her chin against the blade of the sword. "Stand. Up. Now."

Carma sighed, shrugging one shoulder casually. "As you wish." She flexed the muscles in her legs—and in her wings. She focused her power to the edges, the sharp and deadly extremes of her most prized appendages. They tore through the arms of those who held her, sending them screaming and burning to the ground, hellfire licking at their wounds, and devouring the limbs no longer attached. Two more soldiers came to restrain her, but the fire was already in her hands, and it was so simple to spark it to each of them in turn. Their blessed armor caught alight, holding the hellfire at bay only a moment before its holiness began to crumble against the weight of her power.

Gabriel stepped forward as though to attack, but Carma held up a single, blazing hand, stopping her. "Release my soulless and my witch. In return I will recall my fire."

Gaze flicking to her soldiers, four of whom writhed on the ground, batting at the flames that slowly ate away at their armor and skin, Gabriel's jaw clenched. Carma could see the unwillingness in her eyes, but they had fought before, and they both knew how it would end if the fight ever escalated beyond simple testings of strength.

"Release them," she ordered, lowering her sword until its tip touched the ground.

The seraph surrounding Brannick, Mary, and Dorothea were well trained. They did not hesitate. Carma snuffed out the fire in her hand and recalled the flames that burned those of the First File. Aside from the two who had lost limbs, the injuries would be minor.

"Thank you," Carma said with a smile. "We were friends once, Gabriel. I never forget that."

"You betrayed me. You betrayed Haven...and The One. Your friendship means nothing."

"It is a shame you see it that way." She saw Dorothea brush her hands off on her tattered skirt, then begin picking at the bindings on her hands. "I don't suppose you would be open to speaking with me. Alone."

"I do not deal with demons." She motioned for her injured soldiers to be seen to.

"Really? What is all this then?"

"I will find the boy, Carma. I will have him, and he will face the will of Haven."

"Gods forbid."

"He is a threat."

Carma laughed. She couldn't help herself. "Oh, blistering hell, if only you knew how ridiculous you sound. I am almost tempted to let you spend five minutes with the boy. He is a threat to nothing and no one but himself."

"Then why your devoted interest in him? You do nothing without reason, old friend." She leaned on the words, mocking the reference to their past. "If the boy is nothing, then why do you want him so badly?"

"Maybe I just want to him because you do. It is ever so fun to piss you off."

Steel flashed in the sun. Carma grabbed the blade just before the knife could pass into her abdomen and turned it, slamming it into Gabriel instead. Silver blood dripped from the seraph's stomach, just between her breast plate and the belt that had held the weapon now lodged in holy flesh.

No one else dared move.

Carma and Gabriel were so close a kiss could be shared easily, but kissing was far from either of their thoughts. "You just recovered, Gabriel. Do not make me send you back to the infirmary so soon." Gabriel said nothing, instead remaining perfectly still to prevent further damage. Carma did not twist the knife; she had no intention of harming Haven's general. "Funny thing about demons; they know precisely where all seraph weak spots are. You would think the forces of Haven would change their tactics or their armor after a few thousand years of this. Haven needs to change, Gabe. Or it will fall."

Gabriel gritted her teeth, leaning closer despite the blade in her belly, her breath on Carma's face as she spoke. "Finish me, then, and be done with it."

Carma looked her straight in the eyes. She wanted there to be no further uncertainty between them. "As I said, Gabriel, we were friends once. I have not killed you these last years because of it. But if you come after me and mine again, if we meet once more and you have intent to battle with me, I will forget those times of childhood—and I will end you."

Carma retreated in a burst of fire, sinking into Hell's welcoming heat and calling her soulless to her in her next breath. Dorothea appeared beside her in the ensuing instant under her own power. With a sigh, Carma began to walk over the blackened stones and curling vines of Hell's forests. They would have to stay below a while, until she was sure Gabriel had gone. But Gabriel and her First File were the least of her worries.

She had no way of knowing if Pica's untested power had worked. Alec she could still feel, his soul warm inside her, and aware of its body despite the distance between them. Bri was another matter. He was either safe—or dead.

— CHAPTER FIVE —

A lec saw the white wings in the sky. He saw Carma flex her clawed hand and felt the tempting trickle of power on the air as the other soulless around him prepared to fight. His grip on Bri's hand kept him grounded. Dorothea rushed her work, cutting Bri faster and with less care. She worked his blood around into her intended lines as she did so, cursing and muttering to herself the whole time. He heard the tear of Carma's dress as she released her wings and felt the surge in the air as she took flight.

When she collided with Gabriel, it sounded as if Haven and Hell themselves had crashed into one another, screeching and tearing the very life out of the air.

Then Picadilly was directly in front of him, kicking Dorothea away before wrapping her arms around him and Bri.

The whole world went silent and dark then.

Light and sound returned in a pop that sang pain through Alec's head. Grass and stone raked up his back, and he dug his elbows into the ground instinctively to stop the sudden movement. A heavy weight pressed upon his chest. As the colors and lights of his vision dissolved back into a recognizable world, Alec could see Pica's black hair and her pale white arms. He followed the line of her right arm to her hand, where it still gripped the back of Bri's neck.

Alec shoved her off him and sat up, ignoring any and all pain his body complained of. "Bri?" He grabbed him by the shoulders and hoisted him up so he could see his face. He touched one pale and sweaty cheek, relieved when those silver-brown eyes blinked twice then looked at him with full recognition.

"What happened?" Bri shook in Alec's hold, looking ready to be sick.

"I don't know."Alec turned to Picadilly, who had picked herself up off the ground and was busy dusting off her pants. "What happened? What the hell was that?"

"That," she said, flicking a crumbled leaf from her hair, "was a calculated risk."

"What do you mean?" They were surrounded by trees, trees so tall it seemed they reached straight into Haven itself. The forest floor was damp, either from rain or morning dew, and shadows clung to every trunk and every bit of brush that grew around them. The fallen leaves looked like nothing he had seen in Chanae over the past three years. "Where are we?"

"I'm not sure precisely." Pica took a quick turn about the small clearing. "If I remember correctly, this looks to be the edge of the Wilds, close to the border of the Frontland."

"The Wilds?" She had taken them miles north of where they had been. Hundreds of miles, if not thousands. "How did you do it? How did you move us?"

"It's something I've always been able to do myself—you know that. Taking others with me was always a possibility. I simply needed to figure out the right conditions, the proper amount of power."

"Why didn't you tell me you could do this?"

"I didn't know."

"You didn't know?"

"This was my first attempt. It seems to have worked well."

"Well?" Alec stood, careful of Bri's unsteadiness as he did so. "Does this look 'well' to you?"

"We are far from Gabriel and her minions, so yes, it does."

Once glance at the still pale and shaking Bri and Alec went cold with horrible possibilities. He dropped the volume of his voice. "You could have killed him."

"It was a small possibility, yes. But take your complaints elsewhere. I was under orders."

A shame Carma was now so far away. Alec had a number of choice words for their dear demon master. "I assume this is supposed to change nothing? Bri and I still make our way to the mystics from here?"

"Yes."

"If you can transport us instantly, why not do that instead? Hell, why drop us here? Why didn't you just go to the mystics?"

"I'm not so sure how instant the process was. It seems to be morning again. I believe we have lost an entire afternoon and night. As for why I didn't go straight to the mystics, or why I don't take you now—I can't. They're warded. Which is why you're going there, yes? Besides, the boy doesn't look like he would survive a second time."

"I'm okay," Bri said, attempting to stand. His legs gave out, however, and Alec just managed to catch him by the arms and steady him before he fell. Once back on his feet, Bri murmured a quiet thanks.

Alec didn't dare let go of him. Instead, he turned his gaze to what little of the sky he could see through the thick canopy of the trees. It certainly didn't look like the sun had reached its height yet, and the forest smelled of crisp nighttime mixed with morning warmth. "An awful way to travel, if that's the case. I don't remember anything other than nothingness."

Picadilly shrugged one shoulder, wandering to a nearby tree to touch the bark. "It is like that when I travel alone, but it lasts only moments. I suppose the extra weight slowed me down."

Too tired to care—arguing about it would change nothing, only waste time and energy—Alec led Bri to a grassy patch in the clearing and sat him back down. Bri winced, one hand reaching around to sooth his back.

His back. The *labrynth*. Had Dorothea finished, or had Picadilly taken them before the rewriting of the spell was complete?

Cel-Eza, help me.

"Let me see your back, Bri." Alec knelt and lifted the bloodied shirt. He swallowed the instinctive gasp at the near ruin that had become Bri's back, not wanting to alarm him. The runes Dorothea had cut still bled, and had turned red and swollen. It may have taken half a day for them to travel, but their bodies apparently had not registered that time. He didn't know much about *labrynths*, not more than what they looked like, and when they were active, but something about the rune by Bri's left shoulder told him it was incomplete. Maybe it was the way one curl had arched around as though to touch the central line, but had stopped short.

"Is it bad?" Bri asked, sitting stiffly.

"No. Not bad. But we need to clean it up." Alec looked at Picadilly. She turned as though she felt his gaze on her. "What?"

"We need supplies."

"Not my problem."

"You can travel instantaneously. And it's because of your talent that we are here without any clothes, supplies, or money."

"At Carma's order, I'll remind you."

"I promise not to forget. Can you go back to the manor, collect a few of our things?"

Pursing her lips as she thought, Pica closed her eyes and went silent. Though he would have normally been thankful for the blissful quiet from the other soulless, Alec found it grating as he caught sight of the blood running down Bri's back from the last of the runes. Pulling his handkerchief from his pocket, he pressed it against the rune to staunch the flow.

Bri flinched. "Am I bleeding?"

"Just a bit. Hold still."

Like a statue coming to life, Pica breathed and leaned heavily against a nearby tree. "I cannot. I am too weak after transporting the two of you so far. I would never make it back all the way to Chanae."

"Can you manage something shorter?"

"To what end?"

"Never mind." She was right; there was no other option. They were stranded. "How long do you need before you're strong enough?"

"I imagine a meal and a good night's sleep would be a good start."

"Is there a town nearby?" Reaching into his pocket, Alec felt the warm press of coins. Enough for a single night, at least. Or so he hoped.

"This is the Wilds. But I was here once before, as I searched for the best route to your mystics. I believe there is a Frontland town just beyond the border. Half a day's walk westward."

The Wilds were home to hermit witches and gods like the mischievous twins, Keaie and Kesi, who lured travers off their paths to play children's games. They couldn't linger here long.

"Then that's where we go."

—◖●◗—

Though he had spent far more years of his life in Hell than out of it, the heat of this place still made him sweat. How he longed for the comfort of his old workshop, with its glass walls and carefully placed *labrynths*. Here, he had been forced to start from scratch, and while it had taken him substantially less time to acclimate the area to his needs than it had with his first workshop, this spot resisted any cooling spells he constructed.

This one would work if it was the last thing he did.

Sliding the blade across the tips of his fingers, and then arching them over his palm, Kai watched his blood pool in his hand, still fascinated by the sight even after so many years. Satisfied with the amount he had drawn, he turned his hand and trickled the blood over the lines he had carved into the harsh black stone of the floor. Pure brimstone, such as this, was harder to work with, but once it bent to the user's will, its power was uncontested. The *labrynth* burst into life, blue light flooding the dark and humid room. Small crystals of ice began to grow at the spell's edges, reaching outward until they touched Kai's bare knees. He shivered with their cold and pleasure. The light dimmed, but did not fade completely. Touching one ice crystal with the tip of his finger, Kai was pleased when it did not melt or break. The heat on the air, once so thick it caused everything to shimmer and wave like water, broke. A chill swept over Kai's sweating body, and he breathed in the relief of it.

Then he laughed, because even the heat of Hell was nothing compared to his persistence, his power.

Once his amusement was sated, Kai wrapped his bleeding hand so that it now matched the other, as well as his forearms, and stood, ready for the next task. With the first step across the cool brimstone floor, a shiver that was less delight and more a chill ran up his body. In the heat, he had stripped down to work. Now, he sought a comfortable warmth.

Redressing in trousers and a loose white shirt, Kai took a moment to look over the other *labrynths* he had scribed into the walls. Most glowed with a gentle blue or red hue, their twists and turns beautiful and dangerous. That was what Kai loved most about spells: their appearance. To have something so artful, so stunning to the untrained eye, that one might think they were mere decoration, and know that in fact each line spoke a thousand words no tongue could ever mutter. To know that treachery and danger lurked behind each loop—like a trap laid deep within the earth, unseen by its intended prey.

And he controlled them all. Understood. Commanded. It was a heady mix he never tired of.

Shoes back on, Kai crossed the room, heading for the *labrynth* that acted as his door. This was a definite improvement from his last workshop. No one could come in and bother him now. No one. He stopped and brought a hand to the *labrynth* carved into the brimstone just beside the door. He had placed this one here just so he could always check it on his way in and out.

His connection to Bri.

Oh, how fun it had been to taunt his brother the other night. To sneak into the darkness of his room and speak with him as a disembodied voice. Bri's reluctance to accept the inevitability of their union was sweet—an endearing quirk. Kai had no doubt he would see reason soon enough. He touched a finger to the lines, his skin covered in enough residual blood to activate the spell.

The lines remained dark.

Kai tried again, this time laying all five of his blood-coated fingers upon the *labrynth*. Nothing. The spell was cold, dim, and unresponsive. Almost as if—

Bri were dead.

No. No, he wouldn't believe that. Wouldn't think it. His brother was not dead. He would have known. Would have felt it. More bound them together than magic and spells. They were twins, two halves of one whole. Had Bri died, Kai surely would have felt it as acutely as the loss of a limb.

Then what? What could have happened to render his hard-won *labrynth* connection impotent?

The old witch. It was the only possibility. She had found some way to block his connection, to alter the life signature Kai had identified as Bri. Kai leaned heavily against the wall, laughing through grated teeth. His shoulders shook with the laughter, driving his thoughts to darker and darker places. The witch would pay. If she wanted a game, a contest of will and power, then she would get one. Oh, how easy it would be to scribe something that would twist her old bones into spiral toys children would delight at playing with.

His jaw strained and his teeth threatened to crack. With a sudden breath, Kai forced himself upright, and released his rage. For the moment. There would be time enough to plan. And plan he would. The witch would regret toying with him. Bri would be his.

He just needed to maintain focus.

A quick sweep of his hand over the large *labrynth* door caused the wall to shimmer and ripple. He walked through it as easily as if it had been nothing more than air. Hard rock closed behind him once again.

In the dark hall—where he had hoped to be alone for a few moments more—a familiar and unwelcome face awaited him.

Her once black hair was smeared with grey, straggly and without the life and luster of youth. Age spots covered her wrinkled hands and neck, nearly obscuring the thorny vine of Olin's mark. She wore a grey coat over her white dress, always claiming a chill, even in Hell. Because of her, Kai had already started working on a *labrynth* to reverse old age. He'd be damned if he allowed himself to become like that. He had time—witches lived far longer than normal humans— but the thought made the bile rise in his throat.

"What do you want, Xan?" he asked, keeping his distance. He hated the feel of her sagging skin.

She squinted milky blue eyes at him. "Olin is looking for you."

Kai bit down on his impulsive reaction to declare that he did not care. Such things only led to unpleasantness. He had learned over the past few months that if he simply went along, found out what Olin wanted, and did it, he could leave fairly quickly—without a broken jaw.

So, instead of saying something stupid, he decided to focus his annoyance on her. "Why did he send you?"

She lifted her chin haughtily. Despite her physical age, she never stooped or hunched. "Everyone else is busy. He told me to take you by the hand, if need be."

Kai withdrew, giving her a wide berth as he stepped around her and started down the enormous black brimstone hall. "No need for that."

Laughter followed him, then steady, sure footsteps. "Still afraid I'll infect you?"

"Your age is hideous, so yes."

"Old age comes to us all."

"Yes, but you seem to have the worst of it."

"Try and try, child, you will never escape it."

"We shall see about that."

He turned and all but raced down the curling stairs that would take him deeper within the mountain Olin had carved out as his home. The old woman would never keep up. The heat was sweltering here, with so little room for the air to move around. Kai always took the stairs two at a time in order to escape their atmosphere sooner.

He passed numerous doors, which were really more holes cut into the rock, leading to more long hallways that snaked through the mountain in all directions, leading to huge caverns and open courtyards. Kai had been impressed by the structure when Olin had first brought him there after Lillianna's failed ritual. Impressed, though he would never admit it. His admiration for the construction fell short of anything real, however. Each time he walked the halls, Kai could not help but think of how every door, every passage could have been placed in a more advantageous way. The whole place could have been a *labrynth*, and oh the power they would have had then.

Oh well. A thought come far too late. Olin had built this place long before Kai's birth.

Taking the eighth door on his right, Kai slowed to a more leisurely pace as he made his way toward the training yard that lay in the shadow of the mountain on the furthest side from civilization. Beyond, Hell dropped off into a black, cavernous void. One could literally fall off the edge of the world there. As such, not many demons ventured out this far into Hell's wilderness. Even the hellions, who were anything and everything from rodents to humanoid chimera, kept their distance.

That hadn't stopped Kai from throwing one ratlike hellion off the edge, however. Just for fun. He had wanted to see how long it would take for him to hear it hit bottom.

He was still waiting.

The passageway opened up suddenly, light flooding the abruptly wider hall. Kai stuffed his hands into his pockets and slowed his already leisurely pace. He could already hear the clang of steel against steel, the thud of arrows finding their marks, and the thunk of spears and other projectiles hitting the ground. The smell of sweat and blood was heavy on the air. Not for the first time, he contemplated the spells he could scribe into the ground of the training area. Such power would be held there, just waiting to be tapped. Stepping out into the open air of Hell, Kai breathed in the whole of it, then gazed down over the expanse that led right up to the edge of the void.

This overlook gave the perfect view. As far as the eye could see, men and women of all shapes and sizes were locked in mock battle. They growled and screamed, intimidating and challenging one another. Their faces were streaked with blood and dirt, their hair matted. Kai watched one pair that had ventured close to the mountain, the shadow obscuring their features. The man was human, soulless, and had muscles that made him the size of an ox. The other was a hellion, a chimera with four arms and a long, whipping tail that snapped the air. She was scaled all over, though her head resembled that of a wild cat. With a hiss, she dove at the soulless man, claws bared and sharp. He knocked her aside with a strong beat of his sword, then kicked her feet out from under her. It was a good move—until she sprang backward effortlessly, taking him to the ground beneath her and setting her teeth to his neck.

She won. He was soulless, he would recover.

"Kai." Olin came up the black steps that led to the training ground, a giant even among these freaks of Hell. His normally pale skin had turned the color of burned sand in their time here. Those ice blue eyes were cold now, and didn't so much as waver as the hulking, armor covered demon came straight at Kai.

"What?"

"You left Xan behind?"

"It wasn't hard to do. She can't really keep up, even at a normal pace." There was no rail at the edge of the balcony, so Kai couldn't lean, though he would have liked to. Sitting was the only option left to him if he wanted to slouch and display his lack of interest in things, but he didn't dare. The last time he had sat, Olin had nearly kicked him off the lookout.

So Kai leaned against the mountain wall instead.

"I have a job for you. With her."

"Ugh. Why?"

"I do not need to explain my reasons to you."

"Well, she's about ten minutes behind me. What shall we talk about while we wait? Flowers? The meaning of life? The fact that my allegiance was to Lillianna and not to you?"

He knew he had made a mistake the instant the words left his mouth. Oh, well. Sometimes his mouth was faster than his mind. It was a personal flaw he didn't particularly care to work on.

Olin's hand was around his neck and lifting him off his feet before Kai could finish mentally acknowledging his misstep. Kai's ears rang, and his teeth rattled when Olin slammed him back against the brimstone mountain. He clawed at the thick fingers at his throat, but could not dislodge them. Even behind closed eyes, sparks swam in his vision.

"Do not test me," Olin said, leaning close and baring his teeth. "You live by my mercy. Do not forget that."

Kai coughed, his voice appropriately strangled. "I live because I'm useful. You need me. I'm no idiot. You wouldn't have taken me otherwise."

Olin squeezed a little tighter. "True. It would be troublesome to find another witch."

"Impossible. Since you would need someone of equal skill, and I am unequalled."

Another slam against the mountain. Kai's lungs began to burn. He felt the heat of Olin's body and breath close. "I could still break your legs," the demon said. "You don't need those to be useful."

His grip released, and Kai dropped to the ground, the brimstone knocking against his knees. Kai sucked in air and coughed again until his lungs felt normal. Once that had been accomplished, he sat up, brushing his long, auburn bangs from his eyes and looking directly at Olin as if nothing had transpired between them. "Have you ever considered letting me scribe the ground here? I could give your army something to really look out for. Think of the possibilities."

"If I trusted you wouldn't simply blow the entire force of my army to dust, I might."

"You don't trust me?" Kai grinned.

"Not yet."

"You wound me." Clutching at his chest, Kai feigned emotional distress. "I've done everything you ask of me."

"Not without tantrums and complaints."

Kai shrugged. "You haven't made me an offer."

Still towering over him, Olin tapped his fingers impatiently over his thick bicep. "What kind of offer?"

"One that would solidify my loyalty to you, and ensure my cooperation. I work, but I don't get paid."

"You have space for a workshop, and I let you live."

"Ah, but we have already established that I live because you need me. I want something in return. I want to know what I get out of this whole endeavor."

Silence, but for the sounds of training below. Olin studied Kai, searching for the trick.

Kai would never reveal it.

"What do you want?"

Excellent. "I want bodies. Live ones. I need blood, and my own is not enough. I want an unlimited supply for my spells. No questions asked."

"That's all you want?"

"That's all I want." *All I want as far as you need to know.*

"Fine. I suppose you want me to procure these bodies for you."

"It would be nice, but not necessary. I could always get them myself."

"That means having access to the mortal realm."

"Imagine that. I suppose it does."

"That is another negotiation entirely."

"Is it? I don't mind negotiating."

"I will grant you access to the mortal realm in exchange for one thing, and one thing only."

Already Kai was growing bored with his own game. "What's that?"

Olin bent down, putting the two of them face to face. Kai leaned back slightly, but was limited from his place on his knees. He didn't like people so close—well, no, that was a lie. He loved people close, but only when he was the one clearly in control, the one with the power. He never felt that way with Olin. "Bind yourself to me," Olin said. The words tore through Kai's soul. All witches knew of the possibility. Lillianna had not asked it of him because he was too young. And now she was dead. Any witch in the employ of a demon—which was most of them—bound themselves. But it was not a commitment to be taken lightly. Olin knew this. It showed in his face. "Bind yourself to me, so that I can find you if you are gone too long, and so I know you are not aiding other demons behind my back. Bind yourself, and I will believe you trustworthy, and I will grant you unlimited access to the world above."

Unlimited access to the mortal realm. Exactly what he wanted.

"Deal," he said, mocking the words that would never truly pass between them. Demons didn't dare take the soul of a witch; they were useless without it. Bindings had developed instead. Agreements. Nothing like the selling of a soul. The binding was permanent, but not unlimited. Kai would still have his freedom. Olin could find him, but couldn't call him. He could ask things of him, but he couldn't demand them. Likewise, Kai would have Olin's sworn protection.

He held out a hand so they could shake on it. Olin's grip was solid, vice-like. "I feel much better about this whole thing already."

"Good for you." Releasing his hand, Olin stood. The sound of feet echoed through the nearby passage, signaling that Xan had finally caught up. She emerged, her breathing slightly labored from the effort. She glared at Kai, and he simply smiled at her, knowing how impish he looked, sprawled as he was on his knees.

"You are a child of Hell," she said. "There is no doubt about that."

"On the contrary, I'm the stuff Haven is made of."

"Enough, both of you." Grabbing Kai by the arm, Olin hauled him to his feet. "As I said, I have a job for the two of you."

"Together?" Xan echoed Kai's earlier protest.

"Yes. There are followers of mine amassing in southern Vaah. They have built a temple, and I need it blessed."

Kai scrunched up his nose. "Blessed? By us?"

"Xan will go as my emissary. Kai, you will give them a good show. Scribe something so I can appear there easily. I want them entranced enough that they race to convert others."

Boring. Hardly worth my time. But it would put him in the mortal realm. "Fine."

Xan lifted her hands, turning them over as though their wrinkled state distressed her as much as it did Kai. "Must I go like this?" she asked, her voice low.

Olin snorted, waving her off. "Don't be absurd. No one would clamber to worship me if asked to do so by such a worn and decrepit looking thing. Clean yourself up."

She nodded, relief flooding her face.

Kai didn't care.

"You can leave tomorrow. Once you've blessed this one, suggest they build a few more. I'll need followers in numbers if this is to work," Olin said. "Until then," he took Kai by the collar of his shirt and dragged him forward, toward the stairs that lead downward, "get yourself down there. Nallahar has been itching to get his hands on you. If you can't keep your feet against him for longer than a quarter turn, I'll give you to him for the next month for training."

Kai tensed, his legs moving stiffly as Olin manhandled him down the steps. Nallahar was a demon, a former seraph of agility and swiftness. The last time Kai had been forced to train with him, he had beaten Kai bloody. For days he hadn't been able to see straight, and he still had a twinge in his ankle from where it had been broken. Olin insisted he learn how to handle himself on the battlefield, called him weak, and a child for not being able to take a cuff to the head and stand right back up. Lillianna had babied him too long, he said. Kai had been training for the better part of a year now, and as far as he was concerned, he was a proficient genius with a blade. He had disarmed Olin once, even. But he was no match for Nallahar, and Olin knew it. Handing him over to the other demon was most likely the punishment for his earlier smart remark. Perhaps this time the beating would actually enforce some connection between his brain and his mouth.

Not likely.

But if I can stay on my feet, if I can hold Nallahar off for at least a quarter turn, then Olin will consider my training complete. He'd be satisfied. And so would I. If I can do this, then I will be stronger, my blood will be stronger, and my labrynths will be stronger. Bri won't be able to resist me then.

Spirits lifted by those thoughts, Kai shook free of Olin and marched toward Nallahar on his own. He pulled a spear from the ground, testing its weight, then lifted a sword from the body of a fallen soldier who had lost consciousness. Hefting the spear into throwing position, Kai spotted Nallahar among a group of skirmishing soulless, and aimed for his head.

— CHAPTER SIX —

Bri twisted around, not for the first time, to check his back in the mirror. Alec had lied. His back was a mess.

The weeks of rest had helped, and the pain was mostly gone, but that single unfinished rune continued to break open and bleed, and when that happened, it ached like nothing else. The *labrynth* didn't appear to have changed much. Bri knew those lines well. It seemed Dorothea had simply stretched a few lines, added others. The additional runes were the biggest difference. He could see them—five runes, four nicely healed and faded to pink scars, one covered in white gauze that had yet to be stained with blood—their meanings unknown. Over the years, he had learned the purposes of the first runes she had scribed into his back. There had been no time for that with these. Bri pulled his shirt on over his head and turned away from the mirror. No use dwelling on it. He had tested his connection to the myst, trying to determine if the spell still worked. As far as he could tell, it did. He felt its warmth, lending him control when he called for it. Something was different, but he couldn't articulate what. It was like staring at a work of art through clouded glass.

Dressed and grateful for the simplicity of Frontland attire—plain, lightweight, comfortable—Bri grabbed his pack from the edge of the bed and headed downstairs.

They hadn't stayed in one place for very long, but they had been at this particular inn for three days. Alec said it was because they were nearing the edge of the Frontland—slang for Frontier—and supplies and shelter would be uncertain once they crossed the border into

Xia-Lo. Bri knew Alec wanted to ensure that he was healed before moving on. This was the longest they had stayed in one place since the first days, when they waited for Pica to regain enough strength to retrieve their money and a few meager belongings. They had debated searching for a witch to finish the partial rune, but in the end, they had both agreed it was too risky. Witches were almost always working for a demon, and letting a stranger see Dorothea's *labrynth* meant revealing everything about Bri's situation. It was their hope now that the mystics they were searching for would be able to do something.

Descending the steps of the inn to the main floor, Bri's stomach growled at the smell of roasting duck and herbs and spices. The innkeeper here had a wife and daughter who could cook better than anything Bri had ever had before—better even than the food at those fancy parties Carma dragged him to. After only three days, he wasn't looking forward to leaving it behind.

"Good morning, Bri." The innkeeper's daughter, Sharat, smiled at him as she swept the floor at the bottom of the steps. Her coal black eyes sparkled, the same as her long, plaited hair.

"Good morning." Already he had stopped bracing himself for the onslaught of the myst. It was there, of course, but ever since entering the Frontland, Bri had found that the population was so sparse he could manage it with far more ease than in Chanae. "The kitchen smells great."

"Of course it does." She had a slight accent Bri couldn't place, though he thought he remembered hearing something similar once when he was a boy, traveling with the caravan. Somewhere near the eastern ocean? Her skin was a flawless warm brown he rarely saw in Chanae. She stopped sweeping, leaning on the broom as though to tell him a secret. "I added cinnamon to the apples today. I'll make sure you get some."

"Thank you." Stepping around the corner and into the dining room, Bri had to take a moment to let the myst come close. The inn was full, each table bustling with conversation and eating. Bri glanced at their futures, allowing them to pass through his mind and trying to pay little attention to the details. The group all pressed together in the farthest corner were thieves, but they'd had recent success on the road while traveling, and this was their celebration. They would leave the town alone. Bri mentally batted away their plans for the next journey and eased the myst back. It wouldn't recede entirely, but he could get through a meal.

Alec sat near the front door, his plate of food mostly untouched in front of him. A man sat across from him, dressed all in black with a high collar and gold fastenings. Smoke curled from a pipe stuck between his lips, and facial features Bri knew he had never seen before. Small, dark eyes, sharp features, and onyx hair, straight and fine, unlike Sharat's. Alec appeared to be having a heated discussion with the man, and as Bri came closer, he could make out more and more of it.

"There must be a way."

The foreign man shook his head. "I told you. The borders are closed."

"There are always ways around that."

"Not legal ones."

"I'm not afraid of doing things a little outside the law."

At that, the man raised one eyebrow. "Do you mean to insinuate that I am a man who operates outside the law?"

"I am saying you are a man who knows an opportunity when you see it. Otherwise, you wouldn't still be here talking to me."

The man huffed, neither confirming nor denying, though Bri thought he saw the side of his mouth quirk upward for a brief moment. But he had reached the table, and the unknown man turned his gaze sharply from Alec to Bri.

Uncomfortable under that scrutinizing gaze, Bri stumbled over his words. "Did I—did I come at a bad time?"

"No," Alec said. "Sit. Have something to eat. I was just discussing the best route into Xia-Lo."

Bri sat next to Alec, but didn't feel any better.

"This is Enlai." Alec introduced the stranger. "This is my brother, Bri."

Enlai inclined his head slightly in greeting. "Your brother tells me it is imperative that he gets you to Xia-Lo. I have told him this is currently impossible."

"Why is that?"

"Our borders are closed."

Bri hardly noticed when Sharat brought him a plate of steaming duck and sweet-smelling apples. He was alarmed by the news that they may not be able to reach the mystics, but he managed a smile and a thank you before she went back to her chores. "But you're here. You must have come over recently."

"I have been here the better part of a season," Enlai said. "I was attempting to return home myself when I heard the news."

Bri glanced at Alec, who had taken to spinning his fork on his plate, still not eating. "Why have they closed the borders?"

"Xia-Lo is a complicated country." With a puff of his pipe, Enlai reclined in his chair. "My people crossed the sea some two hundred years ago and conquered the native people, who then called the land Gallenar. For the most part we now live in peace, but two hundred years is nothing for two peoples with as much history as ours. Occasionally there are disputes."

Alec set his fork down. "I told you, we have no interest in politics or even the country as a whole. All we need to do is reach a small, reclusive group of people."

"Easier said than done. The border patrols will arrest you on sight."

"There is always a way," Alec insisted. "We don't have to go by road."

Enlai smoked his pipe again. "The woods are a treacherous place. We have many demons and new witches who wander. They hide in our lands until they gain enough power and experience to survive elsewhere. Travelers often end up their victims."

"That wouldn't be a problem for us, I assure you," Alec said.

A ring of smoke preceded the words from his mouth. "You are foolish."

"We're looking for a group of mystics," Bri said on a whim, hoping Alec wouldn't be mad. "Have you heard of them?"

Alec didn't say anything, but Bri felt him turn in surprise. Bri kept his eyes on Enlai, refusing to back down.

"Mystics?" The pipe took a slow journey from the man's mouth to the table. "Not many people know about them. They hide themselves well. How did you come to hear of them?"

"You know them?"

"Answer my question first."

"We—" This time Bri looked to Alec for help. He didn't want to reveal too much, but at the mention of the mystics, Enlai's whole demeanor had changed.

Alec picked up the answer. "We were told to find them. Apparently, they are the only ones who can help us."

Chair creaking, Enlai leaned forward over the table until he was as close as possible, studying Bri's face. Bri remained perfectly still, his hand shaking around the fork he had picked up but not used. "I should have seen it before," Enlai said. "Those eyes. They give him away if one knows what to look for."

Bri could feel both the wariness and the excitement rolling off Alec. "So you do know of them."

"Yes." Leaning back once again, Enlai sipped from his mug. "I know of whom you speak. I can take you to them."

"What about the closed borders?" Alec said.

"Not an issue anymore."

"Why not?"

"Because the border will not be patrolled where you need to go. It is guarded by wards and spells that keep anyone unknowing far from the edges of the compound. Including government soldiers."

"And you are not unknowing?"

"There was a time," Enlai said, "when my family greatly feared the seraph of Haven. We fear them still. For there was once a night when one of my ancestors was visited by one of the holy creatures, and their union resulted in a child. This child was sickly, weak, and plagued by visions. Many times it was thought the child would die. But the seraph returned with a warning: keep the child hidden. If Haven knew, Death would come swiftly. The seraph taught the child to control the visions, and even, it is said, drew what power could be drawn from the child away to lessen the problem. The child survived and had a family. Over the years these Havenly traits have weakened and dissolved in my ancestors. But every few generations one is born who shows evidence of this tainted blood. Never as strong as the first, not even as strong as the second or third, but there nonetheless. These children are hidden as the first was, lest Haven discover them. I know these mystics you speak of, and I know where to find them." He lifted a single finger to point at Bri. "I know what he is, and I know why you seek the mystics. I sought them once myself."

"My son has silver in his eyes."

All further conversation on the matter had ceased after that. Enlai insisted they could not talk in such an open place. Instead, they had finished their food—food Bri had barely tasted around all the thoughts he could not control.

There are more like me.

"Not exactly like you, no," Enlai had said when Bri expressed that particular thought later as they rode on horseback out beyond the town. The Frontland was a vast desert, and nothing here could hear them aside from a few cacti and the occasional sand-skirting lizard. "I have not seen one such as you in my lifetime, and if the records are to be believed, the mystics have not encountered a child born of human and seraph in hundreds of years. Haven has been strict in its law against such things."

They did not point out that Bri was not the child of a seraph and a human, but of a seraph and a witch.

"But your son sees the myst. He has visions."

"Nothing to the degree of what you deal with, I imagine. I noticed the color of his eyes before any other symptoms appeared. My son has a tendency to predict happenings, nothing more. He says it will storm and it does. When asked about it, he shrugs it off as an intense feeling, an itch."

Gods, what I wouldn't give to be able to say this was nothing more than an itch.

"Still," Bri said, shifting in the saddle, "I never knew there were others out there. I thought I was alone."

Enlai laughed, smoke puffing from his mouth as he did so. "Such is the plight of the young." He stuck his pipe between his teeth, still chuckling.

Alec, who rode slightly ahead of Bri, twisted around so he could see them both. "How much farther is it from here?"

"It will take the better part of the day to reach the border. You will see the growth of green things begin long before we reach Xia-Lo. Once we cross, it is another day, at least, until we reach the compound itself. And that's if they let you in."

"I was under the impression that the leader of these mystics wouldn't turn Bri away," Alec said.

"Bri, most likely not. Though the Satguru is a fickle creature, and has been known to do the unexpected. As for you and me, that is another matter entirely."

"I will not leave Bri alone. I cannot."

"Then you will have to hope the Satguru accepts your plea. When I brought my son, I was told I could stay only during the cold months. When the world is warm, it is my duty to roam and guard. But I would not worry too much about the matter. After all, I was waiting for you."

"What?" Bri heard Alec's voice perfectly overlap with his own.

Once again, Enlai laughed. "I admit, I had begun to think you would never come. That it had been a false prediction. But in the spring, before I left as I always do, my son told me to linger in the outermost towns of the Frontland. He said there would be something there for me to collect. Of course, I never dreamed he meant you."

Bri felt the hairs on his arms rise in response to the chill suddenly dancing along his skin, despite the desert heat. "I cannot be seen in the myst. Neither can Alec. How would he have known?"

"I don't think he knew exactly what I would find either, and I don't pretend to understand the workings of the myst. Perhaps it was a change in my future he saw. Perhaps something else entirely. You can ask him when you meet him."

Bri glanced at Alec, gauging his reaction. As he expected, there was a tension in his shoulders that signaled his unease. Yet there was no other choice. They had to proceed. They had known coming here was a risk in the first place, but there was no other option now but to follow through. Hopefully the benefits would greatly outweigh any negative outcomes.

Wiping the sweat from his brow, Bri resisted the sudden, unfamiliar urge to pray. For him, appealing to Haven was the very worst thing he could do.

Rolling over, Tassos stretched and dispelled the remnants of sleep from his body. Reapers didn't need sleep; it was merely a luxury. One most of them indulged in. Their bodies didn't fatigue, but their minds did. Such was life when you lived at the whim of Death. She was a harsh bitch of a mistress, not caring if her Reapers were busy with other things when she called them. They were to go immediately and without question. They listened, for the most part. Death was harsh, but she was also an irresistible beauty—no Reaper felt anything but unconditional love for her.

But, seeing that Death was an incorporeal being, incapable of returning the love given her by her so devoted children, they—like every other being—sought comfort elsewhere.

Sitting up in bed, Tassos yawned and stretched once more until his back cracked and the lethargy in his limbs receded. His long, unbound hair fell around his shoulders, tangled and cool. He ran his fingers through it a few times, sorting out the knots. A brief flare of magic left the black locks silken and tangle-free once again. He tied it back at the nape of his neck, then stood and willed his clothes back into being around his body.

Turning, and loving the way his black robes wrapped about him as he did so, Tassos gave himself a quick look-over in the mirror on the wall. Another little dusting of magic and the violet of his eyes brightened. Satisfied that he was as glorious as always, he searched for any nearby death-calls that might fall to him. When he found nothing, he returned to the bed, giving himself one last look at the creature who still slept there.

Tassos always wished he could watch as they tumbled together. What a sight it must be. Him, all pale white and sharp black, the other golden tones and blond. The mix had to be exquisite. Now, his partner lay sleeping against the white sheets, hair obscuring the gorgeous face and the coverlet hiding the firm ass. Demons didn't need sleep either, not really, but this one had spent the better part of the last thousand years with his eyes closed to the whole world. Once, he had been Lord of Hell and feared by all—in many ways he still was—but something had happened and he had withdrawn, tucking himself away in this small cottage nestled against the edge of the void. No one knew where he had gone. No one knew how to call him. Tassos had stumbled upon him quite by accident, and now was his only visitor. He kept the secret, pretending to know nothing when the subject came up in conversation, but it wasn't easy. One slip of the tongue was all it would take. As a precaution, Tassos didn't join such conversations.

He leaned down and placed a kiss on that golden forehead. A hand shot out from under the blankets, grabbing him by the wrist.

"You're leaving so soon?"

Tassos rolled his eyes. "Isn't that the deal? Don't linger? Wouldn't want to give you away, now would I?"

"What if I wasn't finished?"

"Your snoring indicated otherwise."

Shifting, the golden demon turned his head and opened his eyes. Tassos had always found it difficult to argue with those eyes. Their blue rivaled the sea. "Has Death called you?"

Already he could feel himself giving in. Tassos clamped down on those impulses. "Not yet."

"Then come back." A gentle tug on his wrist.

"Lonely, are you?"

Those sea blue eyes darkened, as if a storm had come on the horizon. It didn't scare Tassos; he had gone toe to toe with this demon enough times to know how the fight would go.

"If you're so lonely, why don't you just come out of hiding?"

"I will not."

"Are you going to tell me why?"

"No."

"Then I am leaving." He touched the air with his magic. "If I do so now, no one will sense me or detect where I came from."

The hand around his wrist released him, grabbing instead the pillow Tassos had laid on and pulling it close. The demon settled back into sleep. "Fine. Leave."

"Fine. I will. But I'll come back."

"You always come back."

"Yes, I do." *Though sometimes I have no idea why.*

Slipping into the space between realms, Tassos grabbed the first wind of Death he felt, and rode it all the way back to the mortal realm, leaving Hell and its complicated inhabitants behind.

— CHAPTER SEVEN—

Gabriel gripped the edge of her desk so hard she felt the wood give way beneath her fingers. The light of Haven poured in from the window behind her, casting her shameful shadow on the pristine white marble floor of her office. That shadow served as a reminder every day of her sins. Of all their sins. There was no darkness in Haven aside from where they walked. They worked tirelessly, every day, to redeem themselves, to cast aside all that made them unworthy. Yet these shadows continued to cling to them. Not the white, spiraling towers, or the modest cottages they called home. The Citadel loomed above the city, blotting out parts of the flawless sky, yet it cast nothing upon the small buildings below.

Only the seraph had shadows, and as such, only they could erase whatever wrongs they had done. Perhaps then, The One would return to them.

Until that time, it was still their job to keep order. And these two who stood in front of her, casting their own black shadows on the floor, had long been under suspicion.

Kadiel had grown used to being called in, and stood with her hands folded over her chest, a stubborn expression already set into her face. Her clothes were stained with ink, as were her fingers and a few spots on her cheeks. The bun that had once held her brown hair out of her face as she read the multitude of books kept within the Vault had fallen free in some places. So much disorder. It was no wonder she continued to act outside their holy law.

At her side, her eldest sister, Oriel, stood tall and confident, though clearly anxious to be back within the myst where she spent the majority of her life ensuring the safe passing of The One's Plan. It was her treachery that was so surprising. Singers were faithful creatures, fully committed to their place. They rarely Fell, but when they did, it was a disaster.

Gabriel was still cleaning up after the last fallen Singer. Hence why they were here.

"Kadiel, you went unaccounted for the other day."

"Did I?" Her feigned innocence was not meant as a defense, but as a knife to twist in Gabriel's weak patience. "I can't imagine why."

"You know full well why. You went to the mortal realm."

"Can you prove it?"

"Where else would you have gone? There is only one thing you care about more than your books."

Kadiel shrugged a shoulder, her gaze wandering away from Gabriel as though nothing important were being discussed. "Even I need a break sometimes."

Stepping away from the desk, Gabriel descended on the younger seraph. "You went to the mortal realm. You warned them I was coming."

"Warned who?" Kadiel did not retreat, even when Gabriel became close enough that little would be able to pass between them but words. "You continue to accuse me, but never use specifics."

"The boy. Your sister's child. The one who sees the myst and destroys The One's Plan. You warned them, and they were ready for me when I came for him."

"I hardly think he 'destroys' the Plan. The world has not collapsed."

"You are too young. Too young to understand the ramifications each breath he takes could have."

Kadiel's brown eyes darkened. "No one called me 'too young' when they ordered me to call Death upon my own sister and her child. I was not too young for that. I am older now."

"Clearly you were too young. That was our mistake. We thought you understood, thought you were intelligent. But you are not. You are weak."

"Bully me all you want, Gabriel. You will not change my mind, and you will not change the past."

The impulse to scream in frustration was nearly uncontainable. Instead of giving into those baser instincts, Gabriel turned momentarily on the silent Singer standing beside them. "And you. You say nothing?"

A gentle tilt of her head was the only physical reaction. "My sister has no problem speaking for herself."

"You told me you understood the situation."

"I do understand."

All that silver began to wear on Gabriel's nerves. Singers resembled the myst they walked in, pale with silver hair and eyes. At times it seemed as though you could look right through them, that they weren't really there. "Then why did you let the boy go?"

Oriel clasped her hands behind her back casually. "I don't know what you mean."

"The boy! He was in the myst! I've had reports. He was there. Fully there. Physically there. Others felt a surge of power, and then he was gone."

"He has come and gone within the myst his whole life, Gabriel. I see no difference in this most recent occurrence."

"So you deny that it was you who helped him?"

"I deny nothing. Your accusation is without evidence."

Kadiel leaned in, smiling. "You can't prove anything, Gabriel. If you could, you would have already had us arrested. Instead, you stand here attempting to goad us into incriminating ourselves. But it will not work. You have nothing, and we all know it."

Gabriel stepped back at that. The blatant audacity of Kadiel's words caused her mind to spin. How could they not understand? This was a matter of The One's sacred Grand Plan. Oriel was a Singer; she had pledged herself and her life to the maintenance of the Plan. Kadiel, a student of the Center of Education, Enlightenment, and Knowledge, had done nothing but study their past and their intended futures. And she was seraph, they all were. Did they not want the return of The One? Did they not want peace and prosperity for the mortal beings that had been left in their charge? Their sister's child threatened all of that. Half-breed children led to destruction. Especially when they were the children of Singers. The future was not meant for mortal minds.

Breathing carefully lest she lose her temper, Gabriel returned to her desk, giving herself time to decide how to proceed. She would convince them. They would hand the boy to her.

"Oriel, I cannot reassign you, as the myst is the only place you are suited for, but I will be assigning a rotation of my First File to guard your actions. Until this child is found and dealt with, you will not be alone."

The Singer said nothing.

"And as for you, Kadiel, you will return to the Vault and gather all the records you can on the forbidden children. You will then report back here to my office, where you will work side by side with me on the matter. You will help me find him, and you will be there when I bring him in. After all, this is your mess I've been forced to clean up. I should have made the decision to make you help in the correction of your mistake earlier."

"Is that all?" Kadiel said, her posture still slouched and indicating no sign the reassignment bothered her. "Shall I start right away?"

"Yes. Now get out, and get to it, before I make you bleed for your mistake."

"I already took my punishment for my actions, Gabriel. It is not my fault you cannot find one mortal child." She turned toward the door.

Gabriel envisioned herself unsheathing her sword and drawing blood as she pressed its edge to Kadiel's throat. But such thoughts were sinful, so she repressed it, making a note to go and repent later. "Get out!"

Oriel had followed her sister to the door and now opened it, ushering the younger seraph out and away from Gabriel's ire.

Gabriel thought she heard Kadiel laugh.

"Why do you provoke her?" Oriel asked once the door had shut and they were safely walking down the long white corridor that led away from the offices and out into the courtyards.

Kadiel shrugged, wringing her hands together and wondering just how close she had gotten to breaking Gabriel's temper. It wasn't really what she intended, but when she found herself face to face with the general, it was like she just couldn't help herself. "I don't really mean to. But I can't stand the thought of Bri in her custody."

"Gabriel is not a bad seraph. She does her job, and she takes it seriously. As do I, and as should you."

Kadiel looked at her sister and wondered, not for the first time, why she had not been born into a life with the myst. Talia had had the same coloring, the same delicate features. Oriel was beautiful, as Talia had been. Kadiel's own skin was more peach, and her hair the rich brown most common among her kind. She looked like their father, who had been a warrior among the First File long before Gabriel had assumed command. An injury given him by the Lord of Hell had resulted in early retirement, and he had spent his last years in study. That was the only way Kadiel had known him, and why she had chosen the path of a scholar rather than solider. He had succumbed to the latent infection of his wound before Talia's Fall. Oriel was always thankful for this, saying Talia's descent would have killed him. Kadiel was not convinced. She had seen how happy her sister was in the mortal realm—any good father would have been content with that.

She was certain he never would have killed her, never would have ended Bri's life. That was why she did what she did and why she never regretted it, because she knew in her heart, her father would have done the same.

"I take my job very seriously. I also take our family seriously. And you really can't afford to lecture me anymore. Despite all your talk of neutrality, you defended him when the time came."

"Do not speak of it so openly," Oriel hushed her. "It was a moment in time, and I had to make my decision quickly."

"You made the right one."

"That is open for debate at the moment."

"Gabriel has nothing. She knows he was there, and that he got away. She assumes it was you because of your connection...and because of me."

They stepped out of the halls and into the bright light of Haven's sky. In the distance, the Citadel sparked, almost glowing. The highest of the high resided there, passing down their decisions and awaiting news from The One. Kadiel had been inside only once. Someone of her rank normally never saw the interior of the Citadel. But when she returned without the bodies of her sister and the newborn child, she had been called in. The lash marks on her back still burned when she looked at the towering structure, and she wondered if her blood still stained the floor of their hall where they meted out their justice. She didn't regret it.

Stopping a moment, Kadiel caressed the white petals of a star-gazer lily. The pink at the center was some of the only color they had in Haven. Most things were white or green or brown or blue. The lilies had been brought up from the mortal realm with a number of other species. Only the star-gazers had survived. Kadiel had looked into why, but not a single book or record had the answer.

Oriel touched her face, turning Kadiel to look at her. "Kadiel, I worry for you."

"Why?"

"You were so young when it happened. Do you not remember Talia's last days with us?"

She thought about it. Talia had been quiet, somber, but most Singers were gentle and soft in everything they did. Like Oriel. Kadiel had been shocked the day her sister Fell. She'd had no idea it was coming. Looking back, she realized Oriel had not been so surprised.

What Kadiel did know was how happy her sister had been afterward. It was the first time she had seen her sister smile. Really smile. That, she could not forget.

"She was melancholy in the years before," Oriel said. "Listless and constantly questioning."

"Did she ever tell you why?"

"No. Though since it happened, I have had time to think about it, and there was a time she saw something in the myst that left her badly shaken. She would never speak of it, and no matter how I tried, I could not find it myself."

"She Fell because of Jaymes. She loved him."

"I think it was more than that. Jaymes was simply the final piece."

"He made her happy. Bri made her happy." Kai had too, but Kadiel could say nothing of him. She had told no one that there had been two. Not even her own sister.

"Yes."

"But you said you worry for me?" Kadiel let her fingers drift away from the petals. "Why?" Oriel's silver eyes were shining more than usual. Tears?

"Because," Oriel said, her hand moving to stroke Kadiel's cheek, "you remind me so much of Talia. When she was young, and in her last days with us."

"I don't understand."

"I fear you will Fall too."

— CHAPTER EIGHT —

The dry heat of the Frontland had turned humid as they reached the border. As Enlai had promised, the dust and sand of the desert gradually turned to something richer. They saw first a few sparse greens, poking up through the cracked ground, fighting for what little water there was. Then the plants grew larger and larger until patches of grass were lined with late summer flowers that cast their fragrance into the bland air. Eventually there were trees and dark soil fit for growing most anything. When the trees grew tall enough that Alec could no longer see their tops, Enlai declared they had passed into Xia-Lo.

The rainstorm had hit in the next breath.

And hadn't let up.

"Quite common this time of year," Enlai had said. "It will go on like this a few days, then we will have nothing for a good long while."

Common or not, Alec was tired of being wet.

They had left the roads behind and had encountered no border patrols. Alec wasn't sure if that enhanced his faith in this stranger or created a place for doubt. What would Ari have made of all this? Long ago, she'd been an excellent gauge of character. He hadn't longed for her input so insistently in centuries. He told himself not to worry about it. Any humans they encountered would be no problem. He could overpower them easily. Witches and demons were another matter.

"How much farther?" he asked, having to raise his voice over the sound of the rain.

Enlai had taken to wearing a wide hat that allowed the water to cascade down, far from his face. "We are almost there. I suspect the first sentries and guards will notice us soon, if they have not already." *Cel-Eza, preserve us.* He was praying to a dead god, but it was a habit he couldn't break. Alec turned in his saddle, looking back at Bri who looked every inch a miserable, drowned thing. "Still all right back there?"

"Not the worst I've been through," he said, wiping the water from his eyes. His short-brimmed hat wasn't doing much to help with the matter. "But I find I'm quickly forgetting what was worse."

At least his minimal sense of humor was still intact. "Keep close. Enlai says we're almost there."

"I know," Bri said. "I can feel the pull on the myst. It started maybe half a mile back. It's almost like Kai's *labrynths*, it can't get through here so well. Like it's being blocked. It's clambering at me for a way in."

At that, Enlai spun suddenly to look at Bri. "Are you truly that strong? Could you bring it here?"

"I think it's more the opposite. If it's stronger than me, it will use me regardless of my efforts. But the—what did you call them? Wards?—are strong. The myst is having trouble getting even to me."

A moment of silence, then a satisfied nod. "Good. If you bring the myst down upon these people in a way they cannot control, they will most likely turn you away."

Bri's face fell, his gaze dropping to his hands where they twisted the reins against the horn of the saddle.

Alec wouldn't let them turn him away. He needed this too badly. Well, he needed what they hoped "this" was. Despite everything, despite how long they had traveled, Alec was ready to fight, if that's what the situation called for.

Enlai slowed his horse and stopped. Doing the same, Alec called out to Bri to follow suit when the boy failed to notice. He listened, but heard nothing over the torrential downpour of the rain. "What is it?"

"They have found us," Enlai said, not a sign of tension in his body. He wrapped his reins so they would not fall, and folded his arms over his chest to wait. "Another moment, maybe two, and you will see."

Searching the darkness of the trees all around them, then the shadowed game trail they had been following, Alec reached for Bri's horse, grabbing the bridal and pulling close. He saw nothing.

"What do you want me to do?" Bri asked.

"Just be ready for anything. The moment I tell you to do something, you do it."

Bri nodded; hands still clasped tightly to the saddle.

The rain continued, soaking them further and pattering against the leaves and branches, filling the air with sound. A spot of light appeared down the path; the rain drops glimmering in the air around it. It wobbled and blurred, growing larger and larger against the darkness of the forest until a man became visible. He held the lantern up, shining the light on their group, squinting, and frowning in the rain.

"Enlai. We have been expecting you." This man looked nothing like their guide. His skin was a rich brown with golden undertones, his eyes dark and his hair black. A deep grey cloak had been wrapped around him as protection from the rain.

"I take it the Satguru saw me coming?"

"Of course. And we were told to expect strangers to be with you." The man turned his attention to Alec and Bri. "Strangers who live outside the myst."

"We mean no harm," Alec said when he saw the wariness in the man's eyes. "My brother needs help. We were told to find your group."

"That there is someone who can tell you of us is troubling," the man said.

"Stories get around and become rumors. We acted on nothing more."

A snort heard through the rain, then the man lifted the lantern higher, casting its light on Bri. He froze, then crept closer for a better look.

Enlai remained calm and relaxed. "The Satguru will want to see him, don't you agree?"

Shaking away his apparent shock, the man lowered the lantern and stepped back. "Yes. Yes, of course. We must make haste." He lifted one hand and snapped a quick rhythm. The pattern echoed back from the woods. "Come," he said. "I will lead the way."

As they nudged their horses back into motion, Alec leaned toward Enlai. "What signal was that?"

Enlai smiled. "To call off the men in the woods with bolts and bows aimed at your head."

"Ah. Terrific."

The ride carried on longer than Alec had anticipated. Eventually the ground grew too rocky and steep, and they were forced to dismount and lead the horses. More men appeared from the shadows of the forest, taking up places on either side, escorting, guarding. One, an older man with that golden brown skin, his hair gone white on the sides, approached Bri with a deep bow, and offered to take his horse in thickly accented words. Though Bri had insisted it was not necessary, the old man had not taken no for an answer. Alec was grateful. Without a horse to lead, Bri could keep closer to him, and with so many strangers about, keeping close was about number one on Alec's list of priorities.

The rain broke, changing to a misty drizzle as they reached the top of the mountain. Some of the dark clouds cleared, allowing streaks of sunlight to filter down to the world below. The valley spread out between the mountains, a river cutting through and glittering by as the rain danced along its surface. Bri grabbed Alec's sleeve as though he might fall. Tucked into the side of the mountain, stretching down to the edge of the winding river, was a temple of spiraling towers and blooming turrets. Polished gates surrounded colorful gardens filled with statues and fountains. The walls of the temple had been carved and painted in every shade imaginable. A paved road led down the mountainside to the entrance where a sweeping arch of sandstone and granite made dwarves of the people milling about underneath. Small sparks of light glittered from each of them as though they had covered themselves in gold.

"Gods, Alec." Bri breathed. "I thought Chanae was impressive."

"All that brick and stone? Smoke pouring from every chimney? Chanae is nothing. You should have seen some of the cities my people built, though even then, this puts them to shame."

"That, I can believe."

Enlai beckoned them onward. "We must keep moving. As brilliant as it is from this vantage point, you cannot see the details of the carvings. Save your awe for then."

The horses' hooves clacked against the stones when they reached the road, and voices from the temple became clear on the air, ringing in multiple languages Bri couldn't place. They were led under the archway, and as Enlai had said, the carvings were awe-inspiring. They depicted scenes of heroes fighting monsters with wings and long necks, of creatures with the body of a lion and the head of an eagle soaring high above the world. More than once a long-necked creature had been carved, clutching an egg close or nurturing it as it hatched. Strangely, the egg produced not another creature like the one that stood over it, but a man. All were painted with bright blues and reds, yellows, and greens.

The people were just as breath-taking. Far from the shades of brown, black, and white fabrics common back home, these people dressed in deep reds, stunning yellows, jewel-tone blues, and most every other color. Some had gold coins hung around their necks and hips, sparkling in the daylight, and jangling as they passed. Many eyes were rimmed with dark lines, and their ears and noses had been pierced through. These people tended to wear high-collared shirts and dresses, where the others donned low cut tops and mid-drift baring attire. So many had darker skin like the man with the lantern, but just as many resembled Enlai more closely. It had been a long time since Alec had seen people dressed this way. At least five hundred years.

They stared as Alec and Bri were escorted inside, whispering and pointing. Some ventured close for a better look. Others hurried off— presumably to gather friends and family or start the spread of gossip. Enlai and the others kept the boldest of the onlookers away, ushering Alec and Bri through painted doors, across a gardened courtyard where bronze statues seemed to watch them as they walked by, and into a quiet granite room, shutting the doors behind them.

This room was unlike the colorful temple they had come through to get there. Bri almost doubted his eyes as he looked at the bare walls and smooth floor. Windows graced the far wall, showing the grey sky and the gentle rain that continued to fall. Between each window a single lamp burned, and beneath it a slender stick had been placed in a carved base, smoking, and casting an unusual, but not unpleasant, scent about the room. A lone wooden door occupied the far right-hand corner. Finally, inside out of the rain, Bri shivered.

The door opened, and a young boy came through, black hair cut short, and wearing the high-collared attire. He smiled when he saw Enlai and rushed toward him. "Ba!"

Enlai embraced him, his own expression mirroring that of the child. He ruffled the boy's hair, then turned him to face Bri. "This is my son, En," he said. Then he spoke to the child in a musical language Bri had never heard before. En bowed. "I have told him who you are," Enlai continued. "He does not speak your Dactic tongue."

En rose and took his father by the hand, tugging on him and speaking quickly in that lyrical language. Bri envied him. To be able to touch his father with such confidence, with such a feeling of safety. Bri had always been able to touch his mother—he wished he had known as a child why she was so different—but everyone else had always hurt so much. Even Ella.

Enlai calmed his son, affection never leaving his eyes. "He says the Satguru is aware of your arrival and will be here shortly."

The door opened again, as though the words had summoned the action. Slippered feet made hardly any sound as they glided in, and the white and silver clothes were a far cry from that of the other inhabitants of the temple. The gossamer skirt flowed like the myst, and the sleeves dripped from the arms. Her hair was silver, tied in a knot on the back of her head, and her skin pale as a cloud. She came straight at Bri, no uncertainty anywhere in her face. She looked no more than eighteen or nineteen years old, but Bri could feel the power rolling off her, the way the myst turned to her first before giving him the slightest attention. She took him by the chin, her nails polished a shining silver to match everything else, and he had no choice but to look straight into her blue-streaked silver eyes.

"I am Iris."

"Bri."

She stood only a few inches taller than him, hardly enough to matter, but Bri felt small in her presence. "I have not seen one like you in centuries." There was something in her eyes that reminded him of Dorothea. That pure interest and concentration. She would study him until she was satisfied, and let him go only then. "Most forbidden children are killed."

"I assure you, it's been tried."

"Yet you escape."

"My mother hid me. Then I made a pact with a demon."

At that she snatched up his right arm, turning it so she could see the mark in full. Its subtle light pulsed against her fingers. Bri felt Alec step closer to him, almost at his back. "You have sold your soul."

"Yes."

"Why?"

"I was dying. The seraph can't seem to finish me, but the myst nearly did."

She dropped his arm. "So then what do you want from me?"

Bri waited a moment to see if Alec would cut in. When he did not, Bri proceeded. "I was told you could help me. Teach me how to control the myst."

"Who told you?"

"My mother's sister. She is the reason I'm alive at all."

"She goes against Haven's holy order."

"It seems so."

"I like her. Who was your mother?"

"Talia."

Iris thought a moment, one silver nail tapping lightly against her pink lips. "I did not know her. But I am very old." Bri's face must have shown his disbelief at that because she continued. "I was very young when I Fell, but now I am very old."

"I don't know how old my mother was."

"It does not matter." She took up his hand again, lacing their fingers together and closing her eyes.

Bri felt his palm tingle, saw the myst charge down from the ceiling where it had waited like an obedient dog and slide along her body. It traveled down her arm and toward his hand. It licked at his fingers, but came no further. Iris jerked it back, her eyes open once again.

"There is magic on you."

"Yes." He choked on the word. "A *labrynth,* meant to help me learn control."

In a flurry of movement, Iris spun him around and peeled his soaking wet shirt from his back. A sound of disgust echoed across the open room, and she released him, throwing her hands up in the air. "You have mutilated yourself. Go. I will not help you." She headed toward the door.

"No!" Bri nearly slipped in the water that had puddled beneath him. "Please! Miss Iris, I need your help."

"Why?" She faced him once again, her expression as cold and unmoving as the stone that constructed her temple. "Why should I help you? You have made your pact with a demon. It will keep you alive, and once your soul is gone all your problems will be solved."

"I have seven years left in my bargain. Carma won't renegotiate. I can't live like this. The seraph nearly caught me the other day, and I have no idea what they will do to me. I can't be in crowded rooms. I have a brother who stalks me through my connection to the myst. I can't even—" He stopped himself. *I can't even kiss a girl.* "Please, Iris. Please. You're the only one who can teach me."

She thrust a finger at his face, the sleeves of her robe rolling down her arm as the myst had. "You defaced your body with mortal magic."

"It wasn't his fault," Alec spoke suddenly, appearing at Bri's side. "It wasn't his fault. He had nothing to do with it. He was thirteen, and attacked while trying to learn how to control the myst. We did it to save him. He would have been torn apart."

"And you are?" Iris regarded him with little more than a tilt of her head.

"Alec."

"And what connection do you have to Bri?"

"I am one of the soulless of the demon to whom he sold his soul. He's my responsibility."

"And you are responsible for the damage that is his back?"

"Yes."

"No, he's not." Bri shook his head, but stopped when more water dripped into his eyes. "Alec has only ever protected me. A witch put the *labrynth* on my back, not Alec."

"I didn't stop her," Alec said.

"You had no choice."

"How sweet." Iris waved a hand, silencing them both. "I do not care. What must be understood is this," she caught Bri in an unbreakable hold of eye contact, "the *labrynth* is irreversible. If it were smaller,

I would cut it from your body, but that is not possible. This witch of yours marked you permanently. Short of skinning you."

Bri shuddered at the thought. "So you can't help me?"

"Of course, I can help you. I was a Singer. I know the myst better than any other creature in this realm. I am Fallen, so my use of it is limited, but I doubt it is more limited than what you have been given. No, the matter is not whether or not I can help you, but if I will."

"Will you?"

"Tell me why." She moved closer, her face nearly touching his, her silver and blue eyes studying him with that unwavering intent. "Why should I hide you? Why should I risk Haven's eye turning my way when I have avoided it so long?"

Bri was shaking so hard he wasn't sure if it was from the cold of being wet, or fear. "I'm not seraph and human. My father was a witch. My brother is a witch, and he works for demons who try to become gods."

That glimmer of curiosity had come to her eyes again. "I heard of this happening. Lillianna, was it not? The Mistress of Hell."

"Yes."

"But she is dead now."

"My brother wants something from me. He's mad. I can't let him have it, whatever it is. But he's stronger than me. I cannot resist him the way I am."

"So you want to learn so you can resist a mad witch?"

"Yes. Whatever he wants to do, it isn't good."

"And that's all?"

"What do you mean?"

She traced the line of his jaw with one finger. "That is the only reason you want to learn to control the myst?"

Bri closed his eyes in embarrassment. *Can she read my mind as well?*

Iris laughed. "Your body tells me the truth. You lean into every touch like a starved child. Who is it you want to touch, but can't?"

Ella. Her name became a mantra in his head, over and over again, until the word sounded like nothing but sweet music. He begged Iris silently not to force him to answer. The knowing smile she wore for him tied his heart in knots. He couldn't admit it. Not in front of so many strangers.

A light smack broke the torturous mantra in his head. Iris stroked the offended cheek, then tapped twice as she nodded. "Fine. You will tell me later. Get cleaned up and dry off. Eat something and have someone show you to your rooms. We will begin tomorrow."

In that moment, Bri felt lighter than ever before. "Thank you." The word was barely a whisper, but he said it over and over again until he wasn't sure he was even using the correct language. He bent over, clutching his own knees for support, and felt Alec's hand on his back.

"As for you," Iris seemed to be speaking to Alec, "I will allow you to stay as well…on one condition."

"What's that?" Alec said.

"Don't cause too much of a ruckus with that face of yours. The girls and some of the boys here are so sheltered they're likely to think you are some sort of god—or a demon."

"I promise not to compromise their virtue."

"Oh no, there is nothing to compromise. We do not have the same stuffy values here as they do to the east. My students are here to seek truth; by all means, help them find it. Just don't cause a ruckus."

PART TWO

— CHAPTER NINE —

She had stained her fingers with ink, having spent the entire night drafting the letter that now lay drying on the mahogany desk before her. The right words had taken so long to come, she feared she had ink on her face from all the times she had succumbed to her frustration. If she did, she would be wise to clean up before anyone saw her. Appearance—her appearance—was nearly the only thing anyone seemed to think about lately.

That, and her safety.

"Marce?" The voice preceded a gentle knock on her door and the sound of it swinging open.

Damnit. Can a girl get no privacy at all? She scrubbed her forearm along her cheeks, hoping she was making the situation better, rather than worse. "I've asked you not to call me that."

Her older brother, Den, shut the door after entering. He was fully dressed, an odd thing for so early in the morning, and not a good sign. His jacket was perfectly pressed and buttoned, the white of his shirt and handkerchief a stark contrast to the black. His light brown hair had been tamed and slicked, allowing no chance of a hair coming out of place. The shine on his shoes caught the morning light coming in through her window. Too put together. It didn't bode well for her.

"Fine then, I'm here to tell you to get dressed. We have an early luncheon to attend, *Marciella*," He placed so much emphasis on her name it sounded more like how their grandmother had said it, with her thick Talconian accent.

She ground her teeth at her full name. It wasn't what she had meant for him to call her, but at least it was an improvement. "With whom? And don't say with that rat of a man, Gattock." Standing from her chair, she swept a limp blonde curl from her eyes.

Den's face fell. "Oh, Marce, look at you! You have ink everywhere!"

"Don't change the subject. It will wash off. Who is the luncheon with?" The washbasin sat across the room. The white porcelain clinked softly as she lifted the pitcher to pour some water into the bowl.

"Well, it's with Gattock."

The washcloth she had wet splashed back into the bowl as she turned on him. "I knew it!"

"He's really not that bad."

"Not that bad? He's old, and he's crude, and he has the face of a rat."

Sighing, Den stopped himself just before he could muss his hair with a frustrated hand. "You shouldn't say such things about him."

"Why not? They're true."

"He's not that old."

"Old enough. Older than you, and you're ten years older than me."

"I just want to keep you safe."

"Safe?" She bit her tongue to keep from launching into the same argument they always had. Grabbing up the washcloth, she scrubbed at her face until her cheeks hurt and the white cotton had turned black. She worked on her fingers to give herself something to do as she carefully spoke. "Safe from what, Den? No one is going to come after me."

"You're a fool if you really believe that. You are the only surviving heir. The throne is yours."

She laughed before she could stop herself. "Throne? What throne? There is no throne. Talconay is dust, and Vaah has taken the rubble that remains."

"The people don't feel that way. The death of the royal family rocked them, but they remembered you."

The water had turned murky, and her fingers were more red than ink-covered. "I was so far down the line of succession no one cared about me. A dozen people would have had to die before I was queen."

"Not a dozen. Just nine. And they did die. And now you are queen."

"Stop saying that. You sound ridiculous."

"Marciella Kalagrey, you cannot deny who you are."

The use of her full name caused her to pause. Den was right. She couldn't deny who she was. Wishing it away did not make it so. She sat on the edge of her bed, feeling the mattress sink beneath her and wishing life was as easy to bend to her will. The throne had never been her dream. It hadn't been a possibility. Then one single night had changed everything. A demon changed everything.

"Why don't you be king, Den? You would be better at it than me."

She felt the bed give under him on the other side, and just as tangibly the change in the air around him. These were all things they had said before, but sometimes she felt like they would never sink in.

"I am not fullblood," he said. "I am not the heir. You are."

"I don't know how to be queen. I wasn't raised for it."

"What do you think we've been doing for the past year?"

Gliding her hand over the rich blue coverlet and under the down pillow encased in silk, she found the single item that had given her some peace over the last torturous year. She pulled the paper out and turned it gently in her hands. The letter had become fragile, the folds likely to tear if she was not careful. She had read it countless times. Beside her bed, a leather book marked with a silver ribbon had ink stains on the edges of its pages and along the binding. She had read it to the point of memorization as well.

"Just come to the luncheon," Den said, all the fight gone from his voice. "Hear what Gattock has to say."

"I can't imagine he has anything to say that he hasn't already said. If he proposes to me, I will never speak to you again."

"He isn't going to propose. He can't propose; you haven't been Presented yet."

"If he proposes at my Masquerade, I will never speak to you again."

"He has no intention of marrying you. If you paid attention to gossip, you would know that. He has his eye on the Lady Fayette."

"Really?"

"I promise." He crossed his heart as they had when they were children. "I won't force you to marry anyone. You're my queen, you make the choice. But you do have to choose wisely, and Gattock is connected and intelligent. He is a good ally to have."

There wasn't a hint of a lie in her brother's green eyes. "All right," she agreed. "Go and let me get dressed, then. I'll meet you in the parlor."

"Thank you." Den stood. "Try to be ready in a half turn?"

"A half turn?"

"I knew that was too much to ask. Especially since you still haven't gotten all the ink off." He wiped at her cheek with a thumb. "As soon you can, then? No more than a turn, please."

She huffed. "I don't need a full turn." She remembered the reason for all the ink. "Send the letter on my desk, please? I'd like it out this morning."

"Another one?" It was mostly a tease. He went to the desk without further prompting, lifting the now-dry paper.

"It's been a month, as usual." A lie. She kept her gaze focused elsewhere.

"No. It's been two weeks. You're early."

"This one is important. I don't want it to be late."

Folding the letter and sealing it for her, Den held it up for her inspection. "I shall get it out immediately then, my dear Marciella."

"Thank you, Denholm."

"I've asked you not to call me that."

"As I have also asked you. If you will not call me by my preferred name, then I shall not call you by yours."

He headed for the door. "Fair is fair, I suppose. I will see you soon, Ella."

She smiled. "See you soon, Den."

He left, and Ella unfolded the delicate letter in the silence that followed. The words had faded a bit with time, though they were still legible. She tried not to touch it so much, but the habit was hard to break. The words always filled her with happiness and hope. As had every letter that had followed each month since. She wrote back faithfully.

My dearest Ella,

Regretfully, I won't be able to see you on your birthday and give this to you in person. I must leave Callay, and I can't say where I will be. Please don't worry. I will be safe, and

HOPEFULLY STRONGER WHEN I RETURN. WE THINK WE'VE FOUND SOMEONE WHO CAN HELP ME WITH MY SITUATION.

I'VE ENCLOSED MY COPY OF AUSTEIRE'S NOVEL, A THOUSAND NIGHTS UNDER THE SUN. I HOPE YOU ENJOY THE STORIES WITHIN AS MUCH AS I DO. I FIND THE WORLD CREATED IN THESE PAGES GIVES ME A SENSE OF ESCAPE WHEN THIS WORLD GETS TO BE TOO MUCH. NIRAH IS MY FAVORITE CHARACTER.

I'LL WRITE TO YOU AS OFTEN AS I CAN. IF YOU'D LIKE, YOU CAN SEND LETTERS TO ME THROUGH MRS. McCALLAHAN AT LOSTLEY HOUSE. SHE'LL SEE THAT I GET THEM.

HAPPY BIRTHDAY, ELLA. I HOPE I SEE YOU AGAIN SOON.

BEST, BRI.

It had been a year since then. A year of nothing but his words to comfort her as she navigated this new and terrifying world she had been thrust into. She was queen of a conquered and decimated land. A life she never wanted. And with her seventeenth birthday fast approaching she would be eligible to be Presented at the Autumn Masquerade. Her adulthood would be recognized, and everyone would know she was of marriageable age.

At least one thing would go the way she wanted it. She would see to it.

It felt good to be in Hell once again. Carma had made many trips in the past year, never visiting the same place twice. She had been to the boiling lakes, where tormented souls swam for a shore they would never reach. The icy glaciers of the highest point, where icicles cut and stabbed manifest flesh while feet stuck to the frozen ground. She had visited the murderers' pit, and watched as they were bet upon to fight to the death as demons cheered and drank. Hell had so many entertainments.

Once, the punishment in Hell had fit the crime, but the High Lord had decided the process was too poetic, too like Haven's orderly ways. Now, a soul's eternity in Hell was determined by any number of things. If you were a thief, you could end up anywhere from the mines where brimstone was chipped away to find black jewels and poisonous dust, to the household of a demon who wanted a servant. A soul could make their way in Hell, earning privileges and promotions. Carma had once met a courtesan who had killed her most wealthy clients for money in life. Hell had placed her first in the airless caves where she had stumbled and clambered in the dark, gasping for air, but she had caught the attention of a certain demon who liked her face. Now, she spent her days scrubbing his floors and cooking his food, and she warmed his bed every night. He killed her afterward, of course, every time. This was Hell, after all. But she had nice clothes and air in her lungs, so she was satisfied. No chance for redemption anyway. That was reserved for those who inhabited The Gated Realm.

Carma, however, was not interested in the afterlife choices of the sinful souls of Hell. She had come for its demons. One demon, in particular.

He was a hard man to find. For every one she found who claimed to have seen him, another ten swore he hadn't been heard from in ages. It made him difficult to track. She had settled for wandering, asking nothing of anyone, and simply listening to gossip and rumors. It had taken the better part of the year, but it had led her here, to the Demon's Bane Fields, where white and pink stargazer lilies grew in abundance. They called them demon's bane, for the flowers grew in Haven as well, and here they served as a constant reminder of what they had left behind. It was here that they had all entered the Demon Realm of Hell after tearing their hearts free of their chests.

Carma ran a hand along her chest, the skin smooth and unscarred. The dead-stillness sat against her hand like a great, resounding tone. She had no regrets, and yet, standing there, remembering the abrupt and violent descent as she had been cast out of Haven by her own hand, she could not help but toy with the idea of other avenues she might have taken.

She laughed. Nothing would make her wish to go back. Nothing could make her want Gabriel's life. Haven was rules and order and holy imprisonment. Hell was chaos and freedom. There was no question in her mind which suited her goals better. None.

She went to a large brimstone boulder and sat. She had left behind her human attire, opting instead for a long, red sheath dress with a tattered skirt that allowed her legs complete freedom of movement.

Her silver hair lay against her back, utterly still in the lack of breeze. The heat of the air shimmered and sat dryly in her throat, but she did not mind. It matched the stillness in her chest. Closing her eyes, she breathed deep, tasting the scent of the lilies. It stirred memories of long ago. Of strong arms and a rock-hard chest that she had always been able to sleep soundly against. She remembered restless nights as he had battled with his thoughts. Conversations they would have well into morning about the state of things, and what was right. A growing obsession with power had come first—though he had always been ambitious. The day he told her what he planned to do, there had been nothing but solid conviction in his eyes. She knew he would succeed. He had torn his heart out right in front of her. And when he threw the organ to the floor, she knew there would never—

No. Such thoughts were not allowed. No lying.

"I do hope you are thinking about me."

That voice. It was like molasses; thick, sweet, and dark. It had been a year since she had heard it, but such time was nothing. "In fact, I was." Carma didn't turn to look at him. She wouldn't have to.

His hands found her shoulders first, then her back, trailing down to her waist before sliding around to lock her in an embrace. She felt his whole body pressed behind her and marveled at how some things never seemed to change. "You are not very subtle, my love. Wandering about Hell, asking about me for a time, then saying nothing at all. It was clear to me what you were doing."

"And what was I doing?"

"Looking for me."

"Why would I do that?"

"The same reason you followed me here all those years ago."

"You mean, because I love you?"

He laughed and pressed his lips to her shoulder. "Love is something of Haven."

"And we are of Hell."

"We are left with nothing but lust."

"I wouldn't call lust nothing." One of his hands snaked downward, between her legs. Carma almost leaned into him. Almost. She turned and faced him, forcing him to release her from his embrace. "Don't distract me. I have things to ask you."

He had always been so handsome. Too handsome. A face like that attracted sin. Vanity, at the very least. His ice blue eyes were a stark contrast to the black of his hair, and Carma had to remind herself of a few very important things to keep from getting lost in them. "You had me thrown into the Inbetween."

"Did I?"

"Yes."

"Can you prove it?"

"Why deny it?"

Olin took up a lock of her hair and let it glide between his fingers. "True. Yes. It was me."

"Why?"

"Because you were getting too close to the truth."

"And which truth is that? That you want to be a god?" She shook her head as he smiled, flashing teeth white as Haven's Citadel. "I have always known that, Olin. Ever since I watched you tear your heart from your chest."

"Even I did not know exactly where my desires would lead me back then."

"Fine, then, but I knew whatever you wanted was no trivial desire."

"Nothing I want ever is. But now I think it is my turn for a question. Why did you then tear out your own heart?"

"To follow you."

"Why?"

"Haven't I always followed you?"

"You are the best at skirting the truth, Carma."

"Thank you."

"Which is why I had you thrown to the Inbetween. I had eyes on you. Even your soulless were beginning to think you were going mad. I could no longer trust you."

"You could have killed me."

"I love you too well for that." He ran a finger over her lips.

"Love is for Haven."

"It is an expression."

She studied him a moment. He was much the same; tall, imposing, and every bit Haven's soldier turned Hell's demon. She could pinpoint nothing different about him, and yet... "You used Lillianna. She was the oldest of us, and you let her be slaughtered like chattel."

"Shall I remind you who it was who did the slaughtering?"

"You helped."

His hand continued to roam her body, stroking her neck, then her collarbones. "The woman was mad. And weak. She was clearly not strong enough."

"But you are?"

"I will not have this conversation with you, Carma. If you force it, I will toss you back in the Inbetween and ensure you do not escape again."

"Once you kept no secrets from me."

"I trusted you once. Now, I do not." His hand wrapped around her waist, squeezing. "Would you like to try to earn it back?"

His touch was becoming harder to ignore. It stirred things she had not felt in centuries. "Do you not fear Luca?"

Laughter filled the field, and his hand fell away, taking with it the physical spell he had begun to weave around her. "Luca is dead."

Carma was literally taken aback, scrambling for purchase on the rock. "You cannot say that. Why would you say that? If the Lord of Hell was dead, we—"

"If the Lord of Hell was alive, we would all know it. But he has not been seen in eons. Demons have searched all corners of Hell and have found nothing. If he were still alive, the death of his sister would have drawn him out. I have nothing to fear from an old, dead demon."

"He and Lillianna were the first. You have everything to fear from them."

"I think we proved otherwise last summer. You and I turned Lil to ash."

"Not alone."

"No, but she is ash nonetheless. I believe that leaves no one in Hell for me to fear."

"There are others. Younger than Luca, but older than us."

"My dear Carma," Olin leaned close, taking her by the chin and running his thumb along her lips, "there is no one in Hell who can give me pause. No one, but you. So, if I were you, I would watch my step, because I will do whatever necessary to achieve my goals. And if that means sucking every last soul from your body, I will do so."

"Careful. You'll forget, as Lillianna did, that what you do to me comes back to you. And you have always gotten seven-fold."

"I never forget. It made sharing your bed so much more rewarding."
His other hand found her thigh.

Carma slid closer to him, hands tracing the lines of his muscles through his shirt. "So is this where we stand? A heartbeat from killing one another?"

"Neither of us have heartbeats."

"Another expression."

He grabbed her by the hips and hauled her into his lap. She wrapped her arms around his neck. "Do not get in my way, Carma."

"Don't get in mine."

"Are you plotting something of your own, my little minx?"

He was moving her dress aside, and she didn't stop him. "Of course. It's what you love about me."

"Again with the love."

"We do both seem to keep making the same mistake." His belt came away easily enough.

"Old habits, I suppose."

"Old habits die hard."

He grinned and lifted her while she did away with the last barrier between them.

They never kissed. Kissing would have been a lie.

And demons couldn't lie.

— CHAPTER TEN —

Blistering hell, Alec. Put some clothes on."
Casually reclined on his bed with a book in hand, Alec turned the page lazily, not surprised by Picadilly's sudden appearance. He had heard her tell-tale footsteps in the hall before she had opened the door. "I am alone in my room, Pica, why should I wear a shirt if I don't want to?"

She flipped the long braid of her black hair over her shoulder. "This place is no good for you. It's made you vain."

"This place is hot. Hotter than hell, one might say if in a bad mood. But the best part is, no one cares if I choose to be half naked, so I choose to be. I'm practical. Now, is there something you want, or did you come for no other reason than to bother me?"

A swift kick shut the door. "I brought Bri a letter, and I thought you might like to know what Carma has been up to."

That got his attention. Alec set the book down and sat up. "She must be doing something very interesting if you're willing to betray her to me."

Gliding across the room in slacks and a dinner jacket that she'd had tailored, Pica went to the glassless window and pushed the curtains aside, letting the sunlight in. "She's been to Hell again."

"Key word, 'again.' That's nothing new, Pica."

"She has Dorothea scribing every night, and she has been drinking human blood."

"Heart's blood?"

"Not that I have seen, but I would not be surprised."

Alec dropped his head into his hands. "She's strengthening herself. Or going mad again."

"She is not mad yet."

"No mutterings about pieces?"

"No muttering, but she leaves for days on end, and when she comes back, she smells of Hell."

"And she's told you nothing?" There was a bottle of bitter amber liquor on his bedside table. Alec reached for it.

"You were always the one she spoke candidly to. Once, I was her friend and equal, but it is not so any longer. She tells me only what I need to know."

"Nothing at all?" Throat burning from his drink, Alec offered the bottle to Pica.

She took it and threw back a mouthful without so much as a wince. "One thing."

"And what's that?" Alec swung his legs around and stood, stretching.

"She keeps telling me to remember the Restorium."

He stilled, arms still raised above his head as he had been working the lethargy from his shoulders. Lowering his arms, he stared at Pica, not sure he heard her correctly. "The Restorium?"

She looked grave. "Yes."

"I thought that was a myth."

"It is far from a myth." Drawing the curtains closed once more, Pica darkened the room as though light and open air would betray their conversation. "It is simply rare."

"How rare?"

"I was a child during the last one, and I am nearly three thousand years old if you include my life as seraph. Before that was the time Lillianna and Luca tore out their hearts and claimed Hell as their own."

Alec sat again. "Only two. All that time and there have only been two."

"There were more before, of course, but as I said, they are rare, and without a schedule."

"Is there one coming?"

"Only Haven would know."

"Then why is Carma talking about it?"

"Perhaps she fears one is coming...or hopes. It would be a perfect time for a demon to act. Haven will take no action."

Alec put his hand out, and Pica returned his bottle to him. He took a long, painful swig of the liquor. The Restorium. A time when all of Haven slept and bathed in pure light, cleansing itself. Those who were weak or of questionable faith were often forcibly turned out, Fallen. Couples would all conceive. When Haven awoke, it was rumored to be stronger and purer than ever. "I've never lived through one. How many will Fall?"

"As many as need to. Iris was forced out during the last Restorium."

"She did not tell me that."

"It is most likely not a point of pride with her, but if you are worried about the number of Fallen that could appear in this realm should there be a Restorium, you would be smart. There has not been a Restorium since The Silent One became so silent."

"I take it there's a lot of shaken faith up in Haven."

"Not as much as you might think, but I imagine some have thoughts they keep even from themselves."

"And if a demon knew this time was coming?"

"As I said," she smiled, "we could run amok in the mortal realm, terrorizing and feasting, and Haven would not lift a finger."

"Even if one attempted to become, say, a god?"

"Even then."

When Picadilly finally left, Alec had a terrible headache and had drained more than half his bottle of liquor. The idea of a Restorium happening in his lifetime, and now of all times, gave him waking nightmares. They knew Olin was up to something, and his most likely goal, but he wasn't the demon Alec was worried about. Carma was. He had no idea what she intended. None at all. And if all the pieces she had been collecting over the years were for some purpose, he suspected he would find out soon.

Which was all the more reason to stay where he was, safe behind the walls and wards of this obscure group of mystics. All the more reason to keep Bri there. Every night, he dreamed of Ariadne and their one meeting that now seemed so long ago. She had said they would find each other again. He had left for the other end of the continent. Needless to say, there had been no further meetings. Some days he woke up tempted to search for her, but the thought always dissipated with the morning fog. Bri was his first responsibility, and Bri needed to remain where they were. Iris had spent the last year working with him, training him, teaching him. He could call the myst to him now when he wanted it, and he could sit in the great hall with the whole of the mystic community while they meditated and focused on the myst without being overcome and ill. There hadn't been a single night after the first month where Alec had to lay awake beside Bri, soothing him as he struggled not to let the myst overpower him and come rushing into the temple.

Of course, a lot of things had changed in the last year. Just not enough for him to start thinking about leaving.

A knock on his door. "Alec?" Bri stood in the open doorway, a stark reminder of everything Alec had just been thinking about. The small, sickly boy he had brought here was gone, replaced by a young man who had broadened in the shoulders, and exercised daily. Iris had been insistent upon that, that he strengthen his body. Every morning Bri woke early and practiced with the temple initiates in the dawn light, going through a sequence of slow, choreographed movements meant to focus the mind and train the body. The result was a lean build, but muscled, and Bri did seem the stronger for it. Alec no longer felt like Bri would snap in two if a strong enough wind came by. He knew if he stood next to Bri the top of Bri's head now reached his nose. Due to that growth spurt, Bri had been forced to adopt the local attire, though he avoided the bright colors. The white tunic and loose-fitting pants made him look like a completely different person from the boy Alec had met some four years ago now. It took work, but Alec was trying not to think of him as a boy anymore. A kid still— Alec figured he would always see Bri as a kid, even in five hundred years—but no longer a child. Regardless, he was glad they had found this place. His only regret was not having found it sooner.

"Can I talk to you?" Bri said. He had a letter clutched in his right hand.

Alec gestured to the letter with his bottle, wincing as the sound of a gong echoed across the valley. "That's the second one this month."

Bri blushed, one of the many things he had still not grown out of, and shifted so the letter was half hidden behind his leg. "Yes."

"I thought you two were on a monthly schedule?" The letters had been the source of a long fight between the two of them when they first arrived. Alec thought it was foolish to have contact with anyone in the outside world. Bri complained that Alec couldn't lock him away forever with no friends. Pica, who had brought the first letter and every letter since, had simply been amused. In the end, Bri had won, and every month he wrote a letter, which Pica delivered. The next time she came to give Alec an update on Carma's whereabouts, she would bring with her a reply.

"We are. We were. Pica came early too, so it's not like it's the only unusual occurrence this month."

"That's true." Thinking of that made him want another drink, but the sound of the sloshing in the bottle was too hollow, and Alec remembered he had already had more than he should have, and so he set it aside.

"What did Pica say? Is everything all right?"

"Yeah, it's fine. Nothing to worry about. She just likes to irritate me whenever possible. What did you want to talk about?"

"I want to go home."

"What?"

Bri had been staring at his feet. Now, he shifted, no longer leaning against the doorjamb, though he kept one hand on it, and looked straight at Alec. "I want to go home."

"I'm not sure I know what that means."

"It means I want to go home, Alec."

"And just where do you consider home?"

When Bri got exasperated, he breathed deep, rocked back on his heels, and made a face that implied the receiver's stupidity, though he would never voice it aloud. He did all that now. "Callay, Alec. I want to go back to Callay."

"What the hell is in that letter that you would want to go back to Callay?"

"It's not about the letter." Said letter disappeared farther behind Bri's back.

"Liar."

"Okay, fine. It has to do with the letter."

"And just what does the fair Lady Ella have to say that would tempt you away from this paradise?" He rose and went to the window, opening the curtains once again and standing in the sunlight. Another gong sounded and chimes followed, signaling the beginning of afternoon rituals.

"It's not just about her letter. I'm ready to go. We've been here a year, and it was never meant to be permanent. Carma must want us back."

"Carma has not asked for us back. Good try, though. You are here to learn, and to be safe."

"I have been learning. I'm much better at everything now—you know I am. It's been months since I've gotten ill."

Alec turned and leaned against the window so he could see Bri. "Maybe so, but there are new complications."

Bri was staring at his feet again. "I don't know what you're talking about."

"No? You mean you forgot how yesterday you thought there were Vaanasian caravan folk walking through the center of the temple, but there weren't, you were just seeing the myst overlaid with reality?"

"That doesn't happen that often." The words were muttered, but Alec heard them well enough.

"I just don't think leaving is a good idea, Bri." It might not happen that often, but Alec thought it happened often enough. It shouldn't have happened at all. "Besides, you've been behind these walls a long time now. The wards protect you from the myst, not just your own ability. What happens if you step outside?"

"I won't know until I try."

Occasionally, Alec missed the small child who gladly went along with whatever decision he made. Bri was growing into a rather stubborn adolescent. Independence was a good thing, Alec reminded himself of that. *Gods, no one ever warned me this would be so hard. Watching him grow up. Being capable of making decisions for himself. Trouble is, he's still a kid in so many ways. Despite what he may think.* "You haven't given it a try yet. I'm not taking you across the continent without knowing you can handle it. Nothing in that letter is worth setting everything you've learned back." All this nonsense made him feel the need for a walk, so he grabbed a tunic from the back of a chair and slipped it on, then headed out, bottle in hand, knowing Bri would follow.

Bri's fist tightened around the letter as Alec moved past him, then loosened when he heard the crinkling of the paper. "That's not fair. Besides, you hate it here." Alec scoffed, taking the steps down toward the courtyard two at a time. "I don't hate it here."

"You do. You're bored."

Bored was an understatement. But it wasn't the point. "I can survive boredom. I've lived through worse."

"Just say yes." They'd reached the bottom of the stairs, and the sun hit them both as they stepped out into the tiled courtyard. The songs and chants of the mystics beyond swept about on the breeze.

"Tell me why you want to go home so badly." Cutting across the brightly colored tiles that formed spiraling designs beneath their feet, Alec headed toward the gardens that led to the market stalls where imports were made available to those staying within the walls of the Temple.

Bri kept up, though he still had to walk faster than Alec to do so. "I don't need to tell you. You've already guessed."

Alec stopped, the bees buzzing behind him, hard at work in the large purple flowers that bloomed this time of year. "So then where's the harm in admitting it?"

Glaring, Bri reached across, grabbed Alec's bottle of liquor and took a drink, all the while looking incredibly defiant. He gasped after swallowing. "What the hell is that?"

"Baijiu." Alec tried not to laugh when Bri coughed, he really did, but success was not his in that moment. Which earned him another glare—which was also rather amusing. Being stared down by Bri was much like being stared down by a kitten. Time and growth hadn't changed a thing about that.

"It's terrible," Bri said.

"I don't think so, but you don't like any alcohol."

Bri coughed once more, then took another drink before shoving the bottle back into Alec's arms. Alec had to admit he was a little impressed by the display. "Ella will be Presented at the Autumn Masquerade."

Alec inclined his head to a passerby. It didn't go unnoticed that Bri still instinctively moved aside to avoid any accidental touch. "All the seventeen-year-old girls will be. I don't see what that has to do with us." Yes he did.

"She's asked me to come."

"I was once given an invitation to the home of a very beautiful and influential concubine. Doesn't mean I went." He started back toward the market stalls, knowing precisely which one he needed.

"You're being difficult."

"Deliberately." He passed the stall lined in beautiful silks and damask, though he smiled at the woman who sold them when she waved. They skipped Bri's favorite, where sweets were lined up on clay dishes, and stopped only when they reached the spot where shelves were well stocked with bottles of all shapes and sizes. The bottle in Alec's hand was almost empty. He'd need another.

"I want to be there."

Alec pretended to think for a long moment, just to draw this out a bit further. He wanted Bri to be absolutely sure before he agreed to anything. He already knew what his answer would be, but this was a lot to risk for a dance and the possibility of another kiss. "All right, then, here's my decision." He made his exchange with the man behind the counter, handing over a few gold coins and returning the old bottle to be reused, before turning toward Bri. "We came here so you could learn to be out there in the world. So you can get through a party without collapsing." Bri's jaw set at that. It was a low blow, Alec knew, but he had a point to make, and he would see that it was made. "Talk to Iris," he said. "If she tells me you're ready to go, we'll go. But until I hear it from her, we're staying." He headed back through the stalls, suddenly in need of food, and the kitchen was on the opposite end of the temple.

"You swear?" Bri followed after him. "If Iris says I can go, we'll go?"

"I swear."

There was no chance Iris would tell him yes.

— CHAPTER ELEVEN —

Bri let himself into Iris's seeing room as he did every day. The noon gong had rung, and the mystics and initiates would be in the center courtyard, chanting, filling the air with their harmonized voices and accompanying chimes. It was a sound he had grown used to over the last year, was comforted by, even. Suddenly the idea of leaving it behind was more frightening than he had thought it would be.

This room here—this was safe. The silk curtains, the damask and gold, the tapestries that hung from the walls. The incense that burned by small altars and statues, sending smoke spiraling toward the ceiling. The delicate chimes that hung in the open window, singing as the breeze whistled past. All these things had become familiar to him, and a sign that he was safe from everything that had plagued him in the past. He had control here. The myst could not harm him, could not touch him if he did not wish it. The seraph could not sense him, and even Carma would not dare call him away. The people here, though human and subject to the myst, had allowed themselves to be marked with protective runes. It made them invisible within the myst, still there, but unseen. Their souls helped Iris peer within, acted as a catalyst for what she otherwise would have lost, but nothing more. Because of this, Bri could sit with them, talk with them, without worrying that he would fall into the myst.

Here, where he was at best a willing prisoner, he felt free.

Leaving was a gamble; he knew that, but it was one he was willing to take.

"Iris?" Bri wandered further inside, stepping around the low, round table surrounded by brightly colored cushions. Cold tea sat in a single cup, while another held nothing but drying tea leaves. Iris often left things out for days. Bri didn't ask why. He had learned from so many years with Dorothea that it was often best not to ask. The unfinished rune on his back itched at the thought of the old witch. They had never gotten it fixed—Iris refused to continue what she called the mutilation of his flesh—and so it continued to bleed even a year later, never fully healing.

White beads clattered on their strings on the red and gold doorway curtain as Iris stepped out of her private chambers. Her silver eyes were streaked with blue—a mark of her partial humanity due to her Fall—and they studied him as they always did, seeming to tear into his soul and leave his every thought bared to her. She couldn't really read his mind, but Bri couldn't help but shiver when she looked at him like that.

"You're late," she said, stepping into the room and letting the curtain drop behind her. She wore a flowing white and blue skirt that hung to her ankles, billowing and reminding Bri all too well of the myst they both saw. Her top was nothing more than a band of the same fabric wound about her chest. With a quick motion, she twisted her silver hair up and secured it in place with a silver stick.

"I know. I needed to speak with Alec."

"I don't care." She knelt at the low table, pushing the teacups aside and placing her hands palms up atop the polished wood. "Come, sit with me."

Bri knelt across from her on one of the embroidered cushions. She immediately wriggled her fingers. He placed his hands in hers, holding her wrists while she held his, swallowing his sigh. Iris closed her eyes and breathed deep.

The familiar tingle of her power crept along Bri's arms, up to his shoulders, along his neck, and behind his eyes, forcing them closed. The myst curled close, touching them both and opening itself to their sight. It wasn't like when he fell in alone; this was controlled, and earth-bound. Iris never left the mortal realm, could not, and so they peered within the myst from afar, seeing the visions only against the backs of their own eyelids.

Usually she showed him towns and families. Country fairs and children playing.

He saw nothing but blood now.

It ran like red rivers through once green fields. Black ash covered the trees and the bushes, smothered the flowers. He heard screams, gut wrenching and throat tearing screams. Everywhere the scent of death overpowered all else. Smoke clouded the sky, and he could taste the ash on his tongue. Bri turned in his mind's eye, searching for any glimpse of hope in all the darkness, and stopped short. He knew the pale pink dress, the dainty shoes, and the white gloves. Golden curls had fallen free of their pins, and had become matted with dirt and something else. Her green eyes were wide open, but unseeing. Bri tried not to look, tried to pull away from the vision, but Iris forced him onward, made him look at the delicate, pale throat.

Torn open.

He gagged, barely able to hold back the retching he so desperately wanted to do. Something grew larger in the sky, approaching quickly. It fell and hit the ground, rolling until it hit his feet. Bri peered down, terrified.

Alec's head.

He cast out the myst and Iris, scrambling back, away from the table and away from her hands. Each breath felt choked, and his stomach still roiled with the memory. Counting as he breathed, the incense not helping to clear his head, Bri reached for the letter he had placed carefully in his pocket, touching the paper and the wax seal for comfort. "You fabricated that," he said once words were once again under his power. "Alec isn't seen in the myst."

Iris had not moved a bit. She sat perfectly still, hands still upturned on the table. "Yes."

"Why?"

"It was something you needed to see."

"That doesn't answer the question. Why? Why would you create a vision like that? Why show me my friends dead?"

"Because that is what will happen."

"No."

"It is what will happen," she repeated, "if you do not leave this place."

"I don't understand."

"Of course you do." She stood with the grace of a dancer and crooked a finger at him. "Come with me."

Bri's knees still felt like they were made of water, and he was shaking all over, but he stood, holding tightly to a nearby chair until the shaking had passed. Iris called for him impatiently, having disappeared around a corner. Certain he wouldn't lose his breakfast after the first step, Bri followed.

Iris stood beside a tall white marble table, atop which sat a stone Kayos board. The twelve-piece set was polished to perfection, smooth and pleasant to the touch.

"You know this game?" Iris asked, circling a finger over the top of a piece called the Prophet.

"Yes," Bri said, annoyed by the question given what she had just done to him. "You have made me play with you at least once a week for the past year."

"I have, haven't I?" She smiled. "You know the rules then."

"Of course." Twelve pieces, and two players who took turns directing whichever piece had the next logical move, determined by the nature of that piece. The object of the game was to get all twelve pieces to the center of the board. It was harder than it sounded; because of the nature of the pieces being so like the nature of people; some would often have no choice but to move backward in relation to another. It was a game of manipulation and strategy.

Bri rarely won.

"When all twelve converge at the center, the world is either remade or preserved," Iris said, lifting another piece—the Martyr—from the board and twirling it between her fingers. "Do you know the origin of the game?"

"No, I don't." The game was so old no one knew where it had come from. But Bri didn't doubt that Iris would tell him.

"It was created by the first witch. His first act with his new understanding of the world."

"That's fascinating, but it doesn't explain why you would show me that vision, or what it means."

Iris smiled. "Of course it does." She set the Martyr piece back down and then traced her finger along the edge of the circular board. "The game is real. And it is in play." She had the pieces scattered about the board, as if half-way through a game. Toying with two pieces that lingered at the edge—the Maiden and the Shadow—Iris watched Bri with expectant eyes.

"You want me to believe I am nothing more than a pawn in someone's game?"

"Of course not. You know how Kayos works. Each piece moves in accordance with its nature. Free will is what makes planning so difficult. One move from the other side can upset all your plans."

Bri studied the board, assessing each piece and each possible move. It took him a while to work it all out. It always did. "There are two moves here. The Prophet, and the Ferryman."

"The Ferryman's move is open. He stands alone on the board, near only the Sun. That move can happen any time."

"The Prophet can go two ways. One space to the left, which secures him in that spot, protected on all sides."

"Or?" Iris prompted when Bri hesitated to describe the second option.

"Or...he can slide forward five spaces, which puts him very close to the center."

"Yes, it does."

"It also leaves him open to influence from the Shadow."

"Very astute of you. You are growing better at this game." Clearly satisfied, Iris swept across the room, pulling on a rope attached to a bell.

Bri turned away from the game, unable to look any longer. He understood now, and he didn't like it. "You've rendered my asking rather moot, but I will anyway. I need to go. Alec says he'll only agree if you approve. You have to tell him I've learned enough to be able to handle things out there."

"It would take decades for me to teach you everything, Bri. Unfortunately, we do not have that kind of time."

"Will you tell him, or not?"

She came toward him, gliding in a way that always made Bri fear he had left the mortal realm. They were the same height now, and when she came to a stop directly in front of him, their noses bumped, and Bri's eyes lost focus. "When you came to me, begging pathetically for my help, you had one goal in mind. You remember it?"

Yes. "It wasn't my only goal."

"It was the driving force behind your efforts. It still is." She stroked his cheeks.

Bri stood utterly still. In many ways Iris was like Dorothea, teetering on the edge. It was best not to push. "I know what's important," he said, "but, yes, it is still on my mind."

"You don't have to go. You could stay here. With me."

"You said I had to go."

"I did not. I showed you what will happen if you do not leave here. I never gave my opinion on the matter. The choice is yours. Left, or forward."

"Was the vision you showed me in any way real?" Her hands had found his throat, caressing and drawing nonsense patterns. Bri broke eye contact, unable to look at her and keep his wits about him.

"Yes."

"Then I have to go."

"I would rather you stay."

"Why?"

"Because. Do you not feel it?" With a gentle touch, she coaxed his gaze back to hers. "Flesh calls to like flesh. And yours is more like mine than any other I have come across in recent years. Fallen since birth."

"I am not Fallen."

"Of course you are. I feel it. You just don't know the difference. But you can feel it in the way your body responds to mine. The trembling, the anticipation. We are the same."

"I have a soul. I am human."

"You delude yourself. You are simply the culmination of the races. And the result is beautiful."

A knock on the door. Iris broke away, and Bri stumbled back, thankfully landing in a nearby chair. Looking smug, Iris said, "Perfect timing," then went to open the door. Bri put his head in his hands, dizzy. He barely heard the murmured words across the room, and only even tried to pay attention when he saw Iris's bare feet in his limited field of vision once again. "I have something for you," she said.

When Bri looked up, he was glad he had sat down. A girl and a boy. Two of the initiates, by the incomplete blood mark on their foreheads. The thumbprint of Iris's blood sat unadorned between their brows. Once they took vows of service, it would be lined in gold and silver, forever emblazoned upon their flesh. They must have been about the same age as himself, Bri reasoned. The girl smiled and blushed, hands clasped behind her back. The boy looked right at him, confident and stoic.

"This is Petra and Tarik," Iris introduced them, smoothing the girl's long black hair over her shoulders. "They have come to help you with your dilemma."

Oh, gods. "What dilemma?"

"The reason you came. You want to be able to be close to humans. To one human in particular. It went terribly the first time you tried. Horribly. Embarrassingly. And to think how many people saw—"

"Yes, okay. That's enough. Thank you."

Iris wrapped herself around the girl from behind, setting her chin on Petra's shoulder. "It would be best to know how successful your training has been before you leave, don't you agree?"

"Iris, I would really rather not—"

"Don't be ridiculous. You're a young man, and such is this time of human life. So here you are: a pure human girl and a pure human boy, still susceptible to the myst. I can see their lives flash before my eyes even now." Iris made a face expressing that it would be ghastly boring. Bri was glad neither of them could see. The girl simply stood there, letting her Satguru do as she pleased. The boy never took his gaze from Bri.

Bri stood, quickly putting the chair between himself and the pair. "It's an intriguing offer, Iris, but I think I'll be all right."

"Nonsense. Pick one. I didn't want to presume your preferences."

Bri stumbled over his words. "It's not—I mean I— I'm not sure—it's just Ella. Only Ella."

"Petra then," Iris said. "You can pretend." She gave the girl a push. "Bri is shy. He needs some encouragement." Tarik's shoulders slumped. Bri felt oddly guilty about it, but Petra was coming closer.

"I don't mind, if that's what worries you," she said, moving around the chair that made such a dismal shield. "It's an honor to be chosen to help you, in whatever way you may need."

"An honor?" Bri backed away, matching her step for step, though he kept stumbling over the many things Iris left laying about on the floor.

"Of course. You are a holy creature of The One."

"I assure you, Haven would not agree with that statement."

"Haven is not The One."

A windowsill bit into Bri's back, leaving him nowhere else to go. The open air at his back was warm and in no way inviting. He knew how high up they were. This was the tallest tower in the temple, touching the sky. Petra closed in on him, eyes still sparkling with her genuine smile. Bri's heart slammed away in his chest, everything he learned in the past year seeming to fly out the window at his back. All he could think of was the party, Ella's lips, and the darkness that followed.

Petra had outstretched her hand. "Here. Take my hand first."

Damnit. What had Iris told her? The whole temple knew to be cautious of touching him, that was no secret, but something in this girl's eyes told him she had been informed of far more. Her hand lingered there, taunting him. It was just a hand, nothing frightening, yet there he was, shaking like a leaf. He hadn't spent the last year growing stronger just to falter now.

But Ella…

It's just a hand.

Without giving himself enough time to change his mind, Bri set his hand in hers, and braced for the worst.

The myst slid close, curious. Bri told it to go away.

Away it went. Back to whence it had come, leaving him without even the smallest vision of Petra's life.

A strange sound, like laughter and shock and relief all bundled into one. The sound had come from him. Bri clasped his hand tightly around Petra's, marveling at the feel of his bare fingers against hers. Yes, he had touched Iris, and Alec and Mrs. McCallahan, but this was different. Petra felt different. Alec and the others were so silent, completely devoid of the myst, but Petra hummed with it. It was like a second pulse, a life force that drummed against his hand, yet remained within her. Leaving him alone. He took up her other hand, completely enthralled by the feeling.

Petra took a single step toward him, lifting their hands so they became settled between their chests. "See? You can do so much now. You don't have to be afraid."

Meeting her deep brown gaze, Bri couldn't find any words that satisfied this experience. Petra kissed him then, remaining still a moment, as if giving him time to adjust or change his mind. Bri closed his eyes, knowing better than to fight. He tried to think of other things. Of blonde curls and green eyes, instead of silver. When still the myst stayed away, Bri relaxed.

Then his chest began to tighten, and he felt a single tear slide down his cheek. All his life, a simple touch had been painful, dangerous. The caravan folk who had raised him hadn't cared. They had abused him, taken what they wanted, all the while forcing the myst and its visions upon him. He had spent so many days ill, barely able to get out of his bed. On those days, they had dragged him to his tent, forcing him to entertain the curious visitors who wanted a glimpse of their future. Now...

Petra must have sensed the change in him because she broke the kiss, but didn't draw away. Gently dislodging one hand from his desperate hold, she wiped away that first tear and the ones that followed. He stared at her, bewildered, and out of his element.

I can touch people. The thought alone was so long dreamed about, it terrified him.

He slid to the floor, unable to stand any longer, and Petra followed, wrapping her arms about him and laying her cheek against his head. The urge to run through the temple, shaking hands and embracing every person he came across rushed through Bri's body with such force he feared he might start laughing in hysteria.

He didn't know how long he cried, but Petra held him the whole time, and when he finally had enough wherewithal to look up and find Iris watching him from across the room she said, "I'll tell Alec you're free to leave."

— CHAPTER TWELVE —

Her attentions were sloppy and inexperienced, but for what she lacked in knowledge she made up for in enthusiasm, so Kai had deemed her not a complete waste of his time.

Time had become such a precious commodity.

The binding to Olin had been both tedious and painful. Tedious, because it required spending an extended period of time—an entire day, so that both the sun and moon could stand witness—with nothing to look at or talk to but Olin, and painful, because, well, it was always painful to trade flesh. Their hands and forearms had been bound together with snakevines, which dug their teeth into both demon and witch flesh. Kai had then drunk from a vial of Olin's blood, taking the demon's power into himself, only to have it surge through him and back to Olin through their joined hands. Twenty-four times he had done so, gritting his teeth so Olin would not see the pain, and hating every moment of the demon's thrilled expression.

Bindings were only painful for the witch.

When it was over, Kai had torn the snakevines from their arms and left for the mortal realm immediately. That was what he had wanted, after all. The seasons had turned since then, shifting from autumn breezes to winter cold, through the gentle warmth of spring and back into the blazing heat of summer. In that year, Kai had divided his time between Hell and the mortal realm, searching. His supply of blood was never low now, and he had even collected a number of bodies for experimentation, but he didn't have what he wanted most.

His brother was nowhere to be found. Nowhere. Between his necessary trips to Olin's temple in Vaah, Kai had scoured the countryside of Chanae, seeking anything that might give him a clue as to what had become of Bri. Carma—that shrew of a demon Olin seemed obsessed with—had remained in the manor he had once invaded, but never spoke of Bri or the soulless who was always at his side.

Unfortunately, spying on her household had become impossible, as that ancient, irritating witch of hers had sensed Kai's presence and had thrown up so many wards and traps that Kai had no choice but to retreat. The first and only time he had tried to break through, she'd had him coughing hornets for the better part of the evening. The damned things had stung his throat on the way up. Breaking her wards wouldn't have been impossible, but it would have been time consuming. And time was short, not to be wasted on something that didn't seem to be rendering him anything useful anyway.

So this time, he had gone into the city and awaited the gossip. He had thought about using his face to get what he wanted; after all, it was Bri's face as well, but talk of his brother being seen in the city would have caused nothing but trouble. Sitting and drinking got boring quickly, however, and so Kai had enlisted this exuberant young woman to entertain him.

Which was now also growing boring. With a harsh shove, Kai rolled her off him and pinned her beneath him instead, stroking her neck with his thumb. She squealed in surprise and tensed at his hold on her throat, then relaxed and drew a foot up his leg. "Ready for something else?" she said, batting her lashes in what she probably thought was a provocative manner.

"I'm thinking about it." The pulse beneath his thumb was strong, surging from their activities.

"Was it not to your liking? I know a few other things I could try."

"Don't. Just...stop talking." It would be so easy to open her. He had more than enough vials with him; he could take her life's blood back to Hell and make her far more useful.

The girl didn't say anything more, but her hands roamed around his chest and hips. Normally, such advances were welcome, but Kai found himself irritated and impatient. He bit his finger and scribed a *labrynth* onto her cheek. "Go learn how to do this right, and we'll try again next time." The fewer people who saw him, the better.

He tossed the girl from the bed, and by the time she was finished bouncing off furniture and had found her feet, the *labrynth* had sunk into her cheek, now nothing more than pale white lines. It would be invisible soon. Kai buttoned his pants and straightened his shirt, having never gotten undressed in the first place, and went to the door. "Oh, and keep this to yourself."

A blank stare changed to an idiotic smile. Satisfied, Kai pulled his hat down over his eyes and stepped out into the sunlight.

The city was alive. A huge difference from the cities of Vaah and Talconay, where he had been spending most of his time. Talconay was dead, barely more than rubble and ash. The people there dragged through the streets, dirty and hopeless. Given how they had treated him as a child, Kai thought it served them right. Vaah was better, thriving on its victories over Talconay and profiting from the spoils of war, but it was still a place of death and darkness. War had that effect.

But Callay—oh, Callay. The sunlight gleamed off the roofs and glass windows. It had just rained, and smoke rose from thousands of chimneys, darkening the blue of the sky, but it didn't serve to diminish the glory of it all. People filled the streets, chatting and nodding politely as they passed. The bakeries smelled of cinnamon and fresh bread; the butcher's smelled of blood and meat. Kai stood at the window of one such place, watching as the burly man behind the counter raised his cleaver and brought it down to bite into a thick piece of cow flesh. Kai had always marveled at the act of slicing meat. It was so different from when he cut into his own flesh, parting skin and letting blood run free. He had just about made up his mind to go inside and feign an innocent interest in the trade when he heard someone stop behind him, and a tentative voice.

"Bri?"

Interesting.

Carefully schooling his expression to one his brother might use, Kai turned. The girl was beautiful. He didn't think that about many things, but it was the only word that came to mind. Petite, her heels placed her at a height that complemented his own. Blonde curls framed a delicate face, not a scar or blemish to be seen. Her lips had been painted a soft pink, but other than that there seemed no other enhancements. The dress she wore was a dusky blue, and the square neckline framed an equally entrancing chest. Kai met her green gaze—wondering if he had ever seen anything so green before—but stilled and silenced the words he had been about to say.

One look was enough to know. She knew he was not Bri.

Very interesting.

"I'm sorry," she said, taking a step back. "I thought you were someone else."

"A common mistake."

"I imagine." She stared at him as though he were a puzzle she could not make sense of.

Kai couldn't decide what angle to play. An odd feeling, to be so unsure. "You sounded surprised before. This person I remind you of—you weren't expecting to see him?"

"No. He's away. Though it would have been nice had he returned."

"Bri, you said? How fortuitous, really. I'm looking for him myself."

"You know Bri?"

Kai gave her his most charming smile. "With a face like this, it would be odd if I didn't, don't you agree?"

That seemed to put her more at ease. The tension in her shoulders leaked away. "I suppose so. A brother?"

"Twin."

"Ah."

"Were you headed somewhere? I could walk you."

"Oh, well, I—" She glanced around. Checking for someone else? "I was just on my way to the library."

"Allow me to escort you, then." Kai bowed in a sweeping gesture, and was rewarded with a cautious smile.

"All right. It's not far. Just around the corner."

"Sounds perfect." They began walking, matching the pace of the others navigating the streets. "So you know my brother well?"

"That's a rather forward question." Her words were polite, her tone was all warning. Yet that told him everything he needed to know.

"My apologies. I didn't mean anything by it. Perhaps my command of the Dactic tongue is not as perfect as I like to believe."

Her curiosity showed in a quirk of her eyebrow. "You speak other languages?"

"Just two." Two human languages. "Dactic and Talconian."

"You have no accent."

"My teachers didn't believe in accents. You either spoke properly, or not at all." He slammed a bladed hand into his other palm, then brushed it away as he said it.

"They sound dreadful. I sympathize."

"Dreadful teachers of your own?"

"Many." She smiled. A genuine smile, and Kai had the sudden urge to run his fingers over those pink lips. He restrained himself. "But to answer your question," she said, "yes, I know your brother."

"I can't seem to find him." They stepped aside to let another young couple pass by without traipsing through a puddle. "You wouldn't happen to know where he is?"

"No," she said, "but he's been gone a year."

"No word when he'll return?"

At that, she lowered her eyes, studying the stitching in her gloves. "Unfortunately not."

"Well, that's a shame. I have so much I need to tell him." Spotting yet another errant rain puddle, Kai took the girl by the elbow and steered her around the offensive water. She thanked him, then came to a stop.

"This is it," she said.

Kai craned his neck to look up at the brick building, its entrance designated by two white columns. At the roof, a half-dozen gargoyles stared down at him as though issuing a challenge. Kai would have liked to see them try. "Impressive place."

"Yes. It's my favorite." She climbed the first step, then stopped. "I'm so sorry, I've been rude. My name is Ella. Thank you for escorting me, Mr...?"

"Kai."

"Kai. Yes, well, thank you, Kai." She said his name as though testing it, tasting it.

How he would have loved to have given her more to taste.

Propriety, Kai. Think of propriety. He hated propriety. But he knew a lead when he saw one. Taking up her hand, he placed a kiss on the back of her glove. "It was my pleasure, Lady Ella. I hope we meet again."

"If you stay in the city, I imagine it will be inevitable."

Kai watched her disappear into the library, and stood there even long after she had gone. The scent of her lingered on the air and on his hand where he had touched her glove. A sweet, sensual fragrance that caused his thoughts to catch fire.

Oh, Bri, what taste you have. If you stay away from that much longer, you're more of a fool than I thought.

Bri was driving Alec crazy. Yes, he was glad Bri could finally interact with the people they encountered without fear of an accidental touch throwing him wildly into the myst. Yes, it made him happy to see Bri so happy, so relaxed. When they had reached the first town on their journey back home and Bri had volunteered to be the one to pick up their supplies from the merchants, Alec had gladly let him go, not even pointing out or caring that he had no idea how to haggle and paid far too much for what they needed. Money didn't matter.

That had been eight towns ago. Alec schooled his patience, had taught Bri the finer points of dealing with merchants, and had even ignored the first time Bri had completely made up a reason for them to stop at a town they could have simply passed by.

Now, here they were again. Alec leaning against the outside of the stables, having already spoken with the man inside about buying passage on a coach that would take them to the next town. Bri had gone inside the general store, once again with a fabricated list of needs, claiming he would only be a short while.

That had been over half a turn ago. Such was becoming the pattern of their life. Alec pulled his hat down over his eyes, squinting in the sunlight as he watched the door. Nothing seemed out of place, and there hadn't been any unusual sounds coming from the little store. He wasn't worried. Yet.

Finally, Bri emerged, arms piled high with brown packages and small paper bags. He juggled the items rather expertly, having gotten much experience in leaving with more than he came for over the past weeks.

"Are you done now?" Alec asked, pushing away from the wall, and plucking the topmost package from Bri's pile. It felt too light to be the jerky Bri had gone in for.

"I think so. Is there anything else you need?"

"No." Definitely not. He plucked a book from under the crook of Bri's arm. "Another one?"

"I finished all the others." Looking disappointed that Alec didn't have any other shopping needs, Bri carefully set the remaining packages at his feet, then suddenly scrunched his nose and wiped at his face.

"Are you all right?"

"It's raining," Bri said, turning his gaze upwards.

There wasn't a cloud in the sky. Alec was still squinting in the sun. "It's not raining, Bri."

"No?"

"No."

"Oh."

"Think maybe you overdid it back there?" Bri no longer grew ill from the touch of a stranger, but instead he often mixed up the myst with reality. As if instead of violently pushing it away, he simply let it slide over the real world until he didn't know one from the other. It wasn't the first time it had happened, as Alec had pointed out when Bri first wanted to leave Xia-Lo, but it seemed worse when Bri spent an extended period of time with myst-bound humans.

"Maybe," Bri agreed reluctantly. His cheek twitched, and Alec saw him stop himself from wiping away another phantom raindrop. "It's going to rain, though. Hard. There will be flooding."

"We should get going, then."

He had bent down to retrieve some of Bri's packages when he felt the familiar burn of Hell power on his skin. One package under each arm, he stood as Picadilly came around the corner of the stables, dressed once again in Callay's corseted fashion. "You can't just appear like that here, Pica. Someone might see."

"And what will they do to me? These Frontier people believe in everything from ghosts to mountain trolls, and snakes that will steal their babies. The soulless are the least of their worries." She tilted her hat to shade her eyes.

"We weren't expecting you," Bri said, arms full once again. "Has something happened?"

"Not exactly, but Carma needs you." She addressed Alec.

"We're due to be home in another week or so. It can't wait?"

"Would I be here if it could?"

No, she wouldn't. Pica didn't do anything unless absolutely necessary, not if it didn't benefit her. "We can't get there any faster than we already are."

"I can take you. Have you forgotten that?"

Not forgotten, exactly. Repressed. Selectively ignored. The last, and first, time Pica had forcibly moved them across the mortal realm, it had been neither instant, nor pleasant. Alec had escaped fairly unscathed, but Bri...

"I don't think that's such a good idea."

Pulling at the fingers of her gloves, Pica made a sound of disgust. "He's still alive, Alec. I didn't kill him last time. I won't kill him now."

"I can do it, Alec," Bri said, all that newfound confidence bolstering his voice. "I'm stronger. Besides, last time Dorothea had been cutting into my back. I'm not injured now."

"See? He's healthy as a horse. He'll be fine."

Cel-Eza, help me. Things were easier when Bri hung on my every decision. "I still don't think it's a good idea."

"Duly noted." Pica shoved her now removed glove into the bodice of her dress and held out her hand. "Shall we go? I've been practicing. I can move you far more smoothly now than I could a year ago."

Bri took her hand without hesitation.

Alec finished going over everything that could go wrong in his mind before he placed his hand atop theirs.

It felt like sliding, as if ice had formed beneath their feet and a wind had skated them across. The world went dark, then burst with white light. Sunlight returned, warm and welcoming. Birds chirped as a light breeze rustled the leaves around them, harmonizing with the hum of bees at the flower beds. Alec opened his eyes, seeing first the cobbled drive that had grown familiar over the years, then the stone and brick of the manor house he hadn't seen in a year. It was later in the day here, with the sun partially behind the manor, casting a large shadow over the lawn.

It hadn't hurt a bit. Pica's practice had clearly paid off.

"Go ahead," she said smugly, releasing their hands, "compliment me."

"You've certainly improved upon the whole process."

"My power grows. There are days I feel almost my old self."

"I am overjoyed on your behalf." Alec looked at Bri, who hadn't moved or said a word. "You okay, Bri?"

"Yes. I'm fine." His voice was thin.

"You sure? You don't look fine." In fact, he looked rather green.

"I'm perfectly fine." A slight pause. "Excuse me." Shoving the belongings he had carried into Alec's arms, Bri walked at quite a normal pace around the corner, toward the backyard.

The sounds of retching followed.

"So," Alec said, not at all surprised, "you said Carma wanted to see me?"

"No," Pica said, leveling a serious expression in his direction, "I said she *needed* you."

— CHAPTER THIRTEEN —

Her room was black as pitch, curtains drawn tight, and not a single candle lit. The light from the hall spilled in as far as the edge of the rug, but no farther. It was as if a wall had been erected, keeping out all illumination. Alec stayed in that small space of light, straining to hear even the slightest change in the darkness, any sign that she was there.

"Carma?"

"Alec." His name was a whisper on the still air. In the far corner, something rose slowly, a sliver of silver in the darkness. Then she was on him, the door slamming shut, casting out the meager light, and leaving Alec blind. The length of her body pressed against his, clawed hands digging into his shoulders. Something stirred the air at her back—her wings? She kissed him, and she tasted of blood. Alec's soul twisted about within her, powered by whatever she had been doing, and jumping at the closeness of the body it had once inhabited.

Alec grabbed her face with one hand and wrenched her mouth away from his. Her cheeks felt leathery, and his thumb caught on a fang. "Carma, what are you doing?"

She pressed against his restraining hold, her chest rising and falling heavily beneath his arm. "Preparing."

"Preparing for what?" In this form she was far stronger than him, yet he held her back. Something kept her from acting at full strength.

"You know for what," she said, still straining against him. Her tongue darted out, touching his lips.

There was not even enough light to see her blue and sapphire eyes. Alec wished he could. Maybe then he could more accurately judge her mental state. Instead, he had only the trembling body in his arms to gauge by. "Pica says you've been going on about the Restorium."

"I have lost time." Carma went abruptly still. "I was not expecting you."

"I'm home early. You've lost nothing."

"Early? Then let us make good use of the time." The claws on his shoulders dug in deeper as she pulled herself closer.

"Carma, stop. Listen to me." Her lips and fangs closed over his throat. "Stop it." *Damn you, Picadilly. You just didn't want to deal with this on your own.* Drawing power, letting it surge into his arms and legs, Alec shoved the demon back. Cold rushed against him immediately as all her hellish power stumbled away. It was not, perhaps, the smartest thing he had ever done, but it was too late to change even the recent past.

He heard Carma stumble once, then growl low. The sound vibrated on the air. Alec did not release the power he had called to himself. It would make him look more of a threat, but it would also give him the weapon he needed if she attacked. When she attacked.

"You should not have done that, soulless."

"You won't kill me. I'm one of your precious pieces. Something tells me you don't have time to wait for another."

She roared. Like a beast in the wild. The walls shook, and something in the room fell and shattered. The air shifted and popped with the beat of her wings. Alec stood perfectly still, and waited. The room was nothing but blackness to him, but she could see. She would not miss.

Pain lanced through his chest. Suddenly Alec's shirt was soaked and clinging to him. He twisted at the last possible instant, ensuring that he went down on his back. With all her weight pressed upon him, heavy as a brimstone block, her teeth sank into his shoulder. Gritting his teeth, Alec struggled not to give her the cries of pain that she wanted. They would only spur her on. Instead, he slammed his hand into her face and pulled more and more power until he smelled flesh burning. Carma hissed and reared back, her fangs tearing away from his shoulder. Blindly, Alec sat up and grabbed for her, hoping and praying he would reach what he wanted. He felt cheeks and lips beneath his fingers, and held on tight. The scent of more burning flesh followed.

Claws punctured his back. Breathing became difficult. Alec slammed a shoulder into Carma, forcing her backward. He felt her land on her back beneath him. Something snapped—most likely a wing. Flesh still sizzling beneath his hands, he changed his grip to her throat and leaned forward, navigating her body by memory.

He kissed her, ignoring the flaking feel of her lips. She bucked beneath him, but did not snap. Her fingers flexed, claws tensing where they were still buried in his back. Then, slowly, she relaxed. It started in her shoulders, the tension of the fight leaking away. Alec felt her flesh shift, soften. She arched against him, then lay flat back against the floor—wingless. As she exhaled, the light returned to the room, gradually, as if the sun were rising.

Alec drew away, releasing the power he had called to himself. Her bronze skin had already healed, showing no trace of the burns he had given her. Her hair was silver, though he knew it had been red in the darkness. The fangs were gone, but his blood still coated her mouth, and when she brought a hand around to touch his face, it, too, was red with blood.

"Alec."

"Oh good. Do you know who I am now?" He leaned heavily on one arm as he sat.

"I always knew who you were."

"My apologies. Do you *care* who I am now?"

Silence. Her fingers traced down his throat and to his shoulder, where she then touched the wound she had made there.

He winced. "What the hell have you been doing this past year?"

"Growing stronger," she said, meeting his gaze. "I am much stronger now, Alec."

"I noticed."

"You broke one of my wings."

"I'm sure it's healed already."

"It has, but you still broke it. You are stronger, too."

"Can't imagine why. I didn't do anything this past year but lay around."

"I think you lie to me."

"It's possible. I'm not a demon." Alec pulled himself to sit against the nearest wall, gritting his teeth through the pain as torn muscles stretched and pulled.

Carma did the same, though no signs of pain plagued her movement. Her red silk dress fell like water around her, darkened in places with blood. "There is something different in the way you taste."

"I assure you, Carma, I didn't do anything out of the ordinary."

"Something has changed."

"Yes, something has. You. What the hell are you doing? Whatever it is, it's enough to make Pica worry. She came and brought me back."

"Pica." Carma scoffed, standing. "She should know better. She was demon once."

"She says you're going on about the Restorium."

At that, Carma stilled. Anyone unknowing would have thought her a statue. "Did she?"

"Yes. You're pushing yourself too far again, if you didn't realize it. She also told me you're drinking blood."

"Demons drink blood, Alexander. It is how we grow stronger."

"Blood and souls. But you haven't acquired any new souls, have you?"

She waved it off. "I have enough souls for now."

Letting his head fall back against the wall, Alec closed his eyes. "What a strange thing for a demon to say."

"How is Bri?"

"Bri is fine. Shaking hands all over town. Don't change the subject."

"What do you want from me, Alec? I am a demon. I do what feels good, and what feels necessary. It had been a long time since I had lived inside my true form. It's exhilarating."

His shoulder ached, thumping with the beat of his heart. "Just tell me about the Restorium."

"What would you like to know? It is a time when Haven rids itself of impurities. The whole realm sleeps, and they wake up brighter and hopefully sin-free. Some wake up here, in the mortal realm, deemed unworthy of Haven's light."

"And during that time, Haven completely shuts its eyes to the mortal realm."

"Indeed it does."

"Allowing demons to run amok."

"If the demons knew when it was happening, yes. But no one knows exactly when the Restorium will hit."

He opened his eyes to look at her once more. "Then why worry about it?"

Sweeping her long silver hair over her shoulder, Carma knelt in front of him. "Because some of us have ways of knowing when it will come."

"How?"

"A connection to the holy realm."

"You no longer have that." Alec coughed. His hand came away bloody. Breathing was still difficult, growing worse. His next breath wheezed.

Carma moved him and laid a hand on his wounded back, fingers prodding the places where her claws had dug deep. "No, I do not. Not personally. But I possess someone who does."

She pressed hard against the damaged flesh, and Alec gasped, then coughed again. Drops of dark red spattered Carma's skirt. The pain did not serve to drive away the realization of what she meant. It made the meaning of her words clear and unmistakable.

"Bri."

Her smile was one of tactical pride. "Yes."

"It always comes back to Bri."

"He is a remarkable child."

"Not so much a child anymore."

"I suppose not. It appears I punctured a lung. You should not have let me do that. We will have to have Picadilly tend to it."

The thought of Pica's ministrations could not distract Alec from the fears curling around in his head. "None of this would be happening if Bri didn't exist. You wouldn't have what you need. Is this why Gabriel hunts him? Because of your plans?"

"Gabriel hunts him because he was born. It has nothing to do with me."

"And what about Kai?"

"What about him?"

"Gabriel doesn't hunt him."

"Gabriel doesn't seem to know about him."

"Olin has Kai. And you have Bri. You and Olin. It always comes back to that, too, doesn't it?"

"I think the pain is playing games with your mind, Alec. You are leaping to conclusions."

The pain wasn't playing games. It was clearing away all extraneous information. He knew, sitting there, forcing Carma to maintain the eye contact she would clearly rather break, both of them covered in his blood, that she worked to circle the truth. She wanted to lie, but couldn't.

"It's almost as if Bri and Kai had been born on purpose," he said.

"Perhaps they were."

In the darkness, the thud of bodies sounded like little more than an off-beat drum. Glad for the training he had been undergoing, Kai hefted one of the larger bodies over his shoulder, carrying it to his pile and tossing it with the others. These were all soldiers, fallen in battle against Vaah. Talconian muscle. It hadn't been enough, but Kai only wanted them for an experiment, a theory. He only picked the ones that hadn't been horribly maimed, the ones that still had faces and intact skulls. Four limbs were a requirement as well.

He looked at his companion when she cursed, stumbling and tripping over the longer legs of the body she dragged across the blood-soaked ground. The moon was half-full, giving them more than enough light to work by. Xan wasn't at her most hideous, but Kai still hated every wrinkle and crag. There was black streaked in her hair at the moment, and her face didn't look so ancient. Her hands were steadier as well—the only reason she was of any help. Her age fluctuated, some odd twist of Olin's power within her, and so her usefulness varied. Kai wished she maintained more of her youth. He hated staring old age in the face.

"Something bothering you, Xan?"

"Your horrid hobbies," she said, shoving the body onto the pile and giving it a kick. "Can't you be like a normal young man and want to collect tin soldiers instead of dead ones?"

"Tin doesn't bleed."

She wiped her hands on her skirt, making a disgusted sound. "You don't want these bodies for their blood. I heard you muttering to yourself the other day."

"I don't mutter."

"Oh, but you do. Is this enough? Have we gathered a suitable amount of dead flesh for your pleasure?"

"You make it sound so dirty. I like my flesh alive, same as everyone else."

"Ah, yes. How could I forget about that girl you keep as a pet in Callay."

The thought of her brought a smile to his face. Yes, the girl had been next to useless the first time he had encountered her, but ever since he had placed a *labrynth* on her and ordered her to make herself useful to him, she had made it her very purpose to fulfill his wishes.

All right, *he* had made it her purpose. The end result was the same. She provided him with all the latest gossip from Callay and informed him any time someone new came to town. She had also taken all that unfocused enthusiasm and turned it into notable skill.

"Thinking about her now, are you?" Xan interrupted his thoughts.

"How could I not, when you brought her up?"

Xan twisted a piece of loose hair back up on her head with a pin. "Do you even know the poor girl's name?"

"No. I call her whatever I like. She doesn't mind."

"Because you've hollowed out her mind like a pumpkin at harvest time."

Kai shrugged.

He did a quick count of the bodies on the pile. It was as tall as he was, containing at least a dozen dead soldiers. Good enough. Biting his finger, he bent down and completed the final line of the *labrynth* he had scribed into the ground before piling the bodies on top. The lines lit up, and the bodies began to sink into the ground. They would appear in his workshop in Hell in a matter of moments. A decent night's work.

"I take it you're finished then," Xan said. "In which case, I'll be going. I have my own things to attend to."

"I can't imagine what."

"No one asked you to." With that, she blinked out of the mortal realm like a dying star in the sky.

Kai flopped down and lay on his back, looking up at the night sky as his bodies continued to sink away. He would wait for them to be completely gone from the mortal realm before returning to Hell. It wouldn't take long. However, he was in no hurry to leave.

Running his still-bloody finger over the *labrynth* he had carved into his own wrist, Kai studied the lines and turns, hating that they lay dead and quiet on his skin. It was the same one he had used to know when Bri was in the myst two years prior. In its original form, it was ineffectual to him now; Bri had somehow denied him access to the myst ever since their misunderstanding. Kai didn't think Bri actually had the knowledge to block him so purposefully, but no matter how he tried, Kai could not slip back within, nor could he sense when his brother traveled there.

So Kai had altered the spell. It wasn't a hard thing to do, to pull the lines into new patterns on his flesh. As long as he used his own blood, the *labrynth* served as a natural part of him, and the pattern could be shifted without any damage. Not like the *labrynth* that old witch had scribed into his brother's back. The one she had somehow changed to keep him from feeling Bri's presence at all. That *labrynth* would have to be systematically cut from his twin's flesh if Kai wanted to be rid of it. Just the thought of it made his hands shake with rage. The old witch had defiled Bri. Kai would have to spend painstaking months, if not longer, correcting her doings.

If only Bri would just see reason and come with him. Then this might all be done with and behind them by winter. All he need was for Bri to say, "yes."

He squeezed his bleeding finger, drawing even more blood, enough to coat the *labrynth* on his wrist. Around and around he swirled the blood until his entire forearm was red. He almost longed for a spell that would drain him to the point of dizziness; it made him feel powerful. It had been so long since he had needed that much blood. The lines of the spell connected to his brother stood out darkly among the blood.

Then, just for a moment, it sparked with light.

Kai stilled. Waited. The dull light pulsed again.

He sat up, staring off to the west where he knew Chanae lay beyond the mountains. The tug, the pull, from that direction was slight, but it was there. Kai knew it anywhere, like a limb of his own body.

Wherever Bri had gone, he had returned.

Shadows were a reaper's best friend. One could stand in them and be seen or sensed by no one at all, aside from another reaper. Tassos had watched the young witch for hours, with none the wiser. He had gleaned the souls from these dead as the sun set, and just as he had sent the last of them down their intended path, the boy had arrived with a soulless in tow.

Lillianna's boy. Kai. The sadist who had trapped living souls inside tormented bodies in Hell. But Lillianna had been destroyed, so who held his leash now?

It was a question better asked by someone in a position to do something about it. Reaping the boy's soul had been a temptation of Tassos's for years, ever since he had met the deranged child. But Death wanted nothing to do with him. Tassos had tried to call her, to entice her—she refused. However terrible Kai was, the mortal realm was not done with him yet. Either that, or he was so twisted that even Death could not bear the thought of tasting him. Often times Tassos believed the latter the more likely scenario.

When Kai started to bleed himself, Tassos chose to take his leave. He had seen many a witch bleed and scribe with their own blood; the nature of the act did not bother him, but he had never seen a witch take such pleasure in it as did Kai. The look on his face as he drew the life-giving substance from his veins was...perverse.

All the realms were open to him, even one level of Haven. Tassos preferred to travel at the edge of the mortal realm, where it was dark and cold and quiet. There, he did not have to worry about running into inquisitive seraph, or plotting demons. It seemed only reapers were comfortable there, where the realm of those who existed in finite time met the vast expanse of the Inbetween. They had no fear of falling within. They could simply walk back out. They were the only creatures who could.

That night, Tassos went elsewhere.

Though he could feel the ward that turned others away, none the wiser, Tassos glided right by, into the heat of Hell, and toward the small stone cabin that lingered at its edge. The yard was nothing but dirt and blackened brimstone; not unusual for Hell, but the lack of symmetry or controlled chaos told of the neglect. The owner rarely ventured outside. Tassos opened the heavy stone door and walked in without announcing himself.

Mugs and empty bottles littered the front room, tipped over on the single table or tumbled to the floor. A half-eaten meal of bread and red meat sat on the counter by the fireplace, sniffers and other rodent hellions nibbling at the remains. The hearth was cold, though a pot of something hung over it. Tassos chased the rodents away as he passed, giving one a swift kick when it hissed at him after falling to the floor. They all skittered away, leaving through a hole in the far wall where it seemed one of the stones had come loose. It hadn't been so long since he had been here. At least, he hadn't thought so. Crossing into the back bedroom, immediately tripping over discarded clothing and broken bottles, Tassos wondered if perhaps he had lost track of time again.

The bed was empty, rumpled and half torn apart. Nothing like the last time he had seen it. Its usual occupant stood at the window, looking out over the great void that some believed would one day swallow them all.

"Out of bed, I see." Perhaps a good sign.

The Lord of Hell leaned heavily against the windowsill, stark naked, his knuckles a striking white that contrasted with his golden skin and hair. "She is gone," he said.

"Who is?"

"Lillianna. They have torn her from me."

Perhaps not such a good sign. "That was two years ago, Luca. Are you only noticing now?"

"I feel the loss of her like a hole in my chest."

"Oh good, I see we've reached the stage of melodrama and self-pity. I don't know what I would have done had I missed it."

Luca turned to him, those blazing blue eyes shining with unshed tears. "You mock me."

"Not at all. Luca, you do this to yourself as surely as the sun rises and sets every day. You have spent thousands of years not giving a damn about anything. Occasionally it catches up with you, and we have an episode such as this." He plucked one broken bottle shard from the floor. "Have I come in time for the beginning, or the end?"

"There are things stirring out there," Luca said, gazing once again out the window. "I can feel them."

Tossing the shard to a far corner, Tassos gave a futile look around for something easily tidied. "How astute of you. I have been trying to tell you that for decades."

"Someone is gathering power. Amassing a force unlike anything we have ever seen. It will turn the world upside down."

"Are we getting serious suddenly? Because I could tell you of a certain little witch who gives me nightmares, and he's loose in both the mortal realm and Hell."

Slowly, as though the weight of the three realms pressed down upon his shoulders, Luca drew away from the window. "I feel him. He changes things. Many will not survive." He crossed the room, heading toward his bed, barely noticing the debris all over the floor.

Only thousands of years' experience kept Tassos from grabbing Luca and shaking him. "Are you listening to yourself? You are the Lord of Hell. Do something about it."

Luca lifted the covers of his mangled bed and slipped underneath. "There is nothing to be done."

CHAPTER FOURTEEN

A quick knock on the door and Bri felt all of his hard-won courage leave him. He stepped back and away, nearly bumping into the opposite wall. His room was not very far. A mere ten steps to his left. If he hurried, he could be there and safe before Alec had a chance to—

"Come in."

Oh, damn. Gods on high, help me, I am a coward. Refusing to let himself think and back out, Bri quickly grasped the handle of the door and let himself inside. Lamps burned brightly, despite it being mid-morning. Alec's room was on the west side of the house, and so didn't get much light until the afternoon. Bri had always loved this room, something in the simple way Alec kept it, necessities only, and all in soft, earthen tones. A desk sat in the corner, but he had never seen Alec use it for anything other than piling knickknacks and knives. A distinct contrast to Bri's own desk, which held paper and ink and books. Now, Alec reclined in one of the armchairs by the windows, leaning over the small table where a Kayos board sat out of play.

Just looking at the game made Bri's nerves rattle. He remembered all too well Iris's fingers touching each piece as she explained the reality. A game. The whole world was a game. And someone, somewhere, was moving the pieces.

Bri intended to be the master of his own decisions.

He crossed the room and sat on the large bed, taking comfort in the way the mattress sunk beneath him. It was a familiar feeling, one that had often soothed him when he was younger. Now it served to remind him only of his past dependence, and his fierce desire to put that behind him.

Alec idly moved one of the pieces and leaned back in his chair. "Is something wrong?"

"No."

"Bri, you look absolutely terrified right now."

"The Masquerade is tonight." He blurted it out before his nerves could get the better of him.

"Yes. I know."

"I'm going."

"I should hope so. It's the entire reason you made us come back here."

"I'm going alone. You can stay here. I'll be fine." He made it halfway back to the door, attempting a quick escape, before Alec managed to respond.

"You're what? Hold on, Bri."

Bri stopped. This was the part of the conversation he had hoped to avoid and had known there would be no avoiding.

"What do you mean you're going alone?"

"Just that. I'm going alone. I don't need a chaperone." He didn't dare look at Alec as he said it.

But that didn't stop him from hearing Alec stand and walk toward him. "Do you think that's a good idea?"

"Yes."

"What if something happens? What about the myst?"

"Nothing is going to happen. I can touch people now, and everyone will be wearing gloves anyway. The myst won't give me any trouble."

"You haven't been in a crowded ballroom since your training with Iris. It could be different."

"It won't be different. It's not different. I know the myst and how it works. I can control it." Had that always been the pattern of the rug? Did they get new rugs?

Alec walked around to stand in front of him, but Bri continued to stare at the floor. "I don't know about this, Bri. I think it would be better if—"

"No." Using every bit of courage he possessed, Bri looked up and met Alec's gaze. "I have to do this. I have to go out on my own. No safety net. If I don't, I'll never believe that I can, and I'll spend my entire life afraid. I'm not a little kid anymore. I can't spend every day hovering at your side, ready to grab your hand. Please, Alec. I need this."

For the longest time, Alec said nothing. His arms were folded across his chest, and one finger tapped against his bicep, a clear signal he was thinking and carefully schooling his reaction. Bri held his breath while he waited, afraid to say anything more. *Gods, please. Alec, please. You have to see how important this is. I need you to say yes. Because if you insist...I'll let you come. And then I'll hate myself.*

The silence dragged on and on between them. Eventually Bri had no choice but to breathe, though it came in a short, gasping action that did little to really relieve the pressure building in his chest.

"All right."

"Alec, you have to—what?"

"I said, all right. You can go alone."

Bri didn't see any telltale sign of Alec messing with him; no arch of the left brow, no slight pull at the corner of his lips. "I can?"

Now though, Alec looked wounded. "Cel-Eza. You look so surprised. What am I, some heartless jail keeper?"

"No! No, I just—I didn't really expect you to agree."

"Carma won't like it."

"Carma left for Hell this morning. She won't even notice."

Alec let his arms slide free from each other. "That doesn't have anything to do with her liking it."

"But I can really go? Alone?" He wanted to jump, to shout, to throw his arms around Alec and hug him until his arms hurt. But all those things would have been counterproductive to his purpose, which was to prove to himself and everyone else that he was no longer a child. So, he kept still.

"Yes. But I'm going with you to see you safely there, and I'm returning at the end of the night for the ride home."

"Fine. Yes. That's fine."

"And you have to do one more thing."

"What's that?"

Alec smirked. "Admit that the real reason you don't want me along is because you don't want an audience while you try to woo Ella."

Words tried to stumble out of Bri's mouth, but he stifled them all. Grabbing for the door, he opened it and hurried out of the room before the blush he felt heating his cheeks could grow any worse. All the while, Alec laughed.

Carma had to work hard at not letting her true form slip free. Here in Hell, the power that gave her life pulsed on the air, calling to her and lacing energy through her entire body. With all the blood she had been drinking, she could have spent the majority of her time in her true form, but it was not yet time for that. If she unleashed the hold she kept on her own power, all those in Hell would feel her presence, and as Olin had said, there were few who could give them reason to pause. Attention would come swiftly, from weaker demons either out to find a protector to whom they could be useful, or, if feeling ambitious, looking to make a name for themselves by besting a stronger demon. Carma had no interest in such politics.

Some wretched soul dragged himself to her table, setting down the mugs of blood-laced ale she had ordered. His shoulders were hunched with the weight of the chains that hung from his body, twisting and wrapping around his chest and waist, then swinging freely by his legs where heavy weights bruised his thighs. Carma reached out and touched the back of his hand lightly, seeking out the sins in life that had led him to this place. He had been handsome once, a charmer and a user. A con artist who had weaseled more than one woman and man out of inheritance and possessions. In the end he had agreed to kill one woman's husband in exchange for her hand and a life of luxury. She had turned him in and seen him hanged instead.

"Has she died yet?" Carma asked. "The woman who outsmarted you?"

The man looked surprised, drawing his hand away quickly. "How?"

"It is a gift of mine," she explained. She would give him nothing more than that. Not all demons could read sins, but since she had once been responsible for the justice of such things, sins, as well as good deeds, were hers to be seen.

"No," he said, drawing a deep breath, and setting his mouth in a hard line. "Not yet."

"I think I would like to be around when that happens. Will you seek her out?"

"It is part of my arrangement here."

"How delightful. Give my compliments to your master." She waved him away, taking her first sip of the warm blood ale.

Picadilly returned to the table as the waiting soul hobbled away. "What was that?"

"Just some entertainment. Did you discover anything?"

"Not much, though there are fewer and fewer reports of Hellwalkers around." She drank from her own mug.

"They will not want to be here when the event hits." Carma was careful not to say Restorium in mixed company. "If they are, they may never be let back through the shining gates."

The crowded tavern hummed with raucous laughter and yelling. Pica leaned forward over the table to be better heard. "There are also rumors of an army."

"What kind of army?"

Off in the corner, a fight broke out. Bottles smashed, and the sound of flesh hitting bone clapped against the walls. Pica ignored it, as they all did. "No one knows exactly. It arises mostly in cryptic conversations about being able to find work if one wanted it."

"No one works in Hell," Carma said.

"That is a terrible falsehood, and you know it. A demon owns this tavern. And there are those here who need purpose in order to stay alive. They seek out the patronage of more powerful demons. Such as yourself. You forget that not everyone was blessed with as much power as you."

"Your power was never anything to scoff at."

"But I lived for the possibility of battle and its wounded. You think I did not work to instigate such things? Souls were never enough for me."

Carma took another drink. The blood laced in her ale seemed to shimmer with power as it entered her. "I do forget my advantages sometimes. I forget not all demons are charming enough to garner themselves large numbers of souls."

"Then there are those who are too weak to resist the call of a *labrynth* and human demon raising. More still hide in the mortal realm their first years, as they grow and gain strength."

"So many options." They paused a moment in their conversation as Pica's drink arrived, then waited until the waiter had gone again to speak more. "Did you hear nothing else of this army?" Carma was almost certain she knew who would be raising an army in Hell.

"The hellions speak of it as well. Equal opportunity."

"Now that's interesting." Together they leaned back, drinking well from their mugs, just as one of the fighting demons came flying through the air and landed on their table.

They left the tavern not long after, staying only long enough to see the end of the argument. The smaller of the two demons won, strangely enough. He, apparently, had arms of plated spikes when in his true form, and had torn through the rib cage of his opponent. The other patrons had a good laugh at the hollow chest, heaving with the task of breathing and bleeding black blood heavily. Carma could see Pica practically salivating at the sight of the wound. She could have gained such power from healing it. But they had things to do, and so Carma insisted they move on.

They walked the streets of the small town, everything brimstone and rock. As much as Carma loved Hell, she did prefer the soft wooden structures of the mortal realm. Such things would burn in this place. Giant horse-like hellions stomped at the hard ground with their tough hooves that gleamed like steel. Their eyes burned red, and their coats were black as the void. Carma wandered close to one, tied to a post where it waited impatiently for its master. It tugged and pulled at its reins, the stone post creaking under the force. Some of these creatures were little more than beasts, but some—like this one— had intelligence. She looked it in the eye, unafraid of the sharp teeth that lay only inches from her now. Only the dumb ones bit. Its nostrils flared, and it shook its head once, then held her gaze.

Because she could, and because she felt like it, Carma flicked the fastenings of the bridal loose and pulled it off. The hell horse nickered, the sound a harmony of low and high sounds all at once, then tore off down the street, knocking down anyone in its path down. Carma smiled to herself.

Pica drew up at her side. "Why did you do that?"

"Why not? There are plenty of dumb beasts in this realm, and only a few that truly deserve the life flowing through their veins. When Lillianna and Luca breathed life into this place, they blessed some more than others. That one was chosen; it doesn't belong here, fettered and captive."

"You speak of Lillianna as if she were a god."

"She was our mother. We cannot forget that."

"You killed her," Pica said.

"You helped."

"She had gone mad."

Had she? Carma often wondered. "We did what was necessary."

"I don't detect regret in your tone, do I?"

"Never. But she has my respect. Come." Carma led the way down the street, following the path of the freed horse. "It will seek the best freedom to be had. We shall follow."

The walk was long, but they did not tire. The horizon eventually swallowed the town, leaving Carma and Picadilly alone on the winding road with only the tell-tale hoof marks in the dirt at their feet. Thick forest grew up on either side of them, casting thick, dark shadows. Bright red and yellow eyes peered out at them from the darkness, while hisses and growls made up the song of the forest. Something somewhere burned, the smell of smoke and meat carried on the breeze. Carma looked to the sky—which was all oranges and reds, as always—where she could see through the breaks in the trees a tendril of black smoke weaving its way across.

Far off, the sound muted by the distance, the horse nickered and snorted, then screamed.

Carma and Picadilly split without discussion, one going left, the other right. Stretching her wings easily, Carma dove in between the trees and other growth, her feet touching the ground only to make quick turns and hops. The cries of pain came from the horse again, and she slowed, able to judge its nearness. Light filled a clearing up ahead, and the smell of meat had grown stronger, thicker. A raven cawed overhead, displeased and probably hungry. Clinging to a tree still well within the shadows, Carma stopped and peered beyond.

A fire burned, encircled by stones of matching size. Orderly. A rudimentary spit had been made, and the roasted carcass of some small, four-legged creature burned over the flames. Firewood sat off to the side, arranged carefully, and stacked neatly. No one in Hell liked things *that* neat.

But Hellwalkers were usually better at covering their tracks.

The horse limped and stumbled in the clearing, red eyes burning, and black coat dripping with sweat. It struggled to put weight on its front left hoof, and it was easy to see why. A short, gleaming dagger had been driven into the horse's shoulder, crippling it, and smoking against the unholy flesh. A blessed weapon.

This was a trap for something. Or someone.

Only one way to find out.

Maintaining her level of power, Carma strode out from the shadows and into the clearing. Picadilly would keep watch from the other side. Without fear, so the hell horse would not attack her, she walked right up to the creature and grabbed the blade, ignoring the pain that seared up her arm. As she pulled it out, her own flesh burned. The wound had not been enough to kill, just to irritate. The blade was short. Which gave rise to a dozen more questions.

"Who are you, and where are you?" Carma called into the shadows, dropping the blessed blade, hearing it sizzle even against the ground of Hell. The horse continued to thrash beside her, stretching its muscles as they began the steady process of healing. She placed one comforting hand on the creature's neck.

No answer came. Carma waited, giving ample time for an ambush to burst forth. Nothing. The forest sounded normal all around her, and even the raven she had heard before became brave enough to swoop in and begin pecking at the discarded meat over the dying fire. Perhaps this Hellwalker was simply a coward, or new and unsure of himself.

"Picadilly." She called her soulless when she did not appear on her own. Enough time had gone by to prove there was clearly no threat. "Pica," she called again when still she did not come.

Leaving the horse to its own devices—it had calmed—Carma moved toward the other side of the clearing, where Picadilly should have been waiting. Once more, she called out to her. Still nothing.

"Picadilly, come to me." Drawing on the power between them, Carma ordered her to her side, the same as she would have had they been a great distance apart. Pica should have appeared instantly. She did not.

Carma turned her attention inward, to the swirling mass of souls that lived within her, warm and pulsing like two dozen hearts. Pica's was there, brighter than most of the others, stronger. Her body, which Carma could always detect, always feel as though she were an extension of her own body, was nowhere. Gone.

— CHAPTER FIFTEEN —

The ballroom was a swirl of color, all greens and golds and reds and blues. Jewels sparkled on hands, around necks, and on the ears. Masks hid faces with feathers and silks, some so elaborate they seemed to hold expressions all their own. As one of the girls to be Presented, Ella's mask was gold. Driven by nerves in the early evening, she had hardly been able to stop touching the soft silk, and the peacock-colored jewels that lined its cat-eyed shape. It matched her dress perfectly, all deep turquoise blues and a rich purples. Den had made a gift of the dress, calling in the most well-reputed seamstress in Chanae to design and tailor it specifically to her. The result was beautiful, with an elegant line all the way to the floor, and a bodice trimmed in gold. Ella smoothed her long gloves along her arms and took another sip of wine. Den had perhaps done too good a job in dressing her for this evening. She felt as though every eye in the room looked at her.

She danced, as was expected, twisting along choreographed lines, her hands alighting with others as partners came and went. Every girl was smiling, and Ella found their enthusiasm contagious. The young men of the city bowed and said charming things as they danced with the girls, most able to lift their partners easily when the dance called for it, though Ella had run across more than one who seemed nervous, out of their element, and hopelessly clumsy. She tried to smile kindly at them, but did not want to give them the wrong idea. This whole evening was a means for the unmarried men of Chanae to meet the newest girls of marriageable age. They would come calling on any young lady who caught their attention. As of yet, Ella had not seen the one young man whose attention she desired.

The dance ended, and everyone clapped politely. Sometimes Ella wondered if anyone else ever got tired of the protocol that dictated so much of their lives. Yes, she was enjoying herself, but her responses were already carved out by social convention. She would have clapped even if the dance had been dreadful.

The band took up a waltz, and Ella excused herself from the young man—who looked to be nearer Den's age—who had inched closer, presumably to ask her to join him. A table of delicacies and sweets had been laid out under the wide windows overlooking the gardens. She selected a slice of apple that had been smothered in caramel and took solace in its sweetness.

"Not in the mood to dance?"

"Not at the moment." She wiped her mouth with a napkin before turning to her brother. His mask was all black, simple, hugging the curves of his face. Small silver stones had been set into the edges, giving the look of the night sky. Ella had always thought her brother looked handsome in a suit. "Why are you not dancing? You're unmarried. The girls here are all for your choosing."

"You make it sound like we auction you off." A waiter happened by with fresh glasses of wine, and Den took one with a nod of thanks.

Ella grabbed one hurriedly before the waiter could finish wandering away, taking a rather unladylike drink. "What?" she said, setting the already half empty glass down and observing her brother's shocked gaze, clear even through the mask.

"Nothing. I just don't think I've ever seen you drink so much. And so quickly. Are you sure you're all right?"

"I'm fine, Den. Really. I just—I wish—"

"You wish you had more than the letter stuffed in your purse."

Ella instinctively clutched the small purple bag where it hung from her wrist. Though, in fact, the letter had been slipped within her corset, for fear of losing it otherwise. "How did you—?"

Den laughed. "You're predictable, Marce—Ella." He finished his own glass of wine. "I'm going to dance. Why don't you do the same?"

With that, he disappeared into the churning crowd, undoubtedly finding a dance partner within moments.

The wine tasted sharper than Ella normally liked, but she drank it anyway. When it was finished, she ate a small cucumber sandwich to help settle her stomach, then went to brave the swirling mass of people nearest the dance floor. Staring at all the masks and the uniform suits of the men, she began to worry. It had been a year. Would she know him if she saw him? What if she had already danced with him but had failed to recognize him? How rude she would have appeared, writing for a year and forgetting his face. She could remember the last time she had seen him so clearly. The way he blushed when she sat beside him. The slight tremble in his hands. She loved the way his hair fell so freely over his forehead and occasionally into his eyes, not all slicked back and tamed the way most men wore their hair. She remembered, too, the softness of his lips when she had so boldly kissed him on his birthday, the utter stillness and shock that had run through him before—

"Would you dance with me?"

The voice was almost too quiet to be heard over the chatter and music of the ball. Ella followed its sound, stopping and causing another roaming partygoer to nearly trip in the process. She was fairly sure she managed to mutter some sort of apology.

He stood there, amidst all the other young men and women. Flesh and blood. Real. There was a small shift in his feet, and his fingers twitched at his sides. His shoulders held a certain level of almost wary tension as so many people passed around them, bumping him on more than one occasion. He looked elegant and mature in his suit, and far more comfortable in it than before. So far he hadn't pulled at his tie or collar once. His hair had darkened some, she thought, more chestnut now than auburn, but it fell in that same haphazard way. She moved closer to him, one hand reaching out to softly touch the lapel of his jacket, assuring herself he was real. His mask was silver, and adorned only with delicate silver swirls that almost seemed to move when she looked at them, like mist over water. Silver-brown eyes gazed back at her. "It's you," she said with unwavering certainty, feeling the smile that stretched her cheeks, already threatening to remain and never give her face a reprieve.

His smile was more nervous relief. "I was afraid you wouldn't recognize me."

"I'd always recognize you." She touched the mask, wishing she could pull it off. Instead, she took him by the hands and drew him closer to the dancing. "Dance with me." She placed his one hand on her waist and set her hand in his other.

They fell into step with the waltz easily, gliding along with the other couples seamlessly. Ella didn't say anything more, and neither did Bri. She focused instead on the feel of having him in her arms. Each letter that had come over the past year had been like a long-awaited visit, but now, having him there, she realized the letters had been a poor substitute. His letters had explained his reason for leaving—his illness could be helped, but only in a far-off country on the other side of the continent. He had gone into detail as much as he could, though there was much he could never risk putting in a letter. He had been growing stronger over the year, healthier. She could feel that just in his touch, and in the muscles of his shoulder under her hand when she dared touch him instead of holding her skirt. But still he braced himself whenever someone came too close; she could feel that as well. So many questions, yet she wasn't ready to give up the dancing—the only social reason for being so close to him—just yet.

"You didn't say in your letters that you learned how to dance," she said, hoping to keep his mind busy and free from whatever worry plagued him.

"Alec taught me. It was...embarrassing." That lovely blush had come to his cheeks. "I try not to think about it."

Ella could picture it all. His older brother, Alec, giving instructions while Bri stumbled and stepped on his feet. There was no stumbling now. "Well, despite that, he seems to have done a good job."

"I'll tell him you said so."

"I was afraid you wouldn't make it tonight." Afraid that in this room filled with acquaintances and connections and society-climbers, she would be completely alone.

"So was I," Bri said. "I almost didn't. We weren't really supposed to come back so early."

"You mean from the place where you sought help?"

"Yes."

"Are you really all right to be here? You shouldn't have cut your healing short on my account."

Bri missed the third step of the waltz and had to catch back up. "No. No, it's nothing like that. I'm all right. Much better. I'm sorry. I didn't mean to imply that you had disrupted existing plans. I'm strong enough to be here. Being here was my only real goal."

That made Ella miss the second step. But she didn't try to restart the pattern, just stood still in the middle of the dance floor, staring at Bri and hoping her heart wouldn't flutter right out of her chest. Breathing suddenly seemed difficult. "Let's go somewhere," she said once she remembered how to speak. "Somewhere we can talk."

At his nod, she took him by the hand and led him through the crowd of dancing couples, past the people who simply mingled at the edges of the room. One set of glass doors stood open, and she headed for them, thankful for the fresh air that hit the moment they stepped through. She had realized just how warm it had become inside, how stifling the air was. Her shoes clicked against the soft grey stone, and she saw immediately that no one else had ventured outside, for which she was grateful. A stone bench sat between two bushes that were out of bloom, and Ella reasoned that the colder night air and the lack of flowers was at least partially responsible for no one visiting the garden. That, and the fact that everyone had only one thing on their minds that night—meeting and courting.

Bri stood at her side, hand still tucked securely in hers. "This is where we first met."

"It is, isn't it?" She pulled him to the bench and sat.

"We have a habit of meeting in gardens," he said, sitting beside her. "I'm usually ill though."

"Change is good." She took up his hand again. "I want to know everything. Where were you? What were you doing? Your letters said so much, and yet, I could tell they said little. You mentioned not wanting to put some things in writing. Can you tell me now?"

He was staring at their joined hands, his thumb moving lightly over the back of her hand. "I can tell you. Where would you like me to begin?"

Start simple. Don't be pushy. Den always says you can be too pushy. "Where were you? All your letters said was 'west.'"

"Xia-Lo."

"Xia-Lo?" She clamped a hand over her mouth when she realized how loudly she had spoken. "I'm sorry," she said, whispering. "So far. And so strange a place. I hear they walk around half-nude most of the time."

"Some of them do, but not all. It's different, but fine."

"And did you...try this fashion?"

"No," he said, almost laughing. "No, I did not." Something in his eyes told her his thoughts had suddenly turned darker; his smile had slipped.

She quickly changed the subject. "Was it beautiful there? I have seen paintings. Everything seems so brightly colored."

"Very colorful." Some of the dark thoughts dispelled from his eyes. "More so even than here tonight. They favor red and gold, yellows."

"I hope someday I can see other places and peoples."

"You will. Traveling is not as hard as some make it look."

It is when it's forbidden. Now it was her turn for dark thoughts. Den would never allow her to go so far off. The only traveling in her future was to Talconay—a place she had never been, and a country that had been destroyed by war. "Perhaps someday we'll go together."

"I would like that."

She refused to let herself think it nothing more than a pleasant fiction. "And your health? You do seem much better."

"Yes."

"What is it? What makes you so sick?" She had looked through many books in the library, searching the symptoms she had seen him display. Nothing ever seemed to add up. "Please tell me," she said when he hesitated.

For a long moment, he looked nowhere, off to the side, at the ground. His eyes had gone unfocused, seeing nothing. Ella waited, willing to let him have what time he needed to work up the courage to tell her the truth. After all, she had her own secrets, and they were never easy to share.

Finally, he breathed deeply, and looked at her. "You know about my mark. On my right hand?"

The demon's mark. The one that meant he had sold his soul to a demon. "Yes."

"You asked me once why I did it. Do you remember my answer?"

Yes. She remembered it as clearly as a wound on her own heart. She had been so young at the time, so unable to understand. She prayed to The One she had gained enough wisdom to understand now. "You said you did it to live."

"I was dying," he said. "I've been dying my whole life. This thing that plagues me... You know about the myst?"

"Of course." The place where The One wove their futures, and where the Singing Seraph carefully guarded and cultivated all lives.

"I can see it. I see it everywhere, all the time. It clings to people, and to cities, towns. If I keep my distance, I've always been all right, but if someone touches me..." he paused, his gaze flicking down to their hands once again. "If someone touches me directly, skin to skin, I was always thrown into the myst. Forced to see their future."

"How is that possible? How can you see into Haven?"

"That is a much longer story. But the myst, it's stronger than anything a human can control or handle. As a result, going in and out of it made me weak, and ill."

So much made sense now. "When I first met you here, at another party, had you seen something?"

Bri nodded, playing with the hem of his jacket. "I was really no good at controlling it back then. A room this large, full of so many people constantly bumping into each other, was a nightmare for me."

"And last year. At your party. After I—" Guilt crept in and kept her from finishing her sentence.

"You caught me by surprise, is all. Had I known, my reaction may not have been so bad."

"Why didn't you tell me? Had I known, I never would have—"

"It's not exactly the kind of thing one goes around telling people," he said, smiling. The smile served to set Ella somewhat at ease.

"Well, I'm glad you told me now."

"So am I. It's nice to be able to tell someone, to not have to hide."

"So, all this time, you've been learning to control the myst?"

"Control my connection to it, yes. I've come a long way. I could show you, if you'd like."

"Show me?"

That element of shyness that had first drawn her to him had returned. "Would you mind removing a glove?"

She pulled the sheath of fabric from her arm without another thought. Bri pulled his left glove off, folding it and putting it in his pocket. Then, slowly, the sounds of his breathing careful and even, he reached out and set his trembling hand in hers.

Ella marveled at the coolness of his hand, despite having been inside a glove. Tiny scars ran along the tips and backs of his fingers. She wanted to ask what they were from, but the question floated away as she flexed her fingers beneath his, feeling the softness of his skin, and the way her own skin tingled at the touch. She met his gaze, surprised to see such wonder there that she felt it must have surely matched her own. And suddenly her heart ached, realizing that this boy, this beautiful boy who was so unlike anyone she had ever met, who made her heart flutter just with words on a page, had spent his whole life afraid to do something as simple as touch another's hand. Carefully, cautious of his reactions, she turned her hand and wove her fingers together with his, giving his hand a gentle squeeze.

He let out a shuddering breath, moving his fingers back and forth along hers. "You have no idea how long I wanted to do this."

"I wanted it too," she whispered, sliding closer on the bench so that their knees touched.

He tore his gaze away from their hands and looked at her. "How did you know it was me? We haven't seen each other in a year, and with this mask..."

"You knew me."

"True."

"But if you must know, it was your eyes. No one has eyes like you."

"Except maybe one," he muttered the words, almost to himself.

But she heard him all the same. "You mean your brother?"

"My brother?"

"Yes. Kai."

All the color rushed out of Bri's face. "You've met Kai?"

"Only briefly," she rushed to assure him, not knowing why he would have such a reaction. "On the street in the city. I thought for a moment he was you, but as soon as he turned around I knew he wasn't. He said he was looking for you, too. You never told me you had another brother."

"We only recently met," Bri said, sounding bitter. "He didn't say anything to you, did he? He didn't do anything?"

"No. He was a perfect gentlemen. Would he not be?"

"I have no idea."

Her stomach seemed to have hollowed out. "Should I be worried?"

"No. No, I don't think you have any reason to worry." He was twisting the ring on his finger.

"You look worried."

Bri smiled, but it appeared false. "I'm not worried."

Ella wasn't convinced, but she didn't want to ruin their first evening together, so she let it go. They would have all the time in the world to argue later. "All right, then. No one's worried."

He tightened his hold on her hand slightly.

"Can we try again?"

"Huh?"

Ella couldn't help but giggle. The look on his face when caught by surprise was just too adorable—especially when he had been so serious only moments before. "Can we try again? I feel I still owe you a birthday present, since last year's didn't go so well. And you've had another birthday since then. We both have."

"Would you think less of me if I told you that's all I've been thinking about for the past year?"

"Not at all."

She rose up enough to press her lips to his. Instantly she felt the need to breathe deeply, as though she wanted to breathe him into herself. He remained still a moment, and for a moment Ella worried they had gone too far for him. But then he exhaled, and his gloved hand touched her cheek lightly, before his lips moved beneath hers, tentatively, cautiously.

She wanted to melt into him, to draw herself closer and closer, until she lost track of where she ended and he began. Forgetting that they were in public, that at any moment anyone could wander out into the garden and see her pressing her free hand against his chest, feeling his heart beat wildly beneath his jacket and shirt. She felt lightheaded and dizzy, but in a way that only made her want more. It seemed as though the whole world would tilt, and she and Bri would simply slide off into oblivion.

Then it did.

The world rocked violently, throwing them from the bench in a tangle of limbs. Her ears rang from the explosion, and she felt sharp and hard rain sting her skin as it came down upon them both. Smoke filled her lungs, and she coughed, struggling to sit upright.

Bri grabbed at her, pulling her up and yelling to be heard over the commotion—or perhaps his hearing was simply as muddled as hers. "Are you all right?"

A thin trail of blood ran down his cheek, and she reached to touch the small cut it spilled from. "You're bleeding."

"Are you hurt?" he asked again, his hands and gaze wandering her body in a way that would have made her blush before, but now seemed only clinical. There was shattered glass all around them. The large windows of the ballroom had been blown outwards.

"I'm fine," she assured him, feeling nothing more than a few scrapes. "I'm fine. Are you?"

He nodded, then turned to look at the ballroom, where black smoke poured through the broken windows and people screamed and cried in horror.

"What happened?" Half of her felt like running; the other half knew she was too shaky to successfully get very far.

"Bri!" a voice called from inside the ballroom, louder than any of the screams. "Brishen! You show yourself to me right now, or I will kill everyone here!"

— CHAPTER SIXTEEN —

No. *It couldn't be.* A terrible hallucination, a figment of his mind in the aftermath of such a shock.

"Bri!"

Kai. Heedless of all the glass surrounding him, Bri stood, unsteady, looking toward the chaotic ballroom. The smoke was beginning to clear, and people were rushing back and forth within, crying and shouting. The bright colors of dresses had become muted, and the crisp, clean white shirts were now grey.

Another flare of light, and Bri heard something shatter. More screams followed. "Bri! I know you're here!"

Helping Ella from the ground, Bri tried to think rationally. "Come on," he said, pulling her toward the large outer wall of the ballroom. She clung to him, tripping over the debris though he did his best to avoid it.

"What's going on?"

He held a finger to his lips for her to be quiet, and pressed her up against the wall. Two large hedges grew on either side of them, hiding them from plain sight. Peering around the edge of one, Bri could see straight into the ballroom.

Kai hopped atop a table, his lightweight clothing a far cry from anything anyone else wore. The white shirt hung partially open, exposing his chest and the lines of a *labrynth* he had carved over his heart. His right hand dripped with blood. All around him, the people of Callay struggled to sit up, to get away from him, their masks fallen away, or torn and dirty. Kai grabbed one young woman as she stumbled past, dragging her by her neck up onto the table with him. He held her there, kneeling at his feet, his bloody hand wrapped around her throat as she whimpered in fear. "Come on, Bri! Don't you want to see your dear brother? It's been so long."

Ella clung to Bri's side, following his gaze. "My gods...What is he doing?"

"Trying to get my attention."

"But why? Is he mad?"

"To say the least, yes."

Kai tore the golden mask from the girl's face, revealing tear-stained cheeks. With his thumb, Kai wiped away those tears. "So beautiful," he said. "You really shouldn't cry. You have no need to. As long as my brother comes to me, you'll live."

A strangled, panicked sound escaped her throat.

Ella gasped, a hand going to her mouth. "He wouldn't!"

Bri said nothing. He knew Kai would.

"You hear that, Bri? Her life is in your hands! Quickly now. What will it be?"

There was no other choice. He pushed Ella back between the hedges. "Stay here. Do not come out until he is gone."

"What? What about you?"

"I have to do what he says."

She grabbed his sleeve, holding tight. "You can't mean to go with that mad man! He'll kill you!"

"He won't. He won't kill me. He needs me." Of that, he was sure. "Promise me. Don't let him see you."

She pulled her mask from her face, then grabbed his wrist. Her green eyes shone with tears, and there was a tiny cut just above her mouth. Despite the ash and glass slivers that had sliced and stuck to her dress, Bri still thought she was the most beautiful thing he had ever seen. "There must be another way."

"No other way."

"I'm growing impatient, Bri!" Kai's voice continued to be louder than humanly possible. No doubt enhanced by some spell of his.

Before he could second guess himself, before the fear sitting like a rock in his stomach could have a chance to disperse to his mind, Bri kissed Ella one more time. He swore to remember the warmth of her lips against his. "Tell Alec," he said.

"What?"

"Tell Alec. And don't let Kai see you." With that, Bri pried Ella's fingers off his arm and moved out of the shelter of the hedges, into the doorway of the ballroom.

There was a snap, and the frightened sounds of the girl cut off sharply. She fell with a dull thud to Kai's feet, her head at an unnatural angle. Bri went cold all over.

"Did you think I wouldn't do it, Bri?" Kai called out, still unaware of Bri's arrival. He toed the poor dead girl. "I said I would, and I do what I say."

The cold horror was replaced by blazing rage. Bri stepped over a fallen plate of food and gently moved a terrified older gentleman out of his way. Untying his mask from behind his head, he let it fall to the floor. "I'm right here, Kai. Why did you do that?"

When Kai saw him, his face lit up like a child given a sweet. "Bri!" He jumped off the table and shoved a few shocked guests out of the way as he crossed the room. "There you are."

"Kai, what have you done?" The ballroom was in complete disarray. Tables overturned, food and drink splattered. The paintings on the walls were darkened by smoke and ash, and everywhere injured people huddled together. No one seemed to be dead. No one but that girl. "All these innocent people. Do you not care?"

Kai made a face like Bri was the one who had gone mad. He threw his arms in a wild gesture to include the entire room. "It's all replaceable!"

"She's not." Bri pointed over Kai's shoulder to where the girl lay dead on the table.

Without even bothering to look back, Kai shrugged. "That's debatable."

"You didn't need to kill her."

"You didn't need to take so long."

"Well, here I am. What do you want?"

"Same thing I always want. For us to be together." Kai clasped Bri on the shoulders. "You hid yourself from me this past year. I don't know how, but you did. I didn't like it."

"We spent fifteen years never knowing about each other, Kai. One more is nothing. Couldn't you handle it?"

"I see you grew a backbone in the last year. Good, you'll need it. You need to be strong." He gripped Bri's face in his hands. "We have much to do."

"You talk as if you're certain I'm going with you."

"You are. Because if you don't, I'll kill everyone here, and I know you don't want that."

If he fought Kai, he wouldn't win. Kai was the stronger, the more ruthless. He could never win a physical altercation with his brother. Any victories would have to be had in other ways, over time. Running seemed cowardly, and Bri had long ago decided to leave that part of himself far behind. All around him, people tended to one another, shaking in fear. Their lives had only become this hell because of him; because his brother was a madman. He could save them, if not himself.

"Let's go then. Leave these people alone."

"I *knew* you'd see it my way." Patting Bri's face two quick times, Kai reached into his pocket and withdrew a knife. "Give me your hand."

"No. No, you don't get to mark me. I'll come with you, but no marks."

"Oh, Bri, are you really going to be like that?"

"Yes. That's my deal. You want me to go with you, then agree to it."

Kai spun the knife in his hand with a dramatic sigh. "You make everything so difficult."

Bri was about to respond when he saw the movement. A man, rising quickly from behind an overturned table, a large carving knife in his hand. He charged Kai, yelling like a warrior from the northern past. Bri shouted for him to stop, but it was too late.

Kai flipped his knife from one hand to the other, and without blinking, slammed the blade into the man's throat. A choking sound came first, and in his shock, the foolishly brave man dropped his weapon, the edge catching Kai's pants as it fell, putting a small, clean slice in the fabric. With a quick tug, Kai split the man's throat wide open, and he fell to the floor, blood bubbling out, gushing all over the front of his once pristine suit. Kai looked utterly disinterested.

"That was self-defense, wouldn't you agree?"

More screams and cries rose up from the ballroom.

"Kai, please. Let's just go, now." Bri wanted to cry for the man dying on the floor, but he couldn't, couldn't let Kai see how it bothered him.

"And look at my pants! They'll have to be mended now."

"Kai."

"Oh, all right. Do you know how to sew? I don't. I suppose I'll have to have Xan do it." Kicking the dead man out of the way, Kai used his foot to scrawl a *labrynth* into the blood that had spilled everywhere. It took him no time at all. "Shall we go, brother?" He held out his hand, covered now in both his own blood and the man's.

Bri reminded himself to breathe, and took the offered hand. They fell through the floor together.

Stories of magic were told to children as the sun went down, as a way to frighten them into good behavior and moral decisions. No one questioned its existence—there was no point. Magic was real, and its users often fell into madness. But witches were still sought out—by kings and queens, the rich, and demons. Since the demons had lost some of their foothold in the mortal realm not one hundred years back, magic had become something less visible, something kept behind closed doors.

Ella had never seen it work firsthand, but that didn't mean she didn't know it when she saw it. She had watched as Kai scrawled in the blood on the floor, then took Bri's hand, drawing him to stand on the *labrynth*. Then the two had slipped easily into the floor, through the floor, disappearing from sight.

It took all of two heartbeats afterward for the ballroom to erupt in cacophonous panic. People called for loved ones, shouted for help. Ella emerged from her hiding spot and joined the chaos inside, careful of those who ran and stumbled by, as well as those who could not move from the floor. The worst of the injuries seemed to be ragged wounds to the legs and arms, most likely from the initial explosion; no one seemed in mortal danger. The two poor souls Kai had selected among the hundreds of guests would be the only casualties. Ella could not bear to look at the man on the floor, his blood staining the marble. She did not know him, and she thought for a moment that it was probably for the best. The ache in her heart was enough already. The girl was a different matter. Ella found herself moving without thought toward the table, drawn there by some unseen force. She had known her. Sarina. Pretty, with deep brown eyes and rich brown hair. Seventeen, she had also come to be Presented. This night should have been full of excitement and dancing. Instead, she had gotten death. The Presentment had not even gotten a chance to take place. Somewhere, a bell rang in a careful rhythm. Ella counted the chimes. Twelve. Midnight. They would have been Presented now. The dance involved a constant changing of partners, a swirl of young ladies and young men, mingling and barely touching gloved hands to gloved hands. At the end, all masks would have come off.

A flood of people suddenly converged on the table where Sarina took her final rest. Her family, Ella supposed.

Den.

She turned in a sweeping arch, looking over the entirety of the ballroom, and shouted for her brother. He wasn't dead, she was certain of that, but in her certainty she had forgotten to worry that perhaps he was one of the worst injured. So she shouted for him again and again, hoping he would hear her over the cries of so many others.

"Marciella."

Her chest felt lighter in relief, and for the first time she was glad for the use of her full name. It was unmistakable in all the noise. Den stumbled over bodies and debris behind her, rushing to her side. Ella met him halfway and let him catch her up in an embrace that was altogether too tight to be comfortable, but assured her of his wellbeing. "You're all right," he said, finally pulling away and checking her for injuries.

"Yes, I'm fine. Hardly a scratch. You?" There was a dark purple stain down the front of his shirt, suggesting he had been drinking wine when the explosion hit, but there seemed to be nothing more.

"I was far from everything when it happened. What *did* happen? All I heard was a lot of yelling."

"It's a long story. First, I think we should try to help who we can."

Den didn't argue with her. Together, they went around the room, giving kind assurance to those still shocked with fear, and pressing napkins and shreds of tablecloth to the bloodiest of wounds. Not long after, royal guards flooded the ballroom—those who hadn't been in attendance in the first place—asking questions and helping with the injured. An inspector arrived and started asking questions. He never got to Ella, but she overheard the answers others gave. A witch, and the Dusombré boy who had been out of town for the past year. More than once Ella almost approached the inspector of her own accord— but she always stopped, not sure what to say. There was nothing the inspector and the guard could do to help Bri.

She was carefully feeding water to another of the gold-masked girls when she heard his voice. It had been more than a year since she had heard it, but there was no mistaking the name it called over the sounds of the ballroom.

"Bri!"

Tell Alec. That had been Bri's only instruction. Ella followed the sound of his voice, sorting her thoughts as she went, deciding exactly how to tell him what had happened. She found him by the main entrance, making demands of some poor servant who probably knew nothing more than he did.

"Alec," she called to him as she approached, stumbling over debris, her hands trembling as they held up her skirts.

They met still close to the doorway, the cold night air drifting in and causing Ella to shiver. "Ella," he said. "You're Ella. Where's Bri?"

"He told me to tell you."

"Tell me what?" He hadn't dressed for the occasion, his shirt untucked and his shoes half tied—as though he had come here in a rush. "I heard the explosion even from the manor. What happened?"

"Kai." The moment she said his name Ella knew it was explanation enough, but she continued anyway. "Kai was here. He did this. Bri went with him so he would stop."

Alec had gone eerily still, his face ashen. "He went with him?"

"Yes. Kai threatened to kill everyone if he didn't."

"Gods damn it, blistering hell and godflesh, that son of a whoring—" Alec came to life again with each curse, his knuckles turning white and his face flushing with anger. He continued on, and Ella let him, though she blushed at a few of his more creative maledictions. Eventually he finished, and breathed deeply before apologizing.

"Don't. You're not sorry, and neither am I. I share your sentiments."

With a nod, Alec seemed settled on the matter. "Is there anything else? Anything either of them said? How did they leave?"

"I couldn't hear very clearly, I just know Kai wanted Bri, and Bri gave him what he wanted. They left using a *labrynth*." She got no response, simply the feeling that Alec was thinking about the implications of what she had said. "I want to help."

"I don't think there's anything you can do."

"Still. If I can help, I will."

For what felt like the longest time, Alec studied her. Ella wondered if he could see straight through her, down to her soul, or into her mind, verifying her sincerity, her trustworthiness. He would find nothing but certainty.

Finally, he nodded. "All right. Until then, keep your eye out. If you see either of them, let me know."

Alec arrived home that night feeling tired and old. Tired because he had spent the past turn going over everything in his mind, and coming up with nothing, no way of finding Bri immediately. And old, because despite the carnage Kai had left behind—the injured and the two dead—none of it had bothered him, hadn't given him a second thought. Two thousand years of demon activity was too much. No one could live that long and remain unjaded.

He went to the parlor and threw himself in one of the armchairs, shutting his eyes and berating himself for the millionth time. *I never should have let him go alone. I knew it was a bad idea. Damnit, Bri, why couldn't you just have agreed to let me come along? I could have made him agree. He wouldn't have fought me if I had insisted. This is my fault.*

Carma would kill him. And he would never forgive himself. He had only one saving thought. *Kai won't hurt him. At least not yet. I have time.*

He didn't know how much time had gone by when he finally felt Carma's return. Hell clung to her, and the scent of it stirred his own yearnings to call power and hold onto it until his entire being burned with potential, and the anger of it consumed him. The heat would concentrate in his hands, spread outward through his arms to his shoulders and down his chest. Strength would flood his muscles, and perhaps he could simply open up a hole to Hell and drag Bri back out. If that was where he had been taken. Olin had Kai, or at least, he'd had him after Lillianna's death. Olin and Kai. When Alec found either of them, he would tear their heads from their necks and—

"It's unusual for you to be bathing in power like that, Alec. Something bothering you?"

Carma stood just in front of him, dressed for Hell and looking haggard. Her expression was one of remote curiosity and more intense concern. Alec had to think hard about her words.

His palms burned with power, as did his chest, and even his mind. He hadn't just thought about pulling power, he had actually done it.

Panicked, he cast it away, forcing it to leave his veins and go back where it belonged. A place in his mind mourned the loss, poked at him with already awakened cravings. No. He would not be a slave to the power. He would not.

Needing a momentary distraction, knowing telling Carma what had transpired that night would only incite his anger and frustration and invite the power back, Alec studied her unusual expression once more. "What about you? You look ready to tear something limb from limb." Her hands were taloned claws, and her hair was red to her shoulders.

"Picadilly is gone. I don't know how. We were ambushed—or she was. I was distracted." Her disgust at that was clear.

"Pica's gone?" Alec felt the weight of impending doom settle on his shoulders. "Who took her? Do you know?"

"No. Nor do I know why."

"I think you do."

"And what foolishness makes you think that?"

"You've been going to Hell nearly every day. You have Dorothea locked in her workshop, scribing and experimenting. You're planning something. And the Restorium is coming. Some suspect you are up to something, and my guess is they aren't wrong."

"You think Pica was taken to stop me?" She moved toward the other chair, but did not sit.

"It would make sense. And considering what happened tonight, it can't be coincidence."

"What happened tonight?"

"I hope your connections in Hell are better than you thought and more trustworthy than they appear, because we're going to need help."

"Alec, just tell me."

Courage was in short supply, but Alec used what he had to look Carma straight in the eyes. "Kai took Bri."

— CHAPTER SEVENTEEN —

Market Day in Haven was always an event not to be missed. Since they had no need of farming and industry like the mortal humans, seraphs never spent their days supplying their cabinets and ensuring they had necessary provisions. However, it was impossible not to watch the humans and their daily activities without admiring the exoticism of it all. So, once a year, the seraph had their own market. Guardians and Ceeks traveled to the mortal realm throughout the year, collecting odds and ends, trinkets and baubles. Anything humanity created that was not naturally provided in the holy realm. They set up tents and tables along the main streets of Haven, bathed in the white light and under the watchful eye of the Citadel. Seraph children especially loved the strange toys the human children played with—hoops and ropes that could be jumped, and dolls that stared back with black button eyes. Grown seraph tended toward things that reminded them of the humans they watched over daily. A bangle meant to bring luck, or a stone set in silver to be worn around the neck for clarity in love. These items drew the seraph who cultivated such things, and they collected them with a sort of condescending amusement. A stone did not bring love or luck. But Gabriel had always bit her tongue when the subject arose, for while the seraph claimed it was they—by will of The One—who brought such blessings, they were often drawn to humans who possessed the trinkets, knowing it as the prayer it was meant to be, and would give their blessing. As Gabriel saw it, that made the stone damn successful.

Wandering through the crowds, grateful for the break from the halls of her office within the headquarters of the First File, Gabriel didn't actually look at many of the wares being sold left and right. Humanity's goods didn't particularly interest her. Not unless one of the vendors had brought back a myst-seeing boy.

A year of nothing. Nothing. It was the worst streak she'd had since his birth now seventeen years prior. She told herself that at least if he was truly missing, she had reason for not catching him, but the assurance fell flat. Not so much as detecting him was worse.

Under a bright banner that proclaimed the presence of baked goods, a group of children squealed in delight with each bite of some fruit-filled, sugar dusted confections. Gabriel remembered the first time she had tasted one. She had been ten, and her father had given it to her to celebrate her acceptance into the University's military academy. Chocolate, he had called it. Humans found it near intoxicating. Gabriel had thought it divine. But that was the last time she had ever tasted it. Such things were to be avoided. Sweets were a human weakness. She watched as the children rushed to eat more and more of the tiny squares. *May The One give them the strength to walk away.* Chocolate, some thought, could be enough to cause a Fall. Still, Gabriel smiled at their enthusiasm.

"Gabriel!"

Kadiel came running up the street, face streaked with ink as always, hair falling out of what should have been a secured knot at the nape of her neck. In the year since Gabriel had taken Kadiel as her assistant—the only real way to keep an eye on her—she had been adamant about cleanliness and uniformity. The First File was not a center of learning; it was a place of law, and rules and order. It never took more than two turns of the glass for Kadiel to look like a wind-blown haystack.

Gabriel stopped and waited for her to catch up, awaiting the salute she had insisted upon. It never came. Kadiel stopped, half bent over, hands on her knees, gasping for breath. Gabriel made a note to begin requiring Kadiel to run every morning and build stamina.

"Hell below," she cursed. "I thought I would never find you."

"Watch your language. What do you want? I thought I ordered you to stay in the office?"

"You did."

"Then why are you here?"

Kadiel drew herself upright, chin lifted. "Because I got another order that superseded yours."

"Don't look so smug about it. From whom?"

"Michael. Michael wants to see you."

Michael. Commander of the Legions. Her mentor. If he had come down from the Citadel to see her... "How long has he been waiting?" Gabriel wasted no time in heading back toward her office, shouldering past the worry-free market goers.

Kadiel kept pace, though she struggled to. "I left as soon as he asked for you, but it took longer to find you in these crowds than I thought it would. I had been so sure you would be down by the human weapons, not the sweets."

She had been planning on going there next, after she had cleared her head. The fact that Kadiel knew her that well made her uncomfortable. No one knew her habits and interests outside of her job—except a perhaps a few old friends who no longer walked in the light, and Michael.

"Please tell me the office is actually in order and not the site of a twister cloud."

Kadiel's guilty silence was answer enough. For every stack of papers Gabriel got in order, neat and tidy, Kadiel had seven spread out over the floor, her desk, and atop numerous open books.

The further they got from the market, the easier it was to get through the streets. Eventually the vendor's voices were too far to be heard, and the constant motion of curious seraph was gone as well. When Gabriel entered through the front door of her building, she felt as though she and Kadiel were the only ones in the realm. Not a sound came from any room, leaving their footsteps to echo harshly through the hall. The door to her office was wide open, and she gave herself no time to hesitate before going in.

Michael had not changed in the near two millennia she had known him. Of course, seraph did not age as the mortals did. They reached adulthood and then aged as they pleased. The only changes by which time could be marked were scars. Michael had few. He was a gruff-looking man, with a square jaw and thin lips. He always kept himself impeccably groomed—a trait which he had passed on to Gabriel in her training. Even without his armor, he was broader than most, with thick arms and strong legs. So tall that he towered over everyone else when meetings were held, he had a commanding presence that was only enhanced by the severity of his gaze and aura of power he exuded. The one scar he did carry, a cross mark by his left eye, pulled his lid downward slightly and made him look dangerous. Most human accounts of encounters with him were littered with words of fear and trepidation.

Gabriel never used to fear him. He had been her teacher, her mentor, her confidant after her father had been killed in a raid on Hell. But she knew when he got that look in his eye, that darkened shine to his normally bright grey eyes, that it was time to use caution.

He had that look now.

"Michael. You wanted to see me?" She saluted as befitted his station, clasping her fist over her heart.

"Yes, I did." His voice was like gravel, a memento left behind from a fight with a demon who had tried to carve out his throat. A flick of his gaze over Gabriel's shoulder told her Kadiel had reached the doorway. "Leave us."

More echoing footsteps, and Gabriel and Michael were alone. Truly alone.

"Close the door," he said.

Gabriel did so, though there was no real reason to. Everyone else was at market. "Something serious must be going on for you to come here on Market Day. What is it?"

"It has been confirmed," he said, straightening one of Kadiel's many haphazard piles. "The Restorium is coming."

"That is no surprise. We have been hearing rumors for some time now."

"Rumor no more. It will come."

"Technically, it could be said that it is always coming. We never know precisely when."

"Before the seasons cycle again in the mortal realm, we will have our time."

He continued to pick at Kadiel's mess, and Gabriel had the strong urge to begin cleaning up, but she had learned to squelch that impulse. Kadiel was messy, but methodical. If Gabriel moved something, she could set back Kadiel's research by days, if not longer.

Living with the mess had become an unpleasant, but acquired, taste.

"Is there something you need me to do in preparation?"

"Yes. I need you to find the boy."

Of course. It had been a false hope to think this meeting could have been about anything else. "I am working on it, Michael, you know I am. He has powerful allies now. They have ways of hiding him."

"Seventeen years, Gabriel."

"I know."

"When I gave you this task, I did so because I believed you could handle it. It was a matter that needed to be dealt with quickly, and I had faith that you would not fail me."

"And I won't. I know it's taking longer than we all thought, but I assure you, it is my every thought, my every effort."

"Including all this?" He gestured around the room, nose wrinkled in disgust.

Gabriel resisted the urge to tidy. "Kadiel got in my way too many times. With her here, I can watch her more closely. Besides, she is a master of research, and she should help clean up her own mess."

"You believe she will not try to thwart you at every turn? She has before." Michael lifted a notebook from the floor, reading over the page that had been left open.

"I believe she can see reason. If she knows the consequences of her actions, of the boy's continued existence, then perhaps she will understand why she was asked to end this in the first place."

"You've had her for a year now." He tossed the notebook back to the floor. "Has there been any change?"

"Unfortunately, the boy has been missing for the past year. Even the Singers have not seen him."

"Has he died?"

"I have Reapers watching for that sort of thing. He will not pass without our knowing. Besides that, I have reason to believe he has made a deal for his soul."

Michael stopped short of shifting through another of Kadiel's chaotic piles. "So he could be soulless now?"

"It is a possibility, but I do not think so."

"You cannot let a demon have his soul, Gabriel."

"I know."

Michael came toward her, reaching out to touch her face gently, as he had so many years ago. Gabriel closed her eyes a moment, remembering things she would do better to forget. "You are named for the best of us. I served with your grandfather when he was general of the First File, and I was at his side when he passed at the hands of Luca and Lillianna. I had great hopes for you when you came to me. You were so young, but so spirited, almost as if The One had seen fit to return your grandfather to us, through you."

"I know. I am sorry I have disappointed you."

"I still believe you can end this, but I must give you a deadline. Any longer, and The Citadel will step in."

Holy One. If the Citadel took up the task of searching for the boy, they would unleash the Legions on the mortal realm. All humanity would know that Haven wanted something. They would tear the delicate realm apart until they found it. Until they found him.

"I understand."

"The Restorium is coming, Gabriel. Soon. He must be ours by then; otherwise, he could wreak such destruction on the realms. Find him. Bring him here. And do not rely on your pet Ceek. If we are lucky, the Restorium will met out the justice we could not. Our weakness will be gone, and if we must obtain the boy with our newly restored strength, we will."

"Haven't you found him yet?"

"Hush, boy. Do not rush me."

Flexing his fingers with the urge to throttle the old witch, Alec swallowed his own frustration and forced himself to walk away. Just to the other side of the workshop, but far enough to avoid anything he would regret.

He didn't know how much longer he could stay down there. He didn't know how Dorothea stayed down in this place day after day, night after night. The air was stale, smoky, and filled with so many aromas Alec couldn't place a one of them. The bitter taste of blood was always on the air, dancing across his tongue every time he dared to speak. It was like living in a soup of magic, and all the spices were harsh and uncomplimentary of each other.

"I am not rushing you," he said once he had calmed some. "It has been days. I can't wait forever."

"I cannot find what cannot be found," Dorothea said, swiping her arm across the table and clearing away all the lines she had drawn over the past turn.

"That isn't helpful."

"His brother, Kai, is a powerful witch."

"So are you."

"Aye, I am. But this child gives me a challenge."

There it was, the gleam in her eye that Alec had been waiting for as confirmation. "You're enjoying this."

"Only a little."

"That is a lie."

Dorothea smiled, and her ancient shoulders shook with pleasant mirth.

Alec crossed the room, slamming his hands down on the table, not caring when they smeared with blood. "This is not a game."

The old witch shrugged, unfazed by him. "I did not say that it was."

"Find. Bri."

"I am working on it. He is not so easy to find. It is what has kept him alive this long." She batted his arms away from her workspace.

"I thought he was hard to find because you made him that way."

"The seraph couldn't find him long before I came into his life. It is not my magic that hides him so well."

"Then whose is it?" Alec demanded.

Opening a large jar of sand, Dorothea dumped it on the table, where it immediately began soaking up the blood. "There is another *labrynth*, you know. Carved into his flesh. Like mine, but not. Bri has no idea it exists."

"What? Where? Who put it there?"

Dorothea tapped the back of her head. "Right here. Under all that lovely hair."

"Why didn't you ever say anything before?"

"It did not matter before. The *labrynth* works. Bri is kept hidden. That is all that matters. Your knowledge of it makes no difference."

"Of course it makes a difference! Now we can't find him because of it! You should have done something."

"What would you have me do?" She stalked around the table, smoothing the sand with her hand, the red tinge following its path. "The spell is his best defense…and a gift."

Alec didn't move when she reached him. He didn't care if he stood in her way of resetting her workspace; it was tit for tat. "Who put the *labrynth* on him?"

"A very old friend of mine. A great witch. Very powerful. He would have been better than me had he not died so tragically."

"Who, Dorothea?"

"His name was Jaymes. He had a terrible weakness for one particular woman. A woman he should have stayed clear of. As a result of their irresponsibility, the world will suffer."

"Why would he hide Bri?"

"All of Haven searches for him, with the intent to kill. What parent wouldn't?"

This time, when she shoved Alec aside, he let her. "You knew Bri's father?"

Dorothea swatted the air. "We all knew Jaymes. He was going to be great. The best of us. Instead, we are left with his abomination of a son, Kai. Powerful, but dangerous."

Damned witches and their secrets. "Does Bri know?"

"We spoke of it once."

There was an ache developing just behind his eyes. Alec rubbed his face, then raked his hands through his hair. "Why does everyone in this house insist on keeping secrets?"

Dusting the sand from her hands, Dorothea pulled a knife from her belt. "That question can be answered easily enough. After all, you keep your own."

"I have no secrets."

"The locket you keep in your pocket tells a different tale."

Suddenly the object spoken of seemed to weigh the same as a boulder where it sat against his thigh. Ariadne had been on his mind ever since they had returned. He wanted to find her again, but Bri was more important. "I don't know what you mean."

"Fine. I will let you play it that way. Give me your hand."

"What? Why?"

"You are family. I need your blood. Give me your hand."

Had she gone mad—der? "Bri is not my blood, Dorothea. You know that."

"So smart about everything, are you? Bonds go deeper than what nature creates, and family can be chosen. Would you say a husband is not family to his wife?" She gestured for his hand once more.

Surrendering to the logic of a madwoman, Alec set his hand in hers. Immediately she dug her blade into his heel of his hand and cut him open so deeply that blood pooled and spilled over onto the sand in mere moments. Alec thought she would collect the blood, begin scribing, but she did not move, simply held his hand over the table, squeezing to keep the flow heavy.

His blood hit the sand, splattering and sinking into the already reddened substance. But it did not spread. Regardless of the amount that dripped down, it pooled and flooded one area, darkening the sand until it was almost black. Alec began to feel dizzy, blinking to clear his vision. He tugged on his arm, but Dorothea would not release him.

Balancing the knife on the table point up, she pricked her own finger and let one single bead of blood collect before she delicately set it atop the pile of sand saturated in Alec's blood. It sank within, and for a moment, the workshop seemed to go completely still. She let Alec loose, and he stepped back, clutching his hand to his chest and quickly searching for something with which to staunch the blood. He wrapped a long piece of linen around and around until it felt tight enough that his fingers grew tingly. The lightheadedness began to recede. "Did you really need to take so much?"

"No. That was for rushing me."

She leaned over the table, drew a deep breath, and began to blow. The bloodied sand scattered as though it were dry and warm. Gracefully, it spread across the table, carried by Dorothea's power-filled breeze. It settled in places, skipped across to others, and slowly, a pattern, an image, began to arise. It was a well-known *labrynth*, one Alec had seen many times. In fact, he remembered, he had seen it the very night this all had begun four years ago, on the night of the storm in the ruin, when Carma had returned and Bri had sold his soul.

An entrance way to Hell.

"There is your answer," Dorothea said, her back cracking as she straightened.

"How is that my answer?" Hell was vast. Huge. It wasn't like telling him to search a particular city. Hell was an entire realm. Another world.

"I cannot give you anything more than which realm to search. Instead of three, you now have one. You are welcome."

He stared at the mark in the sand, drawn in his blood. If only it would shift, give him some further clue...but it did not. "How am I supposed to search all of Hell?"

"My advice?" She drew a crude stick figure beside her *labrynth.* "Get a guide."

— CHAPTER EIGHTEEN —

Bri had not left the room Kai had deposited him in for three days. He wasn't sure what he had expected. This was Hell, the demon realm, the place of torment for the sinful dead. He certainly hadn't pictured a paradise, but Carma always spoke of the place so fondly, he'd imagined there was at least something pleasant about it.

How very wrong. The ground was black, ashen, and cracked, as though it had not seen water in millions of years. The air shimmered with heat, making the distance appear as though through imperfect glass. Kai had brought him to the base of a looming brimstone mountain, surrounded on one side by a lake that boiled and churned. On the other side, Kai had told him, was the void, a black abyss that no one returned from. The halls and stairs within the mountain wove back and forth like a maze. Bri had no clue how to retrace his steps even if he wanted to.

But all those things were not what kept him huddled inside the simple, unadorned room. No, he stayed inside because of what roamed those halls. Creatures that looked like men, but had tusks growing from their mouths, and horns from their heads. Hooved, four-legged things with tails like snakes, and heads like cats. Rats and other rodents skittered about the halls, their flesh scaled and burned. They brought back memories of fire, of a manor burning to the ground while a seraph attacked. It was a horror show he had never imagined.

The single window in his room overlooked the void, and Bri had to wonder if Kai had chosen that purposefully. There was nowhere to run. Literally. But Bri had no plans for running. No. If he had to stay here, in this sulfur-smelling, oppressive place, then he would make the best of it. He would learn about Kai, gain a measure of trust, and he would find a way to stop him.

Such thoughts made Bri feel brave. And foolish.

He sat on his meager bed, and, not for the first time, tried to assure himself that he had a plan.

At least Ella and the others were safe.

The door opened, and Kai walked right in. It had been a day since Bri had seen him. He had changed his clothes, wearing a crisp white shirt and loose linen pants. His hair looked damp, but it seemed to be drying even as Bri watched. White bandages wrapped his hands, as always, and an extra strip hung from the waistband of his trousers. The shoes he wore were the most substantial thing on him, thick-soled things that would protect his feet from the hot ground.

"All right, I've let you sulk long enough," Kai said, tossing a pile of clothes down on the bed. "Get changed. I want to show you something."

Bri stared at the clothing that seemed to be a perfect match for what his brother wore. The last thing he wanted was to be mistaken for Kai in this place. "Don't you have anything else?" He had sweated though his expensive suit, having long ago discarded the jacket and tie. The white shirt and pressed pants were ruined.

"If you're a good boy, I'll take you to town and you can pick out whatever you want. But until then, no. You'll wear what I give you." He grinned as though he had just gifted Bri with a beautiful present, not made a subtextual threat.

At least he would be cooler. "Fine."

"What?" Kai said when Bri didn't move. "Are you shy? I'm not leaving. We're brothers, and twins at that. I'm sure you don't have anything I've never seen before."

"That's not the point," Bri said, even as he stood and undid the buttons on his shirt. "I've been here three days and I haven't run. You don't need to watch my every move."

Kai shrugged. "I walked all this way and I have nothing to do until you're ready, so there's no point in my going."

Bri tossed the shirt to the bed and turned to grab the new one. Kai caught his wrist, stopping him.

"Wait."

"What is it? Oh," Bri said, when he felt Kai's fingers touch his back. "That. You know about that. I told you when we first met."

"It's different now. She changed it so it would grow with you. And this rune—"

Bri winced and twisted away when he touched the unfinished rune. It still hurt, and occasionally it still bled. "It's fine. Leave it alone."

"I could fix it for you."

"No."

"Bri, it must be painful. And it's starting to bleed."

"No." He faced his brother, wanting to be sure there was no misunderstanding. "I don't need you to fix it. You don't get to mark me, even to repair old marks. That's my deal. I'll stay here with you, but no marks. No runes. No *labrynths*."

"Are you really that stubborn?" Kai's gaze flicked to the side, trying to see Bri's back again, his eyes alight with hunger.

"I don't trust you. You don't get to write your magic into my body."

"Fine, fine. At least let me bandage it for you. If it bleeds, there are things here that will come at the smell of blood."

"I imagine it's something of a common smell here."

Kai held up his wrapped hands and wiggled his fingers. "Occupational hazard for some of us. But I don't want them seeking you out. I want you safe."

If I'm going to gain his trust, it's going to take a bit of compromise on my end. A difficult thought to swallow. "All right. Bandage only."

Kai produced one between his fingers as though by magic.

Once bandaged and changed, Bri followed Kai out into the halls and down a number of stairs. Kai pointed things out along the way, like the path to the kitchen and another to the baths. Bri couldn't make sense of any of it. It all looked the same. Kai was busy explaining the pathway leading to the training grounds when an old woman emerged from that very place.

She was tall, and she maintained that height despite her age. No hunch to her shoulders or spine. Though wrinkled and dotted with age spots, Bri thought she had probably been very pretty in her youth.

Her hair had gone mostly grey, but there was evidence still of the rich black it had once been. She wore a white silk dress that reminded Bri of some of the things Carma wore, and it fluttered about her in the hot air, looking cool and comfortable.

Kai groaned in disgust. "Can't I go anywhere without running into you?"

"Apparently it is a curse we both suffer," the woman said. "I tire of your face. And now I see I shall have to look upon it twice as much."

Bri said nothing.

"You should count yourself lucky," Kai said. "We're so handsome, many would kill to stare at us both so leisurely."

"I doubt that."

"Bri, this is Xan. She's hideous and old, but sometimes useful. One of Olin's soulless."

Hoping to distinguish himself from his brother, Bri held out his hand. "It's a pleasure to meet you."

She took his hand, her thorny demon's mark on her upper arm looking particularly dull so near his own pulsing mark. "Perhaps I will like you better than your brother. As you can see from his horrified expression, he won't even touch me."

"Why not?" As the handshake ended, Bri saw that Kai did indeed look horrified.

"She's so *old*," he said. "Her hands are all squishy and wrinkled." He shuddered dramatically.

"You can't be serious."

"I don't like it. But occasionally she's not so bad. Her age actually changes. So don't worry if you see her tomorrow and she resembles something a bit more human. It's normal."

Unable to believe he was actually hearing the words coming out of Kai's mouth, Bri gave up on him and turned instead to Xan. "Your age really changes?"

"An unfortunate side-effect of the power granted me by Olin. It is not so bad. The discomfort it causes Kai is worth it most days."

Kai snatched up Bri's wrist. "We're busy, Xan. Go away."

"My pleasure. Though it may interest you to know that Olin has returned."

"Not interested." He pulled Bri along, down the twisting and confusing halls until they reached what Bri reasoned was somewhere deep within the mountain, perhaps even underground. It had been some time since he had seen a window.

Nervously, Bri spun his mother's ring on his left hand and asked her for strength.

"This is my workshop," Kai said, finally. There was nothing but wall all around them, and the stairs from which they had come. "I expected something...more."

Kai rolled his eyes. "Not *here* here. Here." Grabbing Bri once again, Kai set his hand to the wall in front of them and stepped through.

Now this was what Bri had expected. *Labrynths* everywhere; on the walls, on the floor, on the table at the center of the room. Books were stacked in the far corner, and bottles and vials sat both full and empty on the table. More than one had tipped over. Torches burned at steady intervals around the room, lighting the otherwise dark place. It had much the same feel as Dorothea's workshop. What was it with witches and clutter?

"Come see here," Kai said, already pushing papers about on the table.

Bri went to his side, but the papers were jumbles of lines and loops, sometimes at the center, sometimes only drawn along the edge. Everything was in ink, not blood. "What am I looking at?"

"Our future."

"Kai, I don't understand. You can't speak in riddles all the time."

"Look," Kai said, only barely hiding his exasperation. He pulled two papers close to each other, shifting them carefully until the lines of one matched up with the other. "It's a *labrynth*, or it will be. I have to construct the pieces carefully, separately. I wouldn't want it accidentally activating before it was truly time."

"Time for what?"

"For you and me to take back what's ours. I've told you before, Bri," Kai leaned heavily on the table, causing it to creak, "we were not meant to be apart. We're stronger together. And this spell will correct that."

The lines on the page seemed to swirl in Bri's vision. "We're two separate people, Kai. We can't be one."

"Who says we can't? Your power and mine, combined. No one will be able to stand against us."

"I don't care about that kind of thing."

"I do." Kai slung an arm around around Bri's shoulders. "And you're going to help me."

It always felt odd when Kai got so close, when Bri could feel their chests rise and fall together with their breath, feel Kai's excited pulse, as if it were trying to get in time with Bri's own. "What makes you so sure about that?"

"I know how to make you cooperate, brother. I made you come here with me; I can make you agree to more."

Through threats and violence. Kai didn't have to say it for Bri to know it. "How is it we are so different, despite coming from the same womb?"

"A miracle. I know." Kai hurried away, excited and enthused by the prospect. Bri inhaled carefully. His brother didn't know anything. Nothing good. When Kai returned to the table, he had a large jar made of green glass in his hands. "Here. Watch this." He set the bottle on the table and pulled Bri to stand directly next to him. Pulling the cork free, and unwrapping his right hand, he slipped that hand into the neck and splashed about inside for a moment. When he withdrew, his fingers had turned green, but did not drip.

"What is it?"

"A camouflage. I created it. There's a *labrynth* carved into the bottom of the bottle, and the liquid inside is turned into more of a paint. You could color your entire body and hide in the grass in plain sight! I have other colors too."

"What do you use it for?"

Kai shrugged. "Spying. Hiding. Any number of things."

"How long does it last?" Experimentally, he touched his brother's hand, expecting it to be wet and cold. It felt no different. Warm, smooth flesh marred by scars.

"A couple of turns. It depends on how long you soak yourself. But I have another concoction that will remove the color as well."

"Very clever."

"Isn't it? Oh! And this!" Hand still green, Kai ran to one of the many disorganized corners of the room, rummaging around until he found a cloak and then holding it up proudly. It looked just the same as every other cloak Bri had ever seen. "I spelled it to keep cool in Hell. Genius, right? Put on a cloak, get cooler."

"It makes no sense."

"It doesn't have to! That's the best part! I have another one for keeping warm. Well, I spelled it to keep warmer, since cloaks normally warm in the first place. I can make more for you, for when we travel to the mortal realm. It will be winter soon."

Things continued on like that. Kai turned his workshop upside down, selecting things to show Bri, then simply discarding them to move onto the next. By the time he was finished, Bri had seen hats with portals attached to them, stones that could be thrown as exploding weapons, oil lamps that burned twice as long, and an assortment of other things that seemed to have no real purpose other than to expand Kai's repertoire. Despite Bri's caution, his brother's enthusiasm was contagious, and he felt himself begin to smile.

Somewhere along the line, Kai had come across the potion that returned his hand to its normal color. After tossing aside a book that held a spell for creating an army of tin soldiers, Kai rushed back to Bri, taking both his hands and squeezing them tightly. "Don't you see, Bri? Nothing is beyond us!"

"It seems like nothing is beyond you alone. You don't need me. You did all this without me."

"Child's play!" Kai spun away, arms stretched wide. "Making toys and turning myself colors. This is just how I entertain myself when I grow bored. But with you, I can try what I've always dreamt of."

"What's that?"

Calm once again, but grinning, Kai clapped him on the shoulder. "Now, Bri, I can't very well tell you that yet. It would not do to expose all my secrets so soon. After all, we don't yet trust each other. But we will. And then I will tell you everything."

Kai left Bri to his own devices not long after, claiming some all-important errand elsewhere. Unfortunately, he had also slipped through one of his many portals before Bri had a chance to remind him that he did not know his way around. He tried one hall, then another, before experimentally climbing a staircase. Brimstone walls were all that greeted him. There was a door, but Bri didn't dare open it. He knew he hadn't come through it and didn't want to know what lay beyond. The door had been reinforced with metal bars. With no other option, Bri began to retrace his steps.

The sound of light footsteps coming his way froze him in his tracks. He had no idea how the others of this place would react to him. Leave him alone? Mistake him for Kai? Torment him just for fun? He wished Alec or Carma had told him more about Hell and its inhabitants.

But the silk dress that drifted around the corner was familiar, as was the face and the wrinkled hands. Bri relaxed slightly. Xan, at least, didn't seem hostile toward him.

"Lost, are you?" she said as she approached, sounding not the least bit surprised.

"Kai took off before I could ask him how to get back."

"He is inconsiderate like that. Selfish to the core. Be careful he does not leave you somewhere dangerous one day."

"Meaning this place isn't dangerous?" With demons and hellions everywhere, dangerous seemed an appropriate word.

"Not compared to the outside. Here, you are safe." She crept closer than was comfortable, taking Bri's chin in her hand and turning his face this way and that. "You really are identical," she said after a long moment. "It is only the scars that set you apart."

When she released him, Bri took a step back. "It's more than that. I'm not like my brother."

Her lips curled. "Yes. That much is clear in your eyes. You do not have his madness."

"You don't like him."

"Neither do you." She shifted where she stood, as though her back were growing stiff.

"True enough. But I don't think it's all his fault. His childhood was…difficult."

"And yours was any better? Do not fool yourself. Kai has been mad since the womb, that much is clear. Life simply made him worse."

Bri did not disagree, though the thought made him sad. Had their parents known? Was that the real reason for splitting them up?

Xan stared at him, studying him like some specimen on a witch's table. He fidgeted under her gaze for a long moment. "What is it?" he asked when he could not take the silence any longer.

Something had changed in her face. Her expression had softened, and her milky blue eyes had gone unfocused, as if she saw something other than the present. "Hm? Oh." Closing her eyes and giving one quick shake of her head, she squinted at him as though he were suddenly hard to see. "Nothing. It was nothing. For a moment, I thought you reminded me of someone."

"Someone from your past?"

"A past far gone from me."

A child, perhaps? Or a friend, maybe a lover? Bri didn't ask. She had sold her soul, and he had learned from Alec that the circumstances under which most people did so were often the last thing they wanted to talk about.

More footsteps echoed against the walls, these heavy and with an even, swift stride. Xan stiffened, then smiled. "Here comes my master. Have you had the pleasure of meeting him yet?"

"Once, briefly, some time ago." That dark night filled with death, when he had first seen *labrynths* as Kai saw them; alive and vibrant.

"Well, aren't you in for a treat, then." She turned just as Olin appeared, coming around the corner in full armor, his knuckles bloodied and his face covered in dust and dirt. He looked much the same as when Bri had last seen him, standing over them as he and Kai struggled to find their equilibrium after their first real battle of wills. This demon had lifted Kai as if he were nothing more than a doll, and had taken him away without so much as a struggle from Bri's brother.

Where Carma elicited the images of a cunning and seductive demon, one who could convince you to sell your own children for just a moment of her time, this man, this Olin, whose name Bri had heard only in whispers and angry yells, brought to mind what people meant when they said "demon" in a hushed voice, afraid of the dark. Dangerous, violent, mean, yet charming and capable of a misleading smile. Carma might tear your heart out, but you'd smile while she did so. Olin would make sure you screamed the whole way through.

Bri tried to will himself into the wall, wanting nothing more than to disappear. Olin went straight to Xan, taking her face in his hands almost lovingly and kissing her on the mouth. She gasped, arched into him, then settled back to her feet. When he drew away, Bri could feel a tingle on the air, and Xan, though still elderly, looked younger than she had before. The lines in her face had smoothed some, and her grey hair had become a streaked black. She gazed at Olin in pure adoration.

"I have a job for you," Olin said. "Go wait for me in my rooms."

Xan went without question, without hesitation.

Leaving Bri alone, with nothing to stand between him and this demon.

Pulling a handkerchief from inside his breastplate, Olin began wiping the blood from his knuckles. "Kai searched for you a long time. When he was a child, I endured hours of his tantrums whenever you slipped through his fingers."

What does he want? An apology? Bri bit his lip so he wouldn't say anything stupid.

"Have you ever wondered why?"

"Why what?" Bri's voice sounded thin and unformidable even to his own ears.

"Why, that night that Lillianna was killed, and you and Kai lay helpless on the ground, I did not take you as well? I could have."

"It crossed my mind."

Handkerchief now red and black with blood and dirt, Olin slipped it back within his armor and looked at Bri for the first time. His icy eyes seemed to smolder with promises of danger. "It was because I do not need you. Kai needs you, or he believes he does, and I need Kai, but you—you are an extravagance. If having you makes Kai more productive, then I welcome your presence. But make no mistake, young seraph child, the moment you get in my way, the moment you become a hindrance to my plans, I will end you. As I said, I have dealt with Kai's tantrums before. I can do it again. So do not think his reaction would keep you safe. It will not. You remind me of what I left, of what I intend to destroy. And I know your mark all too well." Suddenly he had Bri by the wrist, jerking him forward, his fingers cutting into the thin muscle and flesh of Bri's arm. "You are Carma's creature, and I do not trust her. I will not allow you to go back to her, to tell her of what you see here. When Kai is done with you, I will kill you, and leave her no soul to collect. That is, if Kai hasn't swallowed it already himself."

Olin released Bri, tossing him into the hard brimstone wall. Bri clung to that wall as the demon walked away, leaving him alone. Breathing hurt and came in difficult, struggling bursts. Bri fought the panic, but only just managed to prevent it from overtaking him. For the first time since he had learned the truth, he longed for the safety of being with Kai.

Kai didn't like being kept waiting. He especially didn't like waiting with Xan. Even if she was a bit younger at the moment. Olin's rooms were stark and unadorned in many ways. No extraneous belongings. Just the heads of a few enemies on the walls, along with the horns and teeth and other various parts of creatures he had hunted down and claimed as trophies. Another wall displayed the sword he had carried as a seraph in the Legions. If he touched it now, it burned his flesh, and as it was, the very air of Hell smoked around the blessed thing, but Olin kept it. He said it served as a reminder, not of what he had given up, but of Haven's weakness.

Kai really didn't care. He had flopped down in the only plush armchair Olin possessed, kicking his feet up over one arm and reclining against the other. That left Xan with no other place to sit but one of the hard stone chairs that were placed evenly and strategically around the room. She hadn't chosen one, and had instead taken to wandering, looking at one head, then a set of teeth, then the entire jaw of a monstrous hellion that hung over Olin's desk.

"Where the hell is he?"

"Are you ever going to be anything more than an impatient child?"

"I already am. There are a number of young women who can attest to that. I can be very patient when I want to be." A lesson Lillianna had beaten into him. He knew the value of patience now, but he still didn't like it.

Xan made a sound of disgust. "I suggest you develop a taste for it now, then. When I saw him, he was about to speak with your dear little brother."

Kai stilled, then lifted himself on one elbow to see her better. "Bri? Olin is with Bri?"

"Oh, what's that? Do I detect a hint of concern? I didn't think you had human emotions such as that."

"I'm not concerned. What was he doing?"

"I left, Kai. I don't know what Olin did with him. If you don't want others playing with your newest toy, perhaps you shouldn't leave it to wander around on its own."

Kai snarled at her. He hadn't given a second thought to leaving Bri alone. He had forgotten his brother didn't know his way around. Oh well. Something to correct at another time.

But he didn't exactly trust Olin.

The door opened, and the demon in question entered his rooms just as Kai debated leaving and going in search of Bri at the risk of not being there when Olin arrived. A moot thought now. Olin crossed the room without a word, removing his armor and depositing it on a long side table to be cleaned. Xan said nothing, but Kai had never been one to wait.

"Where the hell have you been? You asked me to meet you here almost a turn ago. And I, being the considerate man I am, got here on time."

"What a miracle," Olin said, flexing his shoulders once free of all the heavy armor. "Lucky for me, since I expected you to be late. I'm sure you enjoyed waiting."

"Much longer and I would have made rubble of your furniture."

"That would have been foolish, since I'm sure you remember what happened the last time you did so."

Now that he mentioned it, Kai did remember, but the memory of all those broken bones and the time it had taken to set them had somehow eluded him before. Odd how that happened. He shrugged it off. "Where is my brother?"

"Exactly where you left him, wandering the halls. But, while he is what we are here to talk about, I wish to speak with Xan first."

Kai knew this game all too well. Olin loved to make him wait, to push his limits. Kai worked hard at looking like he didn't care.

Xan swept her way across the room to her master, face alight with the promise of his attention. "You said you had a job for me?"

"Yes. And one I think you'll find quite appealing. That boy, Bri, he is Carma's, and I know her well enough to know that she will not let him disappear. She will search for him. Send her other soulless after him. I need you to make sure they do not find their way to him."

"You want me to lure them away."

"I don't care how you do it. Just keep the search party away from me and my plans."

Kai closed his eyes. This was all horribly boring.

"You know who—" Xan said.

"Yes," Olin interrupted. "That's is not a problem, is it?"

"Of course not. But...I..."

Silence strung out for some time. Kai kicked his feet where they hung over the edge of the chair, imagining Xan's struggle with what she so desperately wanted to ask. It was amusing. When he was bored enough. Which he was.

"Say it," Olin said. "Ask me."

"You will lend me power, won't you? Enough to prevent the change?"

"Of course."

In the next bit of silence Kai could hear Olin kiss her, and he had to choke back on his gag reflex. Magic touched the air, light at first, then a flood as it filled Xan's body. Kai contemplated taking a nap.

"There," Olin said. "Go now. I want no time wasted."

Xan rushed from the room, her steps light and quick, more like those of a girl. It happened. Nothing to be curious over. With her gone, Kai would be next, and that was more important.

"Is it my turn now?" When a shadow passed over him, Kai cracked open one eye. Olin loomed, sneering.

"Oh, yes. It is your turn. Don't worry, I won't take much of your time. I just want to make sure we are clear on something."

Kai closed his eyes once again. Acting indifferent always pissed Olin off. And that was always fun. Until it wasn't. "Well, out with it then."

"You have your brother now. Get to work."

"I am. You know I am. But I need his cooperation, and that's going to take some time."

"I don't have time, Kai. We are on a deadline. The Restorium could come at any moment. You need to confirm it with him."

He could hear Olin coming closer. "Yeah, yeah."

"And you need to finish the *labrynth*."

"What is it exactly we're clearing up here? You haven't said anything new."

A steel-toed boot nudged his shin. A warning. "Get it done, Kai. Get it done quickly, or I will begin breaking your brother's bones, one by one."

Kai cracked one eye open, willing himself to remain otherwise still. He refused to give Olin the satisfaction of seeing him squirm. "You say that as if I am supposed to care."

Olin gazed down at him, as unreadable as ever. "You care. He's the only thing you do care about, other than power and yourself. But, if that is not enough incentive for you, then I offer you this. Get me my *labrynth* or I will tell your brother what you really intend to do with him."

That bore sitting upright. Kai turned in his chair to face the demon, almost nose to nose. "That will only make him less likely to cooperate, and if he doesn't cooperate, then you may not get your *labrynth*."

"Oh, I'll get my *labrynth*, I have no doubt of that. You will make sure of it. But if I tell him the truth, he will make your life far more difficult than I ever could," Olin smiled. "And that will be satisfaction enough for me."

— CHAPTER NINETEEN —

Alec had always hated Hell. The screams always on the air, the places of torment and suffering, the heat—it was all too much. Every time he was there, he lived in fear of turning a corner and seeing someone he'd known in life. No one could ever be sure what they had done was enough to grant them entrance to Haven. That was left to the discretion of the Reapers. When he had first sold his soul, he'd had nightmares that his brother Marc had been thrown to the fires, made to carry heavy loads through burning cinders, or forced to swim in treacherous waters for all eternity.

Those nightmares had never come to pass. When thinking clearly, Alec knew Marc had been too young, and too kind, to ever end up in Hell. But nightmares were never reasonable. He knew that because the dark dreams had returned in the past days. This time with Bri. And this time, no amount of reasoned thinking could dispel the images. Bri was in Hell; there was no doubt about that.

And Carma had sent Alec alone to find him.

"Go to Hell," she had said. "Leave no stone unturned. Find him. Olin is amassing an army. It's hidden and secret, but there will be trails. And Kai is anything but subtle."

"I am only one man, Carma. How am I supposed to search all of Hell on my own? How am I supposed to find what cannot be found? Bri is with Kai; Kai is with Olin. No one can say where he is."

"Then that gives you a good place to start, doesn't it? Clearly he isn't in the towns and other populated areas."

"And just what will you be doing?" He had seen Dorothea packing up her odds and ends in her workshop that morning.

"Searching for Picadilly. Finding allies. We are running out of time, and without Bri, we have no way of knowing when the Restorium will hit."

And so there he was. Alone. In Hell. He could feel the pull of the place on the empty space where his soul once sat, and the screams of the damned rang in his ears. Shouldering his pack and biting down on his resolve, telling himself over and over again to think not of Carma and her schemes but of Bri, he headed into town. Carma had given him one useful piece of information. Before Pica had disappeared, they had heard something about an army amassing. Alec wanted to hear that gossip for himself.

Three turns of the glass later, his fifth mug of ale empty on the stone table in front of him, Alec had heard nothing. Nothing. Not a damned thing. Four bar fights had broken out over various things—a misplaced word, an incorrect drink, and a case of being in the wrong place at the wrong time. Outside, a pack of canine hellions had charged through the streets, tearing limbs and stealing livestock. Demons and hellions had taken the stage beside the bar, dancing and smiling and then finding themselves laps to sit on while the patrons bought them drinks.

There was no talk of armies. Not even a whisper. Alec tossed his coins onto the bar and stood, heading outside where the residents were still collecting their misplaced hands and feet for reattachment. No one said a word to him as he walked past, quietly heading out of town and onto the open road.

He hoped he didn't run into bandits.

Five days and nothing had changed. Alec trudged over the bare brimstone roads that connected one Hell town to the next, the emptiness within him straining to be filled. He had barely slept. When he did, the power in the air used the moments of his deepest sleep to try to slip within him. Too many times he had woken to burning palms and a swirl of heat in his chest. He could not be overcome by the power. So he slept as little as possible, always sitting up, so that when he drifted off the sag of his head would wake him once again. It wasn't a perfect plan, but it was all he had.

A small penance for being stupid enough to let Bri go off on his own.

As he walked, the air shifting from hot to cold with little warning, he saw a group moving against the horizon. Maybe a dozen, judging by the size and shape. Almost certainly a group of mercenaries or bandits. His hope to avoid such characters had gone unfulfilled. The long cut along his left bicep twinged with the memory of the first group he had encountered. There would be no avoiding this one. On the left side of the road, a lake of steaming lava churned and boiled, popping and jumping up at the souls who had been stranded on small islands throughout. Some screamed—the newest, most likely— but most sat silently, used to the torment and subdued by it. To the right, a crater sank into the ground, so deep that its bottom could not be seen. Gusting wind swirled about within, picking up anything in its path and tossing it about. These souls reached out for help despite years of knowing none would come. At times, one would come close to the road, a hand only inches from Alec's side. He did not acknowledge it. Nothing could be done to help, and he would only get himself sucked in.

He hoped Kai was wise enough to keep Bri from trying to help all the souls of Hell. If he wasn't, then Bri was already lost to both of them.

Alec could not feel the heat of the lava, or the force of the wind. The cold air of the road sheltered him from both. The group up ahead grew closer with each step he took, dressed in thick furs and heavy boots. No doubt they knew quite well how to throw any wandering traveler into either of the torments nearby. But why were they standing in full view of any who came by? Why not hide in wait?

Another dozen steps and the reason became apparent. They were already busy.

Their taunting and demands became distinguishable above the holler of the gusts and the screams of those surrounded by lava. A lithe body was tossed about between them, jostled and spun around until, no doubt, they lost much sense of balance and direction. Alec had sworn to himself that he would not get involved with anyone else's problems. Finding Bri was all that mattered.

But he wouldn't be able to get by without being seen.

He walked up to the group of bandits, casual and without a word. A hellion with burning red eyes and the beak of a hawk noticed him first, squawking and looking him over carefully. "Well, what have we here?" he said, the words sounding funny coming from a mouth with no lips. No doubt someone had given him the ability to speak human languages with a *labrynth*. "Going somewhere?"

"Just passing through," Alec said, adjusting the weight of his pack on his shoulder.

Another bandit, this one a demon with ashen hair and skin, joined his beaked comrade. "There's a toll for passing through here."

The entire group turned their attention to Alec now, ceasing their mistreatment of the other, smaller traveler. Their victim hung limply from the arms of the largest of the bandits. Long hair covered the defeated face, but Alec could see now the skirt that covered slim legs, and the slender fingers of one hand that had lost its glove. A woman.

Suddenly Alec had three more bandits closing in on him. "I really don't want any trouble," he said.

"Then make this easy on yourself and hand over whatever you have of value." The hand extended to him was taloned.

A warmth pulsed in Alec's palms. "I have nothing."

"Nothing? Then what's this?" A small bandit, no taller than Alec's hip and covered in scales, darted toward him, then back again. Alec felt the slightest touch at his pocket before it was gone, and the clinking of delicate metal reached his ears. The little hellion grinned as he held up his stolen prize, and Alec's chest twisted with shock, fear—and burning anger.

His locket.

"Give that back."

"No," said the small hellion.

"That should do as payment," the beaked one said.

Alec shook his head. "I cannot leave without it."

"What are you going to do about it?" He didn't see who had spoken, but they all laughed in response.

He didn't give them a second chance. It was so easy to flood himself with power, to let it slide up his arms and into his legs. The scaled flesh of the bandit who had taken the locket smoked as he burned through the wrist, forcing him to release it. The first two bandits who tried to stop him went down with powerful kicks to their cores. It had been so long since Alec had used the power this way, let so much of it in, yet the feeling was as familiar as breathing. He fought off the next attacker, then shoved his locket deep within his pocket once again. He could not lose her again, would not.

The glint of light on steel. Someone had drawn a blade.

"Stop!"

That voice...

The woman, still held tightly by the largest of the bandits, pushed her hair back from her face and stood tall. Her blue eyes seemed darker in Hell, and the light of the lava pit reflected off them and her ebony hair. She looked right at Alec, and his heart stopped. "He's with me."

"Ariadne."

More laughter erupted from the group, and for the first time the giant, hairy hellion that held Ariadne opened his mouth. "What does that matter? You'll just make things worse for him, admitting that. You owe us, and we can take it from either your flesh, or his. Or both."

Damnit. What the hell had she gotten herself into?

"I told you, I can get you what you want. But I need more gold first."

"No. No more gold. You've run out of time, girl."

"You're being foolish."

"Don't make bargains you can't keep." He lifted a knife in his oversized hand.

Alec remembered another time, a time long lost to the past, when he had come across a girl making foolish bargains that ended with her on the wrong end of a blade. He had broken his rule of non-involvement then, too.

The Hell-power burned as he called it again, washing over his mind until thoughts were nothing more than sharp commands. He took out three more bandits before they had time to react. Taking a fallen dagger from the ground, he rammed it into the throat of the hellion holding Ariadne by the arm, then grabbed her himself as the giant fell to the ground.

"Run," he said.

She did so.

The bandits gave chase, but the road was narrow and so two could move through far more easily than half a dozen. Alec led Ariadne down around the gusting crater, away from the lava pit and toward a dense forest. The air grew even colder, then absolutely frigid. Ice gathered on the ground, causing them to slip. One particular corner they took too fast, and with their balance lost, they skidded around, knocking into a thick black tree that grew along the edge of the road. Even then, Alec couldn't help but note how the lines of her body still fit so well against his.

She steadied herself with a hand on his chest, then caught her breath. "I can still hear them."

"They'll chase us for some time I imagine."

"There's a place we can hide. Come." Grabbing his hand, she led him back to the road. They ran another treacherous course over the ice, the cold air making Alec's lungs burn. Then, without warning, Ariadne turned off the road, twisting through the trees. Alec tripped and fell, rolling and landing square on his back in some deep hole beneath a fallen tree. Ariadne came down on top of him, smiling.

"What the—"

"Shh." She silenced him further with a kiss. It was like fire in the cold. Alec leaned into her, wrapping his arms tightly around her and pulling her close enough that he was sure she could not disappear without his knowing. The warmth of her body called to his, and the power he had called earlier slipped away.

Only after the telltale sounds of the bandits running past and away had come and gone did she break their kiss and allow them both to breathe easy once more. "Just like old times, huh?" she said with a wide smile.

"The first time was understandable, but I taught you better than that."

She shrugged. "Conning has been a bit out of practice for me."

"Even as a soulless?"

"Even then, if you'd believe it. How did you find me?"

He couldn't stop touching her. Only now did he realize he had begun to think that night on the bridge a dream, an imagining. Her skin was soft under his fingers, her pulse strong at her throat. "I didn't," he said. "That's not why I'm here."

She drew back. "Well, that's disappointing."

"That isn't to say I'm not happy about it."

"For two people no longer aligned with Fate," she said, "we certainly do keep finding one another."

"A sign?"

"I should hope so." Shifting her weight—and pressing parts of them together that gave rise to distracting feelings in the process—she arranged her hair over her shoulder, out of her face. "So what *did* bring you here, then?"

For a brief moment, he'd almost been able to forget the constant anxiety of his mission there. "Bri. He's been taken. I need to find him."

"Taken?"

"It's a very long story."

"One you'll have to tell me. But I don't think it's quite safe for us to leave here yet, and we'll freeze to death if we don't do something about it." One of her legs wrapped about his.

"We can't freeze to death, we're immortal." Facts couldn't distract him from desires.

"Play along, Alec. I've missed you." She kissed his cheek. "I searched for you again after that night, but you were never in Callay."

"I had to leave rather suddenly."

"But you're back now."

"Yes."

"And we've found each other again."

"Yes."

"If we're stuck here," she said, kissing his neck, "we might as well celebrate."

Alec's first instinct was to protest—Bri was more important. But she was right, they couldn't leave yet. Enough time hadn't passed. They would only run into the bandits again. And it seemed her hands had forgotten nothing in two thousand years. Nor had her lips. Other instincts rose up, squashing the more logical ones that had cropped up first. Grabbing her by the waist, he flipped their position, pinning her beneath him. To keep her warm, of course.

— CHAPTER TWENTY —

Bri, you're not concentrating."

"I am."

"You're not. I can feel your thoughts all over the place."

"I am not a witch, Kai. This isn't exactly my area of expertise."

"No, it isn't, is it? You're far more experienced in completely losing yourself and falling in and out of visions so fast you make *my* head spin."

They had been at this for more turns of the glass than Bri cared to count. And it wasn't even the first day. It was the seventh. Each day Kai brought Bri down to his workshop, sat him atop a *labrynth* scribed into the stone floor, knelt in front of him, took his hands, and demanded Bri's full concentration. Nothing ever came of it other than arguments. The *labrynth* was supposed to let them access the power of the other, but Bri never felt anything more than the discomfort of sitting on unforgiving stone. Kai had bled them both, first in small amounts, then larger when that didn't work. The spell remained quiet and inactive.

Bri wrenched his hands from his brother's and stood, his muscles protesting after so much stillness. "This isn't working, Kai. Try something else."

"The *labrynth* should be good. It should work."

"But it's not. Maybe you made a mistake."

A visible tension ran through Kai's body at that. "I do not make mistakes."

"Then what do you call this?"

"Your lack of focus."

Yes. My lack of focus on your power which I have absolutely no interest in. Bri bit his tongue so he wouldn't say any of that. It wouldn't do him any good. Kai had already made it quite clear he didn't care what Bri cared about. Bri was supposed to care about what Kai wanted for them both, and nothing more.

"Kai, we've been at this for days. Neither of us is at his best anymore. Let's take a break."

"We don't have time for a break."

"Of course we do. We'll get something to eat, and then we'll try again."

"I'm not hungry."

"Well, I am." He looked at his hands. They shook even when he tried to keep them still. "I'm not used to living in this realm. It's taking more out of me than I thought it would."

At that, Kai stood and came to him, taking his brother's hands in his as though holding them would allow him to feel the tremors. "You should have said something."

"I just did." These were the times Bri hated the most. The times when he could see something of genuine concern in his brother's face. He hated them, because he so wanted to believe that Kai could feel things, that they could have a normal relationship despite the madness that infected him. He hated them because in these moments, Bri almost believed he could save his brother. Almost.

"If you'd let me mark you—"

And then there were moments such as this. "No. No marks. That was our deal."

Kai dropped his hands, shoulders slumping in exasperation. "Bri, I could make things so much easier for you."

"No marks."

"Why are you so stubborn?"

"Apparently it's a family trait."

"Fine," he drew out the word into a whine. "Be difficult. At least let me scribe something into your clothes." He reached for Bri's sleeve.

Bri stepped back, angling his arm out of reach. "No. Not until I can understand what you're scribing."

"Do you really have to distrust me that much?"

"Considering the fact that the only reason I am here is because you threatened innocent people, yes."

"Always bringing that up. And here I thought we were finally getting along."

There was no response to that. Nothing that wouldn't escalate the conversation far beyond this sibling banter—if that's what it could be called. Bri breathed deep and shook out his hands, pacing the length of the room and putting as much distance between himself and the *labrynth* as he could manage. He had been in Hell with his brother for nearly two weeks, and he was at his wit's end. His days were spent with Kai, watching him scribe and pretending to focus on whatever it was Kai wanted. In truth, he had felt the spark of what he suspected Kai wanted him to latch onto after only the first day, but he had refused to touch it, feigned ignorance. The longer he could keep Kai wandering about in the metaphorical dark, the better.

At night—the nights Kai allowed him to sleep—he thought of Ella and the others he had left behind. She was safe, he was sure of that. It was all he would allow himself to believe. He had kept her out of sight, fearing what Kai would do if he saw them together. He hoped whatever meeting they had had on the street was brief enough that Kai suspected nothing of their friendship. If Kai knew...

Thoughts like that were quickly done away with. He had to keep a clear head.

Ella would have told Alec what happened. Surely Alec had already started looking for him. Would he know to look in Hell? Even if he did, how long would it take to search? Hell was an entire realm; Bri knew that. What he didn't know was just how large it was. As big as the mortal realm? People claimed there were lands beyond the sea no one had ever laid eyes on. In all of history, no mapmakers had ever filled in what came after the sea. In Xia-Lo, Enlai had told him that his people had come from a large island nation to the west, and there was even more hidden behind the horizon. If Hell was as large as all that, it would take an eternity for Alec to find him.

Which meant he had to do something to help himself.

"Kai, you said there were towns."

"Yes. What about them?" Kai stood over his *labrynth* once again, chewing his fingertip bloody as he spent most of his attention on the lines and turns he had drawn. Bri had learned to recognize the degrees of his brother's concentration. At the moment, Kai was listening with only a small fraction of his attention, far more engrossed in his own thoughts than Bri's words.

Perfect. "Take me. You said you would. I could use a meal other than the gruel the cook here makes, and I'm tired of these clothes. I want something of my own." He still wore Kai's clothes, and every time he looked in a mirror he nearly jumped out of his skin thinking Kai watched him from the glass once again. He needed to look like himself again. "And I dare say you could use the time away as well. Clear your head. Get a fresh look at things."

Kai said nothing, his gaze completely glazed over as he saw things few others would understand. Blood ran down his hand to his wrist.

"Kai." Bri put some force behind his voice. His twin's constant disregard for bleeding unnerved him.

"Hm? What?"

"You're bleeding."

"I'm always bleeding."

"Fine, then, but it's wasted at the moment. It won't help you think. Wrap up your hand and let's go."

"Go where?"

"To town."

Kai dislodged his finger from his teeth and crinkled his nose in confusion. "We're going to town?"

The benefits of dealing with a mad person. Bri thought all his years with Dorothea had made him grow used to it, but looking at Kai now he couldn't help but feel a little sad. That didn't stop him from proceeding. "Yes. You just said you wanted to go to get something to eat."

A low growl echoed through the room. Bri knew it hadn't come from his stomach, though he shared the sentiment. "Well, all right then. Let's go." He brushed past Bri, heading straight for the portal that would let them out into the hall beyond.

They took another portal into town. Bri was getting used to the strange feeling of slipping through reality, disappearing in once place and reappearing in another, but he didn't like it much. It reminded him too much of falling into the myst.

"Is town really so far that a portal is necessary?" Bri asked, taking a moment to steady his legs.

"This one is." Kai picked at the fresh bandages on his hand.

"What do you mean?"

"I mean, this town is very far away from where we were." Something in his voice indicated that they were not to use specifics when speaking so far from Olin's lair. "There are, obviously, towns that are much closer, but I don't like them as much, and it's better not to be seen in the same place over and over again."

"I didn't realize you were hiding."

Kai shrugged. "I don't care one way or the other, but I have my orders. Come on, the walk from here isn't long. I know a lovely little tavern run by a young demon girl who makes the very best pie."

Suddenly Bri worried about Hellish cuisine. Carma generally ate the same as they did at home, but that didn't mean it was the same for demons in Hell. He hoped he hadn't made a mistake.

The town reminded him of the settlements in the Frontland, neatly spaced along a straight road, every other building a tavern or inn. Everything was made of stone to prevent burning. The heat rose off the streets, making it hard to breathe. Already, Bri could feel the sweat running down the back of his neck. Hellions wandered, some nothing more than beasts of burden, resembling horses and oxen. Others walked upright, nodding to those they passed and engaging in conversation. Bri had to remind himself not to stare when he saw one particular hellion with large antlers, thick tusks descending from her lips and a whip-like tail curling in the air behind her.

Kai grabbed him by the elbow and steered him away. The doors to the tavern swung open, then closed again on their own once they were through. Bri was struck immediately by the sudden change in the air. It was cool. Comfortable. More like the mortal realm on a spring day.

"Friends, I have returned!" Kai announced himself, flinging his arms wide.

The tavern patrons gave an uproarious response, cheering and raising their classes. Laughter followed, along with the splashing of drinks and the thumping of fists.

Grinning, Kai led Bri to the bar where a pretty demon girl leaned far over on her arms, emphasizing the swell of her breast for her patron. "Little Kailas. It took you long enough to return to me." When she smiled, her teeth were all fangs behind black lips.

"I am sorry, my dear," Kai said, approaching and leaning over the bar in a mimic of her own posture. "Business. You know how it is." He curled his fingers into her long, loose, black hair.

She crooked a finger under his chin, running a single claw back and forth. "That I do. What can I get for you?"

"My brother and I are in sore need of a decent meal."

"Brother?" A flick of her eyes left Bri on the receiving end of a cat-like gaze. "My, my. Two of you. I didn't know life could be so generous."

"He's not as much fun as I am," Kai said.

"What a shame." She flicked her tongue over Kai's lips, then slid back off the bar. "I'll get you both something. Don't go anywhere."

"Wouldn't dream of it." Kai sat on a nearby stool before patting the one beside him. "Sit, Bri. You're in for a treat."

"I thought you said it was better not to be seen in the same place over and over again."

"It's not. I haven't been here in some time. But a man needs somewhere to go for companionship. This town is mine. No one will speak a word of my presence."

"And why is that?" Bri joined his brother and sat.

"Notice how lovely it is in here?"

"You mean the temperature?"

"Of course."

Bri breathed deeply of the cool air. "I take it that's your doing, then. A *labrynth*?"

Kai nodded. "Everyone loves me here. All the businesses have this little spell."

"A bribe to keep quiet."

"One favor for another."

"Friendship is more than a series of favors."

"No, it isn't. And don't go all serious on me, Bri. I want to actually enjoy my time here."

Deciding it would be best not to push his twin's limits, Bri ran his hand along the bar idly. Then stopped. He had been so distracted by the people and Kai's antics with the barmaid that he hadn't noticed before. Hadn't noticed the nature of the stool he sat upon. Wood. Everything was wood. And it didn't burn, because of Kai's spell.

"See?" Kai said, apparently noticing Bri's admiration. "I do such nice things here."

In return for their vow of silence regarding your presence. Bri followed the grain with his fingers, marveling at the smoothness. It had been polished and treated in the same manner as in Callay. Not only that, but not a single patron had defaced the bar in any way. No chips, no carvings, no evidence of brawls involving knives. At least they appreciated what Kai had done for them.

But that gave Bri an idea.

The demon girl returned, placing two mugs of ale down in front of them. "There you are, boys. Food will be along shortly."

"Thank you, love," Kai said, charming as ever. He took a drink, wiped his mouth on the back of his hand, staining his bandage, then crooked a thumb at Bri. "Let me introduce you properly. This is my brother, Bri. Bri, this is Fauna, prettiest thing this side of the void."

"He thinks his flattery will keep him in my good graces," she said, once again settled on the bar.

"Well, I certainly don't want to be anywhere else, do I?"

"Life is more fun when we're not trying to kill each other. Though those times do have their moments," she allowed.

"It would be a shame if I had to kill you, darling," Kai said over his mug.

"A bigger shame if I had to kill you. My bar would be hot again."

"Gods forbid."

Laughing, she retreated once again to the kitchen.

Kai leaned close to Bri, whispering, though Bri doubted he would be heard by anyone else anyway. A loud argument had started up behind them. "She was a seraph of chastity, of all things. Most days I hardly believe it."

"That's none of my business, Kai."

"Sure it is." He clinked his mug against Bri's. "Drink up. I'm hoping you're more fun drunk."

"I think I'll leave the fun to you, thanks."

Kai groaned. "You're so boring. Always serious and brooding. Cut it out. Spend an hour with Fauna, that should fix you right up."

"No, thank you."

"You're right. I don't really want to share her anyway. I'll find you someone else." He began twisting about on his stool, searching the room for a candidate.

Bri let him. It gave him the chance to experimentally dig his fingernail into the underside of the wood. Soft. Pliable. Good.

Fauna brought their food. Just the smell of it made Bri's mouth water, and any fears he had of Hell's food being much different from the mortal realm left him the moment he saw the potato and steak. Imported from the mortal realm? He cut his meat quickly, while Kai and Fauna engaged in more flirtation. Once finished, he tucked the knife subtly into his other hand and under the edge of the bar. As he ate—the food even better than it smelled—he began carefully, quietly, digging the tip of the knife into the soft wood.

"People are saying you're up to something," Fauna said, now actually sitting on her bar, right beside Kai's plate of food which he yet to barely touch.

"Me? Up to something?" Kai ran his fingers up and down her thigh where a slit in her skirt left it exposed.

"That's not the part that surprises me. You're always up to something."

Kai chuckled. "Then why bring it up?"

"Because people are talking. They don't say your name—they don't know it—but the rumors speak of witchcraft all over Hell."

"That's not me." He sounded oddly sincere.

"No?"

"Nope. I've been keeping to myself as of late."

"Then what other witch is here?"

Another witch. Dorothea?

"Good question." Kai tilted his head to the side. "What craft is happening?"

"Traps. Locator spells. Hellions vanishing in plain sight as they walk down a crowded street."

"Oh, wait. Some of that is me."

"Only some?"

"Only some," Kai admitted. "Old games I used to play as a child. I had forgotten about them."

"Well, they're drawing attention now. What if this other witch is looking for you?"

"Darling," he drew himself up on his stool, kissing the side of her neck, "there is no witch in any realm who can stand against me. I made sure of that long ago. I have nothing to worry about."

The atmosphere degraded from there. Bri finished his work beneath the edge of the bar and set the knife down so he could use that hand to block his view of his brother and the demon girl. He knew better than to say anything about it. Kai would only ensure he grew more uncomfortable.

To distract himself, he ran his thumb along his handiwork beneath the bar, checking the accuracy and detail. It was clear enough. Out of sight. He would have to hope that if it were detected, it would be only by the one person he intended it for.

— CHAPTER TWENTY-ONE —

The laughter coming from the workshop beneath the manor had escalated from annoying to irritating. Carma had put up with it for nearly a week, but now she was finished. Done. There would be no more.

Dressing gown wrapped tightly about herself, she made her way outside in the dead of night. She had been awake, thinking, planning. Decisions needed to be made, and she had to make them, no matter how much she wished it otherwise.

Staring into the flickering flame of the single candle that had lit her room, she had realized what needed to be done. The very thought alone put a bad taste in her mouth. Her plan was most likely suicidal. She would try, regardless.

But first, she had to deal with the witch.

"Dorothea!" Carma stormed down the steps into the workshop, nearly stumbling on a number of vials that had been smashed along the way. The room was brightly lit, fires burning in every corner. Fires, not lamps. Dorothea's long scribing table was caked with wax and blood, and bowls filled with dark liquid had been lined up along one side. The witch stood before that table, stark naked, hands covered in blood, laughing.

"Blistering godflesh, what the hell are you doing? Are you mad? Trying to kill us all?"

Dorothea's laughter cut off short. She snapped her head around so quickly Carma was surprised she didn't break something. Clarity blazing in her grey eyes, she dropped her bloody hands to her sides. "The residents of this place are not so easy to kill."

"You could still burn the entire place down around us. Put out those fires immediately."

"I cannot."

"Why not?"

Dorothea's lips curled in something that might have been a smile, and it chilled Carma's normally hot blood. "Because I am not done playing with the naughty little witch."

"The naughty little—stop this immediately. He has Bri. Do not anger him."

"He is a child, and he must be taught that there are consequences to the kind of magic he seeks."

"Let nature dole those out," Carma said. The last thing she needed was any of the game pieces shifting too far too soon.

"So careful," Dorothea said, though she swept a hand over a *labrynth* on the table and the fires went out, plunging the room into a dimly lit darkness. "You always were a cautious one. Your recklessness an act."

Carma bristled, feeling her power creep across her skin, changing her form slightly, and bringing her claws to her hands. "Just because we are alone does not mean you can speak truths."

"Do not worry. I do not know your truths any better than Alec. I simply have different information from which to glean my conclusions." Walking around the length of her table, she dragged a finger along the edge, small sparks of magic jumping between her flesh and the wood.

"You are clear tonight. Why?"

"Because I must be."

"Have you found Picadilly yet?"

"No." Dorothea stopped, fingers working against the table top a moment, then going still once more. "I have locator spells all over Hell, but they have detected nothing."

Carma cursed, clenching her fist until she felt her claws appear and dig into her palm. "Where in all the realms could she be?"

"We are pawns in a dangerous game, Carma. And I feel the end nearing."

"We're not ready."

208 • KATE MARTIN

"You are not ready. I am ready when you are."

A stillness came over the room at that. Carma went over the fading words in her mind multiple times to be sure she had heard them correctly. "You did it? You have the *labrynth*?"

"I have the shell with which to confine and redirect the *labrynth*. I can do what you asked of me."

The feeling bubbled up from inside her. Slowly at first, then faster and steadier. Her chest shook, and her power gathered more strongly. She covered her mouth with her clawed hand as the laughter came forth. Such relief.

Dorothea huffed. "And they say *I* am mad."

Collecting herself was more difficult than Carma would have anticipated, but she did not care. Dorothea had the *labrynth*; they could change the course of the future. All she needed now were her pieces in the proper positions. Which meant taking back what had been stolen from her.

"Well done, Dorothea. I knew you would not fail me."

"Bah." The old woman waved her off and began wrapping her bleeding hands.

"And your timing is perfect. I reached my decision concerning our next move just tonight."

"And what move is that?"

"Have you ever met a god?"

Days were difficult to track in Hell. In some places the light remained unending, and in others there was total darkness. Then there were the spots where light and dark mixed and flashed together, lasting a turn here, two there, then perhaps twelve, never the same. As such, Alec found it hard to know how long Bri had been left in Kai's clutches, and his worry and anxiety over what that mad witch might be up to kept him from getting much sleep.

Wound together with those dark thoughts, however, was the strange and dreamlike joy of having Ariadne back at his side once again.

The town they were currently passing through had a market at the center that boasted trinkets and delicacies from the mortal realm, and dark potions and scheming tricks constructed by witches who hid in The Wilds. They had hoped to find something that could aid then in their search for Bri, but so far, nothing of real power and turned up. Ari had stopped at one stall that claimed to have vials of hair from the gods, including their own god Cel-Eza, who had been dead and gone for many centuries.

She held up a vial for Alec to inspect, the gleaming hair within suspended in a blue liquid. "Do you think it's real?"

"How could it be? Inaseri threw Cel-Eza's head into the sea, where everything then burned. I don't see how any hair could be left after that."

The hellion selling the hairs leaned over his table, one crooked horn making his one crooked eye look almost centered on his green face. "Perhaps my stock predates the god's death, eh? Ever think of that?"

Alec looked over the scrying bowls and baskets of teeth that accompanied the remainder of the hellion's merchandise. "I think you've clearly been questioned before and you're smart enough to have ready answers."

The merchant just laughed. "You've been around a while; I can see you'll be hard to convince. I'll make you a good deal on it."

Alec wasn't interested in buying.

"How much do you want for it?" Ariadne asked, clearly not of the same mind.

The hellion turned its sights on her. "Ah, a lady of good taste, and quick timing. You are smarter than your lover here."

Ariadne leaned forward a bit, lowering her voice as though they shared some secret. "I would be a fool to take a lover otherwise, would I not?"

Alec held his tongue. Her words smacked of familiarity. Old, ancient, a game he hadn't strategized in a long time.

"Indeed, lady, indeed. I shall make you an even better deal. One time only. Just for you."

"Name your price then," she said, rolling the vial between her fingers.

She'd noticed something, something of value, and she was giving Alec the opportunity to investigate without the hellion noticing. Alec ran his gaze over the table once more, wondering what he had missed, shifting his weight so that he mirrored Ari's angle, hoping it would reveal something previously hidden.

"For you, miss," the hellion merchant said, "the vial will cost you only two single strands of your own beautiful hair."

Hell had no currency other than secrets and power.

Ariadne shook her head. "Unfortunately, that is not something I can pay. I have a master, you see, and my body is not mine to barter away. Might I make a counteroffer?"

Alec bristled at the reminder of her demon master, of the fact that she had sold herself away in order to search for him, and now answered to some creature she refused to reveal to him.

But Bri was more important in the moment, and when he shifted his weight once more, he noticed a flash of light behind one of the scrying bowls just at the edge of the table.

"The lady may counter," said the merchant, "but I cannot promise I will accept."

"Of course not," Ari said. "But I think I can entice you well enough." She looked around quickly, then leaned forward on the table, her one hand pushing aside the bowl Alec had just taken notice of. A smaller bowl, made entirely of gold, its center no bigger than the pad of Alec's thumb became visible. It hummed with power when he focused on it.

"How about a secret?" Ari offered. "I have many, and they are tied to powerful things and powerful people."

The hellion seemed cautiously intrigued. "I would need to hear the secret first, of course, to determine it's worth."

"But once you have the secret, you'll have your payment, and I intend to get what I paid for."

"I'll let the lady leave with something, no mistake," the merchant said, his single eye sparkling with delight. "But it might not be that particular vial."

Ari seemed to consider this a moment, then nodded. "Agreed." Then she leaned in close to whisper in the hellion's long black ear, choosing the side that then hid Alec from view.

He pocketed the small bowl.

A gasp escaped the merchant's lips as Ariadne drew back once again, turning into a delighted laugh. "Oh, my lady," he said, clapping his six-fingered hands together, "if that is truth then you deal in far darker dealings than I!"

Ariadne smiled, still leaning against the table, "This is mine then?"

"A fair trade, a fair trade," the merchant said, nodding and waving her off. "I do hope we have reason to do business again someday."

"We shall see about that," Ari said. "Come, my love." She took Alec by the arm, leading him away from the stall.

Alec knew his part was not yet finished. "What did you tell him?" His voice was low and dark, and he glanced over his shoulder at the satisfied hellion for good measure, receiving a wave and a grin in return.

"None of your concern, dearest," Ariadne assured him. "It had nothing to do with you, certainly."

They traveled the market and turned two more corners and streets before Alec dared to think they had enough space between themselves and the merchant. "What did you tell him?"

Ari spun around, a length of red silk stretched between her arms, hiding the bottom half of her face. "A secret too scandalous to speak aloud in a market for sure," she said. "But it will certainly start a few rumors, hopefully they will outpace anything we are about to do. You got the bowl, I presume?"

Alec patted his pocket where the small bowl sat, warm and humming in wait. "It's been a long time since I've done anything like that."

"That's a surprise. You were always so good at it. And after all," she pulled two vials from her pocket, letting the red slip drops over her arm, "you were the one who taught me."

"A second?"

Ariadne shrugged, setting two giant emeralds inscribed with runes down in exchange for her silk. "Just in case they're real. Cel-Eza doesn't deserve to be used by his kind down here. We were devoted in life, and perhaps in this afterlife as well, we are the better caretakers." Vials safely back in her pocket, and silk wrapped about her shoulders, Ari took his arm and led him out of town. It was a clean escape, but Alec couldn't help but think of how many times they'd had to run from a con, ending breathless and laughing with their plunder safely in hand.

"Now," she said once they had left the market behind, "let's find a quiet spot and see if that scrying bowl can tell us anything."

Three more turns and one loop and it was finished. Kai admired his own handiwork in the dim light of his workshop, impressed with how swiftly he had solved the problem of intertwining two forces that were so fundamentally different. Magic—*labrynths*—was a source of life. It was one of the reasons why a witch became useless if a demon took their soul. The soul charged a body with life, animated it and sustained it. When one became soulless, the soul was exchanged for the power of Hell and the demon master. That became what gave life to the body, but it was an illusion, a life not true, and could only be maintained as long as the original soul still existed. Some demons ate away at souls, consumed them, leaving the soulless to wither and die over time. The smart demons had found a way around that problem.

Death would take what was hers. She did not like being cheated. And Kai had long ago sensed her mark on his brother. She pulled at him, drew him closer and closer to the edge even though she would never successfully pull him over as long as Carma's deal held power. This made Bri weak, ill, in a constant state of struggle against that which was natural. Everything died. Even seraph. Even gods. Only The One stood outside the cycle, though some argued otherwise. The Silent One had been silent for some time. Perhaps even the Great Maker had to die.

Bri would not die. Not if Kai had anything to say about it. This *labrynth* was the first step. Kai could hold things alive within his *labrynths*—that was easy. He had done so many times, keeping hearts beating for Lillianna, and binding the life force of nine people to her as she ascended to godhood.

Only to be killed by Carma and her friends. And Olin. Kai would not soon forget his betrayal. He thought of the ashes down below, hidden well within the depths of Hell's substance. The Mother Demon had seen better days, but there was progress. Most days he could make out the shape of fingernails and individual strands of hair among the ash.

This *labrynth* would help with that too.

"Bri! Bri, come here and see."

His brother picked himself up from the floor, having propped himself up against the far wall of Kai's workshop. He looked terrible.

Pale and exhausted, moving so slowly he could have been a corpse. "What is it?" Bri asked, sounding just as tired as he looked.

"You look awful," Kai said.

"Yes, well, I'm not accustomed to living in Hell. Nor am I as good at being bled every day as you are."

That drove Kai's attention to the bandages he had wrapped around his brother's hands and forearms. He couldn't help but be a little pleased. They looked so much more alike now. As promised, he had taken Bri to buy clothes, despite the lack of necessity. His clothes fit his brother fine. But Bri wanted his own, and he had done everything he could to look as different as possible. Which wasn't very different at all. There were few choices when dressing to fight the heat. Bri had ended up with a white shirt, loose like Kai's but with a higher neckline that could button at the throat. Kai had never seen it done up. Their pants were the same light, brown linen, and now with the bandages, there were few differences to be seen.

"I forget you can be so fragile," Kai said, though he was glad his brother had given him little resistance when he wanted so much of his blood. "I haven't bled you too badly though, have I? I know a witch can give more than a human, but you are not human either."

"It makes me tired," Bri said. "And the pain from all the cuts doesn't help matters." He leaned heavily against the table, closing his eyes and taking a deep breath.

Pain? Kai never felt any pain. It had never occurred to him that cutting could hurt.

"Don't you feel it?" Bri said after a moment, staring at him with a look sad disbelief.

"Feel what?"

"The pain."

"No. Why would I?"

"You cut yourself and feel nothing?"

Kai began to answer quickly, then stopped himself. Something in Bri's expression made him think carefully about the matter. Nothing obvious came to him. He had felt pain plenty of times, mostly at the other end of Olin's fists, but never when he scribed. If he concentrated very hard, he supposed there was something of a dull ache in his fingertips and along his arms. Nothing worth calling pain. "No. Nothing."

"I guess I shouldn't be surprised. Dorothea never seems aware of it either. I suppose you can't be, if you need to cut into yourself as much as you do."

"Not all witches are as active as I am. And I can bleed myself further than any other."

"Such a thing to be proud of."

"If you're finished being judgmental and whiny, I have something to show you."

Bri gestured for him to go ahead. Kai stepped aside enough so that his brother could see what he had scribed into the table. "Here," he said. "Look."

Still using the table for support, Bri leaned over, squinting his tired eyes. "What am I looking at? Aside from yet another *labrynth?*"

"See this here?" Kai pointed to one particular turn in the spell, where it backtracked over itself, but maintained two distinct lines. Two lines, occupying one space. "It calls Death."

"Why would you want to call Death?"

"To kill."

"You can't tell Death who to kill."

"Of course I can. As surely as I can drive a knife through a man's heart and bring Death upon him, so too can I use this *labrynth* to do the same."

Bri went very still at his side. "You've created a weapon."

Sometimes Bri had a strange way of labeling things. He'd created a *tool.* There were a number of ways to use it. "All someone would have to do is walk across this, and he would drop dead instantly. No explosion, no light or fire or anything else that could be seen. Just Death. Or, at least, that's what I'm hoping. Want to go with me to try it out?"

His brother had pressed his lips very tightly together before he spoke. "You used my blood for this?"

"Yes. Yours and mine. Death marked you, so your blood gave me the link I needed."

"Meaning you need my blood to make this work?"

"No. Not anymore. I just needed your blood to decode Death this first time. Why don't you look happier about this?"

Bri had sunken some while Kai spoke, both arms straining to hold him up as he leaned heavily on the table. Now, he turned just his head to look at his twin, paler than he had been before. "You want me to be happy? Happy that you used my blood to find a new way to kill people?"

"Don't you understand what this means?" Kai grabbed Bri by the arm, standing him up and pulling him close. "It means I can command Death. I can call her. And if I can call her, then I can send her away." He made sure to punctuate his last words carefully and waited for their meaning to sink in.

Bri gaped. "You did this...for me?"

"Yes. Can't you feel it? Death pulls on you constantly. I can find a way to make her let go."

Bri pulled away violently, nearly tripping himself in the process and shattering Kai's hopes for a cheerful thanks. "I never asked you to do that."

"You don't have to." Was this not what brothers did for one another?

"Not at the expense of others. The last thing this world needs is you having the knowledge to beat Death."

"You're sick, Bri. Not thinking clearly. And because of that, I will not take offense and instead will wait for you to come to your senses."

In a movement more graceful than Kai would have thought he had the strength for, Bri grabbed Kai's hand and wiped the blood from it with his own. "Then you'll have a long wait. I'm never letting you cut me again." Then he went to the wall, smeared Kai's blood over the *labrynth* that acted as the door, and exited the workshop without so much as looking back.

For a long moment, Kai didn't move, didn't go after his brother. He didn't get angry. Instead, he drew in a deep breath and curled his hand into a tight fist—which he then slammed into his scribing table, grinding his knuckles into the grain of the wood.

Bri was a fool. He had always known that. Too much like their father, really. But Kai could change that, fix that. Bri just needed a bit more time. He would see, eventually. Until then, Kai just had to be tolerant of his poor, affected brother. Life could be such a challenge when your twin was mad. It was nothing Kai couldn't handle, though. He and Bri were beyond such trivial things.

Perhaps Bri simply needed some incentive. Or something to cheer him up. It wasn't easy living in Hell, Kai knew that, and Bri had been growing more and more despondent with every passing day. What kind of brother would he be if he didn't do something to reverse that? A gift was in order.

— CHAPTER TWENTY-TWO —

The scrying bowl had been a complete dead end.
Either their power just didn't cooperate with whatever magic ran through the bowl, or the scrying wasn't strong enough to break through whatever spells and wards Kai had up around Bri.

Alec didn't care which, it didn't matter. The end result was the same, and he still had no leads.

But he was deep enough now that he was willing to sell information and secrets if it meant getting something in return.

Which had led him to this tent, where he sat across from a demon withering with age and lack of souls, who traded in information, and the occasional tormented soul who escaped their prison. The tent was lit by flickering candles and ghostly orbs that shone by *labrynth*. The demon's clothes were tattered and dirty, but Alec had begun to suspect that was simply part of the performance. There were enough jewels scattered about to buy any number of frocks or suits, whatever the demon preferred.

Gesturing to the empty chair opposite, the demon sat, long grey and brown hair falling over one shoulder. "What brings two soulless to my door?" they asked, their voice crackled and broken.

Alec sat. Ariadne lingered by the tent flap, her opinion on coming here refusing to let her be any further involved. This demon had a reputation for devious and underhanded deals, but that's exactly why Alec had sought them out. If he was going to find Kai, and thus Bri, he needed to search the very underbelly of Hell.

"I'm looking for someone," Alec said. "A witch."

"Ah," said the demon, leaning forward, smiling a crooked smile that revealed missing teeth, "not many of those down here nowadays. Most have taken to hiding in the mortal realm."

"This one doesn't have many qualms about making himself known."

The demon chuckled. "I think I have some knowledge of who you speak, but people only see him once it is said. Either because he never rarely to the same place twice, or because they end up dead at his hands."

A crash sounded outside and Ariadne used a finger to peer beyond the tent. Alec saw her frown, but she didn't try to order him away, so he paid the subsequent crashes no mind.

"You can tell me where he is then," Alec said to the demon. His hands were filthy and shook with the need for the Hell power he was constantly resisting now. It had been too long since he'd come here to find Bri. Any time with Kai was too much, too risky, too dangerous. Alec couldn't shake the feeling that he was failing again.

"You'll need to name a good price," the demon said. "I have no desire to have my own existence ended by that witch."

Though she said nothing, Alec could feel Ariadne's silent warnings from her post. She hadn't wanted to come here, to this place where the air smelled like brimstone and death, where demons who had fled the mortal realm instead worked to prey upon the tortured souls of the deceased, making them something other. Dead souls powered a demon differently than live ones it seemed, but beggars could not be choosers, after all. But this demon seemed an exception.

Alec clenched his fists once, just to relieve the itch there. "I have information worthy of your knowledge."

"You came to me. You pay up first."

And here was his gamble. "Haven hunts a boy. For years, they've failed to find him, to bring him in. What they don't know, is that there are two of them. If they knew, they would raze the realms."

A dense silence stretched out between them as the demon considered this information. They leaned back once again, long limbs stretching out before them, one hand tapping their chin. Slowly, the haggard and dirty facade began to fade some, and their true form flickered through. Golden skin, black hair cut short at the nape and longer at the top, eyes like two ringed emeralds and rubies. "This is very interesting. I have heard of the boy Haven hunts. He sees the myst."

"Yes."

"And there are two?"

"The witch you spoke of, the one I'm looking for, he's the second."

"Alec," Adriadne hissed.

Alec ignored her.

The demon's gaze flicked to her, then back at Alec. "I think I have heard of you as well."

"I've made my payment, it's your turn."

The demon smiled. "There's a town here in the lower realm where they say the residents live in mortal comfort. Cool air, wooden furniture, and relative wealth. No one speaks of it, and yet the silence is just as telling as words would be. The town is under his thumb. Should you find it, I suspect you might find your quarry."

A bewitched town in Hell. "Can you tell me where it is?"

"Do you have another secret?" The demon looked once more to Ariadne where she stood at the flap, dark and silent. "Perhaps your companion has something to offer."

Alec stood, knowing their time was up. "Thank you for the exchange," he said, watching as the demon once again assumed their worn and torn appearance.

"Bring me a soul and I can tell you much more," they said. "I enjoyed our chat."

Ariadne all but hauled Alec out of the tent and down the road, saying nothing as they circumvented the fight between two bull-like hellions that the demons and other hellions had taken to betting upon in the street. They were nearly alone on a brimstone path leading out into the wilderness of darkness and stone when she finally stopped and spoke. "That was dangerous."

Alec knew that look; it was the same one she'd given him two thousand years ago when he had risked stealing from a wealthy merchant's cart in the bright light of day. She'd been certain he'd be caught and lose a hand. But he hadn't then, and he hadn't now, and his body buzzed with excited hope. "It was worth it. A town, Ari. A cool town. We can find that. We can find Bri."

"And what? You're just going to ask everyone we pass if they know where this town is?"

Alec started walking. There was smoke on the other side of these boulders that made up a sort of strange rock forest before them, which meant either some burning torment, or another town. "It's the best plan we've had so far," he said.

She didn't catch up with him right away, didn't take up his hand once she did.

"I'm here to find him, Ari," he said when the silence between them started to feel like an argument.

"I know," she said, pausing in a way that felt like she was choosing her words carefully. "I just wish you would rest."

"Bri doesn't have time for me to rest."

Bri peeled the bandage from his left arm, wincing as the dried blood pulled at the sensitive skin. It had been days since he had let Kai cut him, but the wounds were taking longer to heal than Bri had expected. Longer than normal. Something wasn't right. He didn't react to Hell the same way his brother did. Every day he spent there he felt weaker, heavier, like he was being drained away. The myst couldn't penetrate this realm, and so he had no visions or "slips" to worry about, yet he felt worse. He had never thought it possible, but he actually *missed* the myst. For all that it tormented him, it was familiar, a part of him. Hell made him feel cut off from himself.

Kai didn't understand at all.

With the bandage undone, Bri tossed it aside, choking back the instinct to be sick when he looked at the raised red skin on his arm. He washed it carefully, wishing for someone with healing knowledge he could trust, then wrapped it once again with clean linen.

The hot air made it difficult to breathe, but Bri did his best to draw a deep, calming breath. He sat outside, on the opposite side of the mountain from the training yard. The clash of steel and the yelps of pain could still be heard even at this distance, but vaguely. Bri could almost pretend he was elsewhere. The temple, perhaps, with birds singing, and the people chanting their mediations and prayers. He counted his breaths as they taught him, in through his nose, out through his mouth, and pictured the temple in his mind.

It was little use. The small copse of trees granted him some shade and a sturdy trunk to lean against, but that was where the illusion ended. There was no grass, only dirt, and brimstone pebbles to poke him.

Footsteps crunched over those pebbles as they came closer. Kai's gait was familiar now, unmistakable. As such, it was no surprise when his twin rounded the edge of the small wood and stepped into the shadows.

"There you are," Kai said, looking at ease as always. "I've been looking everywhere for you."

Bri set the small bowl of water he had brought out with him aside, out of the way. "I couldn't stand to be inside there another minute. I needed some time away."

"You could just ask. I'll take you wherever you like."

"No, you won't."

"You're right. Not anywhere. Only places where you can't do something stupid."

"What do you want, Kai? I told you I'm done playing your games. If you want more of my blood, you'll have to just kill me."

"You're always so morbid, brother. Do you really think that's all I care about? Your blood?"

"Yes."

"That hurts me."

"Nice to know something can."

"And here I spent my whole day procuring something nice for you."

Bri hesitated, his mind coming up with a hundred different scenarios that Kai would think were "nice" that were in fact the opposite. "What do you mean?"

Kai leaned against the nearest tree. "You've been unhappy lately. I'm not blind. I can't imagine what's got you so melancholy, but it's irritating. So I got you a present."

"I don't want a present." He didn't want anything from Kai, not at all, and especially not when he had that gleam in his eyes.

"Well, I can't take it back now, so it's too late. You'll have to just accept it and be grateful."

"Kai, what have you done?"

Reaching behind the tree, Kai pulled his present into the clearing.

She was dressed for a cool autumn day, her sleeves long and the fabric of the dress thick enough to keep her warm. The color was a golden orange, which complemented her blonde hair. But her face had turned red in the heat of Hell, and a fine sheen of sweat could already be seen on her brow. All her blonde curls had fallen free of their pins, hanging half in her face as she scowled at Kai, fighting his hold.

Kai turned her sharply, forcing her to face Bri, and when she saw him, she stilled. "Bri."

"Ella."

Yanking her arm free, she ran from Kai and to Bri, her skirts catching on the rough ground and nearly tripping her. Bri caught her, intending to do nothing more than steady her, but she wrapped her arms around him, holding him tightly.

She said nothing, so Bri simply returned the embrace, hardly believing she was really there, and looked instead to his brother. "Why have you brought her here?"

"A present. As I said."

"Ella is not a present. You take her back right now."

Kai waved away his concern. "Nonsense. I can see how happy the two of you are to be together again. That won't happen if I take her back."

"I don't care. She doesn't belong here. You can't just kidnap people."

"Apparently I can."

Ella was so hot against him. Too hot. She needed water, different clothes—she needed to be back in the mortal realm. "How did you bring her here?"

"Really, Bri, are you still so surprised by my talents? I can bring whomever I like, wherever I like."

A terrifying thought crossed Bri's mind. His hands began to shake, but he steadied them, not wanting Ella to see or feel any uncertainty from him. Gently easing her out of the tight hold she still had on him, Bri brushed her hair from her face and whispered, "Stay here." At first, he thought she would protest, but then she nodded and let her arms fall to her sides.

Bri looked at her for one more long moment, then turned on his brother, meeting him on the other side of the clearing and speaking in a low tone so that Ella would not hear. "You can't do this. Take her back."

Kai smiled even as Bri got close enough that they were practically nose to nose. "No."

"Is she dead?" He choked on the word, hating the mere thought, but he put nothing past Kai. "Did you kill her to bring her here?"

"Gods, no. What do you think I am? A monster?"

"Yes."

"Such ill trust, brother. You should work on that."

"If she's a living soul, she should not be here."

"We'd better work fast then. The sooner we finish, the sooner we can all return to the mortal realm."

"Take her back now. Take her back, and I'll do whatever you want."

"She's staying. I brought her here because *you've* been unhappy." He poked Bri in the chest with one scabbed finger. "What kind of brother would I be if I didn't do everything in my power to fix that?"

"Take her back and I'll be happy. I swear it."

"It's too late now, Bri. She's seen too much, knows too much. I can't just have her running around, free to tell anyone where you are, where I am." Kai leaned in closer, taking Bri's face in his hands. "So she stays, and you will be happy. Or I will kill her. Your choice."

How casually he threatened such horrible things. Bri couldn't say anything in return, couldn't find his voice. Kai was mad enough that he would do just what he said, all for the sake of his supposed happiness. Twisting his mother's ring on his finger, Bri prayed for the strength to protect Ella, to find some way to get her out of Hell.

Kai smiled. "That's what I thought. Now, why don't you take her inside and help her settle in. I'm sure the two of you have a lot to catch up on. I'll come find you both for dinner." Delivering two light smacks to Bri's cheek, Kai stepped back and waved to Ella. "Lovely to see you again, my dear. I look forward to getting to know you better."

Bri remained perfectly still until Kai was completely out of sight, until he could no longer hear even his footsteps along the ground. Ella came rushing toward him the moment he moved.

"I'm sorry," she said, throwing her arms around him once again and half sobbing into his shoulder. "I'm sorry. I don't know what happened. I was walking down the street, on my way to the library when I saw him standing on the steps. I don't remember anything after that."

"You have nothing to be sorry for," Bri said, feeling awkward as he tried to soothe her. "It's all right. Kai is...difficult, and hard to resist. He always knows how to get what he wants."

"What does he want?" She wiped at her eyes, then tore her gloves from her hands, throwing them to the ground.

"My help. I withdrew my cooperation the other day. I should be apologizing to you. It's my fault you're here."

Ella pulled her hair from her neck, strands sticking to the sweat that was growing worse in the heat. "What is he?"

"A witch. He's mad, Ella. He works for demons and experiments with the darkest magic. And he wants me to help him."

"How could you help him? I don't understand. Bri, where are we?" She pulled at her clothes, too restricting and too hot in this environment. Bri took her hands in his, trusting that the myst wouldn't assault him. It normally couldn't breach the walls of Hell, but no one here was any longer a subject of the myst. Ella was. Still, he focused hard enough to keep it out if need be.

There was no need. He felt the myst like a distant roll of thunder, struggling to find its hold on her, but it could not see through into Hell.

"Let's go inside," he said. "I'll get you some water, and some cooler clothes. Then I'll tell you everything. I swear."

— CHAPTER TWENTY-THREE —

Ella plucked at the thin fabric of the dress she now wore. Little more than a shift, really. She felt naked and exposed, but at least she was cooler. How like the demons of Hell to dress in such a way. But she refused to seem ungrateful. Bri had gone through some trouble to get her something to change into. She had heard him arguing with some unknown creature in the hallway while she waited inside his room.

Wanting more time to process all he had told her, she began arranging her hair at the back of her head, using nothing more than a piece of string. It would never pass for proper at home. It was good enough for Hell.

Bri had told her everything, just as he had promised. She hadn't doubted that he would, but she had never expected the tale he had shared. Forbidden love between a fallen seraph and a powerful witch. Twin boys, the powers of Haven and Hell twisted and torn between them. He had told her of his childhood with the caravan, and the ritual that had driven him so close to death that his only escape had been a deal with Carma. She had managed not to cry throughout most of it, though she thought the tears might finally come when he told her of Kai's first betrayal, when he had learned his brother was not everything he had dreamed. The story had culminated in her arrival. Leverage against him. A way to force him to comply with Kai's wants.

"Is it too much?" Bri asked, his voice quiet, uncertain.

Ella shook herself lightly, dispelling the stillness that had claimed her. She wiped at the single tear that had trailed down her cheek. "No. No, it's just, I never imagined the truth. Even with the pieces you had offered me before."

"Most days I don't believe it myself."

She looked at him. He stood by the lone window, hands folded behind his back, pinned to the wall. She expected to see him differently now, to see everything in his life on his face, in his eyes. She didn't. He was still the same boy—young man—she had met in the garden. Someone who had spent his life afraid of his own shadow, but had begun to learn how to face danger head on. It was like seeing courage grow in a garden like a flower. It fascinated her. How many times had one event changed his entire life? And each time he had taken it in stride, learned to adapt, and accepted his new circumstances.

If only she could do the same.

Rising from the bed, she crossed the room to stand in front of him. Her instinct was to touch him, but years of training and lessons in propriety kept her hands at her sides. "So what do we do?"

"I won't let him hurt you."

"I know." *I won't let him hurt you either.* She glanced at the bandage on his arm, thinking of how he had told her about the bleedings for Kai's *labrynths*. How anyone could do such a thing baffled her. "Tell me what to do, and I'll do it."

Bri sighed and shook his head. "For now, do what he says. Within reason, of course. He's far easier to be around when he's getting what he wants. I'm working on a way out, but I need him to let his guard down first."

"Make him trust us."

"Yes."

Ella nodded. She could do that. Kai wasn't the only man in the world with an ego. She had met plenty of his kind before. None of the uncertainty she felt at that moment had to do with Kai.

She was alone with Bri. Barely dressed. And every instinct in her body screamed for her to touch him. Her brother, Den, always insisted on having chaperones about when men came to court her. She had never really understood why, figuring it must have had something to do with the "desires of men" her governess had always been on about.

Not once had she ever had a thought beyond the words she spoke to them. In fact, most of the time she could not wait for them to be gone. Standing there with Bri, she understood her brother's caution.

Fires burned everywhere. Smoke thickened the air, choking him with each hard-won breath. There was a pain in his head that rivaled anything he had ever felt before, and when he tried to move, it felt as though something tore through his gut.

Alec forced his eyes open, hands groping about the moist ground beneath him and along his own body. Cold steel and leather brushed against his hand.

A knife. Between his ribs. Driven in up to the hilt.

He wrenched it out without a second thought, coughing blood and screaming at the pain. He rolled over, clutching his stomach, feeling weak. Screams carried through the air, mixing with the chanting that droned on and on like terrifying music.

"Alec!"

Ariadne. Her voice—no, her scream, pierced the air, and his heart. He struggled to move, to find her, to turn his head. Through blurred vision he found her, held down between a circle of men, thrashing and kicking. One man stood over her, a long dagger in his hands, pointed down at her chest as he chanted.

She screamed for him again.

His body wouldn't cooperate. Wouldn't answer him when he commanded himself to stand. What little response he did receive landed him face down in the muddy grass. On his second attempt he saw the other body. Smaller, younger. Still, unmoving.

"Marc!"

His brother didn't answer him, didn't so much as stir. Alec shouted for him again, then coughed more blood.

The chanting paused. He had drawn attention.

"That one's still alive."

"He should be dead."

"Leave him. He'll be dead soon enough. Finish the summoning."

The chanting picked up. Ariadne's terrified screams did too.

What had happened? Alec couldn't remember anything. They had been traveling, resting a moment in a field...

The air suddenly changed. Something surged, running along his skin, tickling, and leaving him numb. His vision cleared some, and in the grass just beyond his face he saw something.

Lines.

A *labrynth*.

The blood on his arm grew warmer. Beckoning him to act. To use it.

"Alec!"

Mustering every bit of strength he had, Alec began dragging himself closer to those lines.

"Alec!"

Hands on his face, stroking his hair. The voice was frantic, but not terrified as it had been before.

Alec sat up, gasping for breath. He clutched at his ribs, but the pain and the blood was gone, nothing more than a memory. The smoky air and the fires had disappeared as well, along with the bloody grass and the lines burned into the ground. Instead, he saw crisp white sheets, and slender hands. Hands that stroked his arms, his face. Alec breathed in deeply, holding it.

"Alec?"

He let that breath out slowly, carefully, calming himself. "I'm all right."

"A nightmare?"

"A memory."

"Which one?"

"The last night we were all human together."

She said nothing at that.

Alec rubbed his face, dispelling the dream and the memories it conjured up. Marc's still body flashed before him once more—then traded itself for an image of Bri.

A warm glass was pressed into his hand. "Here. Drink."

He stared at the contents of the glass a moment. Just water, but warmed by its presence in Hell. He sipped it, hating the flat taste. Ariadne sat on the edge of the bed, her hair brushed smooth and once again dressed in the trousers and fitted shirt she had worn earlier that day. Clothes Alec remembered tearing from her body only hours before. The meager sheet of the bed was not enough to disguise his own nakedness. "Are you going somewhere?"

"We both are. Are you steady again? The nightmare gone?"

Out of habit, Alec glanced at the window, but night and day were not an element of Hell. Some places were in perpetual light, others darkness. Some existed in a constant twilight, like this town where they had stayed while waiting for word from the second of Ariadne's contacts. The first had flatly refused to meet with them. "How long has it been?"

"Only two turns. But we must go, and we must be quick about it. Your nightmare gives me reason to worry."

Finding his shirt at the bottom of the bed, Alec pulled it on. "Why?"

"Do you have them often? Dreams of what used to be?"

"No. Not recently. This was the first in a long time." And it still clung to him. He could feel it, like a cold sweat.

Rising and throwing his pants at him, Ariadne moved about the room, shoving any and all of their belongings into her pack. "Then we have no more time. Hurry. We may have to find another way." At the window, she leaned far out, looking in all directions.

"Why? What do you know?" He pulled on his pants and sought his shoes.

"There is a Hellwalker. A seraph of memory. He likes to make sinners relive their past. Our paths have crossed before. I have no desire to meet him again." She pulled herself up onto the windowsill and gave him a coy smile over her shoulder. "You aren't afraid of a little drop, are you?"

"No, but—"

She jumped. Clothes on, but twisted and uncomfortable, Alec rushed to the window. When he looked down, Ariadne stood in the street below, beckoning him silently and indicating for him to be quiet about it.

They were on the third floor. A long drop for a mortal. Still a long drop for a soulless, though his life wouldn't be in danger. Broken bones could still be a problem, however. Unless, he pulled power.

Taking a deep breath, Alec stepped onto the window ledge and tried to judge the distance. He let a small bit of power into his body, hating the thrill it gave him, the welcome of the warmth that spread through his limbs. He jumped, and landed smoothly on the balls of his feet, using only one hand to steady himself. His heart pounded, feeling large and so very alive within his chest. His blood sang with the power which he then pushed away.

Ariadne grabbed his hand, her power still thrumming through her veins. They ran through the alleys created by homes and businesses. This town had no order to it, thriving instead on the chaos of dead ends and diagonal streets that intersected with others. But Ariadne knew her way through the confusion and disorder. Alec allowed her to lead, all the while marveling at what she had become. She had always been strong, always been capable, but as a human she had never been the one to lead them away from whatever danger chased them. The change, the knowledge that she had taken care of herself for so long, made him love her more—and made him trust her less.

Between the baker's and the butcher's, they slowed their pace and began to walk more leisurely, as if they had not a care in the world. Alec squeezed her hand and pulled her closer so he could whisper in her ear. "What was all that about?"

"I told you. A Hellwalker."

"And how did you know he was coming?"

"You weren't the only one with a nightmare. He knows I'm here, and he made his point very clear."

"What point?"

"That he's here for you."

Ari jerked to a halt when Alec stopped walking without warning. "What do you mean?"

"Please, Alec," she said, pulling on his arm to make him start walking once again. "Please, we don't have time."

He would not go. Not yet. He drew her closer, until they were face to face, not caring that they were in the way of others making their way up and down the street. "No. You tell me. What does a Hellwalker want with me?"

"I don't know, Alec. I really don't. I just know him, and he knows me. He can get into my mind, use my memories against me, and leave me messages. He's here for you, that's all I know."

"Why can he do all this?"

"Alec, please, we don't have time for me to explain now. We have to keep walking."

It wasn't anything about her plea that made Alec agree, despite the desperation in her eyes. It was the sudden flash of the fires and Marc's blood that popped into his mind.

They walked casually, as though nothing were chasing them. Ariadne was tense beside him, visibly working at not checking every corner and doorway they passed. A pair of young hellions came running past, knocking into their legs and sending themselves spinning even as they laughed and carried on. Two boys. Identical. Each with skinless wings and a long, scaled tail.

A chill came over Alec, even in the heat of Hell. "Ari, how much of my memories can he see? Only my human years?"

She took them around a corner, and the hellion boys disappeared. "No. He sees everything. Every memory you have can be his."

Then he could see Bri. "How do I keep him out?"

"You won't like the answer."

"Tell me. Haven cannot know what I know."

Another corner, leading to the last road that would bring them out of town and into Hell's wilderness. She stopped and looked him straight in the eye. "Hell power can create enough of a barrier to keep him out, but it needs to be enough to really burn him when he looks. A lot of power, Alec."

More than I'm comfortable drawing. Alec closed his eyes and thought long and hard about the decision placed before him. He drew a small amount of power, just enough to warm his palms and accidentally force Ariadne to release him, testing his resolve.

Cel-Eza, it felt so good. He drew a little more, swirling it about his heart until he felt as though he had run halfway across the world without the slightest fatigue. More, and his head began to swim pleasantly. He felt strong, he felt powerful. He wanted to take Ari, slam her up against the nearest wall, grind his hips against hers, and drink power from her mouth until they were one single entity.

"Alec!"

Her voice shattered his power-induced trance. Opening his eyes, he saw nothing but her face, framed by the blackened bricks of the building behind her. He had one fist buried in her hair, his other hand locked around her hip, fingers digging into soft flesh.

Alec broke away, breathing hard as he tried to drive the power back to whence it had come. It refused to leave completely, enough remaining to make his whole body tingle and shiver.

Ariadne peeled herself from the wall slowly, cautiously. "You really don't do well with the power, do you?"

"It's harder here. In Hell. Everything is magnified."

She touched his hand, just a finger brushing over his knuckles. "I'll help. We can find your balance."

"I would rather just keep myself empty."

"Empty isn't balance. It's simply the other extreme."

A footfall, low and heavy, joined her whisper on the air. "Extremes. Something demons and their soulless do well, in my experience."

Ariadne stilled, her gaze fixed over Alec's shoulder. Her golden skin turned ashen, and Alec would have sworn he heard her heart quicken.

"What name do you go by now, Ariadne? Out of courtesy I shall defer to your preference," the voice came again, a melodic tenor, full of light and power.

"Ariadne will do fine. It is my true name, as well you know."

"I do know you better than most. Now, if you would be so kind, do introduce me to your companion. I have so longed to meet him."

Her breath was shaky when she inhaled. "Alec, this is Zachriel. Whatever you do, do not look into his eyes."

— CHAPTER TWENTY-FOUR —

Now that's a rather rude thing to say, wouldn't you agree?" The seraph's voice belied the good will the words implied.

Ari ignored him. "Alec, draw power. Do it now. I know you hate it, but it is the only way to keep him out. Once he makes eye contact, he will begin to strip you bare."

"I don't have time for your games, Ariadne," Zachriel said, sounding more impatient than his words indicated.

"No games. Just precautions."

It felt as though his power lingered close by, having resisted leaving when he pushed it away. Despite his fear of having been overcome by it only moments before, Alec opened himself to it.

It flooded back in. His pulse surged, his palms warmed. The air around him soon felt cooler in comparison. He felt full, complete. No emptiness lingered in his chest.

He turned and faced the Hellwalker.

Zachriel was tall, like most seraph. He had the earthly coloring so many of them were born with, all brown tones and golds, but one look was not enough to tell anyone that he was a Havenly being. Hellwalkers strove to blend into their surroundings, and Zachriel did it well. His clothes were loose, simple, and nondescript. A scar ran the length of his face, stretching from his left ear to the right side of his throat. Peeking out from under the collar of his shirt was a burn mark in the shape of a hand.

The eyes were a deep brown, and Alec instantly felt the seraph trying to worm his way inside what memories he had. He hadn't meant to make eye contact.

Alec pulled more power.

Zachriel smiled. "It is a good attempt. We will see if it is enough. Ariadne has never been able to keep me out, not truly, though she does her best."

"What do you want?" Alec said, resisting the urge to fall into the heat of his power completely. It would have been so easy, just a tiny shift of his weight, so to speak.

"I want what Haven wants," Zachriel said. "Peace, harmony, an adherence to the Grand Plan."

"I mean, what do you want with me?"

"Ah, Alec. I have seen you so many times in Ariadne's memories I feel as though I already know you. Let us speak as gentlemen first. If we cannot reach an amicable conclusion, then we will turn to our other options."

"Fine. Talk."

"Somewhere more private, perhaps?" Zachriel motioned for them to follow as his long stride took him down the street, toward the edge of town. To the thick woods where little could be seen or heard, aside from the fights and couplings of wild hellions.

Alec had already begun to follow when Ariadne grabbed his arm. "Alec, wait."

"You heard him. He wants to talk."

"He doesn't. You can't trust him."

"I'm not sure I can trust anyone, but I need information. Maybe he has some. At the very least, I can find out what he wants with me, and avoid him in the future."

She tugged him to a stop once again when he tried to move. "Please, Alec. I'm worried."

"About what?"

"You. He'll tear your mind apart if you let him."

"Then I won't let him."

"We should run. Now."

"I can't pop in and out of existence like you can, Ari. I have nowhere to run to." He moved again, and this time he used an extra surge of power to drag her along when she tried to hang back. It felt fantastic to use it so freely, to not calculate and always be ready to push it away.

The giant trees cast thick shadows over the road. Zachriel stood just outside the tree line, waiting with crossed arms. Alec had Ariadne by the hand, and she clung to his side when they stopped, facing the seraph who most likely meant them much harm. He could feel her own power pulsing against his.

"Well, here we are," Alec said. "Talk."

"I want the boy," Zachriel said.

"And now we're finished. Can't say it was a pleasure meeting you." Alec turned to leave.

"You don't even know my purposes."

"I don't need to know them."

"He will destroy us all."

"I think you have him confused with someone else."

Zachriel stepped forward. "Give him to me, and we can end all of this."

"There is nothing in all the realms you could offer me that would convince me to give him up to you."

"Not even peace? The continued existence of the mortal realm?"

"Not even that."

"Then you are either mad, or drunk on this power you so desperately gather to yourself."

The power Alec had traded for in order to protect those he loved. "Pick whichever you like. It doesn't matter to me."

Zachriel smiled, then turned his attention to Ariadne. "Does it not concern you, Ariadne, that your dear lover does not even question how I came to know his relation to the boy?"

All the heat rushed out of him, and Alec felt suddenly very cold. His power fell like a stone to the pit of his stomach, and he tightened his grip on Ariadne's hand. He should have noticed that. Should have kept his mouth shut and denied everything. Now the seraph knew, without a doubt, that he could get to Bri. "What have you done?"

Running a hand over his closely cropped hair, Zachriel looked the very picture of relaxed. "I have my sources. I have seen the boy in memories. He is outwardly a quiet thing, gentle and kind. But he has power that he cannot control, and he brings destruction to the lives he touches. He was never meant to live, never meant to exist. His continued presence in the mortal realm jeopardizes everything."

"He's a kid. And there's nothing 'outwardly' about what you saw. He is gentle and kind. He deserves your protection, not this ridiculous hunt."

"I will find him, and I will deliver him personally to the Hall of Judgment where the elders will strip him of his stolen power and unmake him." Zachriel moved quickly. He threw Ariadne to the ground, hard enough that something cracked. Then his hand was around Alec's throat, squeezing and raising him to his tiptoes. Alec clutched at that hand, neither of them burning one another with simple touch. Pulling back the power he had before he lost his grip on it, Alec thrust one hand into Zachriel's throat, gathering more and more until smoke began to rise from the holy—but unblessed—flesh. Zachriel did not flinch. In his shock, Alec locked eyes with the seraph and did not break away fast enough.

Bri spun his mother's ring on his smallest finger. It was a nervous habit he had picked up over the months in Xia-Lo. "Some days I feel like it would just be easier to give in and let Haven do what they want with me," he said.

They were sitting outside as they did most nights, enjoying the spring air as it chased away the last bits of winter. "Easier," Alec said, "but not better."

"I could give myself over to Kai instead. At least it doesn't hurt when he's around."

"Does it hurt now?"

Bri put his head in his hands, lacing his fingers through his hair. "It hurts all the time."

"Why didn't you say something?"

"Some days I hardly notice. Other days it's worse."

"Like today?" Alec could see the tension in Bri's arms, his legs. Looking closer, he had even curled his bare toes tightly. Bri's silence confirmed what his body showed. "What makes today so bad? Maybe we can avoid it in the future."

"I don't know. Iris wanted to talk about Kai today. Talking about him is hard." Bri sat up suddenly, shaking his head as though he could shake away everything that bothered him. He smiled at Alec, but it didn't reach his eyes. "I'm sorry. I'm just feeling sorry for myself."

"Why is talking about Kai so hard?"

"Please, Alec. I'd rather just forget about it."

"Tell me. Maybe I can help."

Bri sighed and said nothing for a long while. Alec didn't push; he knew Bri would talk eventually. "It's just—it bothers me how things worked out for us. My power hurts me, weakens me, makes me feel out of control. His power makes him strong, makes him feel invincible."

"But he's mad."

"Yes. And that's what bothers me. He's mad, and I'm not. Or at least, I think I'm not. But I can never decide which of us got the worse end."

"Kai got the worst of it."

"How can you be so sure?"

"Because, despite looking just like you, he's nothing like you. And I know a lot of things in your life are hard, and being sick so often is frustrating, but you have a good heart. And you're getting stronger, you work to be the master of this ability rather than let it control you. I know it seems like I worry about you a lot, but I never worry about whether or not you have a good heart."

"Really?"

"Really. So you can stop feeling sorry for yourself. Spend it on someone else."

"I guess I should feel sorry for Kai."

"If you think he's worth your time."

"Do you think things would have been different if we had grown up together? If we'd had the chance to really be brothers?"

"Who knows. The bond between brothers can be a powerful thing."

"I know. That's why I'm always grateful for you."

"There are two."

The voice didn't match the images Alec was seeing. It wasn't his, and it wasn't Bri's. It belonged to no one in Xia-Lo at Iris's temple. A familiar, yet normally unwelcome presence lingered just beside him, begging entrance. Alec touched the power, let it drift over him. Just a small amount, not enough to consume him.

A scarred face he did not recognize appeared before him. Something pressed against his mind, trying to force its way inside. Another image rose, this one of Carma's manor, the hallway dark, and the boy in front of him acting strangely. Not Bri. Kai.

He couldn't let Haven know there were two. Couldn't let them find Bri.

That ever-present power flooded him, burning up his veins and driving a steady beat into his heart. The scent of burned flesh coated the air, and the sound of bones popping and breaking became an eerie music. He tasted blood, felt it running over his hands.

Then all went dark.

"Alec! Alec, stop! That's enough."

Something pulled at him. Hands on his arms, his shoulders. He shoved them away. They were too cold for this fire that consumed him. He refused to let go.

"Alec, please. You'll kill him."

Kill who? And would that be so bad? It felt so good to burn away at the flesh beneath his hands, to tear at the strong muscle, to claw at the soft parts.

The hands returned, getting in his way, trying to draw him away from his prey. He twisted out of reach and ignored what he could not avoid.

"You must stop, Alec! We have to leave. You don't want to do this. Think of Bri."

Bri? A whip of cold snapped through him, but was quickly swallowed by the heat. Everything urged him to continue existing through feeling alone. The hunger. The burning. The drive. The vengeance. He was owed this. Everything had been taken from him. His life, his soul, his heart—his love.

But that single thought was enough to let others through, and suddenly Alec could no longer see anything but that which he felt. He saw a boy with silver-brown eyes, and Marc, still and unmoving. He saw a woman, tall and beautiful, smiling in a way that promised everything.

A hand on his face. A voice—that same voice—pleading with him to stop.

The power left him, dying like a fire that had been doused with water. His vision returned. The dark, burned road of Hell. The giant trees that loomed overhead, casting long shadows in the perpetual dusk. The woman stared at him with wide, worried eyes, her black hair half hanging in her face as if she had been a part of some struggle. He reached a hand toward her, but stopped.

His hand was red. Red and black. Burned and bloody.

"Ariadne," he said her name as though it were the question that would give him all the answers.

She took his bloody hand in hers and pulled him to his feet. When had he kneeled? "Come, Alec. Come with me. Don't look."

"Don't look?" Of course he tried to move his head, but she grabbed his face and held tight, refusing to let him see anything but her face.

"Don't. He's still alive. That's enough. We need to go before he wakes, before someone finds him." She tried to lead him away.

Alec would not move. Could not. "What do you mean? What have I done?" His entire body tingled with the after-effects of power. His ears rang, and his heart pounded. It had been centuries since he had felt this way—so alive. So out of control. "Ariadne, what happened?"

"Later. Please, Alec."

"No." He grabbed her hands, forcing her to release his head. Before she could stop him, he turned.

The body on the ground was Zachriel, but the seraph did not move. His face was streaked with silver blood, his arms blackened and twisted. His shirt had been torn open, and a fierce black and red handprint smoked just over his heart.

Alec knew if he were to lay his hand over the mark, it would be a perfect match.

The shaking began at his feet, rising through his body until he thought he would no longer be able to stand.

Ariadne took him by the arm, pulling on him until he took one step away, then another, and another. Alec let her continue to lead him in that manner until the sight of the seraph on the ground faded into the distance.

But it didn't fade from his mind. Nor did one terrifying piece of knowledge.

His trouble with Hell power was more than a simple addiction.

— CHAPTER TWENTY-FIVE —

Kai watched the two of them from the top of the mountain. This far up, they were little more than half-recognizable, but it was enough. Bri and Ella moved through the east garden of the compound, talking and laughing together amongst the thorns and thistle. Just as Kai wanted it.

Or so he had thought. He had brought the girl so Bri would stop being so difficult and melancholy, so they could start their work again. Scribing had resumed, and Bri had let Kai take small amounts of his blood once again, but despite getting closer and closer to having the *labrynth* he needed to satisfy Olin, Kai felt something else dampening his mood.

Something beautiful and blonde. Something his brother had, that he wanted.

Ella had insisted on having her own room. Kai had obliged, all the while thinking Bri the fool for not taking what was so obviously available to him. Now he valued the distance between them.

They had eaten their meals together for the last week. Ella was intelligent and quick witted. She didn't back down from challenging him, but didn't withhold niceties when earned either. She thanked him for the clothes he had brought her from town, dresses that covered her enough to satisfy her sense of decency while still keeping her cool in Hell. She had even accepted when he offered to scribe a cooling spell into the fabrics. Kai felt a certain amiability growing between them. He liked her. He wanted her.

But she refused his offers when he invited her to walk with him privately, and whenever he sent for her, she always came with Bri along. Never alone.

So Kai watched, studying her interactions with his brother for clues as to how to get her to spare her attention for him instead.

"Kailas."

Ugh. He rolled onto his back, staring up at Olin and the looming shadow he created. "What do you want? I'm busy."

"You brought a human girl here." Olin was filthy, his face bloody and his armor bent and twisted about his body.

"What happened to you?"

"Nallahar and I had some business to attend to. Don't worry, it doesn't concern you."

"Wonderful."

"Now, explain yourself."

"What? The girl? She's leverage."

"Not some game?"

"All life is a game, Olin."

"I will not tolerate frivolity here. If you want to bed human girls, go to the mortal realm."

"Oh, I do. I assure you. But she's not here for me. She's here for my brother."

"You can take him to the mortal realm for that as well."

"Ah, how I wish." Kai rolled back onto his stomach, watching the two wandering below. "Alas, my brother is a gentleman and does not indulge himself."

"Then what is she doing here?"

"Bri didn't want to cooperate and help me anymore. She's here to make sure he does."

Olin laughed. "You are far more ruthless than I ever thought."

"My fits of mass killing weren't assurance enough for you?"

"I admit I worried you were developing a soft spot for your brother."

"I can control him."

"You had better. Remember what I told you. If I don't get my *labrynth* soon, I will start breaking his bones."

Try as he might, Kai couldn't keep that thought from making his gut twist. He'd break Bri's fingers himself if he had to, but for some reason, he couldn't stand the thought of someone else threatening him. "You'll get it."

"By the next full moon."

That had Kai sitting up suddenly, nearly falling from the mountain peak in the process. "That's too soon. I need more time." The moon had been full just the previous night, but a single month wouldn't be enough.

"You don't have more time. Take him to the mortal realm while you're at it. I need to know when the Restorium is expected, and he is the only one who can see into Haven."

"He won't be easy to convince."

"I thought you said you can control him?"

"I can."

"Then do so, and get me what I want. A little advice?" Olin leaned over, looking down where Bri and Ella still walked about, unaware that anyone watched. "Use the girl to your advantage in another way. Tell her what will happen to Bri if he does not do as you ask. I'm sure she will help you convince him then."

As Olin retreated back down the mountain, Kai considered his words. Ella seemed sensible. It might work, but Kai knew better than to play all his cards at one time. It was better to always have one more move up your sleeve. To always be one step ahead.

The cell was dark, lit only by a single burning torch by the door. A window, no more than a slender slit in the stone just below the ceiling, let nothing but more darkness in. Picadilly had watched the sky through that pitiful opening day in and day out. The blackness never changed. She was somewhere in Hell, then, that much was clear. More than one part of that realm suffered perpetual darkness, so it was impossible to know where exactly, but even just knowing the realm was a comfort. Being in Hell was a comfort. She had always loved Hell—the heat, the sounds of screams on the air, the distinct flutter of sinful souls reacting to her presence. For the two hundred years Carma had been missing, Pica had spent the majority of her time in the lower realm feasting and reveling in all its pleasures. Despite her current circumstances, she was glad to be back.

She heard his footsteps—so familiar now, that steady, strong pace—and leaned back against the warm brimstone wall, drawing up her unbroken knee and making herself look as casual as possible. The door opened, and the solitary flame of the torch lit his face.

Pica laughed.

He frowned, winced, then returned his face to a passive expression. Silver blood dripped from his mouth when he spoke. "What is so funny?"

"The fact that you clearly did not listen to me. I told you he was a force to be reckoned with. Especially when pushed past the edge. What did you say to make him lose it so completely?"

"It does not matter."

"Then why have you come straight to me rather than tend to your wounds first?" He had come fully into the light now, and she could see the extent of his injuries. There was a bloody handprint on his chest, blackened and half turned to ash. Alec had gone for the heart. Picadilly could only imagine how far gone he would have to be to try to deliver such a blow. It had been centuries since she had seen him like that.

"There is a small matter I would like to discuss with you," Zachriel said, holding onto the door still. Picadilly wondered if he was having trouble standing on his own.

"I imagine you have a lot of small matters." She let her gaze flick to his pants, then back up to his face. "I have no interest in them."

"He has a memory," Zachriel said, ignoring her jibe though she could still see the annoyance in his eyes, "of a boy."

"Yes. You took that memory from me as well. It was the whole reason for your going after Alec. You weren't satisfied with mine." He'd infiltrated her mind, but she was strong in her power, a power she'd carefully honed over the centuries, and she'd been able to resist him just enough. Alec had no such control. Letting Zachriel see that had been her mistake.

"Not that boy. A second boy. One that remarkably resembles the first."

Kai. Oh, Alec, you have given up too much. "Alec spends the majority of his time with Bri. He has a lot of memories, I'm sure. What you saw was Bri."

"No. It was very clearly not." He let go of the door, and stepped forward, looming over her. "Tell me who he is."

"I thought Haven was all-knowing."

"Do not make this harder on yourself."

"Your interrogations tickle me. I think I fell asleep during the last one."

"Do you really want to do this?"

"I think it might be fun."

Slowly, though he managed never to take his gaze from hers, Zachriel knelt in front of her. It put him at a disadvantage, but he had no reason to worry about her attempting to flee. He had broken one of her legs, and she had yet to completely heal, so she was too weak to move instantly through the realms. "I think you forget yourself. You are soulless. I am seraph. One of Haven's great warriors."

"You are a Hellwalker. Why don't you take the plunge and do what you really want to do? Hell intrigues you. You want to be here. Yet you won't take that last step. You can't find the strength and the conviction to tear out your own heart. Like I did. Would you like some help? I could show you how, hold your hand."

"Even if I did want help, I wouldn't take it from someone like you. A demon tricked into turning human, forced to sell her newly acquired soul in exchange for a glimmer of her former power."

Picadilly felt her power stir within her, responding to her anger. She often lost her temper over her past, but now, she clamped down on it hard. "Do you know what happened to that human?"

"Please, enlighten me."

"I killed him. With my bare, human hands. The hands he so desperately wanted me to have. As I will eventually kill you. With my soulless hands. Damned hands against your holy flesh. I look forward to the smell of your skin cooking beneath my fingers."

Zachriel leaned in closer. "You certainly speak like a demon."

"I am true to myself." She reached out and touched the burned mark above his heart. "You could do it now. It would be so easy. Alec did half the work for you. Just reach in...and pull."

He grabbed her hand, crushing her fingers. "Tell me about the second boy."

"He would kill you before you got a good look at him. The second one is crafty, and mad."

"You underestimate me."

"You underestimate a boy who stayed hidden from Haven for seventeen years." Wrenching her hand from his vise-like grip, Picadilly flexed her fingers—nothing broken. "But I will propose a deal."

"I don't deal with demons."

"Let me heal you," she said, taking a lock of her hair into her hands, stroking it, already able to feel the power that ran through it. "You'll feel better, and so will I. Then, maybe, I will consider telling you about the second boy."

Zachriel's face was shadowed, the light of the torch gleaming off the back of his short-cropped hair. "Healing me will heal yourself. And I have no need of demonic healing, nor a prisoner with two working legs."

"Then we are finished speaking." Picadilly closed her eyes and feigned sleep.

"You were a child of Haven once. What changed?"

"I walked in Hell, and I experienced the freedom of it. As you do now. You would love nothing more than to beat me senseless, but you cannot. It would not be honorable, to attack an opponent who cannot defend herself on even ground. Simply the fact that you broke my leg to keep me here must keep you up at night. And if it does not, then you are closer to tearing out your heart than you think."

His fist was suddenly in her hair, pulling her head back, twisting her neck to a painful angle. Picadilly gasped, surprised, then reached her own hands back to try to relieve the sharp pull on her head. Zachriel's face was right against hers. "As I said, you underestimate me. Haven has changed since you were last there."

"Haven doesn't change." Even as she said it, she feared it wasn't true. Something in his voice made her formerly human heart thump harder in her chest.

"Allow me to show you just how wrong you are."

Gabriel read the report for the tenth time. She could hardly believe the words, despite the clear, precise scrawl that had been inked into the paper. In all her years of chasing Talia's child, of cleaning up

Kadiel's mistake, she had never dreamed what her operative had discovered.

Twins.

She had sent Zachriel after Carma's soulless as a way to weaken her old friend, to diminish her resources and send doubt and worry into her heartless chest. She hadn't expected the search to turn up information that would change her entire mission.

There wasn't just one child to find. There were two. Talia had given birth to twins. Kadiel had saved her sister and her two sons.

Kadiel had also allowed Gabriel to chase one, leaving the other undetected.

The bookish seraph in question currently sat at the other side of Gabriel's office, hunched over books and stained with ink. The report had come in only a quarter turn earlier, and Gabriel had spent that time reading and rereading it, making certain that she had not misinterpreted the words. Now, Gabriel watched Kadiel scribble and turn pages, her temper carefully in check. There was no longer any room for leniency.

"Kadiel."

"Hm? Yes?" Kadiel looked up, cheeks smeared with ink, her hair clinging to those dark spots.

"Your sister's child…is there anything you have neglected to tell me?"

"Of course there is. I've been hiding him from you."

"True. However, I suggest you practice full disclosure right now. If you do not, things will go badly for you."

"What do you mean?" Her gaze flicked to the report in Gabriel's hands. "Did something happen?"

"I am giving you one last chance to redeem yourself. Tell me everything."

"You know everything that matters to you. Talia had a son who can see into the myst. Because of that, he changes things in The Plan and so you seek to destroy him. What else could there possibly be?"

"Last chance, Kadiel."

Tucking her hair behind her ear, Kadiel sat straight up, folded her arms over her chest, and dared to give Gabriel a defiant expression. "I have nothing more to say."

"There were two children that night," Gabriel said, then paused to watch Kadiel pale. "You and she hid two boys from Haven. Not one."

"Gabriel—" She had lost some of her usual bravado.

"All this time, I have been searching for one, when I should have searched for two." She stood, slowly, hands planted firmly on the hard surface of her desk. "You will tell me everything you know about this second child."

"I will not. I will not aid in your hunt of either of my sister's children."

"You will tell me, or you will tell the Hall of Justice."

Kadiel sat straighter, taller, in her chair, though it only served to betray the tension in her body, rather than give the illusion of confidence. "You cannot scare me. I will tell you nothing."

Gabriel rounded her desk, fingers trailing along the edges of a locked box she'd finally been desperate enough to take out. Kadiel was weak and foolish. Gabriel could make her talk. "Is he another Singer? Another myst-seer?"

"Don't you think you would have noticed if he was?"

"What is he then? Like their father?"

"It would make sense, wouldn't it?"

A witch. Suddenly Gabriel felt cold. "A half-seraph witch? You've hidden an abomination like that all this time? Are you trying to end us all?"

"I was trying to give two children the chance to live."

"Witches are born of demons."

"And demons are born of seraph. Everything is connected in some way."

"Do you understand nothing? Are you really so naïve? Witches are a perversion of our power. To have a creature that is both—" Gabriel couldn't finish her sentence. The thought was too unbearable. "There is no way a being could be both and survive. The two natures would pull each other apart."

"He has lived this long."

"He will tear himself and this world apart. You are doing him no favors by keeping him secret."

Kadiel pushed her chair away from the desk and stood. "You will not convince me to help you. I would rather tear out my own heart."

"It may just come to that. But be careful, your time is most likely limited. The Restorium will come, and you will be cast out, forever Fallen and aching for Haven's light in your life."

"I know my heart," she said, coming round her desk until she stood face to face with Gabriel. "The One knows my heart. I do not fear the Restorium. Perhaps you should, with all your conflicting emotions."

"You will come with me to the mortal realm, and we will find these boys together."

"And just how do you intend to make me do that?"

Gabriel's fingers flexed along the box on her desk. She wasn't afraid of doing what was necessary. No matter the cost. "Divine Order. I shall put in for your bindings this very day."

Kadiel stepped back, face pale, throat taut. "You would take away what will I have?"

"Free will is a luxury."

— CHAPTER TWENTY-SIX —

The sun shone warm on his face, and the gentle breeze coming off the water smelled of lilies and grass. Alec stretched out where he lay on the ground beside the lake, breathing easy and feeling more content than he had in a long time. For a moment, no one was chasing them, no one searched for them, no one wanted to tell them what they could do and where they could be. It had been a good full day since they had seen another living soul, and Alec didn't mind one bit.

He felt Ariadne drop down beside him, smelling like the flowers that grew nearby. She sighed happily, her hip brushing against his. Then he felt water dripping onto his face and arm.

"Ari," he said, opening his eyes, "there's not a cloud in the sky, and yet I seem to be getting rained on."

She smiled sweetly, teasingly, and rung out her long, wet hair over the ground, shaking the last of the water onto him. "How odd. I can't imagine what would be the cause."

He grabbed her by the wrists and pulled her down on his chest, kissing her soundly. Her skin was cool from her time in the lake, and she tasted like the very waters of life. "Enjoy your swim?" he asked, only after he'd had his fill—for now.

"Yes," she said, gathering her hair and drawing it over her shoulder so that it lay in a wet circle against his chest. "I think had I gone any longer without a proper bath I would have begun to take root with the flowers."

"You would fit right in." Alec traced her cheek bones, then her lips.

"You're such a flatterer. My black hair would look dismal beside all these flowers."

"I disagree."

"Then I worry you may be colorblind."

"Doesn't matter, as long as I can see you." He ran a hang along her spine, to her lower back.

She slapped his hand away. "You're incorrigible." With a quick peck on the mouth, she stood, leaving him colder on the grass.

"You weren't complaining the other night."

"There weren't innocent eyes pretending to be elsewhere the other night."

Alec made a pillow of his arms beneath his head. "Is that what he's up to?"

"He claimed to be taking a walk around the lake. I believe I noticed another family setting up camp nearby. They have daughters about his age. He's more like you than he seems." She kicked Alec's hand away when he reached for her ankle.

"You say that like it's a bad thing."

"One of you is enough."

Alec stood, drawing her into his arms. "I love you."

"I know," she said, playing with the hair at the nape of his neck.

"You're supposed to say, 'I love you too.'"

"If I tell you all the time, you'll take it for granted."

"Never."

Ariadne took his right hand and kissed each of his fingertips in turn. Alec watched her lips move against his fingers, mesmerized as a sort of fog drifted over his vision. For a moment, his skin appeared darker, weathered, and he thought he saw a line across his wrist. He reached to brush it away.

"What is it?" Ariadne asked.

"I thought I had something on my arm." The line wouldn't go away. His skin felt raised where he touched it, almost like a scar.

Quickly, Ariadne brushed her own hand over his wrist, her touch tingling. His arm once again looked normal. No scars, no weathering. "I don't see anything," she said. "Your eyes must have been playing tricks on you."

"Must have." His vision had cleared, but the memory lingered.

"Alec!" The scuffle of feet against grass and dirt emerged from the trees that lined the western side of the lake. Long gangly limbs flailed about as the boy ran, then hopped over rocks and flowers as he made his way closer.

"Marc, don't run! You'll fall in."

Marc wrinkled his nose. "I'm not a baby. I can swim, you know." He slowed as he reached them, smiling as he caught his breath. "In fact, in most cultures I'm nearly what is considered 'of age.'"

"You're thirteen," Alec said, having one of those moments where he was suddenly overcome with affection for his brother. Marc's clothes were covered in dirt and leaves, and there was a smudge of mud across one cheek, but he looked as happy as ever. Alec felt a pang in his heart as he looked at those deep blue eyes—their mother's eyes. He worried because Marc was all he had left. Because their parents had succumbed to plague when Marc was still too small to remember. Because he had almost lost Marc as well. It was a miracle he had survived, as small as he had been. Alec thanked Cel-Eza every day, and Inaseri as well, for sparing his brother.

"It's my job to worry," he said. It was his job to keep that smile as carefree as it always had been.

Marc rolled his eyes and ducked away when Alec reached to tousle his hair. He held out a handful of flowers to Ariadne. "Here, I picked these for you."

"They're beautiful," she said, taking them and lifting them to her nose. "You always get me the best presents." She kissed him on the cheek, and Alec saw Marc blush.

"No present for me?" Alec asked.

"I didn't think you'd want any flowers for your hat," Marc said, "but I can go get more."

"Ha ha, you're a funny kid today."

"And you're an overprotective slack today. I must have spent an entire turn in the woods—didn't you notice?"

"I may have fallen asleep."

Marc frowned. "You never let me wander off that long."

"I knew you were safe."

"What if I wasn't?"

"I knew you were."

"What if I was lost? Would you come look for me?"

"Of course. Always. I'd find you before you even knew you were lost yourself."

"Good." As soon as the word was free of Marc's lips, his whole face shifted. His hair lightened, the smile disappeared, and blue eyes became silver-brown. "Alec!"

A swift wind of terror swept him, and then the vision was gone, and Marc stood staring at Alec against the backdrop of lush green, and vibrant crystal blue water, and spring flowers. "Alec?" he said, looking concerned, "Are you all right?"

"Yes," Alec said, closing his eyes a moment to clear his head. He felt a little sick to his stomach, and his right arm burned. "Yes, I'm fine. I just—"

When he opened his eyes, it wasn't Marc standing before him—it was another boy entirely. One with silver-brown eyes that held nothing but terror. There was blood on his face and hands, and lines cut into his arms and chest. The boy reached out to him, saying his name again and again.

"Alec, help me!"

Ariadne grabbed Alec by the shoulders, calling his name and turning him away. "Alec, look at me. At me." The lake and the flowers returned, the sun shining brightly in the blue sky. Ariadne took his face in her hands, stroking his cheeks soothingly. "It's all right," she said. "Look here. Right at me."

Alec felt hot and cold all at once. His hands shook. "What was that?"

"Nothing. Nothing at all. You probably just slept too long in the sun. Let's find some shade and get you something to drink."

She tried to lead him away, but Alec didn't move. He breathed carefully, reminding himself that out followed in, and to repeat. He lifted one shaky hand, and on his wrist the lines he'd seen before returned. More now, more pronounced. Scars, and an unnatural vine, coiled around his forearm.

A demon's mark.

"Alec, please look at me."

He didn't. He stared at the mark, the tiny leaves that appeared so delicate, yet bound him to a dangerous and cursed life. Ariadne's hands were still at his face, trying to coax him to look away. He brushed her off and stepped back.

Marc touched his arm. "Alec? You're scaring me."

His brother. He looked at the boy, and the fear he saw in those blue eyes was too out of place, too painful—the other face appeared again, covered in blood. The two flickered back and forth like two candle flames until they mixed as one, and Marc's face was bruised and bloody.

The lake disappeared, replaced by bonfires and a giant stone slab. Lines had been charred into the once-green grass, and the smell of smoke swallowed the fresh spring breeze.

Marc lay at his feet. Dead.

Alec turned and retched, his knees like water and trembling uncontrollably. Then he heard another voice, just as young, just as precious.

"Alec? Are you going to find me?"

Bri. He was hurt. A *labrynth* had been carved into his chest, dripping blood. As Alec watched, a hand appeared over Bri's shoulder, and then an arm, a head, until he saw the identical, but twisted face of Kai lingering in the shadows at Bri's back.

Ariadne grabbed Alec's wrist, muttering strange words. He felt her Hell power caress his own, and for a brief moment the sky was blue and clear again. Alec wrenched his arm from her grip and tore at his left wrist.

A braided bit of leather broke free in his hand. The sky was red, the clouds black and stormy grey. Brimstone boulders surrounded a churning lake where dark shadows swam beneath the choppy surface. In the distance, a forest burned, and through the smoke Alec could make out the vague figures of people running from the flames. He stared again at the leather in his hand and saw the tiny lines that had been etched into the underside. *Labrynths.*

Ariadne stood before him, against the backdrop of Hell, her throat tense, her eyes desperate and sad. "Alec, I..."

"Did you do this?" His voice hardly sounded his own. Quiet, disbelieving.

Her hesitation may have only been a few beats of Alec's unsteady heart, but it was enough. "Yes," she said.

"What was it?"

"An illusion." She looked afraid to touch him, which was good, because he didn't want to be touched.

"Why?"

"After everything's that's happened...you've been having such bad dreams. I just wanted you to have a moment of peace."

Alec looked at the leather bracelet as if it were a leech that could grab hold of him again. He remembered the day she had given it to him. They had run for days, putting distance between themselves and the seraph he had—he couldn't think of it. In a tiny Hell village, occupied by mostly more calmly natured hellions, Ariadne had purchased the gift and tied it around his wrist. But she couldn't have gotten it there. Hellions were not witches. "Where did it come from?"

"Alec, please—"

"Where?"

His shout sent her back a step and caused her tears to flow freely. "It's something I've had a while now. I bought it off a young witch some time ago. I had planned to use it for myself, when I needed to be back in the past, even for just a moment."

The sky hadn't been red when she had given it to him. They had been in another part of Hell, where it was always night. "How long? How long have I been living that lie?" When she didn't answer, Alec raised his voice yet again. "How long?"

"A week!" She cried the words, repeating them when at first they came out stunted and broken.

Alec's heartbeat stuttered in his ears, Ariadne's frantic breathing a dissonant accompaniment. Hot power bleed into his hands, and he let the leather drop to the ground, stepping on it when he turned so he wouldn't have to see her anymore. Digging his hands into his hair, he tried to remember how to breathe, how to think. A week. A week lost. A week wasted.

A week Bri had spent with Kai.

He heard Ari at his back. "Alec, I didn't mean to—"

"But you did. Don't talk to me right now. Don't talk to me."

She said nothing at first, but he heard her tears and then a whispered, "I'm sorry."

How was he going to find Bri now? He didn't even know where he was himself. She had cost them all valuable time. It was a mistake to be with her. It wasn't about him and his lost past, it was about finding Bri and protecting the future. He prayed his selfishness hadn't caused irreparable damage. If he was smart, he would leave her behind and find Bri on his own. Then, once Bri was safe, he could pursue the past.

Alec walked down the barren road, Hell power burning in his hands, not knowing what direction he was heading, not knowing where it would take him. He simply needed to move. To act. To find Bri. His heart, broken as it was, would have to wait.

But he didn't protest when he heard Ariadne follow.

The brush was thick, tearing at the hem of her pant legs and scratching her exposed arms. Carma remembered this place well; she had been reborn here, a young demon with a gaping hole in her chest and a hunger for something to fill it. A group of idiot mortals had summoned her and granted her exactly that. If memory served—and she was sure that it did—she had met Alec just on the other side of the mountain range that stretched out to the west. So much had changed since then. This place had been a bustling center of civilization. Now, it was The Wilds, overgrown and under-populated. The Burning Sea lay to the north, swirling heat through the region. Carma had been there many times in the past thousand years. It was where Inaseri had tossed Cel-Eza's head after their legendary battle. A battle with no cause. Carma had hoped on all occasions to catch a glimpse of the god's head at the bottom of the sea, but had never had such satisfaction. Perhaps the tale had been fabricated. Wouldn't Alec love that? But, no. Cel-Eza was dead, and the sea burned because of it. There was no denying it.

This time, she hadn't come for a dead god's head.

Dorothea shuffled along behind her, attention constantly being stolen away by the many things they passed in the woods. Trees, rocks, snakes, and bugs—everything had the potential to assist her scribings in some way. Once, Carma had been forced to stop for a whole day just so the old witch could inspect and study the pattern in the bark of an ancient tree.

"Can we hurry things along?" Carma asked when Dorothea slowed once again, hands reaching for the leaves that hung down into the path.

"Do not rush me," Dorothea said, turning the orange leaf over, then pulling it free. "There are secrets to be had here."

"We didn't come for secrets. We came for a god."

"And the trees know where to find them."

"What do you mean?"

Dorothea turned the leaf over in her hands as Carma came toward her. "The lines, the veins, they are language. You simply have to know how to read them."

"And you can?"

"I am a witch. I can read all the lines of the world."

"Then what do they say?"

Holding the leaf between two fingers, Dorothea lifted it to Carma's eye level. When she released it, it remained airborne, spinning in place. "They are here."

The wind blew, but the leaf did not respond. It remained precisely in front of her face, dancing lazily with no indication that it would ever touch the ground. "Who is here?"

"The Twins."

No. Of all the damnable godflesh...

A hand closed around the leaf, brown and long fingered. White lines traced veins along the arm and throat, creating patterns that seemed almost skeletal. Then there were two arms, then three, then four. Feet touched the ground while two more legs wrapped about a waist. A second head appeared beside the first, the faces identical in all ways. Brown eyes, round noses, white lashes, and teeth. The only discernible difference was the length of their curled brown hair—one to the shoulders, the other to the waist. Everything about them seemed to be in a constant state of change.

The hand that had closed about the leaf opened once more, empty. "Cool trick, huh?" said the first head.

"It is no trick to destroy a dead leaf," Carma said.

"But we did not destroy it," the first said. "We restored it," said the second, opening a different hand where the leaf lay, green and fresh as spring.

"A better trick, then," Carma said. "But to what end? Winter is almost here, why should the leaf live once more?"

"Because we will it so," said the second as he hung on his brother's back, though it seemed he may have also lain within his brother's body.

"You should have been witches," Dorothea said, taking the leaf without asking and without resistance. She immediately began reading the lines once more.

"Our parents were witches," the first said. "No," the second cut in, "they were farmers." They both shrugged. "Maybe they were both," said the both of them in unison.

"Are the two of you so ancient now you no longer remember?" Carma knew their legend well. Children who refused to grow up. The sons of a tribal chief back in the days before cities and roads. They had run away into the woods, never to return. But travelers often heard laughter in the air, and the boys were never forgotten. Their story was passed down through the ages, told around campfires and to children as they lay down to sleep. It became rumored that the twins had taken up residence in the forest, playing there eternally among the wildlife and trees. Eventually the people of their land began to pray to them, to beg them to leave travelers be, or to resist the urge to lure their children into the woods with promises of never-ending games. Once enough people believed, the gods were born, taking shape and form, acting out that which they were said to do.

Carma had always wondered what would happen if the bones of those two children were ever to be found. It was her own personal belief that they had died out there, foolishly believing in their own invulnerability.

From the looks on their faces now, she didn't doubt it. Gods made their pasts what they desired them to be, not what the truth had been. "Parents are parents," they spoke together, "a child never cares beyond that."

"And what of orphans?"

They both frowned, and the second one hopped from his brother's back, bouncing on the air just above the ground. "What do you want? Why are you here? It's not often we get visitors."

"The people of The Wilds know better than to tempt you," Dorothea said, running her finger along the veins of the leaf.

"We get lonely," said the first. "Do you want to play?" They both looked at Carma.

"I did not come to play. I am looking for someone, and it is not the two of you."

Slipping the green leaf into the folds of her dress, Dorothea's gaze wandered the wood. "I will play."

The Twins slumped, pouting. "But you're so *old.*"

"One is never too old to play."

"Dorothea," Carma said, "what are you doing?"

The witch held up a single hand. "Hush, girl. I am speaking with my friends."

"Friends?" Temper flaring, Carma felt the claws on her hands stretch and show.

The twin gods bounced toward the old witch. "You would be friends with us?"

"Yes. I know many good games."

"You will tell us your name then?" they spoke together.

"If you tell me yours."

What in all the gods' names is she up to?

"I am Keaie," said the first, the one with hair only to his shoulders. "Kesi," said the second, with hair all the way down his back.

"Dorothea." She reached out both hands to them, and the twins took them, one each. The growth of power on the air was palpable. Dorothea clasped her hands about each of their wrists, her thumbs moving over their darker skin, tracing the white lines that ran all over their bodies. "Tell me," she said, "what happens when a child refuses to grow old?"

"Easy," Kesi said, grinning from ear to ear. "They live forever."

"Maybe so. What happens when those children cannot escape eternity? Can the mind remain young even after living for so long?"

"Of course. As long as people believe it," said Keaie.

"Do you still hear people's prayers?"

"Every day," they said together. "Can we play the game now?"

Dorothea smiled. "We are already playing."

The Twins stilled, then looked at their arms. The white lines were turning red where Dorothea touched them, the color soaking its way up to their necks. "What have you done?" they screamed, pulling to free themselves—but Dorothea was suddenly stronger than they were, and she did not let go.

"I am reading you," she said. "Nothing more. Do not fear it. I am almost finished."

"You cannot!" screamed Kesi. "Let us go!" Keaie screeched over his brother's voice, still struggling against the old witch's hold. They both craned their necks around to look at Carma. "Help us! We are only children!"

"I don't care much for children," Carma said, surprised at the steadiness of her own voice. She had no idea what Dorothea was doing, but she had no doubt that it would get them both killed somewhere down the line. At the very least, the mischievous god twins would make their lives a living nightmare from this point on.

Dorothea shut her eyes and let her head fall back, her grip on The Twins still as strong as steel. Then she breathed and released them. The Twins stumbled backward, falling to the ground and clutching each other. The lines on their arms returned to their normal white color.

"That was not a fun game," said Keaie, his face seeming to shift from ashen to red and back again. "I feel sick," said Kesi.

"You will both be perfectly fine," Dorothea said. "I did you no harm. You have helped me much today. I thank you."

"You tricked us," they hissed together, the hue of their eyes turning darker.

"Not possible. How could I trick the very gods of trickery? And if I had, then it would have been with your blessing, for no tricks are accomplished without you." The old witch smiled at them like a grandmother amused with her grandchildren.

Even after nine hundred years, Dorothea could still curl Carma's toes.

The Twins looked at one another, then at the old witch, then back to each other again. "She could be right," Kesi said. "She could be wrong," Keaie said. "I do feel better now," said Kesi, rubbing his stomach. "My arm is fine," Keaie rubbed the appendage as he spoke. "Mother won't like it." "Father won't either."

"You have no parents," Carma said, not liking the way they spoke of their mother and father.

"Children always have parents." In perfect unison they hopped back to their feet, Kesi once again on his brother's back, almost melting within. "When the birth parents die, someone always takes over." They grinned like a pair of cats about to feast on a mouse. "And ours will not be happy about this game."

"Who?"

"Inaseri." Cackling, they disappeared, their laughter floating on the breeze long after they had gone.

Inaseri. Just who she had come looking for. Though she had hoped to meet on more favorable terms. "What have you done, Dorothea?"

"Inaseri will come now, just as you wanted."

"I didn't want her to arrive angry!"

"There will be no anger. I did not hurt the children."

"They are gods, not children."

Dorothea waved her off. "They are children in every sense. They never age, not even their minds. People believe they are children and so they are."

"What is your point?"

"People's beliefs, Carma. That is what sustains them. They are mortal made, despite what the lines on their bodies would suggest."

"You wanted to see if they had been created by a *labrynth*? The Twins outdate witches and *labrynths* by centuries!"

"That is the tale we are all told, yes. But the truth can be lost to history. You know this." She turned to the closest tree and began tracing its patterns again. "You believe your Olin wants to ascend, just as Lillianna wanted to ascend. I want to know what it takes to make a god."

The words came to her as though they had been placed there by someone else. "Followers. A legend."

"Exactly."

"Olin will need to do something that has people talking of him, weaving tales and fantasies until he becomes something more than what he is now. But that takes centuries. The Twins were surely dead and dust long before they became gods. We know Olin does not have that kind of time. He is acting now."

"He has *labrynths* to help him, and communication is much different now. Stories spread faster than they used to."

"So he could do it. He could become a god."

Her hand going still against the tree, Dorothea looked at Carma. "Anyone could."

Holy One and darkest Hell... It was impossible. No. Possible. Unthinkable. But the only thing she could think of.

Anyone could be a god.

Anyone.

Warm light flashed through the shadows of the trees, then simmered to a gentle hue. "Well, isn't this interesting. A demon and a witch, discussing gods and magic."

She never changed, Carma thought. Just as Haven never changed. The Restorium would do nothing to fix that. Haven would purge itself of everything that could make it grow. "It is a conversation you may want to be a part of, Gabriel."

"Then by all means." Armor creaking as she moved, careful of her sword, Gabriel sat on a fallen log. "Let's talk."

— CHAPTER TWENTY-SEVEN —

A large group had gathered at the front of the tavern, just under the windows so that the bright light of the outside illuminated their coins and mugs. They shouted over one another, cutting in and swapping rumors. Every so often, their voices would drop to a sharp whisper, as though they remembered that their topic of conversation was rather taboo and uncommon. As though they didn't want to bring the subject of the gossip down upon them.

They were talking about Luca.

Tassos tried to bury himself in his ale, to drown out the excited voices with drunkenness, but it wasn't working. It had been some time since he had left the High Lord of Hell to wallow in his misery. Even a reaper could only take so much. He had come to this tavern to escape all that, to drink and eavesdrop and maybe find a pretty face to help him forget. What had he gotten instead? A drunken crowd of busy-bodies passing along hearsay.

"Dead, I say. No way could he hide for so long without somebody noticing."

"You're a fool. You can't kill the High Lord."

"Lillianna was killed, why not Luca?"

"It hasn't been long enough for me to believe Lillianna will stay dead."

"They say the High Lord disappeared at the same time as The Silent One. Perhaps they are having a not-so-silent affair together!"

Laughter erupted, then another cut in, "Hold your tongue. It ain't right to say such things. One of them could hear you."

"Let them hear! At least then we would know the truth of it."

Tassos groaned and took another long drink from his mug. *You're all wrong. The High Lord of Hell is in bed, feeling sorry for himself.* He couldn't stand it. He would need to be much, much drunker if this nonsense was going to continue. When the serving girl came by again, he grabbed her by the wrist. She was a waif of a thing, a soul condemned to service to pay for her sins. Looking at her face, he thought maybe he had been the one to send her here, but it was always better not to dwell on such things. "Bring me as many mugs as you can carry, love. I have a feeling this is going to be a long night."

She scrambled off to do so, but was stopped before reaching the bar. A woman with black hair called out to her from a nearby table, asking for more ale, and water as well. The serving girl nodded and headed off again. Tassos could visibly see her working to remember both orders. They weren't so difficult, but something told him he would be waiting a bit on the rest of his drinks.

The black-haired woman turned in her chair, gathering all that hair and tying it back. A man sat beside her, his head on the table. Tassos thought there seemed something familiar about that head of black hair, but dismissed it. It was simply nice to look at, thick and shining in the candlelight. It probably felt fantastic to run your fingers through it all, to grab and pull just a—

Focus, Tassos. You're letting your mind wander too far. Gods, he needed another drink. Whatever that serving girl was trying to redeem herself for, she wasn't doing a very good job of it. Tassos turned his empty mug around and around on the table, attempting to distract himself.

"You need to relax," the woman said. "You've worn yourself down and it's too hard to fight when you're exhausted. Take tonight to regain your strength."

"I don't have time," the man said, his voice muffled by the table. "I have to find him."

"You have to get yourself back under control."

"I feel perfectly in control right now."

"You're perfectly drunk right now."

The man scoffed and swatted at her clumsily. To the woman's credit, she pushed the issue no further, instead sitting back in her chair and letting her gaze move about the room. When she and Tassos inevitably locked eyes, he smiled and held up his glass to her. She returned the gesture. Beautiful, Tassos acknowledged, in a strong and capable way. This woman was no delicate flower. She reminded him of his Lady Death and how he imagined She would look had She a physical form. *Well chosen, my friend,* he thought to the drunken man.

The crowd on the other end of the tavern erupted with laughter once again, banging their mugs and fists against the tables. As a result, the dark-haired man sat up, rubbing at his face and temples.

"This was a terrible idea," he said.

"I told you as much nearly three turns ago," the woman said, looking relieved when the serving girl finally returned. She pushed the water over to the inebriated man. "Here, drink this."

He didn't drink. "How am I ever going to find him, Ari?" he said through his hands. "It's like looking for a needle in a haystack. I have nothing to go on."

"We'll find him. There's always a way."

"It would be nice if that way would fall into our laps."

The woman—Ari—pulled his hands from his face and shoved the glass of water at him. "Drink."

Tassos didn't hear whatever was said next. He was too busy staring at the man's familiar face. *Sweet Lady Death, it's Alec. What in all Hell happened to him?*

Alec drank the water, but hated every drop of it. In Hell, water was always warm, and the power still coursing through his hands only warmed it further. He had nightmares about what he had done, about the mangled body of the seraph lying on the ground, and the way he felt standing over it. Powerful. Strong. If he called more power to himself, flooded his body with the energy and the heat, the dreams faded away, but then he felt it difficult to feel anything but anger. He hated who he was when using the power.

Ariadne had argued with him countless times, insisting that he master the power, hold onto it, but not give in. It was easier said than done. He wanted it all gone. But when he had driven it from his body completely, emptied himself until he felt that familiar hole that was the place inside him that should have held a soul, he suffered shakes and nausea. Giving it up was harder in Hell; it always had been. He wouldn't be able to truly work on dispelling the power until he was back in the mortal realm—but he couldn't do that until he found Bri.

So the power remained, and Alec hated himself.

"We need to keep moving," he said. "There's nothing here. No sign of Kai or Bri."

"I thought we agreed to rest."

"Don't have time." He stood, having to steady himself as he did so. "I can't sit still. It makes it all worse." Heading for the door, Alec stumbled into a misplaced chair, cursing the stone object and the throbbing that started in his knee.

Ariadne hurried after him. "I don't think this is a good idea. Maybe if you weren't drunk—"

"Being drunk makes me clearer."

"I think you're mistaken."

The itch to fight made his hands curl into fists, but this was Ariadne, and he didn't want to hurt her, no matter what the power wanted. The door was so close now; he had almost made it.

A demon parted from the large group that had been carrying on and adding to Alec's headache all evening. Blue-skinned and black-scaled at his joints, the demon tripped over his own feet, careening into Alec, sending them both knocking into the wall.

"My sincere apologies," the blue demon slurred. "It seems the ale here is stronger than we all suspected." He patted Alec on the chest, swaying and crossing his eyes.

"Just get off me," Alec said, his palms hot enough to burn through flesh.

"As you wish, as you wish." But the blue demon could not back up when he tried. Instead, he stumbled and his lost balance, which sent him teetering into Ariadne—who caught him deftly, and set him back on his feet. "My thanks, pretty lady." He grinned, and all his teeth were as black as his scales.

Ariadne did not respond. Knowing he had only moments before the power made him start a fight, Alec reached for the door.

"It's a shame, ya know," the demon said, hiccuping between words. "Once nothing could be lost in Hell. The High Lord could find anything. Nothing was outside his scope. You had only to ask…and pay the right price."

"What did you say?" By the time Alec turned, the demon was carefully making his way toward the bar, holding onto the tables as he went.

"Just reminis—remin—ah, forget it. Just doing some thinking." Missing a chair, the demon fell into the lap of another patron. "Couldn't help but overhear, ya know." He smiled at the man whose lap he occupied. "A bit of help?"

The patron, clad in black and purple, shoved the demon up and back to his feet.

Alec held tight to a chair, not because he was unsteady, but because the urge to attack and force an answer had grown nearly unbearable. "What do you mean the High Lord could find anything?"

"Just that. They say he knew every inch of this place. No one knows how." At the bar, the blue demon signaled the serving girl for another drink. "Coulda found what you're looking for easy."

"But the High Lord is missing," Alec said.

"Missing. Ha! My bet, he's dead."

"If the High Lord of Hell was dead," Ariadne said, "don't you think we would know for certain?"

"Why? He ain't done nothing for us lately. No one's seen him, and he doesn't ever step in, not even when his sister got killed." Another full mug in hand, the blue demon lifted it toward them in a sloshing toast, then began staggering his way back to the rowdy table he had come from. "Good day to you."

Ariadne set a hand on his shoulder. "Don't think it, Alec. It's impossible."

"So is searching on our own like this. It's at least worth a try."

"We'll never find him. No one knows where he is. He doesn't want to be found. There's no way finding Luca is easier than finding Bri."

The black and purple clad patron stood and headed toward the door. Something about the long black hair that fell down his back made Alec grab him by the arm before he could leave.

"Ow! That hurts!"

"Tassos."

"Yes," The reaper pulled his arm from Alec's grip, inspecting his sleeve. "You've scorched the fabric! It will be irreparable!"

"What are you doing here?"

"Taking in the scenery. I'd say it's lovely to see you, Alec, but it isn't. You look terrible. Which is a shame."

"It's not like you to sit alone. Why not join the fun?" he asked, indicating the raucous group.

Tassos shrugged. "Even I like my solitude from time to time. How is my friend, Carma?" He flicked his gaze to Ariadne. "This beautiful woman is decidedly not her. Have you gone rogue?"

"Wouldn't be possible, and you know it. Carma knows where I am."

"And who you're with?"

Alec said nothing. There were still days where he couldn't reconcile his conscience on the matter of Ariadne. He loved her—he couldn't not. She was Ariadne, a piece of himself. But he knew Carma would never approve, and her suspicion invaded his mind daily.

"Ah, yes. That's what I thought," Tassos said. "Now, if you'll excuse me, I have places to be."

Alec grabbed him again, this time hearing the hiss of the reaper's expensive fabric beneath his hand. "Don't you want to know why I'm here?"

Tassos didn't pull away. "No."

"You're awfully quiet concerning the High Lord."

He looked away, a haughty gesture, filled with denial. "I have nothing to say on the matter."

"Funny. Every other time I've met you, you had plenty to say on any matter."

"I came here to drink, not to gossip."

"I don't believe you."

"Well, that's too bad, isn't it?" Tassos plucked each of Alec's fingers from his arm in turn, his strength surprising.

"Wait." Ariadne stepped in front of the door, blocking Tassos's escape. "Do you really know nothing?"

Turning on one heel to face her, Tassos gave her a glassy stare. "Who are you? Why should I be talking to you?"

"I'm an old friend of Alec's. We were human together."

"Oh, well isn't that sweet. Reunited after so long. Tearful, I imagine. I still don't care." Sliding Ariadne aside, Tassos reached for the door.

"Kai has Bri." Alec spoke on a whim, remembering the first time Tassos had seen Bri, and the reaction he'd had. It was a hunch, nothing more.

And it proved right. Tassos's hand hovered just above the door handle. "What did you say?"

"Kai, he has Bri. You've met Kai before, haven't you?"

Tassos's normally expressive face went stoney. "I have had the misfortune, yes."

"Then you know how dire the situation is. He took Bri. That's why I'm here, but I can't find him. If you know anything, *anything*, please tell me."

Tassos looked at him, and Alec could see the war taking place inside his head. He pinched the bridge of his nose, then grumbled a few things in a language that hardly sounded human. "Fine," he said. "I may know someone who can help, but—" He stuck a finger in Alec's face, "You're going to have to put a knife to my back and make this look good, or I will be in a world of trouble."

— CHAPTER TWENTY-EIGHT —

Bri rushed down the halls of the mountain, knowing his brother would be at the training yard this time of day. Kai had made sure Bri knew exactly how much he had grown over the past year, how much stronger he had become physically. Kai could hurl a javelin clear across the field, and snap a staff with his bare hands. Some of it was natural, earned by months of careful practice and honing of muscles. But Bri knew better than to believe it had all been gained that way. *Labrynths* were becoming easier for him to read lately, and Kai had numerous marks scribed all over his body. More than one was for strength or agility.

But none of that mattered. None of it mattered because it wasn't why he sought his brother out.

Ella was sick. They couldn't stay here any longer.

Stepping outside onto the overlook, the sounds of mock battle filled the air, surprising Bri with the sheer sharpness of most of the noise. Despite having heard it before, it always caught him off guard. He shuddered when someone below bellowed in unexpected pain. There had been a *shing* of steel and a dull thump that followed. Bri didn't want to know what limb had been lost.

Kai was within sight, centered in the field, his hair matted with dirt, and his arms and neck soaked with sweat. He balanced the weight of his sword easily, his stance quick to change as each blow from his opponent came. The demon fighting him was called Nallahar. Bri had had the unfortunate pleasure of meeting him only once, but once was quite enough. Nallahar was cold and sadistic, thriving in battle and conflict. Now, he pushed Kai back, though not down. A fallen weapons rack lay just behind Kai, getting closer and closer with each step. He would trip, stumble, and Nallahar would have him. Bri hoped the demon knew better than to seriously hurt Kai—but things were forgotten when a fight became like this one. Both had fire burning in their eyes. The rack grew closer still, and Kai had only two more paces before he would go down.

One.

Kai's feet stuck, and he went ungracefully backward, landing on the harsh metal rack and the weapons it held. He hissed and went still.

Nallahar approached, laughing. "Poor little Kailas. Fallen, have we? You should be more careful." He raised his sword, ready to strike.

Bri felt his voice stuck in his throat. He wanted to cry out for the demon to stop, but nothing would come.

Nallahar struck.

So did Kai.

Nallahar's sword stilled in the air, held back by Kai's. One of the fallen javelins stuck through the demon's abdomen, coming out through his back. Kai grinned as he released it, shoving Nallahar back and carefully standing from the pile of weapons. "Who should be more careful? You seem to have something lodged in your stomach there. May want to do something about it." With a swift kick that sent Nallahar to the ground, Kai tossed his sword aside and turned toward the mountain—and grinned at Bri, waving.

How had he known I was watching? Awkwardly, Bri waved back.

While other hellions and demons tended to Nallahar, Kai made his way up to the overlook where Bri waited for him. As he grew closer, Bri could see that he had fared worse than it had appeared from so far away. His arms were bruised and bleeding, his shirt was torn, and he walked with a stiffness that indicated more wounds that could not be seen. But he smiled at Bri as he unwrapped the protective leather from his hands. "Hello, Brother. What brings you here today?"

"I need to talk to you."

"Well, that's fairly obvious. About what?"

"About Ella."

"You want me to help you woo her? All right, but just this once."

"Be serious." Any concern Bri might have had for Kai's injuries disappeared. Kai could take care of himself. "She's not doing well. She's sick."

"So get her some remedy. What do you want me to do about it?" Kai headed back inside, so Bri followed.

"It's nothing a tonic will fix. It's this place. She's not meant to be here. She is a living mortal soul; she can't be in Hell. It's killing her."

"Killing her? That's rather dramatic."

"I don't want to wait and find out. Take her back to the mortal realm."

Kai shook his head. "No. I can't do that. She has to stay with us."

"Then we all go."

Kai spun around as they walked, lifting his arms in a grand gesture. "What if I have things to do here?"

A deflection. Suddenly, Bri was afraid Kai wanted to go back to the mortal realm, but it didn't matter. If their goals aligned in this, all the better. "You're scribing. You can do that anywhere."

"You think you know so much about what I do, Bri."

"As you think you know so much about me."

"I do know so much about you. I've spent years studying the matter."

"Have you spent any of that time thinking about what Hell does to a living soul? A good soul who should end up in Haven?"

Kai waggled his finger at him. "Now, now, Bri, that's not for you to decide."

"Think about it. You can't keep her here. Frankly, I'm surprised you survive here as well as you do."

"A witch's power is Hell-based. I can manage here."

"And what about me?"

"What about you?"

"This place isn't good for me either, Kai. I fare better than Ella, probably because our father was a witch and so some of that is in me, but I won't be able to stay here much longer. I can feel it weakening me every day. My power is from Haven, Kai. Hell crushes it." He could feel the brimstone walls of this entire place as if they closed in around him.

"I could change that, if you'd just let me mark you."

"No marks." He had said it thousands of times it seemed. "Come see Ella. Tell me then that we can't leave."

Kai sighed, exasperated. "Fine, fine. Show me your ailing woman." Though he didn't appreciate the theatrics, Bri wasn't fool enough to argue when he was getting his way. They walked in silence the rest of the way to Ella's room, Kai making bored facial expressions and picking the dirt from his fingernails.

Bri rapped three times on Ella's door and waited for her to answer before going in.

In his short time away from her, she seemed to have gotten worse. She sat up when they entered, having given into the need to lay down while alone. Her cheeks were flushed, though the rest of her had gone pale. Sweat covered her brow, and she had pulled her long hair back hastily. Even as she smiled at Bri, he could see her labored breathing.

"I brought Kai," he said, moving to sit beside her.

She took his hand immediately. "So I see."

Kai shut the door and crossed the room, stopping to inspect the few papers on the desk by the window. "Bri tells me you aren't feeling well. You certainly don't look well."

"What a gentlemanly thing to say," Ella said before covering her mouth to cough. "Please don't go through my things. They're private."

Kai picked up one of the many papers. "Journaling your time here?" He began to read. "I feel weaker this morning. As if a weight sits on my chest. I wonder if it is the sins of others who inhabit this realm, or my own sins come to claim me." He pouted. "So dramatic."

"She asked you not to read those, Kai," Bri said.

"And yet I did." He let the paper flutter back to the desktop. "But back to the matter at hand. Bri thinks we should take you back to the mortal realm before you die in this place."

Ella kept her chin up as he approached them. "I would have to admit I wish the same."

"You aren't enjoying Hell?"

"I don't think enjoyment is the goal here."

"Hm. Perhaps not." Kai touched her cheek lightly with his fingertips. Bri bit his own tongue to keep himself from slapping his brother's hand away. Ella didn't so much as flinch. "You are warm, I suppose. Despite my cooling *labrynths*." He looked at Bri. "Some people are sensible."

He wasn't going to say it again. There would be no marks anywhere near him. Cooling or otherwise.

Kai studied Ella a while longer, touching her face, her hands, checking her pulse. He looked her straight in the eyes, and Ella looked right back. Bri had to commend her for that. He knew from experience that if you stared long enough, you could see Kai's madness in his eyes.

"All right, then." Kai stepped back. "To the mortal realm we go."

"Really?" Bri said.

"Yes, really. Isn't that what you wanted? Why are you so surprised?"

"I'm not. I'm sorry, I shouldn't have reacted that way," Bri said, squeezing Ella's hand. "Thank you."

"Pack up. We'll leave before day's end. I have things to do up there anyway. But," he stopped just before opening the door, "if either of you betray me, if either of you attempt to run while we are there, I will make the other eternally sorry." Smiling as though he hadn't just threatened them, Kai left.

Bri didn't breathe easy again until the door shut firmly behind his brother. "That worked better than I expected."

"He's a careful planner," Ella said, pulling her hair off her neck. "He either has plans for the both of us and can't have me dying on him, or he does have simple human emotions and can understand my predicament."

"I think he likes you."

"I don't care either way. Our plan worked."

"The letters on the desk were a nice touch."

"He hasn't seen me in a few days, we needed some way to show that I've been sick for some time."

"You're all right though, aren't you? I almost panicked when I saw you. You look far worse than before."

Ella laughed, then coughed lightly. "I'm fine, I promise. Sick, as we didn't make that up, but not as bad as I look." She wiped at her brow. "It's water. And I pinched my cheeks the whole time I was alone to redden them."

Bri couldn't help but be relieved. "So now we go back to the mortal realm."

"Where we'll both feel better."

"Well, I don't know about me, but you certainly will."

"Why wouldn't you?"

"There's no myst here."

"But you can control it now."

"Better than before, but not perfectly. I was having trouble separating it from reality on occasion."

Ella took his hand and kissed the back of it. "I'll help you."

Bri tried to memorize the feel of her lips on his hand. He hoped he could control the myst well enough that he wouldn't have to give that up.

If Gabriel shook her head one more time, refusing to believe what she was told, Carma was going to tear her head from her neck.

"No," Gabriel said, not for the first time. "That cannot be. If it were true, we would have seen it."

"How would you have seen it, Gabriel? Haven is blind to anything outside the myst. All any of you would have to do is look at the mortal realm, but you foolishly believe that everything is exposed in that gods forsaken twisting mass—"

"Watch your tongue."

"—of futures The One left behind." Carma continued without stopping, keeping a reasonable distance from her old friend; she trusted little after the way she had lost Picadilly in Hell. Dorothea had tried to wander off, but Carma had quickly forbidden it. Now the old witch sat off to the side, where she could be seen scrawling in the dirt and humming to herself.

"We are well aware that demons cannot be seen," Gabriel said, "but gods have always been made known to us. They do not exist outside the Plan."

"There has never been a demon god before, only human."

"Still a god."

"He will become a god, Gabriel, whether you believe it or not."

"It is not in the myst, and the myst shows no forced changes either."

"Then Haven will let itself be destroyed."

"Not possible."

"We shall see." Circling her old friend like a hawk that had found prey, Carma studied Gabriel where she sat so very still. "Why did you come, then? If not to listen to what I have to say? I told you what will happen if we ever come to blows again."

"I need the boy."

"No. You need the boy to stop changing the Plan. There is a difference."

Gabriel drummed her fingers along the hilt of her sword. "No. The Council has demanded he be brought before them, and I am running out of time."

"I will not help you."

"There is another matter I was curious about."

"And what is that?"

"Are you aware that there are two?"

Carma was careful not to react too quickly to that. "Is it the second one you want now? You can have him. He's a thorn in my side."

"He is a witch. He does not change the myst."

"Of course he does. He's not seen in the myst because he is Talia's child. And he is behind so much of the terror befalling the mortals lately."

"We have not seen this."

"And that is why Haven will fall. You are all blind, Gabe. Open your eyes and be the first to see it."

"Like you did? Is that why you tore out your heart?"

"That is my business alone."

Gabriel stood, hands up and spread so to make it clear that she would not reach for any weapons. "Talia's treachery goes deeper than any of us thought. Two children, not one. And a powerful witch-child hidden for seventeen years. She was up to something. Help me find out what."

"Help you?" Carma laughed. "Gabriel, have you lost your mind? Are you really asking a demon for help? The Council will call you before them to answer for it."

"I am asking you to help me discover why these children exist at all. Carma, please." Gabriel reached to take Carma's hands, but stopped herself short, uncertain of the reception. Carma didn't know how she would have reacted either. "Please. These half-breed children are not the first. We both know that. But they are the first to be hidden, to grow so powerful. The first between a seraph and a witch. Talia was a competent seraph from a good line. She must have known what it would mean to procreate with her lover, yet she did it anyway. Why? Haven't you ever asked yourself that?"

The question had crossed Carma's mind before, but she had pushed it aside in favor of other things. Bri was one of the pieces needed in this strange game they all played. Without him, there was no hope of change. But how strange that he existed it all. Had Talia known? Was she a part of this game? This plan? Or was something greater at work? Did it matter? Carma didn't have the time to sort it all out. However, the promise of having Gabriel at her side was tempting. They had worked well together when they were young, and if Gabriel was with her, then she was not hunting Bri. It would buy her time, if nothing else.

As long as she remembered that while seraph abhorred deception, they could lie.

"All right, Gabriel, you have my attention. I will help you solve this mystery if you help me in turn."

"What is it you want?"

"A god."

Gabriel folded her arms across her armored chest. "The gods beneath The One are difficult to control."

"And yet they are still subject to Haven. Having a seraph on my side will lend weight to my argument," Carma said, mindful to keep the notion of Haven's might at the forefront of Gabriel's thoughts.

"And that is?"

"Gods are rather difficult to kill, since they survive on the belief of mortals. It takes great planning, and witnesses, to end one."

"What god do you plan on killing?"

"None already in existence."

— CHAPTER TWENTY-NINE —

Ella awoke, cold and shivering. It amazed her how quickly she had gone from being grateful for the winter air after so many feverish days in Hell, to wishing for a little warmth. Before throwing off her covers, she grabbed her cloak and pulled it tight around herself. She had slept in her warmest clothes and had kept her boots by the bed. She slipped into them now, thankful that one of the boys—most likely Bri—had made sure to get her appropriate clothing. While still in Hell, she had pretended to be sicker than she was, but once they had arrived back in the mortal realm, she had been overcome with illness. As though she had fought through before only because she knew she needed to. Once back in her home realm, she had relaxed, and the ramifications of spending time in Hell had come on her full force. She had spent every moment since sleeping.

Now, she felt much better. She shivered, but that was not the same as the shaking that had afflicted her previously. Nor did her stomach turn and flip. In fact, she was quite hungry. The sun was rising outside her bedroom window, a welcome sight after the lack of daily change in Hell. For a long moment she stood there, watching the golden sun grow over the horizon, the sky brightening in yellows and pinks before turning blue. When the sun pulled that last bit of itself over the edge of the world and hung in the sky completely, she headed out of her room in search of Bri.

She found Kai.

He sat at a small wooden table—how nice to see wood again—sharpening a knife on a whetstone. A fire crackled in the hearth nearby, warming the room nicely. Kai actually had his sleeves pushed up his arms. A basket sat on the table, filled with bread and dried meats. Checking the blade with a careful touch of his thumb, Kai gestured to the chair beside him. "Good morning, Ella. Please, sit. Help yourself."

She considered refusing and searching for Bri instead, but her stomach growled, and so she sat. The bread was soft, and the meat salty. She ate, reminding herself not to rush. Kai smiled, sitting back as he watched her.

"What?"

"Nothing," he said. "It's just nice to see you eat with your hands. You're always so proper."

"There's no one here to impress."

Kai clutched his heart dramatically. "You wound me."

"You don't care what I think."

"Ah, but I do."

"Your smile isn't as charming as you think it is."

He set the stone down on the table and slipped the knife into his pocket before taking a piece of meat for himself. "We'll see."

"Where are we?"

"My home." He kicked his booted feet up onto the table. "Welcome."

Ella moved her food further from his boots. "You mean this house is yours?"

"Who else's would it be?"

Your victims'. Some poor soul you saw fit to steal it from. Someone who died.

"All right, fine," Kai said. "Stop making that face. It used to be someone else's, of course, but it's been mine for the better part of three years now. I like it here."

"And where is here exactly?"

"Talconay. Just outside Tarkava. I actually grew up not far from here."

Talconay. Tarkava. Her food felt like a rock in her throat. She swallowed hard. She had not grown up here, had never been within the borders of the country at all, but it was all she had heard about over the past year and a half. Talconay. The birthplace of her ancestors. Where an empty throne awaited her.

"What's that look for? Surprised I was ever a child?"

"What? No." Ella shook off her shock and schooled her expression back to something neutral. "Not at all. I just—I've never been this far east before."

"Can't get much farther. All that lies beyond is ocean."

"I've never seen the ocean either."

"I'll take you." He grinned once again. "Always happy to broaden people's horizons."

To see the ocean... She had to admit it stirred a child-like excitement in her. "I'd like that. Thank you."

Kai looked genuinely surprised by that. *Good. Glad to know the tables can be turned.* But how sad to know that a simple act of kindness—nothing more than a "thank you"—was enough to render him momentarily speechless.

He cleared his throat. "It would be my pleasure. We can go whenever you like."

"Really? Whenever I like?"

"Well, clearly it can't be when I'm in the middle of something, but other than that, yes."

Ella nodded, watching how carefully he reclined with his feet still up, balancing the chair on two legs. He was still studying her with that bit of shock behind his eyes. She had him on unfamiliar ground. Curious, she pressed a little further. "You grew up here?"

"Yes." The word was deadpan, and his mouth twisted with disgust.

"You don't say that with much fondness."

"Very perceptive."

"Then why come back here? Why live here at all?"

"Because I like the reminder."

"Of what?"

He pulled his feet from the table and let them hit the floor with the front two legs of his chair, bringing him suddenly very close to her as he leaned in. "Of what I climbed my way out of."

It was hard not to move away, but Ella refused to give him the satisfaction. He did not scare her. At least, that's what she told herself. Talk of the past had put a darkness in his eyes, one she had never seen before. So, she changed the subject. "Where's Bri?"

And just like that, the other Kai, the carefree and charming Kai, was back. "Bri. Always Bri. I suppose I should be flattered you didn't ask for him sooner."

She had wanted to, but she had known to wait for the right time.

"Where is he?"

"Outside somewhere."

"In this weather?" Sitting by the fire, she wasn't as cold as she had been, but she had seen the clearness of the sky as the sun rose. The day would chill bones.

Kai shrugged. "I think the cold eases it some. Makes the illness easier to push back. He said he needed fresh air."

Fresh air. The first few times she had met him, he had been seeking fresh air. But, he had said he was stronger now. He had touched her bare hand, her lips... He shouldn't have been sick.

"He gave up his health for yours. How romantic."

"How dare you mock him. He's only like this because you kept him in Hell so long. He was getting better, stronger."

"Oh, aren't we the expert now."

"Hell weakened him. He just needs time to get his strength back." Holy One, how she wanted to go to him. She could only imagine the shock of suddenly being near the myst again. He had told her how it felt to be so cut off from it in Hell. She should have known, should have suspected this would happen. But she had been so sick herself...

"I could give him that strength," Kai said.

"He doesn't want that kind of help."

"He needs it. You don't know the extent of what's been done to him."

It pained Ella to know she we likely never know the full extent of what Bri had been through. "I know enough. I know that he doesn't trust you to mark him without an ulterior motive."

"What ulterior motive could I possibly have? All I want is for him to be strong."

"Strong enough to help you," Ella said. "You've tricked him in the past. You've lost his trust. How is he to know you won't use a *labrynth* to control him?"

Kai scoffed and threw one arm over the back of his chair. "I couldn't even if I wanted to. *Labrynths* don't work like that."

"You're the only one of us who would know. Why should we believe you?"

"Oh, the two of you are a 'we' now, are you?" He hooked his foot around the leg of her chair and pulled her closer to him. "You should believe me, because it's the truth. Yes, a *labrynth* could make a puppet of a man, but not Bri. He and I are too much the same. He is a piece of me, and therefore to place such a hold on him would be to place the same hold on myself. I'd run the risk of him turning around and controlling me."

"How do I know that's the truth?"

"Why would I make it up?"

They were nearly nose to nose now. Kai had leaned so far in, and Ella had once again refused to pull back first. She could play his game. She would win. Or at least, she would not lose. He didn't scare her. If she told herself that enough perhaps it would become the truth.

"Because you're a liar. Because you want what you want, whatever the cost."

The left side of Kai's mouth quirked up in a half smile. "Think you know me so well, do you?"

"Your eyes betray you."

"Ah, yes. That was how you knew I wasn't my brother the first time we met, wasn't it?"

"Yes."

"So, if my eyes are so revealing, what do they tell you now? Am I lying about marking Bri?"

She studied his eyes, so much like Bri's, but so fundamentally different. They were filled with deception. She had yet to see what they looked like when truthful. He had never proven himself to be so.

"Thank you for agreeing to bring me here," she said, testing a theory. "It must have been hard for you to change your plans so suddenly, simply to help me."

"I admit to having planned on coming here soon anyway, but I did not need to think twice about it once I saw how ill you were."

His honesty didn't look much different from his lies. "Why not simply let me think you did this all for me?"

"You wanted the truth. Wasn't that the point of your little test? I am quite capable of telling the truth. I tell it often. But you're right; I lie a lot too."

"It's not my trust you should be trying to earn."

"And yet I still want it."

The door opened, letting a sharp gust of cold air into the house before it shut once again. Ella drew her cloak tight around her shoulders and sat back. Kai didn't move. Bri looked at them both, his cheeks red from the cold, as were his bare hands. He hadn't worn much outside, no gloves, no scarf, no hat. He coughed, and wiped the back of one of his shaking hands across his mouth, then headed toward the back of the house without so much as a single word to either of them.

Ella looked at Kai only after Bri had passed. "You let him go outside like that?"

Kai shrugged. "I told you. I can't control him."

Suddenly angry—at whom, she wasn't sure—Ella stood and went after Bri. She found him in the room beside her own, the door cracked open. "Bri, come back to the front room and sit by the fire, you must be freez—"

Her voice died in her throat when she stepped through the door.

Bri had removed his shirt, his exposed back all she could see. His stories had prepared her, though she thought she had understood what his life had been. His description of the *labrynth* carved into his back had been sparse, and she had feared her imagination made it worse than reality—she had been wrong. Her imagination had not come close to what had been carved into his flesh.

And it wasn't the only mark. Strange letters accompanied the lines of the *labrynth*, his skin raised and pink. Even between those lines, where there should have been smooth flesh, more tiny scars dotted and marred his skin.

Bri had gone perfectly still. Ella crossed the room to him, touching his back with a gloved hand that hid nothing from her fingertips. "So many..."

"They don't hurt. Not anymore."

"That one does." Kai's voice startled her. He had propped himself in the doorway, arms folded over his chest, casual as ever. As if they weren't staring at a history of pain and suffering.

But his words made Ella look at the rune she now realized she had tried to instantly forget. At the top of Bri's back, just between his shoulder blades, one rune was red and raised, as if brand new. He breathed, and it bled, a single drop rolling down his spine. Without thinking, Ella wiped it away.

"It doesn't matter," Bri said, grabbing a shirt and pulling it over his head. His jacket followed quickly.

"It's making your life more difficult," Kai said.

"It's not the only thing."

"You should let me help. At least let me complete it so it heals and stops bleeding."

"No." Stepping away, Bri sat on the bed and laced up his boots after putting on dry socks.

Kai gave Ella a look that seemed to say, *See? See how difficult he is?* She shooed him away, unwilling to admit that he might be right.

He remained in the doorway. "I could always erase the entire thing. The whole *labrynth* gone. Think about it."

Kai left then, and Ella closed her eyes to take a deep breath. The air in the room seemed less heavy when he wasn't around. She sat beside Bri on the bed and waited for him to speak first.

It was a long time before he did. He let out a breath, and rubbed his temple with two fingers. "Are you feeling better?"

"Yes," she said, placating him only because she felt any sort of argument would be unfair at the moment. "But I think I'm the least of our worries. Kai says you're sick again."

He let his hands drop to his lap. "It was my fault. I wasn't as prepared for the myst as I should have been. I'll be fine now."

She didn't like the ghostly pallor of his cheeks. "You should come eat something. Warm yourself by the fire."

"Kai is out there."

"I admit, his company is tolerable at best, but that doesn't change the fact that you need food and warmth." Oh, how she ached to take his hand. "Besides, I think he does genuinely worry about you."

At this, Bri finally looked at her. "He worries about a tool he needs to complete his work."

It was true that Kai saw most people as tools, as things to be used and thrown away once their usefulness came to an end, but she had seen enough to note a difference in the way he looked at Bri. "I think it's more than that."

"Are you converting to his way of thinking?"

"No! No, of course not. And I'll attribute your lapse in good sense to your health." She smoothed her skirt just to give herself something to do while she collected her thoughts, while she needed a moment to look away. "I just think that there may be some ways he could actually help you. He shouldn't be the only one getting something out of this relationship."

"You want me to let him tend to my back, don't you?"

"Bri, I—"

He shook his head, and for a moment looked like he might stand, but he remained at her side. "This is why I didn't want you to see it. It's not as bad as it looks."

"Don't lie to me."

"I'm not lying."

"You are. You're a terrible liar. It shows in your face."

Bri sighed. "I've never lied to you before."

"That's exactly how I know. At least consider letting him do something about that unhealed mark."

"A rune." He said it without judgement; just simply offering her information. "I can't trust him."

"He knows that. Bri," she took his hand then, trusting he would be strong enough—someone had to believe he was strong enough—and he looked at her, "he knows that. It's what we were talking about when you came in. He wants your trust. You can make him earn it."

He gripped her hand as if she were his only tether. "How?"

"I don't know yet, but we'll find a way."

They had been held up for the better part of the day. Alec drummed his burning fingers along the fallen tree he sat upon, listening to the hard, cold wood ring like metal. His entire body thrummed with energy, with power. He couldn't cast it aside. It made him fidget and chew his nails. He counted, breathing in and out in a slow and controlled rhythm. It was the only thing that kept his temper from snapping again. Tassos stood perfectly still at the ledge, overlooking the valley below, his robes drifting lazily in the light breeze. It grated on Alec's nerves like cat claws on pottery. He had to find this person who could help them. Had to find Bri. Had to get out of Hell.

Ariadne came and sat beside him, offering him a handful of berries she had wandered off to pick. They were blood red and plump, some of the juices staining her hand. Alec imagined it was blood, dripping steadily from her palm to the ground, soaking into the blackened dirt and making it even darker. Like her blood had soaked the ground that night so long ago, when he had traded everything so that she could live...

"Alec. Stop. Come back to me."

A single fingertip touched his chin. Alec realized he had gritted his teeth so hard that his jaw had begun to ache. He breathed and loosened his jaw, working out the stiffness. Not daring to close his eyes, he stared at a small rock by his feet. It was harmless enough, and focusing on it allowed his mind to clear.

"It's getting worse," Ariadne said, her voice little more than a whisper.

"I'm fine."

"You're not. Maybe we should take a break. Go above for a day or so, let you get your bearings."

"We don't have time. Bri doesn't have time. Gods only know what that brother of his is up to. I can't leave him."

Ariadne sighed, and offered him the berries again. Alec took one, mostly to appease her. He wasn't hungry, and though the berry was sweet—too sweet, really—he couldn't think of eating more. "What is he doing?" she asked, turning her attention to the reaper where he stood still as a statue. "Hasn't he moved at all?"

"Not a hair," Alec said.

"It's been more than three turns."

"I am very aware of that." He took up his impatient rapping of the fallen tree again.

"Have you spoken to him?"

"Tried once. He ignored me."

"Maybe you should try again. You certainly can't afford to sit still any longer. You'll go mad."

Alec snorted.

Ariadne laid a hand on his arm. "Just let the power in. Let it in, and you'll feel better. It's worse because you resist it."

"I have let it in."

"Not all the way. I can feel it fighting you. You fighting it."

"You remember what happened last time I let it all in, don't you?"

"So there may be one less seraph in the world. We're soulless; that's a good thing for us."

"I don't live that way." The images of the mutilated body of that seraph haunted his nightmares. Not a night had gone by since that he had not relived his brother's death and walking away from Ariadne. Now, beside all the bodies of the foolish humans, were the bodies of Havenly beings—burned by him.

Last night Bri had joined them. Marked almost beyond recognition by his twin brother, and dying from the power he could not control. No. There was no time for anything other than forward movement.

Setting the berries aside, Ariadne drew closer to him, holding him in a half-embrace and gently running her fingers along his face. "I know this is hard for you. I know. But you're not thinking clearly. Let me help. Let me show you how to control the power."

Alec closed his eyes as she traced his eyelids, his breathing shaky. Every touch washed her power over him, and it spoke to his own. It felt like standing at a precipice, balance uncertain, doomed to shatter with a change in the wind. It would be so easy to fall, to let go and tumble over the edge. She was that edge. It wasn't only the power he had been forced to resist lately. Though his heart yearned for the closeness it had so long been denied, and though his body hungered for her like nothing else, he had taken to sleeping alone. He just couldn't control it with her body pressed against his. Her lips stole his breath and his control.

He felt those lips now, brushing against his mouth, her warm breath sending a surge of power through him. For a moment his limbs stopped quaking, and the loud hum behind his ears quieted. The burning in his fingertips grew, expanding to his palms and up his arms. He could feel his own pulse, strong and steady.

He shoved her away and stood, putting distance between them.

"Alec—"

"No. Just—stop. Don't say anything." He ran his hands through his hair, pulling just hard enough to remind himself that he was in control. It was a bad habit he was picking up. If he wasn't careful, he would lose all his hair.

Ariadne didn't listen. Instead, she stood and came to him. "I'm sorry. I shouldn't have done that. I just can't stand to see you like this. I pictured our reunion for so long in my mind, I imagined every possible outcome, but I never thought of this. I feel like there's a gulf between us, and I only want to help you cross it."

"I know. I know. I'm sorry." He didn't resist, didn't stop her when she came even closer, running her hands up his arms. He set his forehead against hers, concentrating on her scent rather than the power she so easily held onto at all times. There was so much of it. So much. How did she do it without losing herself? Truth was, that's what unbalanced him so. He had always thought he had made the right choice. He had resisted, used the power only when absolutely necessary. He didn't want to be like Picadilly, who sought an echo of her old self. He didn't want to be like the other soulless he had met over the years who had been driven mad by the power. But now, it was he who was going mad, and he worried he had in fact made the *wrong* choice.

"I'm going to go talk to Tassos," he said only once he felt steady again.

Ariadne nodded and kissed him once more—this time with no lace of power through it. "I'll make myself scarce. I don't think he likes me much."

Though he didn't know why, Alec had to agree. He waited until Ariadne had disappeared into the woods before approaching the reaper. "I never would have imagined you could stay this still for so long," Alec said, stopping at Tassos's side and gazing out over the vast valley that lay below. A forest consumed in flames burned off to the left, screams and shouts a constant eerie music. To the right, a dark shadow loomed over an even darker lake. Figures splashed about the waters, barely managing to stay afloat, most being tugged below the surface violently, only to rise again and repeat the terror. From this height, Alec could see all too well the outline of the giant creature that swam beneath. He reminded himself that the souls trapped in these horrors had done something to warrant it in their lifetime, but it made watching their suffering little easier.

"Being still helps me focus," Tassos said, sounding as though he enjoyed the songs of birds and crickets rather than the screams of the damned.

"I thought you knew where we were going. Why is it taking so long for you to remember the way?"

"I don't normally walk there, so you'll have to forgive me if navigating the wilds of Hell takes a bit of time. After all, you are the one who cannot move instantaneously. Though I admit, I don't know why your paramour would possess that ability."

"It's just part of the manifestation of the power that comes to her."

"It is powerful, dark power that courses through her."

"It's from Hell. Same as me. We all have it."

"No, you are mistaken. Yes, the power comes from Hell, but it is funneled through your demon master. Carma's soulless have a lighter power than this Ariadne of yours. Whoever her master is, they are a powerful demon with dark intentions."

"Ari's not like that."

"Oh?" Tassos raised an eyebrow. "So you trust her?"

"I love her."

"Not the same thing. Didn't you mention once that you thought she was dead?"

"I sold my soul to save her, so, yes, I thought she was long dead," Alec said.

"Never trust anyone who's supposed to be dead. Take it from a reaper with thousands of years' experience. I can feel the difference. She should be dead. You should be soulless."

"That doesn't make any sense. Selling your soul goes against the Grand Plan. It's why the seraph hate us so much."

Tassos waved a finger in the air. "Ah, and yet, there are some who simply never hold an attraction to reapers. I haven't met many, but there have been a few. Death never wanted you. You were always meant to sell your soul. But her, Ariadne, my Lady Death shakes with anger whenever she is around. She should never have outlived her mortal body."

"What are you saying?"

"I am saying I don't trust her."

It was then Alec noticed that nothing about Tassos moved. Not his hair in the wind, or his clothes as he shifted his weight. It was as if the reaper stood outside of time. Waiting. "Is that why we've been sitting here all day? Because you don't want to take her to your friend?"

"Alec, sometimes you can be as smart as you are handsome."

"What do you expect me to do about it?"

Tassos glanced behind them. "Ask her to wait here."

"I can't."

"No, you don't want to. There's a difference. Look, Bri is your concern, not hers. And I will admit I have a certain fondness for the young boy myself—I certainly prefer him to his brother—but my friend, the one who can help you, I care about him far more. You, I trust. Her? Not in the slightest."

Alec looked over his shoulder into the woods where Ariadne had disappeared. His options were slim. He could tell by the tone of Tassos's voice that there would be no further negotiations. He could go, Ariadne could not. But what would she think when he asked her to stay behind?

She returned some time later. Alec had considered the matter, and Tassos had gone back to his silent contemplation of the view. Ariadne smiled as she emerged from the trees, waving and sitting down upon the fallen log once more. She had brought back a long piece of black rock that glistened in the light. Alec sat beside her, watching as she ran her thumb along the sharp edges of her find. "I was right, wasn't I? He doesn't trust me."

"Yes."

"He won't go any further unless I stay behind?"

"Yes." His tension eased. She made this much easier by guessing.

"Then I suppose we have no other choice. I'll wait here for you."

Alec swallowed the argument he'd cued up, ready for her resistance. "Really?"

"Really. Why do you seem so surprised?"

"I'm not. I just—I didn't know what to expect." With everything that had happened, he sometimes felt like he didn't know her at all, but then a moment would come—one like this—and she would feel like an extension of himself once again.

Ari squeezed his arm and smiled. "Let him take you. We need to find Bri, and if this is the only way, then it's the only way. I'm not worried. I always know where you are. I can find you easily. I've learned what you feel like, much like places. I could leave here, go to the mortal realm, and bring myself back to you wherever you happen to be."

"I've never heard of a soulless being able to do such a thing."

"My deal was very specific."

Her smile was contagious. Alec kissed her, wishing he could do so much more. Someday. Soon. "Thank you. Give us a few days, then come find me."

"Sounds like a good plan."

He held her tight. "And once all this is over, you and I are going to find a quiet place to live, and we'll have no more secrets, and no more lost time."

Ari nodded and kissed him again, but he thought maybe he detected a flash of sadness in her eyes. "Yes," she said. "That would be lovely."

— CHAPTER THIRTY —

Bri approached his brother cautiously. Kai had been out behind the small house he called home for a day and a night, silent and unresponsive to anything that went on inside. Though childish, Bri and Ella had even resorted to knocking things over to see if Kai would so much as look up. He did not. Finally, Ella expressed her concern that nothing holding Kai's attention for so long could be anything good, and Bri had to agree. So, Bri buttoned up his coat, and braved the harsh winter wind.

Kai had not dressed for the weather. He wore a coat, but it was left open, and he had no scarf to protect his throat. His normally bloody hands were red with the cold, bare and victim to winter's chill. Bri made sure to make enough sound as he walked closer to alert his brother to his presence, but Kai continued to sit still as a statue, cross-legged with his fingers dug into the frozen ground.

"Kai?" No response. Bri moved to stand in front of his brother, able now to see his face. Kai's eyes were closed, but his lips moved in silent words. Bri tried again, and again received nothing in return. He bent down, crouching before Kai. The ground was unmarked. No *labrynth*. No blood. *What in Hell has he been doing out here?*

Bri set a hand to the ground to steady himself, and in that moment, Kai's eyes flew open. "Bri," he said, smiling as though their meeting was expected. "Took you long enough. I've been waiting for you."

"We didn't know what you were doing out here. How was I to know you were waiting?"

"You weren't."

Oh, gods, it's like talking to Dorothea. There was that same odd sparkle to Kai's eyes that Bri had often seen in the old woman. A look that meant the magic had taken over, and there would be little sense coming from the witch. "Kai, I don't understand."

"Of course you don't. You're not a witch. But you could be."

"No. You're the witch. You always have been. I have no talent for scribing."

"Lies. You only say that because you've never tried. Here, watch." Kai grabbed Bri's hands and laid them on the cold ground. Despite having been outside for more turns of the glass than should have been survivable, Kai's body burned warm. "You could scribe for me. An extension of my power in you. We could work simultaneously. I could see the myst."

Though he felt the magic buzzing in his brother's hands, Bri felt nothing in the ground. "You're talking about us being one again."

"Yes! I'm so close, Bri. So close to knowing how. I just need your help. I need you to feel what I feel. But there's something blocking us. Something keeps getting in my way."

Me. I keep getting in your way. I've felt you at the corner of my mind multiple times now, and each time I ignore you and drive you away. "I think you've been out here too long. Come inside."

"No. We need to work." Kai dug his fingers into the ground beside Bri's hands and began to pull, drawing lines and tearing his nails.

Bri felt a pull lunge at him through the dirt. The magic tugged at that same mental place where he had felt Kai before, only stronger this time. He watched the lines as they formed in the ground and had to remind himself to blink as his vision began to glaze over until nothing existed but the lines. It was like that time he had taken in Kai's blood. The lines glowed, pulsed with life, and he understood what their paths meant, what the outcome would be.

Kai had figured it out. The *labrynth* that would join them together as one. Bri couldn't let him complete it. He had to distract him.

"Kai, I want you to erase the *labrynth* from my back."

Everything stilled. The energy in the ground, Kai's fingers, even the pull at the corner of Bri's mind. Kai looked at him, and clarity began to return to his eyes. "What did you say?"

"The *labrynth*...on my back...you said you could erase it." Words he'd said in haste, but there was no going back.

"I said that?"

"Yes, you did."

It was like watching someone come back over the edge of a cliff. The hum of power on the air slowly lessened until it completely died away and the familiar light in Kai's eyes returned. "You'd really let me do it? You'd let me help you?"

The power pulling at him slipped back further. "Yes. Help me. You're right, the rune hurts all the time, and the *labrynth* makes it harder for me to control the myst now. I'd be better off on my own. I want your help."

A moment of stillness passed. Then Kai laughed, clapping his hands and rocking backward. It was like two completely different people had inhabited the one body. Kai was back. "I knew you'd come to your senses. I knew it! I'll do it right now. Let's go inside." He stood, then stopped. "No, wait. I need one thing. Wait here. I'll be back." He ran off before Bri could insist he put the proper clothes on.

Sighing, Bri decided it didn't matter. The pull in his mind was gone—that was the important thing. He couldn't lose himself to Kai, and Kai didn't seem to have even been aware of the breakthrough he was closing in on. Bri would have to be more careful in the future. If he wasn't, if he hadn't realized what Kai was scribing in the ground, it would all be over.

Ella was cooking over the hearth when he returned to the house. None of them were all that exceptional when it came to preparing food, but whatever she had in the pot smelled good enough. "Where's Kai?" she asked as Bri sat wearily at the table, dropping his head into his hands.

"He ran off."

"What was happening to him?" Setting her stirring spoon aside, she came to sit beside him.

"I think he was lost in some sort of trance. I've seen it happen to Dorothea before. I snapped him out of it before he could do any damage."

"How?"

"I asked him to remove the *labrynth* from my back."

Shock widened her eyes. "I thought you were undecided on the matter."

"I had to do something to get his attention. He was too close. I could feel his magic on me."

That sent Ella into a flurry of worry. She frowned, crinkling her nose, and reached for his hands on the table. "What do you mean? He hasn't marked you. He hasn't marked any of your things."

"He's obsessed with finding a way to combine our powers. I think he nearly figured it out. Don't worry—I know what it feels like, and I can resist it. But, I don't think he realized what he was doing, and he doesn't seem to remember now."

"We need to get away from him."

"Yes. But we can't. Not yet. As long as I'm with him, I can stop him."

"Stop him from what?" She placed a hand on his, drawing them down from his face.

"I don't know yet. But the myst is strangely quiet. There are fewer Singers there than usual. I think something is coming."

Bri had thought Kai would want to stay inside for the purposes of working on his back, but he'd been wrong. Kai arrived back at the house, excited to the point of bouncing like a child. He had barely greeted Ella before grabbing Bri and dragging him out into the cold afternoon.

They walked a short distance down the road, going further from the nearby city—which Kai had systematically destroyed over the years. Bri tucked his hands under his arms to keep warm, and followed patiently, just glad that Kai seemed to have remained clear.

The smoke became apparent first, drifting lazily toward the cloudy sky. Then Bri saw the flames of the fire, large and snapping at the air. Only one burned, but it was still reminiscent of the ritual that had changed everything for him four years prior. It made him shiver.

The fire gave off enough heat that when the two of them stopped just before it, Bri no longer needed to hold his coat closed tight. He shook out his arms and cracked his neck, releasing the stiffness the cold had brought about. The road ended here, and the ruins of an old house stood there, lonely against the grey winter sky. The charred bones of what had once been someone's home almost seemed to quake in the presence of Kai's fire.

This place is full of terrible memories. Kai stood silent beside him, staring at the burned remnants of the home with a dark look in his eyes. "What is this place, Kai?"

"Eh, nothing. Just some abandoned building. I thought it would be a good place to get things done."

"Don't lie to me."

"Why not? You won't like the truth."

"I thought we were beyond this. I thought we were beginning to understand one another."

Kai always responded to that sort of thing. He threw an arm around Bri's shoulders and pulled him close. "I like us this way," he said. "I like it when we're not fighting."

You like it when I do what you want. "So then tell me. Where are we?"

"Can you feel it? Is there something familiar about this place to you?"

"No. But I can see it in your eyes. This place means something to you."

Kai scoffed. "It means nothing to me. I burned it to the ground."

"Why?"

"Because I didn't want to see it anymore. This is where he raised me. Where he taught me *labrynths* and scribing." He pointed beyond the blackened foundation to where the land stretched on and on to the horizon. "That is where he took my wings."

Bri stood transfixed. "You grew up here. This is our father's house?"

"Not any more it isn't."

"Kai, if you hate it here so much, why bring me here to do this?" He wanted to touch, to explore, to seek out any remaining sign of their father; yet he didn't dare.

"Because our blood has been spilled on this ground before, making it a powerful site. It is here, or nowhere. I'll need that power to erase what's been scribed into your back." He clapped Bri's shoulders a few times, then moved toward the fire, toeing the ground.

Bri tried to imagine Kai as a child, playing in the fields in the summer, rolling in the snow in the winter. He tried to picture him soaring across a blue sky, content and delighted in his wings. Wings. He saw those wings torn from Kai's body, leaving scars not just on his back, but in his heart and mind. What kind of man was their father? Who could do such a thing to their child? Why do it at all? Had Kai been mad before that, or was the madness a result of the trauma? He supposed he would never know. He had to believe their father had good reason to take the wings. He had to, because he knew nothing else about his father.

Kai knelt down, the flames making his hair look red in the afternoon light. He scribed along the ground in the black ash that had been gathered at that spot, mumbling to himself. Bri walked around him, heading to the ruins of his brother's childhood home. He didn't know what he expected to find there—perhaps some remnant of Kai's previous life, a trinket that belonged to their father—but as he stepped over the threshold, kicking up nothing but dust and ash, his expectations lowered to nothing. Kai had destroyed everything. The house was nothing more than a shell, burned out and gutted beyond recognition. The back wall was the only one still remaining, and it looked like a strong storm would do it in.

"Bri. I'm ready." Kai stood over the *labrynth* he had scribed, his face cast in shadows from the flames. Bri gave the house one more glance over his shoulder, then went to his brother. There was no point pondering the past. Kai was what he was, and no memory of their father would change that.

Bri undressed when Kai asked him to, passing his coat and shirt to his brother who then folded them before setting them aside. The huge fire was enough to keep the winter cold away, so the shiver that ran through Bri was something else. The unfinished rune on his back throbbed, hating the exposure. The myst was sparse there, with little to cling to, though it seemed thicker behind the remains of the house. Bri was just about to reach for it when Kai instructed him to stand on the *labrynth* on the ground. Guided by Kai's hand, Bri stepped onto the carefully scribed lines—and felt his entire back go cold and numb.

"Kai?"

"You won't want to feel it. Trust me." Drawing a knife from his belt, Kai warmed the blade in the flames. "Are you ready?"

Bri couldn't take his eyes from that blade. "Yes."

"Then brace yourself." In a series of swift motions, Kai slashed open all ten of his fingers from palm to tip, then placed the bloody knife in Bri's hands. "Hold this."

Bri did, but it took all his concentration not to drop the sticky blade. He gripped it tightly as Kai moved around him, out of sight, each breath stunted by nervous anticipation.

"Don't move," Kai said, and Bri nodded dumbly, stupidly wondering if this was a mistake, if he should call a stop to everything; use the knife in his shaking hands to turn on his brother. Then he felt Kai's fingers on his back, warm and wet with blood, and he knew there was no turning back. The numbness faded to a disassociation. He felt each move Kai's fingers made, but as though they existed elsewhere, somewhere just beyond his body, within the magic that clung to him. They pulled inward, toward the unfinished rune first, enveloping it and quieting the normal scream of its incomplete magic. Bri hadn't realized just what the rune had done to him until it all began to retreat. Like roots beneath the ground, the power curled inward, retracting from his shoulders and spine. Kai forced them to relinquish their hold, to shrink and return to their place of origin. Despite Kai's numbing *labrynth*, Bri felt the flash of heat that came as the rune collapsed in on itself, then the sudden burst as its life was snuffed out.

Bri wished he had something to hold onto for support. Instead, he swayed on his feet, kept standing only by his brother's hands on his back. "It's gone?"

"The rune is. But that was the easy part. Are you ready for the next?"

"Yes."

"Wide stance then, brother." Something popped, like a cork being pulled from a bottle. Bri felt something warm drizzle down his back, then Kai's hands returned. "Here we go."

Blood allowed Kai's hands to glide along Bri's back. He smeared the substance all across Bri's shoulders first, coating him. Bri closed his eyes, concentrating on breathing and the sensation of his brother's fingers. It felt so innocent, like a child painting with mud or water. Nothing hurt, no power changed. Then Kai wrapped his left hand around Bri's chest, hand directly over his heart. Kai braced him, pulling Bri tight against his own body, one leg locked alongside Bri's. His other hand pressed into Bri's back, just below the base of his neck—and then Kai began to pull downward.

The *labrynth* Dorothea had so violently carved into his back popped and broke. Bri felt it like the snapping of wires, each line and turn bursting, then disappearing. Kai's hand traveled all the way down his spine, and the *labrynth's* power peeled outward to both sides. Trailing his fingers along the now thrumming flesh of Bri's back, Kai set his hand atop Bri's right shoulder blade and pressed once more, preparing to drag downward again. As he did so, Bri heard a terrible scream—and it wasn't his own.

It wasn't him. This didn't hurt enough to warrant any sort of sound. Dorothea's scribings in the past had been far worse. The release of power on his back was like having a wound lanced, a great pressure released, but though it stole his breath now and then, it wasn't worth screaming in pain.

But someone was.

"Kai?"

Kai only hushed him and continued his work, pulling his hand down the length of Bri's back a second time. More bursts of broken power buckled Bri's knees, but Kai held him steady. Nearby, the screams continued, terrible and strangled. Bri tried to concentrate, to listen closer, to see if he could tell at least what direction the sounds were coming from. Kai finished the right side and moved onto the left, leaving Bri little concentration to spare. When Kai's hand once again reached the base of Bri's spine, his fingers curled into a fist and, with only a deep breath as a warning, he gave a single, sharp pull.

The *labrynth* burst and was gone. Bri sagged against his brother, feeling lighter than ever and unable to stand. Kai lowered him to the ground, kneeling beside him and shaking out the hand that had done all the work, splattering blood on the ground. "It's done," he said. "Told you I could do it." He pried his knife from Bri's clenched first.

The myst called to him, louder now that it had been unmuffled. Bri reached a shaking hand around to feel his own back and found none of the most prominent raised marks that had been there so long. His fingers touched only a few smaller lines and scars that he had carried since childhood. The screams continued.

"Kai, what is that?"

"What is what?"

"You know what. The screams. Where are they coming from?"

"Aren't you going to thank me for ridding you of that nuisance on your back?"

"Thank you. What are those screams?"

Kai frowned and cracked his fingers. "Nothing for you to worry about."

Panic twisted Bri's stomach. "What did you do?"

"Exactly what I said I would. I cleared the *labrynth* from your back. That ought to show that old bag of a witch just who's the most powerful."

Bri staggered to his feet, catching his balance just in time to keep from tumbling into the flames. The screams had died some, becoming more of a tormented cry. Without the *labrynth*, the few bits of myst lingering nearby were brighter, appearing almost solid. And a large collection still hovered over the back of the house, only now it twisted and writhed, the blue and silver hues turning grey and black.

Kai grabbed for him as he took off toward it, but missed. "Bri! Bri, don't!"

Bri didn't listen. He stumbled around the debris of the house, the sounds growing louder with each step he took. Rounding the corner, he stopped short. A man lay on the ground, shirtless, with his skin whipped raw from the cold. His back was bloody, the thick red fluid running in rivers over his sides and into the ground. Beneath all that blood were raised wounds. A series of lines and turns that Bri knew all too well.

The *labrynth* from *his* back.

"Kai!"

His twin came around the corner slowly, casually, hands tucked into his pockets. "I told you not to go back here."

"What is this?" Bri pointed to the man on the ground, his entire body shaking so hard that he thought his muscles might snap.

"Nothing. No one of importance."

"You transferred the *labrynth* from my back to his! How can you say he's no one? He must have a family, a job—"

Kai shrugged. "None of that matters now."

Bri turned to go to the poor man writhing on the ground, but Kai caught him by the wrist and pulled him back. "Don't. Don't touch him."

Bri tried to wrench his arm away, but Kai was stronger. Kai was always stronger. "Why not? It's my fault he's lying there. Let me help him."

"You always forget. You're not human, Bri. Not fully. You can survive things others can't. It would be dangerous to touch him now." Cold truth crawled up the back of Bri's neck. "Kai, stop it. Reverse it. Now."

"Too late."

The man's screams gained power once again, splitting the silent air and making Bri instinctively recoil. He tried to correct that horrid impulse, but Kai wouldn't let go, leaving Bri nothing to do but watch as the man thrashed and clawed at the ground, then went eerily still. The lines on his back cracked, blackened, then spread outward, his flesh and bone crumbling away. Just as the hole in his back became large enough that the disintegration would go for the man's limbs next, the man twisted around, and his eyes met Bri's.

Then there was nothing left to see but ash.

Kai let go of Bri's wrist. "There. Done with. Now get dressed. You'll freeze to death out here."

Carma heard Dorothea wake in the night. The old witch had nodded off not long after Gabriel had cryptically gone off to retrieve something. In the morning, they would work together to find Inaseri. In the morning, Carma would begin the delicate balance of juggling Haven's strict laws and rigid soldiers.

Dorothea stood and set to pacing about the clearing. Carma watched her, tending the fire. Something was not right. There was no muttering, no twitching of fingers. Dorothea was absolutely silent.

"What is it?" Carma asked, letting her voice drift softly on the air.

The old witch stilled, closed her eyes, and tilted her head as if listening, then turned abruptly. She faced Carma with an expression of horrified wonder—then anger. "He has broken it. Destroyed it."

"Destroyed what? Who?"

"Kai. That naughty little witch. He has found a way around my scribings. He has undone me."

"What do you mean?"

Her gnarled fingers traced patterns in the air. "I can no longer feel my *labrynth* on Brishen. It is gone."

Blistering Hell...

— CHAPTER THIRTY-ONE —

Ella worried the whole time Bri and Kai were away. The stew had grown cold, and the wind had picked up, whistling at the windows, making the shutters tremble. To pass the time, and to keep herself from rushing out into the cold in a futile attempt to find them, she cleaned. The repetitive motions soothed her some, but were not enough to keep her mind quiet. She thought of everything that could go wrong—of Bri succumbing to Kai's dark magic, Kai losing his mind and turning on the brother he claimed to care for, or even Bri being the one to snap and doing something he would forever regret.

She was straightening the sheets on Bri's bed at the back of the house when she heard the front door open. Her heart jumped right up into her throat. No voices, just footsteps. The silence caused her to worry more. Had they failed? Was Kai angry? It was normal for him to gloat about even the smallest things. Uneven steps grew closer until Bri walked through the bedroom's door, one hand gripping the jamb for support.

His eyes were so haunted Ella's heart went from her throat to her feet. "What happened?" She rushed to him, wanting to touch him, to smooth away the distressed lines on his face, but she stopped herself, afraid of what might happen. If something had gone wrong, then there was no knowing what her touch might do. "Bri?"

He started to speak, but his words wouldn't come. With their absence, he was left staring at her like a man lost in the darkness. Ella reached for his hand, giving him time to stop her if touching was indeed a bad idea. When he didn't move, she drew him inside the room, shocked at the coldness of his fingers. She sat him down on the bed and gasped when she saw that the back of his shirt had been stained red.

"Take that off," she said as she went to the wash basin she had just filled and retrieved the fresh cloth. Bri did as she asked, still without a word, staring at nothing. Returning, Ella braced herself for what she would find as she began to wash the blood from his back. But as she wiped it away, uncovering pale skin inch by inch, she marveled at what she saw.

Smooth, undamaged flesh. Nothing but a few small scars, so old they had faded to ghostly lines. "Bri, it's gone. The *labrynth*...it's completely gone. Kai did it."

"I know." His voice sounded hollow.

Cleaning away the last of the blood, Ella dared to run her bare fingers along Bri's bared back. "Then what's wrong?"

"It wasn't worth the price."

"What price?"

He turned, barely looking at her over his shoulder. "A life."

It took nearly a turn of the glass for Ella to get Bri to tell her what happened, and then get him settled enough to lay down and rest. He was frozen from the cold, but Ella felt sure it was more than just the weather that had taken its toll on his body. She had never seen such guilt, and all of it misplaced. Bri wasn't at fault. The poor man's life should not have been on his conscience.

She stayed with him until he fell into a quiet sleep, then left in search of the source of Bri's despair—and her ire.

Her anger had only grown with each word as Bri recounted the events, fueled by the desperation in his eyes. She wanted so badly to turn back the day, to stop him from asking Kai to perform the spell to remove the *labrynth*. But those were foolish thoughts, not only because the past couldn't be changed, but because—much as she hated to admit it, and as much as she wished there had been another way—the *labrynth* had needed to be erased.

Kai stood by the fire, tending it with the iron and adding another log. "Something wrong, my lady?"

"What have you done to him?" She got as close as she dared, wanting so badly to slap him across the face. Curling her fist into her skirt was the only thing that kept her from making such a foolish mistake.

Kai calmly set the poker aside and leaned against the mantle. "Whatever do you mean?"

"You know perfectly well what I mean. How could you do that to him? You know he never would have agreed had he known it meant killing someone else."

"Darling, maybe you should be asking him why he looked when I told him not to. I would have happily left him in the dark when it came to that particular element. I did what I could to spare him. My delicate brother."

"He's not delicate. He's simply not a heartless monster."

Shrugging, Kai sat in the armchair by the hearth. "It was necessary. You know that."

"Getting rid of the *labrynth* was, yes. But taking the life of an innocent man?"

Kai picked at a bloody fingernail. "You don't get something for nothing."

"That's not true."

"Of course it's true. My spells wouldn't work without blood. A person cannot achieve immortality without selling their soul. A seraph must tear out their heart to become a demon. You want a pie from the baker? You'd best have some coins on you. Exchange is what makes the world go 'round, my dear."

She refused to believe it. "There are plenty of things in this world without a price."

"You sound ridiculous. The *labrynth* on Bri's back was scribed by another witch, a powerful witch. She made it changeable, able to grow with him, and able to be adjusted as she saw fit. I couldn't just break it. I had to move it," he said, illustrating with his hands.

"Bri would have waited until you found another way."

"There was no other way!" He threw his arms up, the firelight turning his hair red. "You think I wouldn't have spared myself the brooding we'll all be subjected to now if I could have? My damned bleeding-heart of a brother will be intolerable."

"You insult him at every turn." Ella kept close to the hearth, the warmth of the fire seeming to match and fuel her anger. "Why go through all this? Why not just let him go?"

"Because I need him."

"For what?"

"Oh, no. You won't get that out of me so easily."

"Do you have a price?" She mocked his earlier argument.

Kai leaned forward, smirking. "Would you be willing to pay it?"

"You have a black heart, Kai. And I imagine your soul matches."

"What would you do," Kai stood, closing the distance between them, "to know the truth of what I plan?" He pressed close to her, close enough that she could feel his breath on her face as he spoke. She used every fiber of courage she had to not back away and give him the satisfaction of seeing her squirm. "Whatever you're planning, it probably wouldn't be worth the price you ask."

"My price will be cheaper than what you're willing to pay to my brother."

Ella turned away before he could place his mouth on hers, leaving him nothing to brush against but her cheek. "I don't know what you're talking about."

"The greatest price of all, of course." He ran his fingers up and down her arm. "Love."

"Love isn't a price."

"Of course it is. It's the worst cost anyone could ask. It leaves you vulnerable and weak. It places so much on the happiness and health of someone else."

"You know nothing of love."

"Sure I do. My mother loved my father so much that she fell from Haven. My father gave up everything to be with her. Stopped practicing. Then Bri and I came along, and out of love our parents split us up and tore themselves apart. They're both dead now, and Bri and I would have been too had it not been for the demons that intervened. Love makes people stupid."

"Then why would you ask me for it?"

"I wouldn't. All I would ask," he let his gaze travel up and down her body, "would be for your company."

She shoved him, half hoping he would stumble and fall into the glowing fire. He caught himself with a hand on the mantle, laughing. "I don't know why Bri spares you even a sliver of his hope," she said.

"Dumb love." He said it with no hint of irony.

Ella hated him. Hated him more than she had ever thought possible.

"Someday soon this will all come back to you, and you won't like it."

Kai threw himself back into his chair, kicking his feet up over the arm once more. "I'm not worried about it."

"Clearly. Leave Bri alone for a while. Don't make this worse."

"You're welcome. I single-handedly increased the quality of my brother's life so that he can give you all your little heart desires. Remember that."

"Don't talk to me either. I have nothing to say to you."

"You're forgetting who's in charge here."

"If you want there to be any chance that Bri will continue to help you, you'll let him heal. Otherwise you'll never get what you want." She headed back toward Bri's room, not caring if Kai had any more to say on the matter.

"So what do you get out of it?"

His voice stopped her. There had been just long enough of a pause that it was clear his question was not a response to her last words. "Excuse me?"

"My brother. What do you get out of this little relationship you have?"

"I told you, not everything has a price."

"Nonsense." He stalked toward her, the glow of the fire behind him making him look like some demon risen from Hell. "I know a runner when I see one. We can pick each other out. So what is it, Ella? What is it that being with my brother allows you to forget?"

His words were like a knife through her heart. She knew it wasn't true, wasn't the reason she had been attracted to Bri, wasn't the reason she was falling for him at all. But she was running. Running from a future she had no desire to fulfill. When she was with Bri, she didn't have to think about all that.

Kai would use all of that against her. Against them both. She drew herself up to her full height, which wasn't much in Kai's presence, and forced her expression to reveal nothing. "It's something you'll never understand. And that's what makes you so wrong about him."

"Wrong about what?"

"You call him weak, but he's not. He's stronger than you. And that's why you'll never win."

Ella went into Bri's room and shut the door quickly. Kai didn't follow. She didn't move until her heart had stopped hammering in her chest.

They stood at the edge of a clearing, the torments of Hell far behind them. At the horizon, Alec could see the Void. A darkness that went on and on with no end known. He had seen it only once before, when he had first sold his soul and Carma had brought him to Hell to show him all that was now available to him. It had filled him with awe then, an undeniable testament to the vastness of the realms.

But they had not come to see the Void. They had come for the cottage that sat in the clearing, black hellion birds with teeth lining their beaks sitting lazily atop the roof. A carcass lay half-eaten away in the yard, ribs picked clean while the head decayed slowly. Tassos scoffed in disgust, then began leading the way through the chaotic path to the front door. They stepped over bones and skulls, fallen rocks from a broken wall, and bottles that had smashed just below the front windows.

"Your friend isn't much of a homemaker," Alec said, kicking aside the remains of a green glass bottle, still wet with a sharp smelling liquor.

"He has his moments." Tassos had slowed some, in no rush to get to the door.

"Not recently."

"No, unfortunately not."

"You really think he can help me?"

"If he can't, then no one can."

They stopped in front of the door, but neither moved to knock. Alec looked around the devastated yard once more, not surprised when he saw the birds from the roof descend upon the half-rotten corpse. "Is this really where the High Lord of Hell has been all this time?"

Tassos stiffened. "I never said he was the High Lord."

"No, but that's who they were talking about in the Tavern when you admitted you knew someone who could help."

"Do us both a favor," Tassos said. "Don't let him know you know, all right?" He raised one hand and knocked three times on the door.

The sound was nothing more than dull thuds. Then clattering and cursing came from beyond the door, and a flash of light burst behind the torn curtains that covered the closest window. Someone stumbled and fell against the door, making it shake, then the handle turned, and the door opened.

The demon standing before them was tall, blond, and completely haggard looking. His long hair was tangled and fell into his face, obscuring reddened eyes framed by dark circles. His clothes were disheveled, torn and stained. It took a full sequence of blinking and squinting before he could properly see who stood in his doorway.

"Tassos," Luca said. "I'm not in the mood for one of your rendez-vous today."

"Unfortunately, not why I came." Tassos stepped aside just enough that Alec became visible to the oldest demon in all the realms.

This time, it took Luca no time to realize what he was looking at. "You betrayed me."

"He put a knife to my back."

"A soulless wretch like him couldn't do you any real harm. You gave in because he's handsome."

"Is he? I hadn't noticed."

Luca began to shut the door. Alec wedged his foot in the way. "Wait. Please. I need your help."

The High Lord hung back, half-hidden by his half-closed door. "I don't help soulless. I don't help anyone."

"I just need to find someone. Then I'll be on my way, I swear."

"No."

Tassos reached an arm inside just as Luca kicked Alec's foot away. "Luca, please. Listen to me. This is important."

"You have betrayed me. Why should I listen to you?"

"He won't tell anyone. I know him; he's a man of his word. He simply needs your help. We all need your help."

"And why should I care?" Luca drew the door open just enough that Tassos ended up on the receiving end of a cold stare.

Tassos—much to Alec's surprise—did not flinch. "It concerns those who killed your sister. Wouldn't you like the chance to repay them in kind?"

Silence. The possibility of hope hung so heavy on the air Alec thought he could physically feel it against his skin. Afraid to move, Alec held his breath and waited.

"Fine." The door was opened to them completely, and Luca retreated within, waving a disinterested hand at the both of them to enter. "I shall hear your proposal. Nothing more."

Tassos stopped Alec with a hand on his chest. "Wait. Let me do the talking. Just sit. Not a word out of you unless I say. Understand? I know how to talk to him."

Alec could see enough of the interior of the house now to know it looked little different from the outside. Unkempt and unclean, things scattered and shattered about. "He's a madman," he whispered. "What good will he be to us?"

"And that is precisely why you will sit and look pretty, completely silent. Give me your word," Tassos said through his teeth.

"Fine," Alec said, mimicking the tone of the High Lord. "You have my word. But this had better work. Bri doesn't have much time."

"This is a delicate situation. Be patient. It has been a long time since Luca cared enough about anything to leave this house."

A long time since a demon with the highest responsibility had given even a sliver of thought toward his charges is what it looked like. "And why is that?"

"You've been alive a long time. I'm sure you can figure it out for yourself."

"No. No, I won't do it."

Tassos followed—chased—Luca to the back of his rundown house, barely catching the bedroom door before it smacked him in the face. "Luca, be reasonable for one moment."

"Reasonable? You want me to be reasonable?" Luca went straight to the window. He always went there to think. Tassos wondered what the view of the Void granted him that he returned to it again and again. "I started all this. I divided myself from Haven and reshaped this underworld into what you see today. We have cities and towns, all amongst those The One sees fit to punish. We are free from

Haven's immovable might here. I remade the world. Who am I to say it cannot be remade again?"

"You are the High Lord of Hell. Or, you used to be."

"My sister would have made herself a god."

"And strangely, even with her death, her plan seems to still live."

"Should I have stopped her had someone else not stepped in?"

"You have been around longer than most. What would a demon god mean for this world?"

Silence. Luca's shoulders moved with the intake of breath, then stiffened. "I do not know."

Tassos stepped inside and shut the door. It wouldn't keep Alec from hearing everything if the conversation escalated to furious yelling, but it would create the illusion of privacy. "Think about it a moment. You have seen gods born; you have seen the creation of the demons. What would the two together result in?"

"Gods are powerful because they are believed to be. Your answer lies in what the mortals would believe a demon god to be capable of."

"Nothing good."

"Not likely."

"So help us. Find the boy. He is somewhere in this realm."

"A seraph child would never survive here."

"The Hellwalkers do."

Luca turned, and his smile was one of dark amusement. Normally Tassos enjoyed that expression; in the past it had promised fun things, but now it made his skin itch. "Do they? They become twisted things. Never really belonging in either realm. The Hellwalkers are darker than their Havenly kin, and they never live long."

"They die in battle. Like most seraph."

"But much sooner. And usually because of some mad impulse."

"Are you telling me you believe the boy to be dead already? He would not have died in battle."

"You tell me he is mortal and seraph. He is too light for this dark place. It will crush him."

"Just find him. Find his witch twin. They cannot be together."

Another glance out the window, and Luca shook his head. "I cannot."

"Can't? Or won't?"

"Can't."

"Really? Are the rumors true, then? The High Lord of Hell has lost his touch?"

"I've lost nothing."

"I'd say that's debatable."

That brought Luca away from the window, stalking toward Tassos like a lion on the plains. "Why do you push me? Taunt me?"

"Because I remember who you used to be. Who you could be again."

"If what you tell me is true, these children will destroy everything and nothing will matter anyway."

"Is that what you want? An end to everything?"

"Everything must die. Even worlds."

They stood face to face, so close that Tassos could feel Luca's breath on his cheeks, see his lips move with each word, but he couldn't believe what he was hearing. "Are you serious? Is that what this has been all these centuries? You waiting for the end of the world because you decided we've all had enough?"

"The One has abandoned us all. Haven will not admit it, but I know it to be true. I knew it then, and I know it now."

"Then you are further gone than I thought."

"Enjoy whatever moment you find yourself in, Tassos. There will not be many more." His hands slipped around Tassos's waist, thumbs kneading into his hips.

Tassos was too disgusted to react as he normally would. Both hands planted firmly on Luca's chest kept the High Lord from sealing their mouths together. "It doesn't have to be the end. We can stop it. But only if you help us find the boy. I knew his mother. She was a bit of a revolutionary, and it caused her Fall. She told me once she had seen the end, and that it was her fault. She swore she would find a way to fix things. The last time I saw her, she told me she had found a way. She was pregnant, and I thought her altered by it—by what grew inside her. It wasn't until years later that I discovered the truth. Her children. Two children."

Luca had gone eerily still. Thoughts worked behind his eyes, changing his expression so many times Tassos could not keep up. "This woman, this Fallen, what was her name?"

"Talia."

"She Fell to be with another, then? A witch?"

"How do you know that?" It had all happened much too recently to have reached Luca's attention. He had been a recluse since long before Talia had ever fallen.

"I have had one other visitor in my years here. Just one. And I saw him only three times. A powerful witch, he had sought me out, wanting to be mine. I refused to bind with him. I wanted no connection to the rest of the world. I kicked him out. He returned. Once more I threw him out, and once more he returned. But this last time he begged me, pleaded with me to hear his case. He had married a fallen seraph, and they were to have a child. A child who would end everything."

Tassos waited for him to continue. When he did not, he curled his fingers into the demon's chest as if he could physically wrench the answer from him. "Well?"

"Jaymes said they could prevent it, but they needed more power. He needed the backing of a demon."

"And did you do it?"

"The children cannot be together. I will find the boy you seek."

— CHAPTER THIRTY-TWO —

The explosion rocked the small house. Ella stumbled, grabbing the table to balance herself. Bri fell back against the wall, catching himself just in time to save his head. When the world settled once again, Ella straightened, careful of the shattered jars that had fallen from the table. "What was that?"

Bri closed his eyes—a habit he had picked up recently when dealing with the myst. It eliminated the real world and left little room for confusion. "It's black," he said, opening his eyes once again. "Everything that was there just turned black...or has clouded over."

"A demon? Or...?"

"Kai."

They ran from the house, following the cloud of smoke that rose against the horizon to the east. It was one of those rare winter days that had warmed above the freezing level, and Ella actually began to sweat in her long-sleeved dress, despite having forgotten her coat in their haste. She stumbled more than once, but each time Bri caught her by the elbow and helped her along.

Another explosion. And this time they heard screams and cries of pain.

The city of Tarkava had once been the height of beauty and progress—or so Ella had been told. Den had showed her numerous paintings, all capturing the sparkling blue of the sky and the soft grey and white stone favored by the builders. The palace had sat high above the city, looking out over the walls and ocean, its towers stretching toward Haven as though The One would choose to visit the mortal realm at that spot.

In the weeks she had spent outside the city with Kai and Bri, Ella had only rarely glanced in the direction of the city that had become the focal point of her future. She hadn't wanted to see it. Hadn't wanted to witness what it had become. She hadn't wanted any possible instinctive reaction to the place that wanted to call her *Queen*.

Now it stood before her, a shell of what it had once been. The towers cracked and crumbled, leaning against the sky, always just a breath away from falling completely. Debris littered the road leading into the city; large stones that had once been a part of homes or shops were now nothing more than obstacles along a no longer flat road. Smoke curled into the sky, and the grey clouds overhead promised snow. It always seemed to warm before the snow came. The people who lived—survived—at the outskirts of the city would once again lose their cleared ground to snowdrifts and ice. Ella had done her best not to think of them—a guilt that crept around her head daily. But she had no more choice in the matter. Their faces stared at her as she and Bri ran past, into the bounds of the city. All had sunken cheeks, reddened noses. Children huddled close to their parents, who stroked their hair despite looking ready to shatter into pieces with the next impending explosion.

These were the people she was supposed to lead.

Lead to what? To where? This place was devastated.

An older man pulled her to a halt as she tried to round a corner, grabbing her by the elbow. "Wait," he said. "Please."

Ella stopped, and Bri did as well. She shared a hesitant look with him, but there was something in the man's grey eyes that made her reluctant to pull away. "What is it?"

"You cannot go within. The demon has returned to torment us. It is not safe."

"He's no demon," Ella said, patting the man's hand. Now that she was closer, now that she had a good look, she could see the man was not as old as she had originally thought. Not sixty, but perhaps forty. Circumstances had aged him.

"There are those of us who remember him. Years ago, he was nothing more than a street child, living in the filth. He used to steal from vendors and pick pockets. I was a man of standing; I caught him more than once stealing from my shop. We whipped him, kicked him. Nothing kept him away. There were others, alley dwellers and crime lords—they would abuse him. We all turned a blind eye. He was a child; we should have done something. Now, he extracts his revenge. The One leaves us to him because we are not innocent. We have sinned by allowing a child to go undefended. But you, you have no part in this. Go home, now. Leave, before he destroys you as well."

Ella gave the man's hands a gentle squeeze. "I will not leave. We will stop him and take him away from here. The One does not leave you to him. He is twisted by his past and by his magic. This is his will alone, not your punishment."

The man shook his head. "He was never right as a child. We saw it then. Perhaps we were not harsh enough. Now he destroys our world as retribution. As if this city has not seen enough darkness in the past years. We are nothing now. No king, no city, just the ash left by the war."

You have a queen. If only she were brave enough to accept it. Could she leave these people with nothing? Standing there, looking into the face of a man broken by war and magic, she knew she would not be able to turn a blind eye again. "Have faith," she said. "Things may yet change." Something cracked against the air, and the sounds of more crumbling stones seemed to put a lie to her words. "Take shelter. We will stop him, the both of us." She glanced at Bri, who waited some distance off, listening and turning his head as if searching out his brother's location.

The man saw Bri then for the first time, his grip on Ella's hands tightening. "He looks just the same."

"He is not the same. He is the opposite."

Flurries began to fill the air, and the small white flakes caught in the man's haggard beard. His nose twitched at the cold. "Seraph?"

"In a way. Please, tell everyone you can to get out of the city limits. It will save lives." She smiled and pulled her hands from his desperate grip. He called after her once, urging her to wait, then sent a blessing instead, and she thought she heard him move away.

She caught up with Bri at a corner, a broken sign for a tailor dangling just above his head. "He's at the very center," he said.

"Then let's hurry." This had to end. Kai could not be allowed to continue. It was hideous. Horrendous.

It was worse than she had ever imagined.

They rounded a final corner, and found themselves in the town square not a quarter turn later. A fountain graced the center, barren and crumbling, just like everything else. The snow that fell clung to the holy figure at the center, one arm broken off, the other extended outward as if it had once held something. A large man lay pinned by some invisible force along the edge of the fountain, his arms outstretched and bleeding into the empty pool. His clothes were haggard, but clearly once finely made. There were rings on his fingers, golden and jeweled. Kai stood over him, twirling a gold pocket watch round and round in his hand, letting it swing and wrap about his finger, only to reverse the action and do it all over again. Lines stretched out beneath both their feet.

"Kai," Bri said his name as if it were so much more than a name, as if it were a question and disbelief all rolled into one. "Stop this."

Kai didn't turn. He simply held up a hand, one finger indicating that Bri should wait. "Silence, my dear brother. For I am busy, and we are not speaking to one another. Or have you forgotten that?"

Ella hadn't forgotten. She had been running back and forth between the two boys for days. Ever since Kai had killed the innocent man in order to remove the *labrynth* from Bri's back. Kai had only grown more and more angry with each passing day.

"I have not forgotten," Bri said. "But I can't let you do this."

"No." Kai twisted about to look over his shoulder at them, his foot grinding into the man's stomach as he did so. "No, that is not how this works. You do not get to decide when we are on speaking terms, and when we are not. I have nothing to say to you, my ungrateful brother, so go away." He bent down, crouching over the bleeding man. Ella could not see what he did, but the man whimpered.

Bri's hands had become fists at his sides. He took a single step forward, but Ella stopped him. "Wait. Let me try."

"He's completely lost it, Ella. It's not worth the risk."

"No." She held him close by the arm. "He's angry with you. Not me. Let me try. I won't push too far."

Bri's eyes told her he hated the idea, but he said nothing. Only the slight shake of his head indicated anything. Ella touched his cold cheek and kissed him lightly, then stepped toward Kai with every ounce of courage she possessed held tightly in her chest.

Kai stiffened a top the fountain. "I said no, Bri."

"I'm not Bri."

A different sort of stillness overcame him. Ella held her breath, then thought better of it and breathed carefully and deeply. Kai flipped around, sitting abruptly on his latest victim, who moaned and twisted. In response, Kai thumped him soundly on the throat before smiling. "Ella. My only companion in the irritable silence caused by my brother. Have you come to scold me as well?"

"You have to stop this, Kai. These are innocent people."

"Innocent?" He hopped off his morbid perch, coming toward her with an expression of disgust. She could see now the blood all over his hands, staining the bandages he always wore. "You think these people are innocent? I could spend the next month listing the atrocities they've committed."

"Against whom?" She did not back away, did not flinch when he made a sweeping gesture with his bloody hand. "Most of the people here are children, Kai. Mothers, and old people. These are not soldiers."

"I never said they were. Look." He grabbed her by the arms and spun her around, forcing her to look down the far street, where a pile of bodies lay in the shadows, slowly turning white with the dusting of snow. "Those people there, they spat on me as I slept in the gutters as a child. The woman at the top, she threatened to cut off my hands for stealing from her bakery. And the man beneath her? I remember him. He was out wandering one day and happened upon me while I still lived in secret with my father. He saw my wings, called me a demon, threatened to turn my father into the authorities for harboring one of Hell's creatures."

She tried not to shudder in his hold, to keep her eyes open. "Clearly he didn't. What stopped him?"

"My father. And every coin we had to our name. My father paid him every month until the day he died."

Ella closed her eyes, struggling to control her emotions. Her heart ached at the thought of the child Kai standing wide-eyed as some stranger said terrible things about the wings that graced his back. But it didn't make him right. "Kai, please."

"And this one." He pulled her again, toward the fountain where the man lay bleeding still. With nothing to block her view, she saw the knife embedded in the man's stomach, and the lines drawn into his arms and chest in red wounds. "Do you know what this man used to do to me? When I was a child living on the streets? Do you?"

When he shook her, she gave him the answer he wanted. "No."

"I'd tell you," Kai said, releasing her, "but it would burn your pretty ears." He returned to the fountain, hopping up to perch over the man once again. "The world needs a change, Ella. I'm going to give it to them."

"Maybe that's true, but you could change it for the better. Why align yourself with Hell? Kai, you have so much power, you could do such good. If you looked to Haven instead—"

"Haven?" He ground the knife into the man's stomach as if it would ease his frustrations. "What has Haven ever done for me? For anyone like me?" The man tried to speak, and Kai pulled the blade from his abdomen and pressed it between his teeth instead, silencing him. "Haven doesn't give a damn about people like me," Kai continued, stepping off the fountain once again. "Or people like Bri. They hunt us. Haven wants Bri dead. Is that who you want to place your faith in? The One is gone. The seraph have lost their way, and demons are the only ones who can see anything anymore. I'm going to remake the world, Ella. A world where people like me don't have to hide in the shadows, where Bri would be respected for the power he holds. Where you wouldn't have to feel guilty for the feelings that brought you to this very place."

"I have no guilt for the empathy that brought me here."

"Not the feelings I was speaking of."

He couldn't... Could he? Oh, gods, if Kai had developed the ability to read minds, she was doomed. They all were. Did he know the thoughts that kept her awake at night? The thoughts of what would happen when Bri's ten years were up? Did Kai know it twisted her heart every time she felt the slightest bit of sympathy for him? For a mad witch who had kidnapped and held her captive?

Or was he simply forcing her to question herself, knowing nothing at all?

Kai laughed bitterly and squeezed his hand, dripping blood onto the ground which he then began toeing into a pattern.

"Is that how you sleep at night? By telling yourself all this is for a noble cause?"

"Oh, no. Nothing keeps me up at night at all. I sleep soundly, kept warm by my revenge. Helping free the world from Haven is a perk. The mortals have had their chance; it's time the immortals rose once again."

She could see Bri watching them, ready to step in, but she lifted just a finger, willing him to wait. To give her another moment. "How does that help you? Witches are neither mortal nor immortal. Where do you fit in?"

With a snap of his fingers the *labrynth* at his feet flashed, and the ground trembled. In the distance, one of the towers shook and collapsed completely. "I am creating a new god! I will be the maker of this new world! I will be *more* than a god."

Her heart broke just as surely as the tower. All that art, history, memories—gone. She would never have the chance to walk those halls. "And you think Olin is the one to do this?"

"Well, he wasn't my first choice, but he'll get the job done."

Ella felt herself shaking. "This is all a game to you, isn't it? Nothing more than a way to test your limits. You don't care about remaking the world."

It seemed as if he hadn't moved at all, as if he simply appeared in front of her, nose to nose. "Don't presume to know me so well, sweetness. I could end your miserable life whenever I want. But for now, you're nice enough to look at, so I keep you around. Once you've given in, and I've had my way with you, you'd be wise to watch your tongue."

The smack echoed off the far walls of the city, high pitched and quick. Kai stood absolutely still, his face turned ever so slightly as his cheek bloomed red. Ella's hand stung.

Time seemed to still, refusing to move forward and unable to go back. She couldn't believe she had done it. So many times the fantasy had crossed her mind. He deserved it—he deserved so much more— but to act against him in such a blatant manner...

Surely she would be dead soon.

Kai lifted a hand to his cheek, touching the reddened skin as if he wasn't sure it had really happened. His eyes shifted, boring into her. Ella's stomach turned. Then time surged back to life—and moved too quickly.

Kai's hand closed around her throat and shoved her backward into a hard stone wall. The fountain where they had stood had become distant. How had he moved her so quickly? The shop behind her shook with Kai's rage, and its walls ground into her spine. Bri called after them, but it was difficult to concentrate on his words. There were sparks in her vision, and no matter how she tried, she could not pull in a breath.

Then the pressure on her throat was gone. She coughed, breathing in ragged, hitching breaths. Bri held Kai's wrist in his hand, and had placed his entire body between her and his brother.

"Don't touch her."

"So brave are we now, brother? When did you get that strong?"

Ella knew Bri had been training in the year he had been away, and she knew he had secretly kept up as much as he could when Kai was distracted. Kai hadn't been meant to know about that strength, not yet.

"Must be all the manual labor of living on our own," Bri said.

Kai bared his teeth. "Your woman is out of control."

"You asked for it, and you know it."

A long moment passed between them. Ella didn't dare move. It was as if power somehow passed between the two boys, battling for superiority. Bri's grip on Kai's wrist was sure, but Kai still had a free hand, and it twitched at his side. Rage blazed in Kai's eyes, stirring the madness that was always there, but had seemed to have quieted some before today.

Ella's every instinct screamed at her to pray—but she didn't know who to invoke.

There was such magic on Kai in that moment, swirling the air and humming along his flesh. Bri felt it all like a fine buzzing in his head. Beneath his fingers were the raised lines of a *labrynth* Kai had etched into his own flesh. How many more existed like it? How many spells had been carved into Kai's skin, waiting and ready for his command to call them awake? The answer was probably best unknown. It was easier to be brave when you didn't know exactly what you were up against.

Kai's free hand moved at his side. "I think I've waited long enough, brother. Don't you?"

"Waited for what?"

"For you to come to your senses."

Ella screamed before Bri's mind even had time to register what had happened. He felt hard stone scrape along his back—still sensitive from losing the *labrynth* only days before—and the air knocked from his lungs. The shock jostled his control of the myst, and it slipped in past his defenses as he struggled to pull breath back into his aching chest. So much of it had gone dark, altered by Kai's presence. The futures of those closest—the man at the fountain, the people piled in the street—were slowly fading into nothingness. But there were a few lines connected further out, the futures of those who had managed to stay out of Kai's path—they still contained a dim glow. They could come back. If things changed. If Bri changed things.

Air rushed back into his lungs as pain flared across his arm. Bri jerked away instinctively, but could not move. Kai sat across his hips, leaning all his weight into Bri's arm. When his vision cleared, he saw blood running in rivers from his elbow to the street.

"Kai."

"Too late." He cut into Bri's arm one more time.

Ella grabbed at Kai, pulling at his shoulders. "Kai, stop this. Get off him!"

Kai shoved her, hard enough that she skittered back over the cobblestones until she lay, limp and still, out of reach.

The sight of her there, unmoving in the moonlight, gave Bri the strength to fight back. He lunged forward, his free hand reaching for Kai's throat. They sat face to face, Kai laughing. Bri couldn't bring himself to squeeze hard enough to truly deny his brother air.

"I told you, Bri, it's too late," Kai said, digging the blade into Bri's arm for no other apparent reason than to cause pain. He leaned into Bri's chokehold, as though daring him to go further. "It's already done. Did you really think I wasn't prepared?"

"Nothing is done. You haven't had the chance to scribe anything."

"I scribed before you got here. Time's up. I need information, and I need it now. I was hoping we could have done this more amicably, but you just wouldn't cooperate. So I lured you to me."

"What?"

"Yes, my dear brother." Kai smiled. "All this was for you. None of it had to happen. If you had just ceased your silent treatment, we could have avoided all this death."

The sight of bodies piled and scattered in the streets flew through Bri's memory. People who had died that day. Died because he had been foolish enough to think he could manipulate Kai by refusing to speak with him. Their blood was on his hands—

No. That was exactly what Kai wanted, for Bri to blame himself. Kai was mad. Simple as that. A mad man could not be controlled or predicted. Not easily. Kai had killed those people—Bri had failed to save them.

Blood dripped from his arm, hitting the stone with a resounding *plink* that drew Bri's attention back to the present. He still had his hand locked firmly around Kai's throat, but despite everything he did not tighten it.

Kai smiled as though he had heard every thought in Bri's head in the last moments and was pleased. "Into the myst, brother."

Bri didn't have time to protest before Kai slammed him back to the ground. He felt the lines light up and burn beneath him, felt the magic force open the pathway between his mind and the myst. He fell inside, uncontrolled and violently, as he had when he was a child.

It had been months since he had seen the myst this way. Not since he had retreated there, body and soul, and the mysteriously kind seraph had pleaded with him to stay away. He had been so careful not to draw the attention of the Singers, of Gabriel and her spies. Now the myst clung to him, overeager. Panic seemed close, but Bri held tight to what he had learned and pushed all the unwanted images away. So much of the future was in flux, grey and twisted and in danger of disappearing altogether.

Kai draped himself over Bri's shoulders. "Ah, it has been some time since I've been here. It makes the scars on my back tingle."

"I can't be here, Kai. They'll find me."

"Who will? Look around, Bri. Really look."

He had been looking. Looking was all he could do when he was in the myst. The visions prodded at him constantly, as if they had no one else to torment.

Bri batted away another insistent tendril of myst, going so still himself that the breath in his chest seemed a huge, too-obvious movement. No one else. The myst had no one else to go to. There was not a Singer in sight.

Kai squeezed him tighter, almost like a hug. "Amazing, isn't it? All this time I had heard the stories, but I didn't really think it could be true. All those irritating seraph, deserting their posts? But here it is! The truth of it! Thank you, Bri, this was exactly what I needed to see." He patted Bri's cheek.

Something moved far off in the distance. A silhouette, growing larger, clearer. And another. Bri had seen that enough times. "They're not all gone, Kai. Please, release the *labrynth*. I can't be here."

"Are you finished resisting me?" Scarred fingertips and rough bandages slid against Bri's throat, threatening.

The wings of the approaching creatures were clear against the myst now. For a moment Bri considered calling out to them, pleading for their aid. They would take him away from Kai—and to his own death. He couldn't die yet. At least with Kai, he would have a chance to make things right. *Gods, what kind of world do I live in where Kai is the least undesirable choice over Haven?* "Yes. I'm finished. I'll do it your way."

"Promise?"

"Yes."

"Really?"

"Yes!"

"Swear to me. Swear on Ella's life."

"No. I won't let you hurt her. This is between the two of us only."

Kai shook his head, fingers still playing upon Bri's throat. "If you don't do as I say from now on, her life is forfeit."

"Kai—"

"I already have the *labrynth* in place."

The seraph in the distance were coming faster now. And there were more. At least four. From the outline of the wings, not all were Singers. "What *labrynth*? What have you done?"

"Remember I showed you how I had learned to call Death?" Kai grinned.

"...you didn't."

"Would you like to call my bluff?"

"Get us out of here before we're both dead!"

"I'm not afraid of a few seraph."

"Kai, please!" Panic was a stone in his stomach.

"Swear it. Swear on her life. You do things my way now. Swear it, or I activate the *labrynth* right here, right now."

He remembered the girl at the Masquerade, dead because Bri had taken two seconds too long to show himself. "Yes. Fine. I swear."

"Excellent."

Bri felt the magic holding them both in the myst burst and dissolve. They dropped out of the other realm like a stone in a pond, and Bri woke in his body, still laying on the cold, hard streets of Tarkava. Kai stood immediately, grinning from ear to ear.

"Thank you, brother. That was very helpful. Now, let's pack up and go home, shall we? We'll have guests soon."

— CHAPTER THIRTY-THREE —

Carma studied the ink-stained hands of the sullen young seraph standing behind Gabriel. This one was young enough that she had not yet been born when Carma had torn out her heart and descended, and yet, there was something vaguely familiar about her features. But that wasn't what caused Carma to stare in disbelief. It was the aura she sensed around the young one, and around Gabriel as well.

A twisting together of energies.

"Gabriel, what have you done?"

"That's none of your concern," Gabriel said. She had disappeared for a time, claiming the need to retrieve something important. Carma and Dorothea had waited impatiently, hoping Inaseri would not show up while the seraph was gone. Luck had been on their side in that respect, but now Carma wondered if they would have another problem all together.

"You have bound her to yourself," she accused.

"Yes," Gabriel said, absolutely no hint of remorse in her tone.

"Why?"

"As I said, it does not concern you."

"It does if we are going to be civil and work together for any amount of time. You have taken her free will."

"It is a holy sanctioned act."

"You are a fool," Carma said. The last time she recalled such a measure being used there had been a tribunal first. "It is an atrocity, a perversion of all Haven is. You should save us all the trouble and time and simply rip your heart from your chest now."

Gabriel laughed. "You'd love that, wouldn't you? To have me so disgraced, just like the rest of you."

"It was quite the risk to take, with the Restorium so close at hand." That shook the general's staunch confidence. "How do you know about that?"

"Everyone knows, Gabe. The only secret is the precise time." Gabriel scoffed.

Shuffling along the forest floor, Dorothea crept close to the young seraph, peering at her face, reaching to touch her wings. "Tricky girl," the old witch said, chuckling when the seraph took a step back.

Carma knew those words for what they were. "What do you mean, Dorothea?" There had only ever been one "tricky girl."

"Can you not see it? She has the same eyes, the same proud chin. The coloring is different, but that is all. Though for you, the coloring would be far more the same."

"What are you talking about, old witch?" Gabriel said, taking a step closer to her bound companion.

But Dorothea simply kept her gaze on the young seraph, reaching to touch her yet again. "Come, Carma. Look carefully. You have seen the next generation, if not this one."

It took only a moment more for Carma to realize what she meant. "Gods in Hell. She looks like Bri."

Dorothea smiled. "Exactly that."

The young seraph gasped, then changed everything as she took a step closer to Dorothea rather than away again. "You know Bri. Then you must be..." She turned. "Carma. You're Carma. You've been protecting him."

"Kadiel, not another word," Gabriel said through clenched teeth.

It was as if a gag had been put in place. The young seraph said nothing more, though she clearly struggled against the command.

Divine Order in action.

Carma wanted to wring Gabriel's holy neck. "What does it matter, Gabriel? She has already said enough. This must be Talia's sister."

Kadiel nodded.

With deliberate steps, Carma approached her once friend. "You have bound Talia's sister to yourself. Taken her free will. Why?

Because she opposed you? Because she hid a child from Haven's eyes?"

"Because she hid two children," Gabriel snapped.

"And binding her now that they have been revealed accomplishes what?"

"She cannot be trusted."

"Perhaps not, but she is young and surely inexperienced."

"What is your point, Carma?"

"My point," she drew near to Gabriel, close enough that the words would pass only between the two of them, "is do you really think she accomplished all that alone?"

Gabriel never had the chance to answer. As the words hung in the air between them, the ground began to shake, and the air turned cold, then hot, then cold and back again.

"He comes," Dorothea whispered, her excitement clear in her voice. Carma nearly fell into Gabriel, and braced herself against a nearby tree. Gabriel stumbled and fell. *Serves her right.* In that moment, Carma had no love for her old friend's pride. The air shifted once more, then remained a steady cold. Carma shivered once, then shook the feeling away.

Inaseri stood before them as if he had always been there. His armor gleamed in the last of the sunlight coming through the trees. Unlike the feathered pattern on Gabriel's plate, it was smooth and unblemished. Not a single scar marring the metal, as if it had never seen battle. Yet Carma knew the truth of it. Inaseri had seen more than his fair share of confrontation. The fact that no one ever landed a blow was part of the legend. Perhaps true, perhaps not, but no blow would ever show. He stood before them, perfect and undefeated. With hair black as night and skin tanned by the sun, his blue eyes were striking and almost unnerving. Almost.

Dorothea had already gone to her knees, and it seemed an appropriate action, so Carma did the same. "Inaseri," she said, by way of greeting, "we are honored by your presence."

The god looked them over as if they were insects to be either ignored or squashed. "You are the ones who tormented the twins?"

"No harm was meant, I assure you," Carma said.

"Simply a curiosity." Dorothea's fingers moved against the forest floor, always drawing, always scribing. Carma hoped it was nothing that would insult the god before them.

Inaseri shifted his weight, thick muscle moving in each arm and leg. "You frightened them."

"It is good for children to know fear. It teaches them," Dorothea said without reservation.

"The twins do not learn."

"And as such they are lucky to have a parent such as you, god of the weak and unprotected."

Gabriel took that moment to drag herself from the ground, standing and shaking the leaves from her wings. Kadiel stood close by still, silent, though her expression said a million things she'd been forbidden to voice.

Inaseri looked at them each in turn, stone-faced and serious. "A demon, a witch, and two of Haven's soldiers. An odd company. To what do I owe the pleasure?"

"We need your help," Carma said, dusting off her knees as she stood.

"What help could a demon need from a god? Don't you all believe yourselves infallible?"

"Not in all things," Carma allowed, "There is one matter in which we have no experience."

"And what would that be?"

"Killing a god."

Inaseri drew his sword.

Everyone except Dorothea—who was still kneeling and drawing on the ground—threw up their arms in a gesture of no harm. "Not you or any of your kind, I assure you," Carma said. "There is another, one who will destroy everything if not dealt with."

"Your words make no sense."

"One of my kind," Carma said, hands still held where they could be seen empty. "He intends to ascend himself. To become like you."

Something in Inaseri's face shifted. "This is impossible."

"I am told it is not."

"How?"

"*Labrynths*," Dorothea said, still drawing her fingers along the dirt.

"You mean to say a witch can create a god?" Inaseri spoke carefully.

"With the right lines and the right witnesses, yes." Never did Dorothea look up from her idle scribing.

Inaseri sheathed his sword. Carma breathed in relief, and lowered her hands slowly. "We sought you out to ask for your help. You defeated Cel-Eza, and he is the only god to have ever met his end."

"Others have, but it was due to a loss of believers."

"I fear we will not have time for that avenue."

"You have Haven on your side in this?" Inaseri flicked his gaze toward Gabriel and Kadiel.

"I am hoping they will at least not get in my way," Carma said.

Gabriel snorted. "Haven could deal with a new god."

"Then why doesn't it?" Inaseri asked.

At this, Gabriel kept silent.

Carma wanted to throttle her. "Because the Restorium is upon them. Haven will be useless soon."

"How dare you speak in such a manner!" Gabriel's temper had snapped.

Carma didn't much care. "Is it, or is it not, about to sleep and turn a blind eye to the Mortal Realm?"

Gabriel stood, stance wide, gaze unwavering. "The Restorium is a necessity. Brought about by The One. We trust in The One."

"A foolish, misplaced trust," Carma said, "The One has not spoken to any of you in thousands of years."

"There are more important things than—"

"Than what?" Carma interrupted. "Than helping those you are supposed to love? Than letting everyone know you are at least alive?"

"Enough!" Inaseri's voice carried through the woods, booming as though thunder had struck, silencing both Gabriel and Carma. "The quarrels of Haven and Hell do not interest me. I care only for the mortals here in my own realm. This demon who seeks to be a god, he will not serve the mortals as the rest of us do?"

Carma shook her head. "His goal is power. That has always been his only goal."

The god turned thoughtful, and as Carma watched she swore the line of Inaseri's jaw changed, becoming less square and more angular. He paced the clearing, arms folded across a chest that also seemed to shift. By the time the god stood in front of Kadiel he had become unquestioningly female. The hair had grown longer, and the waist slimmer. The armor had changed to fit over breasts and shoulders that were less broad. "This one," she said, "she calls to me. I sense a kindred spirit in her. What do you have to say about these matters?"

Kadiel said nothing, just flexed her mouth like a fish, glancing at Gabriel, then Carma, then back to the god.

"Why do you not speak, child?" Inaseri asked in a quiet voice that contrasted her previous tones.

"Because I have forbidden it," Gabriel said, quite plainly, with no apology in her tone.

Inaseri looked at her for only a moment. "You, I do not like. Release whatever binding you have placed on the young one, or I will leave, and you will never have the answer you seek."

At first Carma though Gabriel would argue, but then all the tension in her body released, and she spoke. "Go ahead, Kadiel. Speak with the god."

Immediately, Kadiel bowed her head, though she did not take a knee. "Inaseri. I have studied your legend for quite some time. Though we are not to concern ourselves with the gods of this realm, I have always admired you as a champion of those who cannot protect themselves."

"As you strive to be yourself."

"Yes."

"For one child in particular."

Kadiel nodded. "My sister's son."

"Your sister has two sons," Inaseri said, causing Kadiel to startle.

"How can you know this?" the young seraph whispered.

"As I said, I sense a kindred spirit in you." Inaseri's voice remained kind and calm. "I can see who you seek to protect. Your sister has two sons, yet you mention only one. Why?"

"Only one is hunted."

"Hunted? By whom?"

Here, Kadiel hesitated. And Carma knew why.

"Gabriel," Kadiel said. "Though she is under orders to do so, and she takes orders very seriously. I like to think that if she stopped to think for herself for one minute, she might see reason."

"Why, you ungrateful—"

Inaseri silenced Gabriel with a simple gesture. "You are a kind thing," she said to Kadiel. "Now tell me, why is the child hunted?"

"He is human, yet he sees the myst."

"Hm...Yes, that would trouble the winged ones, wouldn't it?"

Kadiel didn't so much as glance at Gabriel. "I kept him hidden for nearly fifteen years, but he is at the center of all this now. His brother...he is a witch, and he works for the demon who would become a god. If the boys are ever together, it would be—"

"The boys are together," Carma cut in.

"What?"

"Kai took Bri weeks ago. I sent Alec to find him, but he has had no luck. It is why I must know how to kill a god. If Kai has Bri, then he presumably has enough power to scribe a *labrynth* that will raise Olin to godhood."

"This child," Inaseri said, "this *Bri*, is he in danger?"

"It is hard to say. I do not think his brother would kill him, but there are things worse than death."

"Indeed there are." The god turned back to Kadiel. "These creatures here. This demon, seraph, and the witch, do you trust them?"

"I trust Carma to watch over Bri. The witch I do not know, though I believe she has also looked after my nephew. Gabriel...she has a good heart, twisted though her priorities may be."

I like this girl. Gabriel looks ready to burn holes through her, and still she speaks her mind. Despite the grim atmosphere, Carma fought to keep from laughing at Gabriel's expression.

When Inaseri turned to face Carma, she once again bore the body he had first appeared to them in. "Only a god can kill a god. And you must make the mortals believe it. Cel-Eza only fell to me because enough mortals believed it possible."

This is what Carma had feared. "Olin is an unknown factor. The mortals have never seen a demon god. Who knows what they will believe."

"You must plant ideas in their heads."

"Such as?"

Inaseri shrugged. "It depends on your plan."

"Will you kill him?"

"I would rather not risk myself. There are too many who depend on me, and as you said, too much is unknown."

"Then who should I ask?"

Inaseri thought on this a moment. "The others will not help you. They will not care. Not unless he insults them directly."

Damn the gods. What good are they? "Then what do we do?"

Dorothea looked up from the ground for the first time since the conversation had started. "Raise another."

Even after nine hundred years, Carma could not always understand the witch immediately. "What?"

"We raise another god," Dorothea repeated herself. "One to kill him."

"Don't be absurd!" Gabriel said, moving closer to Dorothea as if seeing the witch's face would explain things. "We are trying to stop one demon from becoming a god. Why would we instead raise two?"

Dorothea looked at Gabriel as though she were too simple to understand even the most basic of things. "We need a demon god to kill a demon god."

"And just who would you suggest we raise to godhood alongside Olin?" Gabriel asked.

Dorothea smiled, and it was an expression that often sent shivers along Carma's spine. "The same demon that has been by his side all along, of course."

In that moment, Carma felt all eyes on her.

— CHAPTER THIRTY-FOUR —

A lec had heard the argument between Tassos and the High Lord of Hell carry on through the bedroom door. Not the exact words that were said, but the tones, and the intensity. He had gripped his knees until the ache was too great to bear, then set his grip against the worn couch cushions instead—until they had singed and burned. Despite the disarray of the house, Alec had a feeling it would be better not to risk spoiling his tenuous welcome by destroying the furniture, and took to pacing instead.

The argument had ended more than a turn ago, and neither the reaper, nor the demon, had come out. A hell rat scurried across the kitchen floor, screeching as it grabbed a fallen morsel before slipping through a hole in the wall once more. Alec felt like that rat, hoping to grab something and run. It already felt strange not to have Ariadne at his side. He slid his hand into his pocket and ran a finger along the molded silver of the locket. Even since reuniting with her, he had not opened it. But his nail fit into the latch, and the locket released, the hinge gliding effortlessly.

Alec pulled the locket from his pocket and, hand shaking slightly, unfolded the two sides.

Somewhere, though he couldn't see, there were *labrynths* woven into the small paintings to prevent aging and decay. The colors were just as vivid as they had been the day they had been made. On the right side, Alec saw his own face, Ariadne beside him. They both looked young and happy. Alec remembered the day they had commissioned the portrait, just after they had run away together, free from their pasts, and her father. They had the whole future laid out before them, and the promise of whatever life they wanted. It showed in their faces. Alec felt old looking at it now. He couldn't remember the last time he had smiled like that. Perhaps that had been the last time. Ariadne had changed as well. While she was still beautiful, still youthful, time had stolen some of the sparkle from her eyes, as well as some of the width of her smile. Had they both changed so much? Were they really the same people painted here within the locket?

He had intended to look only at the one side—but his gaze wandered to the left, and to the second picture.

Blue eyes, crinkled with happiness, and a smile that stretched nearly from ear to ear. Hair lighter than Alec's, though still dark. Marc looked like their mother. Alec had been so careful not to let the world touch him, and he had done a good job—until that night.

The locket snapped shut with a sound that seemed to echo throughout the empty room. Alec was surprised at how much the loss still hurt. Like a knife twisted in his chest. He shut his eyes and breathed carefully. He couldn't lose again. Foolish, maybe, to think in such terms, but he thought it nonetheless. He would not lose Bri like he had lost Marc. Never.

What the hell are they doing in there?

The bedroom door opened almost as if Alec's silent, angered plea had gone answered. Tassos stepped out, robes neater than when he had gone in, but Alec tried not to think on that. The reaper's expression was one of victory, and he gave a small nod. Alec would have demanded an answer immediately, but Luca appeared in the doorway, and that was answer enough.

The disheveled High Lord had combed his hair so that it now hung neatly around his shoulders. And he had gotten dressed— thank whatever gods for that. The pants and jacket were so perfectly tailored, Alec had to wonder if they had been manifested rather than made by hand. After hundreds of years living as a disenchanted hermit, there was little chance he actually owned anything new and of current fashion. Yet, there he stood, a gentleman by any standard. Around the eyes he still looked tired, and perhaps not quite sober, but it was an improvement. A vast improvement.

"Well, Alec," Luca said, undoing the tie about his neck, "it seems Tassos has managed to convince me of the importance of your plight." Tassos made a sound of restrained horror as Luca slipped the silken tie free from his neck and dropped it on the floor.

"I am glad to hear it, my lord." Alec wanted to ask him to get to work right then and there, but bit his tongue.

"I'm sure you are." Luca undid the button at his throat and worked open the neck of his shirt, allowing it to fall open casually.

Tassos snatched the silk tie from the floor as if he was rescuing it. "We all are. Though I don't see why you can't help properly dressed."

"I don't see you wearing all this nonsense," Luca said.

"I wear what is flattering to my own figure. It wouldn't kill you to do the same."

"I am the High Lord of Hell, as you were so careful to remind me. I think my clothes make the least of my impression."

"Yes, well, whatever helps you sleep at night."

"When someone lets me sleep."

"My point is," Tassos snapped, folding the tie and then vanishing it with a flick of his wrist, "that you should do something helpful now before Alec grinds his teeth to dust in an effort not to scream demands at you."

Alec released his jaw, wincing at the stiffness that had grown there without his realizing. Their banter had indeed worn on his nerves, but now under the careful gaze of the High Lord, he wished they had continued a while longer.

"Yes," Luca said, looking Alec over in a way that made him think his thoughts were elsewhere, "I suppose you are right. I will find the boy, and help you keep him safe from this brother of his."

"And how do you go about finding someone?"

"It is a sense I have long ago turned off, but now that I pull power once again, I am waking to it. Soon I will feel every spark of life crawling about Hell, and then I will sense the differences in them, the demons, the soulless, and the tormented souls. Once that is clear, your little half-seraph will be easy to find."

Alec nodded, relief flooding his veins more powerfully than the heat that always circled like a vulture now. "Thank you. May I ask how long this might take?"

Luca didn't answer. His eyes had glazed over, as though seeing something in another realm—almost the same look Bri got when staring into the myst. Then the look was gone, and clarity returned as though it had never left—something Bri never achieved—and Luca turned his head toward the void side of the house.

Tassos took a step toward him. "Luca? What is it?"

His smile was dark. "A rat."

Tassos reached for him and grabbed only empty air. The weight of power hovering about them was palpable, so heavy any idiot would have known something old and powerful had returned. It took Tassos no more than a heartbeat to regain his balance and head for the back door. Alec followed.

They burst out into the hot hellish air, little before them but debris and the Void. Dead and bare brush lined the limits of the lawn, bones and fur caught in the branches. Luca was crouched at the edge of the blackness that extended on for endless days, his golden hair shining in great contrast and fluttering about as if charged with power. Something, or someone, was pinned beneath him.

"Luca." Tassos approached with barely managed caution, his robes blending into the backdrop of the Void so that he almost disappeared as Alec watched. "What is—" He stopped, not bothering to finish his sentence once finally close enough to see what Luca held.

With a growl, the High Lord shook and slammed his captive. "How did you come to this place? Who sent you?"

Choked coughs were all that answered.

Tassos took a single step back, and Alec thought he looked like he fought between saying something and saying nothing at all. Growing closer with careful steps, Alec could see the slight legs and the wrinkled skirt that peeked out from beneath Luca's crouch. They were legs he would have known anywhere.

"Stop!" He rushed forward, stopping only when he saw her face below Luca's, her cheeks red from trying to breathe, and her dark hair matted and strewn about. "Stop. She's not a threat. Let her go."

Luca's blue eyes were cold fire when they were turned on Alec. He recognized that change; an indicator of true form fighting to get free. "You know this creature?"

Alec chose his words carefully. "She's a friend."

Tassos scoffed at his choice of words.

Alec gathered his thoughts and continued regardless. "Ariadne. She was traveling with me, but she stayed behind when we came here. Tassos thought you wouldn't appreciate too many visitors."

The air around Luca shimmered with power. "Then why is she here now?"

"I don't know. Let her talk. I'm sure she'll tell you."

Luca shifted his grip on her throat, but did not loosen it. "She tried to run when I caught her. Tried to travel as only demons can. She has access to too much power for a soulless. She tries still." Ariadne seemed to flicker, but remained. Alec felt the power stir in the air, then suddenly snap and disappear.

Gods...he can hold her here. If Luca had that kind of power when he wasn't even at his best...

"She won't run," Alec said, making sure Ariadne was listening, addressing her more than Luca. "Let her breathe, and I'm sure she'll explain herself."

Luca squeezed Ariadne a bit tighter, running his thumb along her jawline. Alec could hear her skin hiss at his touch. "What about you, Tassos? Do you trust this soulless?"

"Not in the least."

Traitor. If Alec hadn't been so terrified of Luca, he would have told Tassos just what he thought of his opinion, but it was probably best to remain calm and focused.

"All right, then." Decision made, Luca released Ariadne's throat, and instead thrust his hand hard against the very center of her chest, holding her flat to the ground just as effectively. "You have one on your side, and one against you," he said to her. "You have a very short amount of time to convince me not to kill you. Now, what are you doing here?"

Ariadne coughed, and when she spoke her voice scratched. "I was looking for Alec."

"You are lying."

"I'm not. I swear."

"A half-truth then. Tell the whole truth."

She said nothing.

Her dress beneath Luca's hand began to burn as power built once again.

"Ari, please," Alec pleaded with her.

"I'm here for Alec," she said.

"You were told to wait behind," Luca said. "Why come here? No lies."

Once again, she said nothing.

The air tingled with power. The skin of Ariadne's chest wrinkled and sagged, her ebony hair streaking with grey. Her eyes widened in fright, and she clutched at Luca's hand where it remained steady and hard against her chest.

"What are you doing?" Alec said, fighting the impulse to pull the High Lord off her. "Stop it."

"She is filled with her master's power. I am withdrawing it, that is all. If she answers me, I will stop."

"Cel-Eza, Ari, just tell him what he wants to know."

Her eyes, dulling with imposed age, filled with tears. "I cannot."

"Why?"

"Please, Alec."

Luca pressed against her harder. "Did your master send you here?" Ariadne shut her eyes and bit her lip. Her hair was evenly black and grey now. "Who is it? Who is your master? What does he want with me?" She flickered once more, but Luca growled and held tight. "I will not let you run."

Ariadne continued to struggle beneath him, then suddenly she went still and relaxed. "It does not matter."

"And why is that?"

"Because he has called me." She smiled, and disappeared in a spark of light.

Luca toppled, suddenly off balance with her gone. He hit his knees hard, but caught himself with his now free hand. Then he went totally still.

Tassos grabbed Alec by the elbow and urged him back. "Move away. Quickly. Toward the house. He won't destroy the house."

"The house?"

"Go!"

Alec ran, every survival instinct he had charged by the tone in the reaper's voice. They didn't stop until they were both pressed tightly against the wall of the dilapidated house. Then the ground began to shake.

Luca still crouched on the ground, shoulders stiff and the muscles in his arms straining against the fabric of his jacket. Dark light grew around him, dampening the glow of his golden tones, and stretching outward against the backdrop of the void. Alec could feel the air growing denser, heavier, until breathing hurt. Then the darkness stopped, lingering in a stillness that was more frightening than the expansion. Chest aching, Alec held his breath, and felt his heart wait as well.

The tiniest shift. Everything imploded, collapsing inward on Luca, and kicking up dust and debris in a terrifying silence. Alec threw up his arms to protect his face, turning into the wall of the house for support.

When it settled, and Alec had stopped shaking well enough to move, he had to freeze immediately in order to prevent himself from falling into the Void—which now stretched right to the back of the house. The entire back lawn no longer existed. As far as the eye could see, there was only darkness. Not even the golden High Lord of Hell.

Tassos placed a tentative hand on Alec's arm. "Come. We should go inside."

"What about Luca? What happened to him?"

"Oh, he's fine. Though I suppose he is a bit difficult to see at the moment. Look closely, just there. See how the darkness shimmers a bit, moves? That's him. He'll corporealize again once he's calmed down."

Alec stared at the Void and at the space where the nothingness seemed to be just a bit *more*. "Is that his true form?"

"It's complicated."

"He made the Void bigger."

"Yes, he did. Just as he made the rest of it. Now, get inside. Even I'm not going near him while he's like this. In the meantime, you and I are going to have a little talk. Your girlfriend may have just cost us everything."

"I don't know why she would have come here," Alec said as Tassos carefully led him inside. They had to watch their step.

"I told you not to trust anyone who's supposed to be dead."

The first time he had heard those words, Alec thought Tassos had simply been being paranoid, throwing around old tales meant to scare the common man. Now, he dreaded the truth. If some people were truly meant to be dead, then how had Ariadne escaped?

— CHAPTER THIRTY-FIVE —

P lease just tell me what's going on."

"I can't." Bri watched the gauze as he wrapped it clumsily around his right arm. Anything to avoid Ella's gaze. His hand shook with nerves and pain. So many cuts. So much blood surrendered.

"The hell you can't." Her cursing shocked him into looking up, and she took the opportunity to grab his face and hold him steady, refusing to let him go. "This has been going on for days now. Ever since Tarkava. You do whatever Kai asks, without question. You are covered in cuts and bandages, and the circles under your eyes are so dark you look like a skeleton. Please, Bri, just tell me."

Not for the first time, Bri wondered where that cursed *labrynth* could possibly be. A *labrynth* set to end Ella's life the moment Kai suspected Bri was no longer willing to play the game. "I can't, Ella. Truly I can't."

"I don't believe you." She sat in front of him on the bed, fingers still touching his face, tracing his cheekbones and under his eyes. "Gods, Bri, can't you see what's happening? He's killing you."

Better me than you. "I have it under control."

"You have nothing under control. Look at yourself." She tore the insufficient wrappings from his arm, revealing so many half-healed and new cuts that Bri thought his arm looked like a spider's web—only not as beautiful, and the spider was Kai. What a fitting metaphor. Most days Bri felt as though he were a fly in Kai's trap, filled with poison so his insides would liquefy and Kai could suck them out. That was exactly what Kai wanted, after all. To take Bri's essence into himself. To make the two of them one. As the days went by, Bri worried that his brother's desires were less symbolic, and more literal.

"Just let me finish." Bri grabbed for the bandages again, but Ella held them away.

"No. I'll do it. You're doing a terrible job on your own anyway." That was true. Bri said nothing more as Ella unwrapped his messily done linens and started over.

Wrapping his abused arm snugly, keeping a rhythm steady enough to dance to, Ella's demeanor changed from livid frustration to tired suspicion. "He threatened you, didn't he?" she said, smoothing the bandage gently over his wrist. Bri said nothing, and found himself on the receiving end of one of her more direct and intimidating stares. The kind that seemed to slip into his mind and see answers he would rather keep hidden. "Me," she said. "He threatened me."

"Ella—just leave it be."

"What did he say? Did he threaten to kill me if you don't do whatever he wants?"

"It's not that simple."

"You cannot help him, Bri. You cannot."

"I won't stand by and allow him to hurt you."

"And what about everyone else?" She shook her head, squeezing his hand gently. "We are not the only two people in the world. There are others who matter, many others who will suffer if Kai has his way."

And that was what kept Bri up at night. The knowledge that by saving Ella, he was potentially killing hundreds, maybe thousands of others. Yet, endless nights had not changed his decision.

She finished tying off the wrappings and simply held his hand for a moment. Bri still marveled over the wonderful sensation of her touch. It sent shivers up his arm—in a good way—and made him want to grab hold of her and never, ever let go. Touching her kept him grounded. It made him think that if he died now, he could die a happy man. At least he'd had this much.

Ella sighed, once again making Bri wonder if she could hear his every thought. "Oh, Bri." She kissed him, soft lips warmer than his own. Her fingers caressed his jaw, and though he wanted to keep his eyes open, to see her so close, they slipped closed as he became lost in the only sensation he treasured more than her touch.

"I'm going to talk to him," she said before he could realize the kiss was over. Before his befuddled mind translated the words into something that made sense, she was already gone.

"Ella, no." Scrambling up from the bed, forgetting that Kai had bled his left leg recently until the pain from the cut protested the quick movement. He stumbled down the hall, unable to go fast enough to catch up to her and stop her. By the time he reached the front room, where Kai reclined in a wingback chair by the fire, Ella had already placed herself directly in front of the witch.

Kai laughed. "Look at that expression! Have you come to slap me again? You remember how that worked out last time, don't you?"

"Don't be so smug."

"And just what have I done to earn your ire this time?"

Kai's mood had been good since Bri had started cooperating with him, almost as if he wasn't mad at all. He had been charming and polite, almost a gentleman. The truth always lingered just beneath the surface, of course, but it had been far more tolerable than Kai's anger. "Ella, please," Bri said, hoping to spare them all a change in Kai's demeanor.

That brought Kai's attention over to him. He shifted in his seat, turning so that he sprawled corner to corner in the chair, one arm thrown across the back. "Well, well. My brother is begging. There's a sight we've been without for, oh, five or six turns." He grinned.

Ella scowled. "Don't you dare mock him. He's given you everything you want, when he shouldn't."

"Oh gods, is that what this is all about?" Kai flung his head back in exasperation. "Really, Ella, you're becoming as predictable as he is. Be careful, or I'll get bored with you."

"And then what? You'll do away with me? Kill me? What would you hold over Bri's head then?"

Bri felt the following silence like the chill of Death herself.

Kai went still, then slowly, ever so slowly, he sat up, drawing his legs together, and his arms to his sides. He looked at Ella first, then Bri, as if they were both small, tiny things that he could squash with little more than a flick of his wrist. Flies in a web. "You told her?"

"I didn't."

"It wasn't hard to figure out," Ella said, remarkably brave, considering she was the closest to Kai at the moment.

Kai stood, and in doing so, he put himself nearly nose to nose with Ella. "You remember what I told you? In Tarkava?"

She didn't flinch. "About being useless? About being nothing more than a pretty conquest? Yes, I remember."

"So then you should know better than to press your limits with me."

"Go ahead and kill me. See what it gets you."

"Oh, my dear, there are worse things in this world than death. I have not even begun to threaten you."

"Kai, that's enough." Bri put himself between Ella and his brother. For as steady as she had maintained her expression, Bri could now feel her trembling at his back. He loved her all the more for it, for standing up to Kai even when it scared her to her very core. He needed some of that courage himself.

Immediately Kai was all smiles once again. "No worries, Bri. We were just talking. You can have the afternoon off, by the way. I have company arriving."

"Company? You've been saying that for days. Is someone actually coming this time?"

"Yes. I was sent a nasty little message just this morning." Kai tapped the side of his head. "Apparently a horrid little side effect of binding yourself to a demon. But you would know all about that sort of thing, wouldn't you, brother?"

"It's not the same, and you know it."

Kai waved him off. "In the meantime, eat something. You're looking haggard. But first." He grabbed Bri by the hands and pulled him close. "Do you feel it?"

Bri could feel Kai's breath on his face and his heartbeat thudding excitedly against his chest. "Feel what?"

"You and me. Watch." He went quiet, and kept perfectly still. Bri didn't know what he was "watching" for, what he was supposed to feel—until he felt it. When Kai had first pulled them together, his brother's heart had beat quickly, fluttering away in his eagerness. Standing there now, Bri thought for a moment that Kai's heart had stopped altogether. All he could feel was the steady, nervous beat of his own heart. Then he realized the truth.

Kai's smile widened. "You feel it. I can see it in your face."

Bri just shook his head, horrified, unable to speak. It couldn't be...

"What?" Ella said, pressing herself against Bri's back, one hand resting lightly between his shoulder blades. "What is it?"

"Do you want to tell her, or should I?"

No words would come.

Kai squeezed Bri's hands, then let go, setting his hand instead against Bri's chest, directly over his heart. "We are in sync," he said. "I can match my pulse to his. We're getting closer. Which is good, because I'm running out of time."

Bri felt Olin's arrival. The myst that normally lingered around their small house, wandering by as the future of Tarkava and its people shifted and changed, suddenly retreated, recoiling back as if touched by fire. Kai had gone outside to wait, ordering Bri and Ella to remain inside, out of sight. For the most part, they had obeyed, but Bri had taken up a position at one of the windows. If he kept behind the curtain, he could see Kai at an angle without it being obvious that he watched. Ella, ignoring Bri's pleas to simply go to her room, had taken a seat in a nearby chair, her nervous hands kept busy with a spool of thread she had used just the other day to close one of the worst of Bri's cuts.

Olin looked different in the mortal realm—larger, perhaps. More imposing against the snow and fields than he had been amidst brimstone and fire. In Hell, he fit. In the mortal realm, he stood out, everything about him screaming "danger" despite his mortal clothing and clean appearance. Beside him, Kai seemed smaller, more fragile. But Bri knew that was far from the truth. Kai was stronger than he looked, and smarter too. Olin might be able to snap him in two, but that was only if he could get his hands on him.

"Is he here?" Ella asked, keeping her voice a whisper.

"Yes."

Kai refused to shiver in the cold. Instead, he pulled his coat closer together at his throat, and adjusted his scarf. His gloves were lined, and all his usual bandages added extra warmth, so that was a help, but damn. He had never liked winter in Talconay.

Olin appeared in a cloud of black smoke. So dramatic. Surprisingly, he was dressed as a mortal, his jacket neatly pressed and brushed. What gave him away as something "other" was his lack of extra clothing to guard against the cold. Given that demons lived in Hell, one would have thought winter would drive them crazy, but Olin never seemed to mind.

"You're late." As far as greetings went, it was actually the nicest thing that crossed Kai's mind in that moment.

"I was busy. Busy preparing for things I hope you have prepared by now." Olin toed a bit of the snow at his feet, dismissing it just as quickly.

"I told you days ago I had your confirmation."

"The Restorium is coming?"

"The myst was damned near empty. They wouldn't do that unless their time was up."

Olin nodded. Kai could practically see the thoughts racing through his mind. "Any day now, then."

"That would be my guess."

"And the *labrynth*? You have it?"

Here was where Kai had to watch his words. "In a manner of speaking."

"What do you mean?"

"It's going to take a little something more than we first expected."

"Something more than a mass sacrifice?"

"Simple human blood may not be enough."

"Kailas, we do not have time to change everything now. We will not get another chance."

"I am well aware of that. But that doesn't change facts. I've been building using my blood and my brother's, and my initial scribings work, but that is on a small scale, with non-human blood. The larger scale will likely need the same."

"Then bleed your brother into it."

"Not a loss I am willing to take."

"I am."

"Yes, but you can't scribe without me, and I won't use Bri."

"I could slit his throat over the site and you'd have no choice."

"Slit his throat and I won't activate anything for you. Good luck finding another witch with my abilities who will."

Olin's hands had curled into fists at his sides. Kai kept a close eye on any minute muscle contractions that would alert him to a coming assault, but Olin quelled his temper, breathing deep and stretching out his neck and shoulders. "All right, then. What do you propose? I can't imagine you would bring this up without having some plan to save your neck already in place."

"Actually, I don't. You're the one with all the grand designs, all the thousands of years' experience behind you. I figured you could find something to fit my needs."

"In such short notice?"

Kai smiled. "I have every faith in you."

Olin snorted.

Then he went still, his gaze turning distant.

"Something wrong?" Kai asked, though really, he wasn't interested.

"Xan," Olin said. "She is rapidly losing power."

"Oh, gee. Could it be she's finally actually dying?"

"Shut up, you stupid child. Xan, come to me."

She appeared then, popping into existence as if she had been dropped out of the air. Flat on her back, she coughed and sputtered, her hair tangled and stuck to her face. It was streaked grey, and her skin had wrinkled and cragged as it often did. A burned handprint marred the front of her dress.

Kai would have laughed. Really, he would have—if he couldn't smell the stink of something terrifying on her. Power. Old, strong, and pulsing as if it had a life of its own.

Olin grabbed her by one arm and hauled her to her feet. "What is going on?"

A long burn stood out along her jaw. She coughed once more before speaking. "You'll never believe me. I hardly believe it myself."

"I gave you a job to do, Xan. It shouldn't be this hard. What have you gotten yourself into?"

She grabbed at him, her knees buckling, unable to stand. Olin kept her on her feet, looking annoyed by the necessity. Wrapping an arm around her waist, he pulled her close and kissed her. Kai fought the urge to gag. Olin's power slipped into Xan, and slowly her hair blackened, and her skin tightened. When Olin pulled away, she was youthful and beautiful, and breathing easy.

"Now," Olin said, releasing her, "tell me. Who did this to you?"

"Luca," she said. "The High Lord of Hell."

Bri stared as the face of the woman clinging to Olin shifted and changed. He had met Xan before, and so he recognized her, but she had always been old. What had Kai said about her? That her age changed? He hadn't seen it himself, but he had seen this face. This younger face. Not in person, no, but the memory was burned into his mind. He had been thirteen, traveling to Callay with Alec for the first time, and his back ached from Dorothea's *labrynth*. Even through the pain he could tell something had made Alec sad. Alec turned a silver locket about in his hands, but never opened it. On that day, he had allowed Bri to peek inside.

He was away from the window and through the door to the outside before Ella had time to realize something had happened.

He wasn't dressed to fight the cold, but Bri continued along the frozen ground, ignoring the sharp chill of the air. Ella called to him from the house, but he ignored her as well.

Kai saw him first, annoyed and angry. "Bri! What are you doing out here? Go back inside."

Something caught Bri's foot and sent him stumbling forward. He regained his balance just before running into Olin and his soulless, who he still held tightly to. She looked at Bri with dark eyes, her gaze cautious, wary, and fearful all at once.

"It's you," Bri said, his words fogging in the air. "All this time, it's been you."

Xan tucked her ebony hair behind one ear as she carefully stood under her own power. "I don't know what you mean. Has your time with Kai addled your mind? It wouldn't surprise me. We met before. Surely, you remember."

Kai grabbed Bri by the arm, pulling him back a step. "Bri, go back inside."

"No." He shook free of his brother, still staring at Xan's face, hardly able to reconcile his memory with his vision. "I've seen you," he said to her. "In the locket." Xan paled. "The locket he carries with him at all times. Your face is there. Beside his, and beside Marc's."

Her whole body had gone taught, she shook her head. "Stop. Stop talking."

"You're Ariadne."

She grabbed at her head. "I told you to stop talking!"

"Alec's Ariadne." She flinched visibly when he said the name. "And you—you sold your soul to *him*?"

This time Kai tried to force him back toward the house, using both arms and the weight of his body. "Ignore my brother; he's lost a lot of blood lately."

Bri tried to wrench himself free, but Kai was stronger, and all he could manage was to slow his backward movement. "Have you known this?" he asked Kai. "Did you know who she is?"

"What does it matter to me?" Kai said, giving up on moving Bri and settling for holding him still instead. "I don't even know what you're talking about, much less care."

"It doesn't matter at all," Olin said. "Not at the moment." He gave Xan—Ariadne—a harsh shake. "You said something about the High Lord."

She gazed up at him, and some clarity returned to her eyes. "He's alive. I saw him."

Olin frowned. "Where? How?"

Ariadne seemed to rush to share with him everything she knew. "I was with Alec, just like you asked. I had managed to keep him far from you, far from here, but then we stumbled across a Reaper who seemed to know someone who could find anyone in Hell. The Reaper wouldn't take me along—he didn't trust me—but he brought Alec, and I followed in secret. It was Luca. He's still alive."

"And he is with Alec?" Olin asked.

"Yes."

"And you were caught."

"Yes." She reached for Olin, but her fingers hesitated just short of touching him, as if unsure of her reception.

"So now, not only does Alec, and therefore Carma, have the High Lord of Hell on their side, but you no longer have his trust."

She shook her head vigorously. "No. I don't know if it goes that far. I never said anything, and he doesn't know about you. I can fix things. I can."

Olin leaned in, putting his face close to hers. "You had better hope so. Because if you can't—"

"I can. I swear it." Her words were quick, her nods quicker.

"Good. Kai, it seems we have another factor to consider in all this. We must move quickly."

Kai shrugged. "I already told you; I can move as quickly as you want—as soon as you find me what I need."

Ariadne still shivered in Olin's arms. "What do you need?"

"Not that you can do anything to help matters, but I need a better scribing location than originally planned. I need some place with more than basic human blood." Bri could feel the tension in Kai's body as he spoke to her. There would be no pulling himself free while Kai was irritated like this.

"I know a place like that," Ariadne said.

The whole world seemed to go silent.

Kai scoffed. "No, you don't."

Ariadne lifted her chin and stepped away from Olin. "I do."

"Hell doesn't count," Kai jibed.

"If you're going to be a child," she said, "then I won't tell you."

"You will tell me," Olin said. "Now. Where did you gain this information?"

She gazed at Olin in an admiring way that made Bri's stomach twist, then she turned and looked straight at him. "Alec talks in his sleep."

"No." Bri felt as if it had suddenly gotten colder. "Alec doesn't talk in his sleep. I've known him for years, he never has."

"He does now. Hell power does odd things to people."

Hell power? But Alec never... "What have you done to him?"

"Enough, Xan." Olin's voice was like thunder in the otherwise silent day. "I don't have time for games. Tell me."

"There is a temple somewhere far to the west," she began.

"No!" Bri shouted.

"He took Bri there for training, so he could learn to better control the myst. The mystics are led by one of the Fallen, and she has collected seraph half-breeds over the years, saving them from elimination. That sort of blood should do nicely, don't you think, Kai?"

It felt like the ground shifted like the ocean, and the sky sunk closer, closing around Bri and rewriting the world he knew. Ariadne's face had twisted into a sneer, nothing like the bright smile he had seen inside the locket. How could this be the woman Alec had given up everything for? Had two thousand years changed her that much? Or had she never been who Alec thought she was? Bri couldn't reconcile the woman dooming hundreds of innocent people to a horrible death with the woman Alec loved. This was Xan, not Ariadne. Ariadne was dead.

A low growl indicated Kai's frustration. "Yes," he said through clenched teeth, "I suppose that would do."

"Fallen blood and seraph half-breeds should give you ample power," Olin said. "Where is this *Temple*?" he asked Xan.

"I don't know precisely. I was piecing things together from nights of mumbling. But you don't need to ask me." Her gaze slid away from her master, sly and cruel.

It was an instinct. That undeniable impulse to run. Foolish, certainly, but undeniable. Bri twisted and kicked his brother square in the gut, breaking free and running toward the house. He didn't think further than that.

A hand far too large to be Kai's closed around his throat and threw him to the ground. All the air rushed from Bri's lungs, and the frozen dirt and snow beneath him denied him any protection. He coughed, drawing in hard-won air that burned his throat and chest. Bri tried to turn onto his side, to ease breathing, but Olin kept him on his back with the simple flick of his toe. "Kai is too easy on you, I think," the demon said. "There will be no running away. Only answers."

"If you break him, he's no good to me," Kai said, appearing just above Bri's head.

"I've told you before, I don't care."

Kai crouched down beside him, arms resting casually on his knees. "That was stupid, Bri. You're only making things worse."

"You won't get a single word out of me." Each word felt like barbed wired in his throat.

"Don't make it come to that," Kai said in his smooth 'be reasonable' tone. "Don't make me pull the information from you like the bones of a fish."

Bri said nothing. He wouldn't betray them.

"Stop trying to reason with him," Olin said as Xan joined him at his side. "I don't have time for it. The moon will soon phase, and I want this done."

Kai trailed a finger along Bri's arm in a simple series of lines and loops, as if planning. "Really, Bri, just give in. It will be so much better when you do."

Silence was his only ally.

"Enough." Olin grabbed Bri by the shirt and lifted him from the ground, standing him on shaky legs before taking one of his hands. "I like the image of de-boning. I'll start with his hands. How many bones do you think I can pull out before he starts to talk, Xan?"

Bri could hear his blood rushing behind his ears. His heart beat so hard it hurt, and his lungs seized up. Olin singled out his first finger, and Bri closed his eyes.

"Stop." The familiar feel of Kai's arm wrapped around Bri's chest, pulling him back and away. His hand slipped free, and Bri instinctively put them both behind his back. "You won't get anything out of him that way. He's too noble. And he's forgetting," Kai whispered against Bri's ear, "I have a far better way of getting him to talk. And she's standing right there."

Bri opened his eyes, knowing what he would see. Ella stood against the snowy backdrop of their ill-gotten home, her hair down and blowing in the wind, her skirt catching about her legs. She looked caught between a dozen different emotions. Anger, fear, and so many others. Her posture could have taken her forward or running backward, and it was clear she couldn't decide which was the better option. Bri begged her to run without saying a word. He wanted her to run, even though he knew she had little chance of success.

But when Ella's green gaze met his, he saw her resolve solidify, and she shook her head. She was staying.

"It's your choice, Bri," Kai said, his lips moving against the side of Bri's face. "Tell me where the Temple is, or I activate the *labrynth* and she dies."

One life, or thousands. Strangers, or the girl who meant more to him than the beat of his own heart. One or many—it was his choice.

Iris, forgive me.

— CHAPTER THIRTY-SIX —

I n the time they had spent there, the light in this part of Hell had cycled much as the sun did in the mortal realm, though much quicker. Since Ariadne had appeared and disappeared, and the Void had grown larger, darkness had enveloped the land, and light had yet to return.

Tassos lit a lamp in the far corner of the room as Alec paced the length of the cabin, unable to remain still for any span of time. His thoughts had been nothing but half-sensed notions, never finishing and never giving him any comfort or conclusions. Ariadne had broken her promise to stay behind. Why? Surely, she must have had some good reason. But then why hide, why not come to the door and announce herself and her intentions? Alec grabbed the locket from its place in his pocket and clicked it open, staring at her face from so long ago. It almost didn't look like the same woman.

"Alec." Tassos's voice was soft, calming, as if Alec were some wild animal that needed to be handled with care. "You need to gather your wits. When Luca comes, we will need to stick together and convince him to still help us. We may even have to convince him not to kill us. Well, to not kill you. I can't be killed, though I think if anyone could find a way it would be him."

"Why did she come here?" Alec said, still staring at the painted portraits. "She said she would wait behind."

Tassos sighed. "I hate to be the one to say, 'I told you so.'"

"Which you've already done."

"True enough. But yes, I did warn you not to trust her. You don't know who her demon master is. Until you know that, you can't possibly know her intentions."

The back door opened, and for a moment darkness spilled into the room, dousing even the lamps that had been lit. Then the darkness receded, and the room once again grew warm with light. Luca melted into being from the darkness, as if he were the darkness itself, taking form. All his golden tones returned, but his eyes remained black. "I know her master. And I know he seeks nothing but power and strength for himself. You have exposed me."

"We did not bring her here, Luca," Tassos said calmly. "She was told to stay behind. I knew she would not be welcome."

"And yet she came anyway," he seethed.

"I assume that was at the order of her master, but yes."

Luca crept toward Tassos, like a big cat on the plains. "I have been betrayed, just as I said when you first arrived."

Tassos lifted his hands in a gesture of good faith. "No betrayal. This was not our doing."

"I knew I was foolish to let you come here. No one should have seen me. No one at all."

He rolled his eyes and let his hands fall back to his sides. "Oh, please, Luca, let's not go there. Your sanity would be dust on this floor right now if not for me. You cannot survive completely alone."

"And now I cannot stay here. It is no longer safe."

"You'll hear no arguments from me."

Alec gathered his courage and spoke. "But will you still help us? Will you help me find Bri?"

Luca's eyes were still all darkness, not a trace of his normal blue visible. They reminded Alec of the Void that now lingered so close outside. "I shouldn't. I should find myself a new place to hide and seclude myself there for whatever remains of eternity."

"But you won't." There was something in Luca's tone that made Alec brave enough to acknowledge the demon's choice of words.

"I have felt the young witch in my realm. He brings more darkness than any of my demons or hellions. His power is far too great for one so young. If he attains his brother's power—I fear what will happen. Once I gave my help in preventing this, so now I will give it again."

"What do you mean?" Alec asked, perplexed by this revelation.

"He means the boys' parents," Tassos said when Luca did not explain. "Their father came here, seeking help. Luca gave it."

"He and his fool wife had seen the danger of what they created," Luca said. "They set about to correct their mistake."

The heat that now always flowed through Alec's veins stirred at that. "Bri is not a mistake."

"No," Luca said, going to the far window and opening it wide to the world beyond, "he is part of the correction."

Bri had no other choice but to watch as his blood flowed down his hand, over wrist and palm, pooling on the stone slab that had been brought in and placed on the floor. His vision had blurred, weakened by the extreme blood loss Kai had subjected him to for the past turn. At least, he thought maybe it had been a turn. Maybe it had been more. Or less. Time only mattered now in the sense that he didn't have enough. His blood collected beside his hand while he lay helpless on the floor, unable to move, unable to do anything to save himself or anyone else.

"Bri?" Her voice came softly from behind him. Kai had made sure Bri watched as he scribed the *labrynth* into the floor that would hold Ella in one corner of the room as surely as any dungeon cell. Probably better. Then, once he'd placed her there and tested the boundaries of his spell by asking her to attempt to leave—which she could not—he had turned on Bri, and made sure he could not see Ella after that. "Bri, please." Her voice sounded thick with tears. "Talk to me." *So I know you're still alive*, Bri could hear her unspoken words clear as day.

The problem was, he wasn't sure he had the strength to give her what she wanted. His dry lips peeled apart, but that small pain was nothing to his dulled mind. "Are you all right?"

He heard her sigh in relief, though he didn't feel at that moment he deserved her feelings. "Yes. He hasn't touched me. Bri, I don't think he would actually hurt me. Not when it really comes down to it. You don't have to—"

"He would. Don't," he breathed, "put anything past him."

"Then don't worry about me. Don't let him do this."

"Not letting him do anything." He felt something wet slide down his cheek and was glad Ella could not see his face. He had fought Kai with everything he had at first. He had fought, and refused—but Olin had remained, along with Xan, and together the three of them had overpowered Bri, and once they had their hands on Ella...

Bri was now bound to the floor, weak and powerless not because he had given in, but because he had given Kai no other choice. Kai's holding spells and cuts were so thorough that Kai had left the room to speak with Olin in private, having no worries that Bri would escape.

"Bri, I want to tell you something. I want you to know—"

The front door opened then, silencing them both. The cold winter air whipped through the fire warmed room as Xan entered, her black hair plaited away from her face. She glanced coldly in Ella's direction for only a moment—long enough to see that she remained in her prison, perhaps—then came to Bri's side.

"I was sent to check on your progress," she said. "You seem to be bleeding well enough to me."

It would have taken more strength than he had to turn his head to really see her, so Bri settled for a skewed view. "Are you really her?" Each word hurt.

She raised an eyebrow, as if surprised he would ask such a thing. "Assuming I know who you mean, yes."

"And you've," he swallowed painfully, "been with Alec all this time?"

"Hardly 'all this time.' A few months is nothing after thousands of years."

"Is he all right?"

"No. But he will be. Once we're together again and he learns to accept who he is now."

"If you hurt him..."

"Hurt him? I would never hurt him. And what would you do about it, besides? Lying here, bleeding to death on the floor of some old hovel. You're nothing. Nothing I need to fear, certainly."

"Xan—Ariadne—please. Break the line of this *labrynth*. Let me up. If you ever truly loved Alec—"

"If?" She bent down beside him, careful not to disturb any of the lines that Kai had scribed. "*If* I loved him? I do love him. More than a child like you could understand."

"You're right. I don't understand. I don't understand how you could work against him like this. He must have told you."

Her eyes were tight, her jaw set. "Oh, we talked. We talked about a lot of things. But don't fool yourself, child. You can never truly have a place in our hearts. You are a pale replacement, a shadow of what we once had. You are not Marc."

Tears flooded Bri's eyes. "You're right. I'm not Marc. I've never tried to be."

"Don't think you can fool me the way you fooled Alec. I see you. You used the loss of Marc to worm your way into Alec's heart, but not me. Marc will not be replaced, and *I* will not be replaced. We will have what we once had, exactly as it was."

Somehow Bri felt colder. Ariadne looked so determined, so sad, that he could practically see the twisting of her mind. "Is that what he promised you?" he asked, his voice a whisper that hurt his throat. "To have Alec back? To have Marc back?"

She clamped her hand down around his bleeding arm and squeezed, but all sense of pain had long ago faded in the far reaches of Bri's mind. "Don't get in my way."

Pain could not touch him, but dread could. *Oh, Alec. What have we done that all we love falls into this madness?*

The door opened again. "Xan, I didn't say you could touch him."

She stood, smoothing her dress with her unbloodied hand as her expression shifted to something less sinister. "I don't take orders from you. But, if you ever do decide to kill him, let me know. I'll be glad to help."

Kai had his arms full of clean white bandages. "Get out."

With a smile that made Bri's numb skin crawl, she left without another word. Kai shut the door tightly behind her. "The only one I'll be killing is her," he said to himself before moving to the table that had been pushed toward the back of the room where Ella sat, trapped. "I'd ask you to help with the bandages, Ella, but unfortunately I don't think I can trust you not to do something incredibly stupid at the moment."

"I won't run," she said.

"Running isn't what I'm worried about." Bri heard the soft sound of linen tumbling down onto the wooden table. "No matter, I can handle it all myself. Isn't that right, Bri?"

"Just get it over with, Kai."

"Oh, my poor brother." Kai appeared in Bri's limited vision, leaning over him so that he seemed upside down. "I wanted to do this the easy way. I wanted us to have a proper brotherly relationship, but you've left me no other choice now."

"Brothers don't torture one another."

"I think some would disagree. Now, it looks like you've finally given me enough blood, so let's begin." He stepped around and knelt beside Bri. The blood lay pooled before him, like paint waiting for a canvas. With quick movements, Kai deactivated the *labrynth* that held Bri's arm to the floor and wrapped the fresh wounds to staunch the bleeding. Bri cradled the arm against his chest once freed, but still could move nothing else. "All better," Kai said. "Now, let's find that Temple."

"I won't tell you."

"I don't need you to tell me." He dipped his finger into the blood, then drew on Bri's forehead. "Can't you feel it, Bri? We're not so separate, you and I. Not anymore." He smiled, and with a great, sweeping movement, he began to scribe on the floor.

The lines and turns took shape quickly. Kai's fingers moved like they had a life of their own, guiding and directing Bri's blood across the stone slab. Not once did he hesitate, not once did he stop to think before making yet another loop.

But as Bri watched, he saw the lines lighten and darken in waves. As Kai's fingers moved, the twists and turns became more than mere patterns. The loop at the top meant *location*, and the sharp bend at the bottom signified *travel*. With each pass of Kai's fingers Bri saw the thousands of words built into the *labrynth*, the intentions and the purpose. Just as he had that night so long ago. The night Lillianna had died.

Bri heard a dull thud, like someone knocking against a thick wall. Ella. "Kai! Stop this, now!"

"Be quiet, little bird," Kai said, never looking up or pausing in his work. "It will all be over soon, and you can keep my brother happy for the rest of his life." With a quick pull, he finished. He sat upright, bloody fingers clear of the floor.

The *labrynth* on Bri's head began to warm. Without meaning to, he began to see the exotic trees and strange, colorful flowers of Xia-Lo in his mind's eye. The painted walls of the Temple, and the people's bright fashions. He could hear the birds singing their foreign songs...

"Kai, please."

"Too late, brother. I see what you see."

Bri fought to think of something else. Anything else. The walls of Carma's manor, vines growing around the windows. The streets of Callay, filled with people dressed in subdued colors and hats and coats. But it all faded away, and his mind was flooded instead with memories of chimes and the warm sun that shined for days on end, of training outside in grassy fields, and of sitting on elaborate pillows as Iris spoke in her cryptic way.

"There we are," Kai said, and he leaned over Bri, one hand on either side of his head. "Are you ready to go back?"

The *labrynth* simmered beside them, hissing and popping with power. Ready and waiting. For a moment, Bri thought about breaking it, severing the lines and bearing the consequences of Kai's wrath. In that moment, the *labrynth* quieted a bit. Kai seemed to hear this, and frowned, setting one finger back against the lines and charging them with power. The *labrynth* flared to life once again.

The moment was gone, but it had been enough. Bri knew enough. He didn't understand it, but he knew it.

"Kai, don't do this."

"We don't have a choice. We need this."

He bit his finger and threw his own blood onto the *labrynth*. Light flashed through the small house, and heat raced over Bri's numb body.

Then all he felt was falling.

— CHAPTER THIRTY-SEVEN —

A lec's head was still reeling when they arrived on the strangely cool streets of the town. Not from the method of instant travel that he was still so unused to, but from what he had learned. Bri's father had come to Luca for help, and Luca had given it in the form of a vial of his blood that could be used for scribing.

There had only been one child then.

Luca released the hold he had on Alec's arm. He straightened his jacket and rolled his shoulders. "Ah. I knew I hadn't lost my touch."

Tassos appeared beside them in a puff of black and purple smoke. "Not completely, no. Let's all be thankful you didn't incinerate Alec in the process of testing yourself."

"Was that a possibility?" No one had said anything about that sort of thing.

"No." "Yes." Luca and Tassos spoke at the same time, and it did nothing to ease Alec's nerves. He told himself to concentrate on the fact that he was, in fact, still in one piece.

"It's cool here," Tassos said, after he was finished glaring at Luca to no real end. "But only incompletely. Like it's laced through the air. Yet this isn't one of the cold regions."

"No, it is not." Luca's eyes were blue once again, for which Alec was grateful. "And it is dripping with power not native to Hell. That's why I brought us here. That little witch spends a lot of time within this town."

A cool town. Just like the demon informant had said. This is what Alec had been searching for right before they'd encountered that Hellwalker. "And what about Bri?" Alec said. "Do you feel him here?"

"Neither of them are here at the moment," Luca said. "Regardless, we should be able to get some answers. We'll start at the tavern."

Tassos rolled his eyes as Luca walked down the street. "A fabulous idea. I know I could certainly use a drink."

The door to the tavern opened without a squeak, and cold air hit their faces in such a way that they all stopped upon entering. This was nothing like the outside, where cold wisps had crept along the hot Hell air, teasing and sending shivers. This was absolute, complete, as if the entire place sat not within Hell, but in some autumn-cooled land.

A young hellion girl bounced up to them, her skin scaled and feathered at the joints. "Welcome! And what can we do for you today? Would you like a table, or perhaps you would rather sit at the bar?"

"Where is the owner of this place?" Luca said, looking far too stiff to be casually entering a tavern for no reason at all. His words were stilted, as if he had forgotten how to speak to common people in all his years alone.

The hellion girl, to her credit, continued to smile, unfazed. "Fauna is the owner here. She tends the bar. You can have a seat wherever you like, and she'll be with you shortly." With that, she skipped away, turning her attention to a table full of bull-snouted hellions at the back of the room.

"What is this place?" Tassos whispered as they took seats at the bar. "I have never felt a building like this before. Cool inside while the heat blazes on outside."

"Could it be done with a *labrynth*?" Alec asked. Dorothea had tried something similar once, eight hundred years ago when she was still young. Her experiment had resulted in the icing over of their current home, so much so that it shattered and collapsed around them. Understandably, Carma had never allowed her to try again.

"I would not be surprised," Luca said. "I feel that witch everywhere here. His power drips on the air." He ran a hand along the polished wood of the bar. "Wood. It would not survive here if not for this coolness."

"Indeed it would not." The feminine voice came from behind black lips and pearly fangs. She tucked her black hair behind an ear with clawed fingers, then set her cat-like gaze on the three of them. "My establishment is one of a kind, and I hear you gentlemen are looking for me."

"You are the owner?" Again, Luca sounded stiff and unaccustomed to making small talk.

"I am," the demon said, clearly taking his measure. "But I've never seen the three of you around these parts before. What brings you here?"

Tassos stopped Luca before he could speak again. He smiled charmingly. "We're looking for someone. We thought perhaps you had seen him."

Fauna took three glasses from behind the bar and set them out, filling them with an amber liquor. "I may have. I get a lot of travelers in and out of here."

"He's young. Seventeen or so. Auburn hair, silver-brown eyes. Pretty face. His hands are usually bandaged, and he has many scars," Tassos said.

"Sounds like a witch," she said, pushing a drink toward each of them. "We don't get many witches in Hell."

"So then you would remember him if you ever saw him?"

Alec turned his glass around on the wood bar, not drinking. He watched the face of the demon bartender and saw how carefully she kept her expression still.

"I remember all my patrons. It's a talent of mine."

"Then just answer the question," Luca snapped, earning himself a reproaching look from Tassos.

The bartender just smiled. "Can't say I've seen anyone like that around here. Can I get you boys something to eat?"

Can't say? It wasn't a 'no,' really. Not when you knew how demons always so carefully had to get around lying.

"I think the drinks will be fine for now. But one more question," Tassos said, always charming. "Same description, only this time with a sweet face, and no scars and bandages. Anyone like that around?"

Alec caught himself running his fingers along the edge of the smooth wooden bar. It had been polished and finished, and remarkably no one had caused a single blemish. An amazing feat in a tavern populated by demons and hellions who did little more than drink and fight. *Stop it, Alec, you'll look like you're touched in the head if you keep on—*

There. Something under the bar. A splintering or...

Fauna paused, thinking carefully. "I'm sure I would remember someone like that. Especially if there were two. Now, if you'll excuse me, I have customers to tend to. But please, let me or any of my staff know if there's anything you need."

"Certainly." Tassos's friendly tone never changed. "Well," he said once they were alone enough, "that was interesting."

"She's lying," Luca said. "Skirting the truth."

"We can't know that for certain."

"I can," Luca said, his words clipped.

"Oh, well, pardon me, oh glorious one."

Alec traced the marring under the bar. Once, twice, three times, and then again until he was certain of what he felt. "She is lying."

Tassos tilted his glass back and forth on the bar, but did not drink. "Oh? And what tells you that?"

"Bri." Alec grabbed Tassos's hand and pulled it under the bar in front of him. The reaper sputtered for a moment, maybe even blushed, but then went quiet and still when Alec set his fingers against the carving.

"Good gods..."

"What?" Luca leaned closer, unable to see. "What is it?"

"Bri was here," Alec said. "He left me a sign. He carved his name into the wood. I had gotten information on this place, was looking for it, but she—" She'd distracted him. Led him away. Trapped him in illusions.

The mug in his hand burned hot with his power.

"Alec," Tassos said, gently removing the mug from his fiery grip. Alec was too angry to protest or care.

They left their three drinks completely untouched, stepping outside into the heat once again. Not a one of them said anything until they were clear of the town limits. Alec wanted to tear Hell apart. Hell could pay for this betrayal.

"I could get the information out of her," Luca said, breaking their silence.

"What's the point?" Tassos smoothed back a bit of hair that had gotten in his face. "We know she was lying. Or avoiding a lie. She chose her words very carefully. We know Kai has been to this place— has it under his bloody little thumb even—and we know he brought Bri here at least once. But we also know they are not there now."

"She may know where he goes."

Alec shook his head. "I doubt Kai reveals that much. He doesn't trust anyone. He would never tell her anything that could lead back to him. But then what do we do now?"

Head tilted back so that he could see the sky, Luca considered things—or, at least, Alec hoped that's what he was doing. "We go on to the next site. I know for certain now the feel of his power. Next time he uses it, I should feel it, as long as he touches Hell in some way."

"You mean he's not in Hell now?" *Blistering, damnable—I've been searching here all this time, and Bri's not even here?*

"No. If he was here, I would feel him. I've felt him before, and that was when I was not attuned. That witch is not in Hell. Not now."

Alec thought his knees might give out.

Tassos took him by the elbow, giving him the little bit of support he needed to not fall flat on his face. "Do not despair, Alec. This is a good thing. Bri would not do well here. It's been so long, Kai must have seen that and taken him back to the mortal realm. And if they are there, then we will simply alter our search. Right, Luca?"

The High Lord of Hell grunted in a non-committal sort of way.

"There! See?" Tassos said, all smiles, and misplaced happiness. "Problem solved. Of course, it's winter on the Dactic continent. We'll need a change of clothes."

"No time."

"What?" Tassos and Alec both looked at Luca, whose eyes had turned dark once again.

"No time to change clothes. We need to go. The witch is scribing."

The harsh winter cold disappeared, and in its place, Bri felt a gentle warmth in the air. Not the heat of summer, but something more akin to autumn in Callay. Or winter in Xia-Lo. The grass tickled his bare arms, and a breeze glided across his body, rustling his clothes. Yet despite the lack of bitter cold air, Bri did not feel warm.

Kai stood, hands still bloody, but otherwise looking like a child discovering some new land for the first time. Bri didn't need to look. He knew exactly where he was; the birds singing overhead, and the steady song of a nearby river told him all he needed to know.

They were in Xia-Lo, and as soon as Kai moved to the edge of the mountain they had landed upon, he would see the Temple down below, bustling with people and bursting with color.

"Bri?"

Her voice startled him. "Ella?"

"Oh, gods, Bri." She appeared beside him, clutching his uninjured hand and brushing his hair from his face. Her hair had tangled in her earlier struggle, as they cornered her and Kai had trapped her within a *labrynth*, but she was otherwise unharmed and as beautiful as ever. Bri clung to that as he tried to remember how to breathe normally. "You're cold! So cold." She rubbed his hand between her own, trying to bring some warmth to his fingers. Bri just stared—he could barely feel her touch. "Kai! Find something to warm him up!"

"He's fine," Kai said from somewhere out of sight. "Just give him a minute."

"He is not fine. Bri, can you move? Can you sit up?"

His left arm started to throb where he had it still cradled tight against his chest. "No. The *labrynth*..."

"There is no *labrynth*, Bri. Not anymore. It didn't come with us. Now, come on. Sit up for me."

With her help, Bri rolled onto his right side, his eyes tearing as sparks of pain flared with each movement. He didn't know if he wanted to get warm. If this was how it felt while numb and cold, then he feared what pain would come when he could actually feel again. But Ella coaxed him up until he was sitting, leaning heavily against her while she gently rubbed his arms and back. She smelled like the herbs she had cooked with that morning. Gods, it seemed so long ago now...

Kai stepped out of the brush behind them, pulling at a branch so he could examine the evergreen needles that clung there. Everything was still so blurry; Bri gave up trying to see and closed his eyes.

"Stop coddling him, Ella," Kai said, the sound of the branch bouncing free coupling his words.

"You took too much blood," Ella said, still trying to coax some warmth into Bri.

"He's half-witch. He can take it."

"He's not. You got all the witch blood."

"That's where you're wrong."

"At least give me your jacket if you're not going to help."

Kai grumbled, but then Ella shifted, and Bri felt the body-warmed jacket slip around his shoulders. "There," she said, smoothing it over his back. "That should help. Can you sit by yourself? I'm going to get you some water to drink."

Bri just nodded dumbly. He would probably fall over the moment she left.

"With what?" Kai sounded farther away again. "Did you bring a cup with you?"

"No," Ella said. "You are going to use a *labrynth* to turn one of these fallen branches into one. And don't even try to tell me that the Great and Powerful Kai can't do it."

"Of course I can do it. It's just so boring."

"Do it anyway."

"You are so very lucky I am in a good mood right now."

Ella huffed and murmured to Bri quiet enough that Kai would not hear, "He's lucky I don't beat him with one of these branches."

Don't provoke him. Please. Bri wanted to say the words, but they wouldn't come. Ella continued to hold him close until Kai came near.

"Here," Kai said, presumably handing over the newly created cup.

"Thank you," Ella replied, then, carefully giving Bri time to hold his own weight, she stood. "I'll be right back."

Bri leaned heavily on his right arm, which shook terribly. His left arm he still kept tight to his chest. He watched Ella disappear into the trees, going in the direction of running water. A part of him hoped she would be smart and never return.

Kai whistled. Standing over at the edge of the clearing, he had a perfect view of all that lay below. "Would you look at that! How long has this been here? And no one ever knew. That's some barrier they have all around it. Is this where you hid from me all that time, Bri?"

"I wasn't hiding from you." He so wanted to lie down, but he didn't want to worry Ella by being on the ground when she returned.

"Hiding from Haven, then."

"They'll know you're here. They will have felt you coming through the barrier."

"Then I had better get started, hadn't I?"

"Don't you need Olin to make this all work?"

"Not here. He's where he belongs. Do you want to watch?"

"I want you to not do this."

"It's too late for that." Kai took a knife from his pocket and cut open his finger, letting the blood drip into the ground. "Wish me luck. Once this is over, you and I are going to be what we were always meant to be."

"I hope someone gets lucky and rams a blade through your heart."

"Ouch." Kai came close and drew his thumb across the mark he had put on Bri's forehead earlier. Bri felt the power there fade. "I'll forgive you since you're not yourself," Kai said. Then he kissed Bri's head and slipped away over the edge of the mountain.

Brush rustled, and Ella returned, an elaborate wooden cup in her hand. Apparently, Kai could do nothing simply. She knelt in front of him and helped him to drink. The water was cool and felt good on his dry lips, but Bri coughed with shortness of breath, and had to stop.

"Where did Kai go?"

"Down to the valley. To the temple."

Horror coated her features. "What do we do?"

"I can stop him." As if mocking him, his arm gave out beneath him, and Ella had to catch Bri awkwardly before he hit the ground.

"How? Tell me. What do you need?"

"Food. I don't have the strength to do anything right now. There are winter berries that grow here. They're black, perfectly round."

"I'll find some. Rest here." Gently as possible, she helped him to a nearby tree where he could rest against the sturdy trunk. Bri set his head back and closed his eyes, unable to remember a time when he had felt worse. Then he felt soft lips against his own.

Ella smiled at his shock. "There's more where that came from. But," she pressed the cup into his good hand, "you have to drink this while I'm gone."

"I'm sorry." The words slipped out unbidden, but true.

"For what?"

"This. All of this. For getting you involved. This isn't how your kindness should be repaid," he said, thinking of the first time she had spoken to him when they were children.

Ella took his face in her hands. "You listen to me, Brishen Dusombré. This is not your fault. I made my own choices, and I wouldn't change a single one. Now, drink that water. I'm going berry picking."

She left, and Bri stared at the water within the cup, still and silent because he couldn't find the strength to lift it. He had to think. Had to rest. If he didn't, he would never be able to stop Kai. Already he knew he wouldn't be able to save everyone, but maybe he could save someone.

He steeled his resolve and forced himself to lift the cup. As he drank, the valley echoed with the first scream.

— CHAPTER THIRTY-EIGHT —

They had sealed the gates, but it didn't seem to help. Enlai watched from Iris's tower as below the inhabitants of the temple keeled over for no apparent reason. Everyone had been ordered not to touch the dead, but chaos overtook those still alive, and they ran or huddled together, screaming for lost loved ones, or in fear when the person beside them suddenly fell, blood leaking from their body.

"What is this plague?" Enlai stood guard at Iris's window, watching the horrors below.

Iris knelt at her table, the Kayos game laid out in front of her. She kept her hands in her lap. Enlai was certain he hadn't seen her reach for the pieces, yet they had shifted position. "It has begun," she said. "The Shadow has come, and the Prophet lies enveloped in his darkness."

"What do we do?"

"We wait. And you may hope, if you like. There is little we can do but let the Players play and the Pieces act."

"I don't understand."

"We may live outside the myst, Enlai, but some things are still inevitable."

The screams carried on, and Enlai thought he smelled smoke. He knew the guards had mobilized, yet he heard nothing of steel clashing with steel. Whoever attacked did so with great stealth.

You mean we cannot stop this. He turned back to Iris just in time to see the Shadow move itself across the board.

"I've done all I can to mitigate the damage," Iris said, her tone offering comfort, her long fingers tracing paths on the board. "The children should be clear of the range by now."

Enlai nodded numbly, remembering saying goodbye to his son that morning as they packed off to head toward the sea.

"He comes," she said.

The door crashed open, and smoke poured in from the hallway, thick and black. It clung to the ceiling, creeping along toward the window where it found freedom once again. A young man sauntered in, hands on hips and lips wide in a grin. His auburn hair was tussled, and those silver-brown eyes were unmistakable.

"Bri?"

"Not Bri," the young man said, "though I hope that's not too much of a disappointment."

Enlai unsheathed the sword at his hip, standing to protect Iris from this threat. "What do you want from us?"

"Oh, that's quite simple." He spread his arms wide. "I want you to bleed for me."

It was then Enlai noticed the scars and bandages along this man's arms, the precise patterning and deliberate depth of the lines. "You're a witch."

"Exactly right."

The grip of his sword felt slick against his hand. "You must be Bri's brother. What did he say your name was...Kai?"

"I'm so pleased you've heard of me! It's always more fun when there's a bit of infamy involved." He stalked around the room, heedless of the threat Enlai meant to impose, running his fingers along the curtains and pillows, the chimes and the other artifacts Iris had collected over her many years.

"You scribe quickly," Iris said, still on her cushion as if they had not been invaded.

"Thank you for noticing," Kai said. He touched a lamp and this time, Enlai noticed the quick pull of his fingers, the deft patter as they worked in tandem. This time, he noticed the blood.

"How did you find us?" Iris regarded Kai with nothing more than her usual intent gaze. "Even your brother did not find his way here on his own."

"I had Bri's help. Unwilling as he was."

Iris cocked her head, as though curious of nothing more than a new school lesson. "You have no problem taking what you want, even from your own brother?"

"Bri doesn't understand. It's my responsibility to make sure he gets what he really needs."

"A noble mission."

Kai bowed. "My duty as a brother, nothing more."

Now Iris stood, and when Enlai moved to stop her, she signaled for him to wait. "You have come into my home," she said, walking toward the witch, "and you have killed my people single-handedly, without being seen. You must have an elaborate plan."

"Quite elaborate. And, you see," he flicked a tassel on a lamp, "your temple provides me with the unique makeup of blood I need."

Iris stopped just short of the witch. "Do you understand the game you play?"

"I may be one of the only ones who understands everything," Kai said.

"Then you know there are two possible outcomes."

"Of course. But I know which one will come to pass."

Iris smiled. "Do not be so certain. Your brother understands more than you think."

Kai returned the expression, though his smile was twisted and cruel. "I need your blood at the center of things."

"But of course."

"You understand too, don't you?" Kai glanced over her shoulder at the Kayos board. "That's why you are here essentially alone."

"I know how to play the game."

"And you won't try to stop me?" Their gazes met.

"I have lived long enough."

Enlai stood frozen. It was not magic, but his own disbelief that kept him from acting. *What are you saying?*

"Shall we get to it then?" Kai reached for her chest.

"Here," Iris said, stopping him. "Let me make it easy for you." Enlai had no voice as she drove her hand deep in her own chest. Her flesh parted easily, silver-flecked blood spilling down her dress and onto the floor. With one great tug, she pulled her heart free of her chest, and set it in Kai's waiting hand. "Make sure you tell Bri of this."

The witch didn't so much as flinch at holding a beating heart. "Oh, I'm sure he'll enjoy the tale immensely."

Iris nodded, then she looked over her shoulder at Enlai and smiled. "Do not fear. It is all as it must be." Her body grew darker, blackening, starting at her feet, and rising up her legs toward her torso and then her head. A soft breeze shifted the air in the room, and she crumbled like ash.

Enlai felt tears on his cheeks. He did not wipe them away.

Kai stepped over the pile of ash, weighing her heart in his hand where it still beat. Enlai charged, fueled by rage. He drew back his sword and brought it down, aiming for the witch's head.

Kai caught Enlai by the face, and suddenly his body was stiff as stone, unable to move. "You knew my brother?"

"Yes."

"Then I'm sure he sends his love."

Kai's fingers moved over Enlai's cheek, and then he felt no more.

"It's not enough." Ella held the remaining berries in her hand as Bri coughed. He'd been unable to eat many of the winter berries she had found, and her hand was still quite full.

"No," he said, wiping his mouth with the back of his hand. "It's fine."

"It's not. You need something more."

"It's all right." He leaned heavily against the tree. "The water helped a lot. See?" He held up his hand. "It only shakes a little now."

A little compared to the wracking tremors that had left him unable to hold anything himself. But still too much. "I'm afraid that's not much of a relief."

Bri dropped his hand to his lap. "It's as good as I'm going to get, I'm afraid. I'm running out of time." He closed his eyes, which looked like dark shadows against his pale face. Ella worried far more than she let on.

"What are you going to do?"

"Can you help me get over there? To that patch of dirt?"

She would have rather not moved him at all. Or if she did, in the complete opposite direction. Away from Kai, away from the danger.

But such selfish thoughts were just that—thoughts, and she didn't give them voice. Instead, she nodded. "Of course."

With his arm around her shoulders, she lifted him from the ground, juggling his weight and balance. Not without difficulty, she brought him to the place he had specified, and helped him to kneel once again. He gasped for breath, just from that effort.

"Bri, are you sure? What are you going to do?" She had asked him a dozen times, and each time he failed to answer. She was beginning to worry she wouldn't like it when he did.

He grabbed a rock from the ground beside him, then started pulling away the bandages on his left arm. "I'm going to scribe."

"What? Bri, you can't. You're not a witch."

"Like Kai said, we can use each other's power. He's been doing it to me for years, but I never understood how to turn it around. I do now. All these months with him," he stopped to catch his breath. "The lines make sense to me now. I'd never be able to manage what Kai can, even if I had my health, but I can do something. I can make things harder for him." The fresh wounds on his arm exposed once again, he pressed the sharp edge of the rock against his abused flesh.

Ella grabbed his hand, stopping him. "You've lost too much blood. You can't."

"What other choice do I have?"

She thrust her own arm out in front of him. "Mine. Use mine."

He smiled sadly. "I can't. It has to be mine."

"Why?"

"Because I'm the one with the connection to Death. He's using what he learned from my blood. It has to be mine that stops it."

"But...if you draw Her attention..."

"I won't die. My deal with Carma is strong enough to prevent that. But I'm afraid you will have to look after me once I've lost consciousness."

Gods, Bri... "Is there nothing else I can do to help?"

Carefully, he lifted his wounded left hand and touched her face. It was cold as ice, and trembled against her cheek. "Just being here so that I'm not alone is enough. I don't know if I'd have the courage to do this if not for you."

She held that hand, fighting the tears that tightened her throat. Before she could think twice, she leaned forward and kissed him, silencing the thoughts that suggested it might be the last time. He kissed back, but she could feel the effort it cost him in his body, and she felt a tear roll down his cheek. "I know you can do this," she said, her lips still against his. "Stop him. Then we'll go home."

Without warning, Bri dug the rock into one of his barely healed cuts, and blood began to flow freely once again. Ella watched as he dipped his shaking fingers into his own blood, keeping herself pressed against his side for support. With a deep breath, he set his fingers to the ground and began to scribe.

He didn't work as quickly as Kai, but the lines were nevertheless just as precise. Amazingly, all the shaking seemed to melt away, and Bri drew smooth and flawless twists and turns. A loop flashed with light here, and then a sweeping arc there. All Ella's experience with magic up until that point had been Kai and his destruction; she had never before taken the time to see how truly beautiful a *labrynth* could be.

Only a few people remained, he could feel it. So much blood flowed at his feet, and the screams had died down to nearly nothing. Kai had never felt more alive. He had scribed little Death-calling *labrynths* all over the temple grounds, then started fires and other dangers in order to drive the inhabitants out. As they ran, they touched his spells and that was that. Aside from the Fallen priestess and her single guard, he'd barely had to get his hands dirty.

He let the people see him now, where before he had taken pleasure in being a ghost. It charged their fear to see him standing there with a bloody heart in his hand. A younger man ran past, hurdling the dead bodies at every turn, and looking particularly frantic when he saw Kai so near. Kai smiled and waved just as the man's feet passed over one of the many *labrynths* he had planted.

And the man kept on running. He did not fall down dead.

No matter, another *labrynth* waited just a few strides away.

Again the man did not fall.

Annoyed, though not completely discouraged, Kai walked to the first of his *labrynths* and set his hand to it, testing the power. It lay quiet. Dead. And not the death he wanted.

But then he felt a tingle of something on the air, and a tickle at his wrist—right over the *labrynth* that connected him to Bri.

Now that was interesting.

Kai went to the second *labrynth* and conducted the same test—getting the same results. "Oh, Bri." He laughed. "It took you long enough." Spinning around, he faced the mountain where he had left his brother and shouted, "Good work, Bri! I've never been more proud!" The young man who had escaped death earlier circled around once more, driven mad in panic, or so Kai assumed. "Bri and I are one step closer," Kai said to himself. "Though his interference is a bit of a nuisance. But no matter." He side-stepped and caught the panicked man by the throat. "I'll just have to finish this the old-fashioned way."

— CHAPTER THIRTY-NINE —

Den huddled in the cold streets with the rest of the populace of Callay. They had been driven from their homes, invaded by demons and terrifying creatures with beastly features. They moved with military precision, gathering the inhabitants and ushering them outside without explanation. Den had seen a few people injured—mostly for refusal to comply with orders—but no one had died. Yet.

For the first time in months, he was glad Ella was nowhere to be found. At least she was safe from all this.

Lord Gattock stood at his side. They had been going over the newest plans for the search for Ella when all this had happened. "What do you think this is?" the older man said as they were jostled by the crowd.

"I don't know. It's been over a hundred years since the demons were driven out of the mortal realm. Maybe they're coming back." A number of imposing demons had gathered at the scaffold in the city square. Den remembered a few years back this had been the place where they had burned accused soulless to rid Callay of their taint. He feared things would go a bit differently this time.

"Haven will save us," Gattock said, shouldering aside a man who clung to a crying wife and child. "The One will not allow the demons to take hold."

"Perhaps you should begin praying then."

A giant demon with brown hair and a shaved head made his way to the scaffold, armed with a sword that looked to have seen many battles, and a long spear atop which sat a multi-bladed head. His presence was enough to silence the crowd. Beside him, another demon appeared out of thin air, tall, muscled, with a face that spoke of experience and strength. He was dressed in gleaming gold armor that bore the faces of lions at the shoulders. This demon held out his arms to the people of Callay, and then spoke.

"Good citizens of Chanae. I have come here to honor you with a great privilege. Today, you shall witness the birth of a new god."

The crowd erupted in whispers, and the demon paused to allow for this. Then someone suddenly spoke up, shouting to be heard, "It's Olin! The demon they've been worshipping in the south!"

"I do not deny it," Olin said.

Den had heard the stories. Tales of cults rising up in the southern lands, making blood sacrifices and swearing loyalty to this demon. It was said he had a witch of immense power at his disposal, and an army fit for Hell. No one had thought the epidemic would reach this far north. But looking around, it was clear at least the hellish army had.

"Why come here?" some man from the crowd asked. "Why not bless your followers with such a sight?"

Olin's expression was not unkind, though Den suspected the charm was all part of the act. "Because they already believe, and why should you not believe as well? Watch! As the moon rises over the horizon, I shall be reborn and the mortal realm remade. You humans drove us out once, thinking yourselves stronger than Hell, stronger than desire and passion and the need for more. You think yourselves above the temptation of sin. But you are wrong, and you cannot keep us out forever."

"Haven will come!" "Haven will answer us!" "Surely the seraph will stop you!" All this and more was shouted and met with cheers and steadfast agreement.

"Will they?" Olin said. "Well then, call to your saviors. Let's see them come!"

Prayers went up, both silent and voiced. The people pleaded with Haven, with The One, to save them, to come and defeat this demon seeking godhood. They prayed and prayed—and nothing happened.

Olin spread out his arms, waiting. "Well? Nothing? Just as I thought. It appears Haven will not hear you. As usual."

Panic overtook the air once more. Some attempted to run, but were stopped by the soldiers who had no qualms about putting down any and all opposition.

"Now, now," Olin said, his voice calm, and empty of anger, "do not fret. Haven will not answer you, but I will. I will offer Callay my protection, I will keep you safe. All you need do is pledge yourselves to me. Your souls will be safe, your children will grow in prosperity, and you'll never need fear the power of Hell again. Haven ignores you; Hell listens."

Den felt sick. He couldn't believe some of the whispers he heard around him. People actually considering this demon's words. *You'll all damn yourselves to an eternity in Hell when you die. Which will likely be sooner rather than later if you ally with this creature. Oh, Ella, wherever you are, I hope you're safe. Don't come home.*

"The moon!" That one shout focused the city's attention on the horizon. In the dusky sky, the first glimpse of the silvery moon became visible, full and round, unmistakable.

"It begins," Olin said, turning his hands in front of his face where he could see them. Black flames began to lick their way up his arms, crawling toward his shoulders then across his chest, consuming him. A strange smell lingered on the air, fouler than smoke, more like burned meat or hide. Brimstone, perhaps. *Gods, is this what Hell smells like?* It had been sometime since Den had prayed to anyone besides The One, and he wondered now if the other gods would answer.

People beside him dropped to their knees, clutching their hands over their hearts and bowing their heads. Den hoped they were praying to the lesser gods, and not to this new demon-god being born right before their eyes.

His hopes were dashed when he was suddenly struck from behind and forced to kneel as well. He could hear their prayers now.

They prayed to Olin.

Carma paced uneasily behind Dorothea as she scribed. "Are you sure about this?"

"Absolutely positive. Now stop talking to me and let me work. Time is short."

Inaseri had brought them to a small village in The Wilds. The population was small, but Dorothea and the god both insisted it was enough to start. Carma wasn't so sure. The people here were wide-eyed in the presence of their god, Inaseri. With tan skin, dark hair, and bright blue eyes, they reminded her all too well of Alec. Of course, this was where he had come from. The culture had changed much since then, all the grand cities now nothing more than small villages and smaller houses.

Keaie and Kesi had returned, crouching and hanging in nearby trees, curious and unable to control their mischief for longer than two heartbeats. Currently, they entertained themselves by throwing pinecones at Gabriel's head. Whenever one of them got one through her wings and landed a shot they cheered and laughed. The seraph general glared, but didn't dare raise a hand against the two child-gods. Carma was glad she had that much sense, and couldn't deny that she took some pleasure herself in watching the Twins torment her old friend.

Kadiel swallowed her own laughter. "They wouldn't find the game so amusing if you would just lighten up a bit, Gabriel."

"No one asked your opinion."

"You haven't forbidden it either."

"I still could. Don't test me."

Carma turned her gaze to the west where the sun was just sinking behind the horizon. The moon had yet to rise, but the skywatchers of this village assured them that it would, just as soon as the sun vanished. There would be no sharing of the sky this day. A bad omen.

Inaseri came to stand at her side. He was all male at the moment, though the last time they had spoken, she had worn her more womanly form. Carma thought she was getting used to shifts. "Omens can change," he said. "I have assured them of this. What we do here now will give them hope, and that hope will power your ascension in turn."

"I never wanted anything like this."

"None of us did. We are born of necessity."

"Haven should have acted," Gabriel said as another pinecone bounced off her head. "They must feel all this."

Kadiel shook her head. "They feel nothing. The Restorium has already begun. Haven't you felt it?"

Gabriel bristled. "I have been otherwise occupied." Another pinecone, and more giggles from the trees.

"Well, they are sleeping," Kadiel bit out, "and we are the only ones awake, so we must act on our own."

Dorothea straightened and stretched, cracking her bloody fingers. "It is complete. Inaseri, if you would?"

The god nodded and went to her side, kneeling and offering her hand. "How much do you need?"

"A few drops will do. Though if you could convince the Twins to contribute, it would be that much stronger."

"They will help." With a crook of his finger, Inaseri called the two children down from their tree.

Dorothea beckoned to Carma. "Come. You must stand here."

Carma couldn't remember the last time she had felt such apprehension. Not even the choice to tear out her own heart had been so difficult. Her feet felt heavy as lead as she took each step toward the witch and her *labrynth*. She stopped just short of the lines. "What about my soulless? My demon powers? I do not want to be something other than what I am."

"I have told these good people who you are, and what you will be," Dorothea said. "Your souls will still be yours, as will all your current abilities. Now stop hesitating like a child, and step onto the *labrynth* before you create a chink in the belief of these villagers."

It had been longer still since she had been scolded like a little girl, but Carma bit her tongue and stepped onto the lines drawn into the ground.

Inaseri held out his hand as the Twins joined him on either side. "Like this," he said, and his palm split open like an overripe peach, ruby red blood leaking out thickly. The Twins mimicked his motions, both their palms opening in the same way, without any instrument other than their wills. Together, they turned their hands and let their blood trickle onto the *labrynth* under Carma's feet.

The moon slipped over the horizon.

It started as a tingle in her fingertips. Then that tingle turned to a burning, strangely comforting and welcome. Black flames burst from her hands, licking their way up her arms. Carma watched as her skin took on the deep bronze of her true form. An unnatural wind blew her hair into her face, and it was pure red. She looked at

Dorothea, and the old witch smiled and nodded in confirmation. It was working. The villagers pressed their hands to their chests and began to pray. They said her name over and over again.

"Do you feel that?" Gabriel's voice surprised her over the din of the worshipping villagers.

Kadiel stood from her place at the edge of the forest. "Feel what? The new god standing before us? Honestly, Gabriel, I would have thought—"

"No. Not that." Something in Gabriel's expression worried Carma. The seraph appeared eager all of a sudden, frantic—impulsive. "The boy. His power is surging. I feel him as clearly as I feel the wings on my back." Those very wings stretched to their full span.

"Gabriel," Carma warned, wanting to say more, but in that moment the flames engulfed her completely, and she felt nothing but the fire, the power rushing into her body.

But she heard Kadiel's desperate cry. "Gabriel, don't!"

— CHAPTER FORTY —

I t took no time at all for Gabriel to cross the Dactic lands by air. Her wings propelled her through the mortal realm, moving just at the edge of its existence, where certain rules and laws no longer applied. She could not cut through Haven, not while it was closed to any outside presence for the Restorium. But that did not matter. Nothing mattered. Nothing other than the boy, and the fact that she finally had him.

She landed in the clearing, tucking her wings away from the trees that seemed to reach for her like dark shadowed hands. The smell of magic lingered on the air like burned molasses or the scratch of a match. The boy lay unconscious on the ground, his head cradled in the lap of a young woman with burning green eyes who clutched him even closer as Gabriel's feet touched the ground.

"I won't let you near him," the girl said.

"Don't be foolish, child. I am a seraph of Haven, you know better than to fear me. Have faith...and move away."

The girl did not obey. "No. I know what you want with him, and I won't allow you to hurt him."

Seventeen years... One mortal girl would not delay her any longer. "He is an abomination."

Her words caused the girl's expression to darken. "Then you and I have drastically different definitions of the word."

"Step aside. Before I make you." The girl only moved to put herself between Gabriel and the boy. Gabriel sighed. "If that is your wish. Just remember, you left me no other choice." She grabbed the girl by the front of her dress, lifting her from the ground, sending he boy tumbled limply from her lap, never stirring. The mortal girl struggled, screaming and cursing, kicking at Gabriel's armor-protected shins. Gabriel regarded her for a moment, wondering at how desperately she fought against something she should have been raised to trust. Just another reason why the boy was so dangerous—he changed things; he changed people. She tossed the girl aside, where she narrowly missed hitting one of the ancient trees surrounding them. Her head knocked against a rock, however, and she moaned groggily, not getting up.

Gabriel did not have time to care. Everything she had worked for during these past seventeen years was right there in front of her, ready for the taking, unable to fight back. She had known her perseverance would be rewarded someday. That day had come.

But she could take no chances. Haven was closed, sleeping; she could not bring him immediately to the Citadel and the safe-keeping of the Elders. She would have to secure him here. Ensure that he could do no more damage.

Much the same way she had lifted the girl, Gabriel grabbed the boy by his torn and bloody shirt, holding him up where she could see him properly. He did look an awful lot like Kadiel. A shame, that such holy features had been corrupted so thoroughly. That entire family should have been dealt with. His skin felt cold against her fingers, so cold that she thought for a moment he might actually be already dead. Then he moaned, his head rolling slightly to the side. Still alive. Still a threat.

She reached into her armor and pulled out the instrument she had kept on her desk in a locked box the last two years, just in case. Somehow, she had known it might come to this. The best soldiers were prepared for anything. The silver coil was marked with runes and symbols passed down from the first of the seraph to be created. It had been created to protect against rogue souls, humans who had turned dark and needed to be eliminated more thoroughly than through simple death. Currently, it lay flat, a spiral in her hand. Gabriel pressed it to the boy's chest, just above his heart. The coil shimmered, coming to life; spiraling, shifting, burrowing deep within the human flesh, creating an opening. At the back of that opening, a blue light glowed, cool and warm all at once. His soul.

Finally. This is all over. Talia's mistake is corrected.

Gabriel drove her hand into that opening, reaching for the blue light.

The boy's eyes few open, his hands coming up to wrap around her arm where it disappeared into his chest.

Gabriel stared into his silver-brown eyes, eyes that almost looked like they should belong to one of her kin. Almost. Fear loomed in there in that gaze. Panic and desperation, and also resignation, as if he had known this was inevitable as she did.

"No!"

Another body crashed against Gabriel's, driving her to the ground and forcing her to lose her grip on the boy and his soul. She managed to tuck her wings just in time to keep them from snapping.

Spitting the dirt from her mouth, she rolled, reaching for her sword—and saw Kadiel's face.

"You!" Gabriel's anger burned hot in her chest. "You meddlesome, unholy, stupid girl! I'll have you brought before the Citadel for this!"

Kadiel pushed her back into the dirt. "Just try. I won't let you hurt him. I won't let you do *that* to him. Have you lost your mind? Stripping him of his soul while he's still alive? Don't you know what that would do?"

"Of course I know!" Gabriel sat up, shoving Kadiel off her. "It would solve everything. End the threat he poses. Without his soul he'll lose any power he has."

"And be worse than a demon's soulless! He'll be an empty corpse! Wandering, unable to do the slightest thing."

"Exactly. Now get out of my way." Kadiel wouldn't be able to disobey a direct order.

A pop sounded on the air, and a voice joined them. "Out of *your* way? Why don't you all get out of mine instead?" Another boy entered the clearing, identical in nearly every way to the one lying on the ground, the coil still deeply imbedded in his chest. Talia's other son.

He rubbed his own chest, indicating some amount of pain. "I felt something odd just now. Figured Bri must have gotten himself into some sort of trouble, and to my great lack of surprise, it seems I was right." He stood over his brother, looking down at the coil and the light. "What has happened to you this time?"

"Kai, please..." Bri said, his voice as weak as his body.

"Can't beg for my help now, brother. Not after that little stunt you pulled earlier. A few of those mystics got away from me. I am impressed. Couldn't be prouder, really."

Gabriel sensed a darkness from this second boy, something far greater than anything she had ever felt in her travels. He would do far more damage with Bri's power than Bri ever had. "Get away from him, witch," she ordered, "and I will allow you to live."

"What is this thing?" Kai said, ignoring her offer. "I do believe that is my brother's soul on the other side."

Gabriel sprang up, sword drawn, ready to charge. She would kill the witch-child and bring back the soul of the myst-seer. Certainly then the Citadel would be pleased.

Pain blossomed in her left side, and she stopped short, unable to breathe. She coughed and felt blood spatter past her lips. Kadiel stood, stark still, pale, and tearful, but determined, holding the hilt of a long dagger—which she had driven into the one weak spot in Gabriel's armor.

"I'm sorry," Kadiel said. "I can't let you near him."

All time seemed to stop then, and Gabriel could only watch in disbelief. How could she? The Divine Order should have prevented this. Yet Kadiel showed no sign of even struggling against her binding. The witch moved toward the boy. How could everything have come together so well, only to fall apart so quickly?

Kai crouched down beside Bri. "Can anyone use this thing?"

Bri shook his head, trying to move, but too weak to do so.

The human girl on the ground came to well enough to lift her head and see the two together, Kai studying the coil with a curious finger. "Kai, no!"

"Kai, don't..." Bri pleaded.

"Sorry. It was never yours to begin with, little brother." His fingers slipped past the first rings of the coil, and nothing adverse rose up to stop him from going further. So, grinning, he reached inside Bri's chest.

What they found when they jumped through Hell and up to the mortal realm was not at all what Alec had expected. The familiar woods of Xia-Lo, evergreens and blue sky all around, the sound of the river nearby, unconcerned with the activities of mortals and immortals alike, surprised him because he had thought never to return to that land. But worse than that, was who inhabited the clearing.

Gabriel stood with Kadiel, a dagger through the general's side, silver blood running freely over her armor. Ella lay on the ground, a bit of blood on her head, causing her hair to stick to her face. And Bri, trapped beneath Kai—who had his arm elbow deep in his brother's chest.

"Wretched, blistering godflesh, what the hell is going on here?" Tassos said, having more voice than Alec did in that moment. Alec's only thought was to get to Bri.

Luca stilled him with a hand on his chest. "Wait."

"Like hell I'm waiting!"

His words did not faze Luca, who simply held out his arms and spoke one single word in a language Alec could not place.

Bri disappeared from his place on the ground and reappeared in Luca's arms. Whole, and alive. Kai cursed, a litany of a tantrum. Alec reached for Bri, but again was told to wait.

"How did you do that?" Tassos asked as they both watched Luca delicately remove the silver coil from Bri's chest with a touch of his finger. The coil drew itself out, flattening until it no longer touched bare flesh. The blue light dimmed and disappeared.

"I can summon over short distances. Any who have made a pact with a demon are subject to my call," Luca said. "I am the High Lord of Hell, after all." He passed Bri into Alec's arms, and Alec took him eagerly. Bri was unconscious, but breathing, though he felt far too light, and far too cold.

"He's like ice."

"Nothing some rest won't cure," Luca said, inspecting the coil.

Rest? He needs far more than rest. Bri was cut, scarred, pale and completely unresponsive. He was also far taller than Alec remembered.

"Death clings to him," Tassos said, coming close and touching Bri's face gently. "But her hold is slipping, as it always will. You have no need to worry about that."

Stepping forward, Luca addressed Gabriel. "This is yours, is it not?" He held the coil between two fingers.

"It is." Blood dripped from her mouth when she spoke. No doubt the blade had pierced her lung, and despite being one of Haven's own, she was still capable of being gravely injured. She held perfectly still, as did Kadiel.

"An old trinket. And generally unsanctioned, I believe," Luca said.

"I do what is necessary."

"Don't we all." He flicked it toward her, and it landed dully at her feet. "And as for you," Luca said, turning to Kai. "You have caused quite the commotion in my realm."

Kai dusted off his hands and stood, his temper once again under control. "So what? You weren't around to do it yourself. I certainly wasn't stepping on your toes."

"Hell is for demons and hellions, not witches."

"Hell is for any who can get there, especially when the High Lord is nowhere to be found."

"You enjoy a challenge, do you?"

Kai shrugged. "Boredom annoys me."

"And I have been asleep for far too long." Luca's right hand shifted, changing into the blackness of the Void, then solidifying into a gleaming black blade. "Care to help me stretch?"

Kai laughed. "All right, then. And when I've killed you, I'll take my brother back."

"Fine," Luca said. "But you will have to kill me first."

Alec shifted Bri's weight, holding him closer. "Are they both mad?"

Tassos grumbled as if they were watching two children getting into a bit of mischief. "You know as well as I do that yes, they are."

Kai cut his arm open and spilled his blood into the ground. "Let's get started, then."

All the space around Luca darkened, as if the Void crept up from Hell through the ground. Kai began to scribe with his foot, and the mountain started to shake.

Alec backed away, each step a stumble as the earth quaked beneath his feet. Tassos blinked out of existence, then reappeared just long enough to lift the groggy Ella from the ground before rejoining Alec. "We should find a safer spot, I think," he said.

"You think?" Alec glanced momentarily at Kadiel. She knelt beside Gabriel, who had likely collapsed as the earth shook. Alec didn't care what became of Gabriel, but Kadiel was another matter.

"Go," she yelled. "I can manage."

Tassos led the way back down the mountain, away from the temple and away from the black void that was slowly growing thicker around the trees. "This way. I don't think they'll last long, but it will likely be messy."

Alec heard the air pop and sizzle, and great groans as ancient trees pulled free of the earth, their roots tearing apart the ground as they saw the air for the first time in centuries. The shaking continued, and the air seemed to grow colder at his back.

"You mortals don't move fast enough," Tassos muttered. "Cut to the side!"

"What?" Alec glanced over his shoulder and saw nothing but darkness.

Then the void swallowed them. He saw nothing. Heard nothing. Felt nothing but the shallow breaths and fevered skin of Bri in his arms. The void went on for one breath, two, three, until Alec had lost count.

And then it washed away like the tide, and the world returned in a deafening cacophony of sound and smell and sight. Alec adjusted his grip on Bri, assuring himself he was still there, still alive, still safe.

Tassos shuddered beside him, holding Ella steady on her feet as she clung to him. "I hate when he does that."

The path leading up the mountain was a graveyard of trees, a forest of roots and stumps where branches and leaves should have been. More than once, a barren strip of land cut between them, cleaving trunks in two, and wiping away any greenery, like a blade had cleaved the earth.

Luca stood closest to them, his dark void-blade still in hand, a single cut bleeding black blood down his arm, but he was calm and controlled.

Kai stood further up the mountain, chest heaving as he breathed, his face bleeding along with his hands and arms and legs. He wiped the blood from under his nose with the back of his hand, looked once at Alec, then down to Bri, before kneeling and scribing into the ground.

A burst of light tore up from the earth at his feet, slicing down the mountain, headed straight for them all.

Luca disappeared and reappeared in the light's path, bringing his blade in an upward stroke that peeled up the mountain toward Kai's light.

In that same moment, a flash burst behind Kai, and Alec saw Ariadne. She wrapped her arms around Kai's chest, holding him tightly even as he screamed and cursed her. Looking once in Alec's direction, their gazes met, and she disappeared, taking Kai with her.

Luca's darkness connected with Kai's light even after he was gone, concussing the air, upending the earth, and sundering the mountain clear in two.

Luca growled in frustration, but remained on the mountain top. Kadiel withdrew her dagger from Gabriel's side, and Gabriel fell to one knee, pressing her hand against the wound to staunch the flow of blood. Seemingly convinced that the general would make no other moves, Kadiel wiped, then sheathed her blade.

But Alec wasn't convinced that everything was over just yet. The air felt thick, heavy, as if it had been filled with power and light and darkness far past its natural capacity and would soon collapse under the weight.

The explosion rocked the earth. The mountain trembled violently, and they all struggled to keep their feet. Alec fetched up against a tree to keep both himself and Bri from ending up on the forest floor. Smoke rose from the valley below—a valley Alec knew held Iris's temple and all the mystics she had collected over the years. He didn't want to look. Didn't need to. He knew there would be nothing left to see.

Tassos gently passed Ella off to Kadiel as she approached, brushing the fallen leaves and dirt from his clothes. "I guess we were too late to stop everything."

"The only thing you stopped was Haven's will," Gabriel hissed through her teeth, righting herself and checking her wound.

Kadiel held Ella protectively as the girl struggled to keep her feet. "Haven's will, maybe—but not The One's."

Gabriel chose not to respond.

In the silence that followed, Alec checked Bri for any signs of improvement. There were none. Yet, despite that, he felt relief. Relief in simply having him back.

Ella pulled herself from Kadiel's hold, and stumbled to Alec and Bri, resting her head on the unconscious boy's shoulder. Alec let her be.

"Well, that's that, then." Tassos said, peering over the edge into the valley. "You feel it, don't you, Gabe? A new god is born."

"Not one," Luca said, moving for the first time since his intended prey had escaped, his sword once again a hand. "Two."

— CHAPTER FORTY-ONE —

His head throbbed, his throat burned, each finger ached, and every fiber of his body felt like he had been tossed down a rocky cliff. For a moment he wondered if he'd rather be numb again. At least he wasn't cold. Soft blankets caressed his broken body, and he could feel the sun shining on his face, warming the pillow beneath his head. A bird sang a chittery song somewhere nearby, and he detected the faint smell of freshly baked bread and sesame oil on the air.

Where am I?

Something touched his hand, and Bri's eyes flew open. Gasping led to coughing and a deep ache in his chest.

"Easy, Bri. Easy."

Something touched him. It was a hand. Another hand, holding his own, and now gently pressing him back to the bed by one shoulder.

"It's Alec."

Alec? Bri blinked, trying to truly open his eyes. The room was a bit blurry, the colors blending together into smudges and unshapely things. He squeezed the hand that held his, trying desperately to determine if it really did belong to Alec. It had been so long since he had woken up to that voice, and with everything that had happened since then—he didn't quite trust it.

"Bri? Are you awake?"

He coughed once more. "I'm awake." His voice was scratchy and quiet, as if unused for some time. "Is it really you, Alec? I can't see very well." He supposed that blurry black spot atop the paler splotch could be Alec.

"It's me. Give your eyes a minute, I'm sure they'll be fine. You've been asleep for days."

"Days?" Bri lifted his left arm, intending to rub his eyes, but pain and stiffness flared so suddenly that he had to let it drop back to his side and the soft bed.

"Go slow. It seems you got yourself into a bit of trouble without me."

Bri groaned. "Now I know you're Alec." Though he didn't really want to, he took his good hand from Alec's grip and rubbed his eyes until they felt alive and not so heavy. When he looked again, Alec's face was clearly a face, and clearly Alec's, albeit still a little fuzzy. He had dark circles under his eyes, and he looked pale, as if he had been away from the sun for a long time. His hair hadn't been combed. "You look terrible."

Alec laughed the kind of laugh that was relief and grief all at once. "Thanks. But I think you should look in a mirror, kid. I'm the picture of beauty compared to you."

Carefully, Bri looked down at his arms, but they were freshly bandaged, hiding the dozens of cuts he knew were there. "I guess I let things with Kai get a little out of control."

"You're still alive and in one piece. Let's count it as a win."

"How bad is it?"

"Enough blood loss to keep you out of it for three days. Cuts all over your arms and legs. The healers here say you won't scar too badly, though. They've been dressing your wounds with some salve that will speed the healing process. But Dorothea says the real trouble was something else."

"Other than having people reach into my chest and try to take my soul?"

"Other than that. Ella says you scribed."

"I did." Images of lines carved into blood and dirt flashed through his mind. "Though the truth is, I don't really remember much of it." Just talking to Ella beforehand, and worrying that his fingers would shake too badly to scribe properly. "Can we talk about that later?"

"Sure."

"Where's Ella?"

"Heh." Alec ran a hand through his hair. "Here. Outside. And she's perfectly fine, before you ask. She wanted to be in here with you, but the healers kept chasing her out."

"Why?"

"Because apparently the healers are also great students of other cultures, and they know that a young lady from Chanae should not be permitted in a room with a naked young man."

"Naked?" Bri shifted under his covers. "Oh." He felt his cheeks grow hot. "Then, where are we?"

"Xia-Lo. The city of AnBai. It seemed the best place to get you healed."

"What about everyone else?"

"Well," Alec leaned back on his arms. "Dorothea is fine, as always. If anything, I think she made it through all this stronger. To hear her tell it, it was all quite the adventure. Ella is fine, as I said. A bump on her head, but otherwise unharmed."

"Kai," Bri said, suddenly panicked. "He said he had placed a *labrynth* on her. One he could use to kill her at any time."

Alec shook his head. "She's been gone over as thoroughly as the rest of us. Dorothea had a look at her, since you had both been with Kai so long. There's no *labrynth*."

Relief or anger? Bri wasn't sure which to feel. Kai had been bluffing.

"Ella told us most of what happened," Alec went on. "How he took the *labrynth* off your back, and all the scribing he made you help him with."

"Did it work?"

"Did what work?"

"All his scribing. Is Olin a god?"

Alec's shoulders slumped. "It seems so, yes. But so is Carma, so that should even things out a bit."

"Carma?"

"It's a long story. One I'm not even completely sure of myself."

Bri closed his eyes and breathed deep, enjoying the feel of filling his lungs completely, despite the discomfort it caused. Settling into the pillows, he tried to remember the last time he had slept without one eye open. All he could think about was when he had been little, and he would climb into Alec's bed, holding his hand all night and resting in the quiet.

Now felt a little like that.

"If I asked you to hold my hand while I slept again, would you think me a child?"

"Not if you don't think me overprotective."

"You are overprotective," Bri said, letting his eyes slip closed. "But I don't mind." He felt Alec's hand close around his, and then he relaxed so completely that the stiffness in his abused body seemed to slip away. "We still have a lot to talk about when I wake up."

"Yes," Alec said, and Bri thought he sounded sad. "Yes, we do." Bri wanted to open his eyes, to ask Alec what hung so heavily unsaid, but sleep came too quickly.

The mortal realm had always felt so *small* to Gabriel. Everything was so finite, so limited. The trees grew for hundreds of years, but even then, their leaves and branches died and fell away, until eventually the tree itself began to rot. Birds, squirrels, insects—they all ran around, living their tiny little lives, never seeming aware of how quickly they would burn out, how quickly they could be snuffed out, like a burning candle under a glass. The humans were little better, living no more than one hundred years, most much less. Such a short lifespan. And yet The One had created all of this to house them. This world with its beginnings and ends. The other realms went on in every direction forever, but this one—it stopped.

She picked at the bark on a tree, surprised at its resilience. It had been three days since the boy had slipped her grasp—again. Three days since two new gods had risen above their intended stature. Three days since she had felt the presence of the holy realm above her. She could not wait for the Restorium to end. Only, what then? She would return home with no good news, only news of her repeated failure. The city of AnBai stretched out to the west, its buildings tall and grand, with tiered spires and flags of crimson blowing in the breeze. The boy lay within those city walls, so close, and yet completely out of her reach. Tassos had kept vigil at the boy's bed, chasing Death away again and again so he could heal more quickly. The old witch had placed *labrynths* at his door and all around his room, protecting him from anyone with ill intentions. And that soulless, Alec, had never left the boy's side, not for a moment.

Then there was Carma. A demon god, whose power was now untested and unknown. She had made it clear that if Gabriel so much as walked into the house where the boy slept, she would discover the extent of her new power quickly, and Carma would feel little remorse.

Gabriel may have failed yet again, but she was not ready to quit. Her father had always said stubbornness was her best trait.

"Well, well, you're still here." Carma came through the trees, dressed in a pale pink silk dress, a dark blue robe of the same material draped over her shoulders.

"Where else would I be?"

Her casual shrug sent a flutter through that delicate fabric. "That is a good question. But I hope you're not waiting here, hoping to get a chance to run off with Bri."

Gabriel huffed, retracted her wings, and leaned back against the tree, folding her arms over her chest, taking solace in the feel of her armor still tightly fitted against her body. As soon as she had been healed well enough to put it back on, she had. "You've made it quite clear it would be foolish of me to try anything now."

"I'm so pleased you've decided to listen to me." Carma didn't look any different now that she was a god. The same silver hair floated freely around her, and her skin was still as bronzed as it had been since she had torn out her heart. Her transition from seraph to demon had been a far greater change. The golden skin Gabriel had always known had deepened, and her light brown hair had lost all its color.

"As soon as the Restorium ends, I will leave."

"Are you sure that's for the best?," Carma asked. "Michael will not be pleased with you."

"I can handle the consequences of my actions. It is you who should be worried."

"And why is that?"

"Because Michael will bring the Legions now. I'd like to see you try to stand against that." Carma looked rightly troubled, and so Gabriel allowed herself a bit of smugness.

"You two ladies aren't fighting already, are you?" Tassos came into sight, actually walking up the hill to where Gabriel and Carma stood, rather than flashing in and out as he usually did.

"Gabriel and I are always fighting with each other," Carma said. "You should worry if you ever catch us getting along. I'm surprised to see you here. How's Bri?"

"Awake, actually," he said, standing like a patch of night in the afternoon sun. "Out of any danger. And so my services are no longer needed."

"Thank you for that," Carma said. "What will you do now?"

"Ah, I think I'll keep a certain High Lord out of trouble."

"You always involve yourself with things that are none of your concern," Gabriel said. "You have a job to do. Would it be too much to expect you to do it properly?"

"Of the three of us standing here, my dear," Tassos said, "I think I have the most unblemished record when it comes to getting my job done. So you'll forgive me for not taking your oh-so-carefully-worded advice."

A flash of pain shot through Gabriel's jaw before she realized she had clenched her teeth.

Tassos let out a loud sound of exasperation. "Oh, for Haven's sake, Gabe. Literally. Take a break. You are far too serious for your own good."

She scowled. "And you're never serious enough."

"Ah," Carma said wistfully. "It is just like when we were children, isn't it?"

"If you mean how Gabriel always ruins our good time, then yes." Tassos smiled tauntingly. Gabriel took a step forward, intent on wiping that smile from his face with the armored part of her fist.

A rustle of leaves alerted them all to yet another someone joining them. Kadiel touched down not far from where they all stood, stretching her wings before folding them close against her back. "You are still here," she said in clear surprise.

"Again," Gabriel said, tiring of this game everyone seemed to be playing, "where else would I be?"

Kadiel just looked at her plainly. "Haven."

"It's not open yet. The Restorium still holds us out."

A long silence crept through the woods. Kadiel shifted nervously, looking to Carma and then Tassos as if they might have some answer she desperately needed.

"What? What is it?" Gabriel's temper was thin as spring ice.

"I—" Kadiel's words faltered. "Haven't you felt it?"

"Felt what?"

"The Restorium. It ended."

Carma and Tassos exchanged a glance. "Are you certain, Kadiel?" Carma asked.

"Yes. Very certain."

"You're mistaken," Gabriel said. She reached toward Haven with that extra sense seraph all had, that invisible limb that allowed them to enter and exit as they pleased. She knocked on nothing but a tightly closed door.

"Tassos, can you confirm this?" Carma said, her voice quiet, cautious.

"It's been a while since I've visited the holy realm," Tassos said, looking at unsure as the rest of them, "but I think I can manage. Give me a moment." In a puff of smoke, he was gone.

No one said anything until he returned. When he did, the smoke of his exit mixing with that of his arrival, Gabriel took one look at his face and felt her stomach turn over.

"Gabriel," he said her name as if it were an apology.

"No." She reached for Haven again, reached with everything she had—and fell hard against an unyielding barrier. She banged against that invisible door, slammed all her power against it. It would not budge. Once more she hammered her spiritual fists against the door, and this time the line between the mortal realm and Haven flared with power, knocking her back.

She landed on her knees at Carma's feet.

"No." It was the only word she had. She couldn't think anything else. Anything else would mean...

Kadiel spoke softly. "My binding to you has dissolved. I think it dissolved days ago. On the mountain."

"Don't say it."

Carma knelt beside her and placed a hand on Gabriel's shoulder, which was immediately shrugged off violently. "Oh, my dear friend. I am so sorry."

"Are you?" Gabriel felt her heart pounding in her chest, a heart that would never again know the light of the holy realm. "Are you sorry? Isn't this what you wanted? For me to be like you? For my threat against your precious boy to be eliminated? I have failed too many times." She felt her world collapsing with each word that came from her lips. "I am cast out! I am nothing! I am—"

Fallen.

The latest body lay on the ground at her feet, bleeding black blood that pooled and crept toward her own bare toes. It was only one of many, but already she could feel her strength returning just looking at the deep open wound in the hellion's chest. She plucked a hair from her head and bent down, hearing the rattling sounds of last breaths, and smelling the scent of flesh and blood.

She had so missed the battlefield. So much, that this little hallway would do.

With an expertise developed after centuries of practice, Picadilly began to stitch up the gaping wound, healing her victim, and in the process, healing herself. She had used the first of her guards to correct what had been broken in her knee, the second had righted her jaw, the third and fourth had erased her minor cuts and bruises. This one would reverse the exhausting and draining effects of being locked up for so long. With each stitch, she breathed more deeply, and felt energy and life returning to her muscles. She had stayed here long enough. It was time to go.

Her healing skills were rescinded just before the guard could become a threat again. She closed up the hole in his chest, but left the legs broken and the face bloodied. There was no need to speak with this one. The third had told her everything.

Hellions working for a Hellwalker. It was a riddle she had tried to work out through the entirety of her incarceration here. Now she had the answer.

Stretching her legs, Pica stood. With a deep breath, she reached for the power she had so long been cut off from—and felt it ready and waiting. Nothing kept her from leaving now.

Except that she wasn't ready.

Footsteps echoed through the brick hall, so familiar that Pica smiled at their sound. Zachriel came around the corner, sword drawn, expression cold.

So she smiled at him, smoothing her hair to make sure it hung straight after all the fuss. "There you are. I've been waiting for you."

"Have you now? Interesting. How did you manage to escape?" He set the point of his sword at her throat.

"Escaping was never the trouble. I simply stayed as long as it suited me to do so."

"If that is true, then why wait so long? Why not flee before I arrived?"

"You are a man of business, and I have a proposition for you." With a finger she moved his blade out of her way and stepped forward. "Interested?"

Ella had grown to like Xia-Lo. The stories Bri had told her so long ago in the garden matched perfectly with the trees and flowers that grew here. Color burst everywhere; in the clothes of the people, their buildings and homes, the statues that overlooked their city. So much of what they wore here would have made her blush a year ago. But much had changed since then, and it took more than a woman's bare midriff to scandalize her now. However, she still couldn't bring herself to wear any of it—beautiful though it was. The healers had understood and brought her a long silk dress of pale blue that covered her shoulders. It was so non-constricting without her usual undergarments that it had taken her an entire day before she felt comfortable walking around the city; to know that no one stared at her as if she had gone out in her shift.

Yes, she had grown very fond of this strange new world, but as she stroked the soft petals of a bright red flower, she could not stop thinking of another world, far on the other side of the map, where the land was dark with ash, and the people disheartened and broken.

"It's nice out."

Her heart leapt at the sound of his voice, and her body did too. "Bri!" He stood there, dressed all in white against a backdrop of green and painted walls. She threw her arms around him, not caring if it wasn't ladylike to do so. She had spent far too many days—months, really—watching him sleep, not knowing what would happen when he woke again. He took an unsteady step back at her sudden embrace, but wrapped an arm around her back in return. She felt his breath against her neck and the sensation of him breathing deeply. As if he would disappear if she let go, Ella held on a little tighter.

Bri winced.

"Oh! I'm sorry!" She drew back, and for the first time noticed the cane he held in his right hand for support. "I'm so sorry." Embarrassed and ashamed of not thinking of his well-being sooner, she stepped back.

Bri caught her by the elbow and drew her close again. "It's all right." He smiled. "It's nice not to be treated as if I'm made of glass."

Carefully this time, Ella wound her arms around his waist. "Alec?"

"It won't last long," Bri said fondly. "I'm sure as soon as I'm well he'll scold me quite thoroughly for going off on my own, turning myself over, scribing *labrynths* without training."

"He says he's never letting you out of his sight again."

"I'm sure eventually that will wear on my nerves, but for now...I won't complain."

"He's not watching now, is he?" She glanced over his shoulder, searching the path from the house.

"No," Bri said. "I made him promise to get some sleep. He was starting to look worse than me."

"And he agreed to this?" She couldn't imagine the conversation.

"I had to promise not to leave the house."

"You're outside."

"In the garden. It's part of the house."

Ella laughed at his awkward little smile. She traced his lips with her ungloved finger. "I was so worried," she said after a moment. "After you finished the *labrynth*, you just fell over, and nothing I did would wake you..."

"I'm sorry." All the mirth that had come into him was gone, and Ella felt guilty that she had chased it away. He touched her head, just by her hairline, where she was still bruised. "You got hurt because of me."

"It was just a little scratch."

"Did you really stand up to Gabriel?"

"I did."

"A general in Haven's army."

"It probably wasn't my most genius moment, but I wasn't willing to look into any other options. And despite what she may think, she's not nearly as scary as Kai."

Bri let out a short laugh. "Yes. Another example of your inexplicable need to confront dangerous situations."

She couldn't shove him; it wouldn't have been fair, or kind, so Ella settled for tapping a finger against his cheek. "Do not mock me, sir. Someone needs to stand up to them."

"Most days I'd rather it didn't have to be you."

"Only most days?"

"Yes. On the other days I marvel at your bravery." He reached out and gently touched her head where her wound was still scabbed and bruised. "I wish I had half your courage."

"But you do. Bri. Don't you realize all you've done? Everything you endured? It would have killed a normal man."

He looked at the ground. "I'm not so sure about that."

"Well, I am." And she'd hear no more about it otherwise. "Come on," she said, taking him by the hand. "You should sit."

"I'd rather walk. I've been still for far too long."

"All right, then. But only through the gardens. You have a promise to marginally keep."

"If I get inside before he wakes, he'll never know," Bri said as Ella tucked her arm through his.

"He will if I tell."

"You would betray me to him?"

"It all depends on how this walk goes, and whether or not you should really still be in bed."

They walked, talking about anything other than the most recent days. She told him about the markets in the city and the trinkets they sold there. He asked about the people, how they lived, and what news they gossiped of in the square. When they came across it, Ella showed him her favorite flower that grew in the gardens, and shared her disappointment in finding out from the locals that it would never be able to grow in the east.

When she felt Bri leaning too heavily on his cane, and the tension growing in his arm, she stopped them. "I think that's enough for today."

Bri's forehead creased. A sure sign of his frustration. "I'm so tired of being sick all the time, Ella. My whole life, this is all I get."

Spotting a bench nearby, she led him to it. "That's not true."

"Of course it's true." He sat, miserable and tired. Ella's heart broke, wanting so much to give back that bit of happiness he'd had when he'd first come outside.

"It's not." Sitting beside him, she took the hand that had held the cane, massaging his fingers. "And it won't be like this forever. You're healing. It's been a long winter. Give yourself some time."

He laughed bitterly. "Time. I'm never sure how to think about my time."

The demon mark on his right forearm had never seemed so pronounced before. "You mean because of this?"

"Yes."

His deal with Carma was something Ella tried not to think about. Like Bri, she wasn't sure what thoughts to have. "How many years left?"

"A little more than five."

Ten years, he had told her. Ten years in exchange for his soul. *Is it a fair trade?* Looking at him now, she wondered if ten years wasn't a cruel thing to make him endure.

He sighed, looking away and rubbing at his face. "I'm sorry, Ella. I'm turning gloomy."

"I don't mind." She turned his face toward her with a gentle hand. "I don't mind," she said again, making sure he understood. "I love you, Bri. Even when you're gloomy."

His eyes widened. "You love me?"

"Stupid boy. Of course I love you." And before he could argue further, she kissed him to emphasize it.

She felt hot tears against her hand on his face, then his shaky breath as they paused for air. "I love you too," he said. "More than you know. More than I should."

On the tallest mountain, in the remotest place, Carma looked down over the clouds, watching the birds that dared fly through them, and marveling at how simple everything appeared from such a vantage point. She didn't feel different, yet it seemed the whole world had changed. It was not such an effort to hold her true form back, yet it came the moment she called for it, as if her other skin were nothing more than a thin veil.

Being a god was a curious thing. One she had yet to take full advantage of. Once Bri was healthy again, she would begin acquiring followers. A necessity, according to Dorothea. Her powers and abilities would grow to follow the beliefs of the people who came to know her name, to worship her. And she needed to make it clear that above all else, she could handle whatever the other new demon god threw at her.

She was the god to kill a god. That had to be her legend.

It all sounded like far more work and responsibility than Carma had ever truly wanted. If she were being honest. And why not? She was, at the moment, completely alone.

And then she wasn't.

"And so we meet again." His voice was like dark honey, melting over her bones as it always had.

"You were always good at finding my hiding places."

"You are never truly hidden from me." Olin came to stand beside her, overlooking the world as she did. His hands were in his pockets. Odd, since usually they were always touching one another, even when fighting. "And now here we are, two gods, surveying the land."

He had always been a pleasure to look at. Godlike. Now, nothing could be more true. "How did you find out?"

"I feel you," he said. "Do you not feel me as well? It is as if we are two pieces to one puzzle."

"I couldn't be sure. After all, I knew what I was doing. I knew what the outcome would be, but no one had told you."

"It was a surprise, I'll admit. Clever. But then, I should know better than to put anything past you."

"A mistake I hope you'll continue to make." Everything she'd planned depended on it.

He set his dark gaze on her and for a moment Carma wished things were different. Wished his ambition wouldn't be the end of them both. "You always follow me at every step."

"Oh, trust me, this was not my idea."

"Then why?"

She recalled their days in the bright Haven; no shadows, hearts still beating within their chests. "It seems we are never meant to be parted, you and I."

In one swift motion he grabbed her by the hips and pulled her close. "Join me then. Think of all we could do now."

"We shall see. Do you have my soulless? Picadilly?" It had been too long since she'd felt the former demon's presence, and who else could hold her?

"I do not," Olin said, his curiosity clearly piqued. "Have you lost her?"

"It would seem so."

"Intriguing. Especially given her role in this game."

"Worrisome, indeed," Carma admitted, thinking of that board and the pieces she'd so carefully collected, "but I do not think it will hinder me too much."

"I've warned you before. Do not get in my way."

"Oh, but darling," she went up on tiptoes to place a sweet kiss on his mouth, "if I didn't get in your way, we wouldn't have moments like this."

"I should kill you now, shouldn't I?" he said, even as he leaned in to nibble on her throat.

"You could try. But it would be such a waste." She pulled his face up where she could see it. "Don't you want to give the mortals something to talk about?"

The entire mountain shook when he dropped her down upon it, grinning like a boy. "We are gods."

Carma grabbed him by the shirt and dragged him down with her, the earth quaking once again. "Indeed we are."

— ACKNOWLEDGMENTS —

Books aren't made in a day, or even a few weeks, and in my experience it takes more than a few months as well. This book has been nearly ten years in the making. While I may have drafted it in about four months back in my twenties, I'm writing this now awaiting a new decade that isn't my thirties, and my life has changed considerably since writing that first incarnation.

First draft Kate was single, finding her way, exploring the courage she could find in cosplay and in writing a book that challenged the darkness that took the form of anxiety attacks in her own life, not knowing if this story would ever see the light of day.

Fully edited draft Kate is married, has two kids, works at a wonderful studio where she feels fully herself, and gets the pleasure of knowing this series is making its way into the world and, hopefully, into readers' hands.

So thank you to Past Kate, who was brave enough to write the words, and to send the queries—we did it. All of it. And for any of you out there writing your own books, in the query trenches, amassing rejections and watching your email—keep going. Don't give up.

Thank you to my family, as always. Mom and Dad, who let me put off a "fully adult job" while I wrote books and tried to figure out what path suited me best.

To my brother, who probably won't read this, but if he is, "Hi. Thanks for reading! I know what an honor that is."

To my husband and partner, CJ, who fell in love with a geeky girl who really likes hugs, and supports me in every way—Thanks for sending that follow up email. I'm eternally glad our bookish-selves found one another. Love you lots.

And my girls—I edited this book while they slept, while they climbed on the chair and couch behind me, and jumped on my bed. I'm not sure what they think it means when I say "I'm writing" but I hope they come to appreciate it someday. I certainly love them more than I can put into words.

To Taylor, who has talked me off many a writerly ledge, let me bounce ideas off her, read first drafts, and is generally the best first reader anyone could ever ask for.

My publishing team at Outland Entertainment is really something special. I've gotten to watch this group grow and develop over the last few years, and I am so proud that I get to call myself a part of that team. To Jeremy, always manning the helm. My editor, Scott—thank you for your insight and understanding of this story. Your input has been invaluable. And Alana, you're always ready to answer an email and sort things out, thanks for that, you're like a key on the map that is this crazy thing called publishing.

Writing can be a solitary endeavor, and with new motherhood in the middle of it, I fell into that isolation a bit. But there were writers on social media who gave me the feeling of being a part of a community even though I'm sure they had no idea they were basically my imaginary friends. Thanks to all of you.

And lastly, but certainly not least—to you, the reader. You are the ultimate dream. That this story can now live in your imagination as it did mine; it's what I always hoped for. Thank you for reading, for talking about these books, for forcing your friends to read with you. I hope you enjoyed this installment of Bri and Alec's story, and that you don't have to wait too long for book three. I'll see you there.

— ABOUT THE AUTHOR —

Kate Martin lives in Connecticut with her husband, two wild little girls, and one disgruntled cat. When not writing fantasy of all shapes and sizes, she can often be found reading, dancing, or watching the local wildlife.

You can connect with her on Instagram @katemartinauthor, TikTok @katemartinwrites, and through her newsletter at Substack: katemartin.substack.com.